Raising Cain

Previously Published as The Color of Seven

By Gail Roughton

Print ISBNs
Amazon 9780228627333
Ingram Spark 9780228627340
Barnes & Noble 9780228627357

BWL Publishing Inc.

Books we love to write ...
Authors around the world.

http://bwlpublishing.ca

Dedication

For Daddy and Mr. Emory and all the hours spent on the banks of Stone Creek Swamp.

Table of Contents

Chapter One

Twin dirt bikes tore through the night, shattering the stillness of the woods. Nightmare visions chased the riders, visions of a skeleton sprawled across a cave floor, a rotting stake lying against its rib bones. Visions of the resurrection begun when they'd pulled that stake from its resting place.

Back in the cave, that resurrection accelerated. Arms and legs rippled with muscle. The rib cage re-fleshed itself as the face re-formed. The skeleton moved its arms and worked its mouth. A croak issued from newly formed vocal cords. A shout split the dark.

"I'm alive!!"

The echoes bounced off the cave walls as the figure inched forward and stood. The man, a coal black giant with shaved skull and massive shoulders, tore off the rags clinging to his new flesh and stood naked in the night. His new body raged with thirst. He sniffed the air, catching the scent of prey.

The man didn't know where he was, though he knew where he'd been. He knew who'd drained his body of life-sustaining blood and buried him in the cave. He didn't know how much time had passed but it didn't matter. If he was alive again, then his nemesis, that interfering highfalutin' white doctor, the recipient of the dark powers he himself had unleashed—he was somewhere near as well. And by all the dark gods, he would find him. But first, he must have blood. He sniffed the air. He cared not if the prey was animal or human. He must hunt. He must stalk and capture, bite and tear. And drink. And drink. And drink.

He stood, naked under the moonglow, and reveled in his rebirth.

"I'm aliiiiiiiive!" he shouted again. His laughter rushed out over the woods and moved on further, filling the deepest reaches of the swamp. Night fishermen, tending their lines along Stone Creek, stopped dead in their tracks and shivered. The night noises of the frogs and crickets ceased. No hoot-owl or whippoorwill sent forth their distinctive calls. Even the swamp snakes ceased to slither. The heartbeat of the woods and swamp stopped. It took a remarkably long time for it to resume.

* * *

As it had always done, the late summer sun beat down on the streets of Macon, Georgia in brutal attack, and as it had done since its construction so many years ago, the house on Orange Street endured as it sat and waited.

While it waited, it remembered the glory of its early years. It felt unloved and unwanted as it sulked within the narrow boundaries of its city lot, pouting in the humid haze of the July heat.

The gracious two-story brick had been such a happy house. In its past life, its rooms were open and airy, painted in light colors, with golden woodwork and scrolled mantles over the fireplaces. A fitting haven for the golden couple who laughed within its walls.

The succession of owners hadn't been kind to the house. They'd partitioned its interior into apartments and later into offices, allowing it to slide into shabby disrepair. Its spacious rooms were now small and dark, the glowing woodwork raped by paint. The hardwood floors lay hidden beneath cheap carpet. The ceilings looked down on the walls and floors and sighed.

Still, the house hoped. Perhaps it had absorbed into its bricks and boards the optimism and vitality of the young doctor who'd been its first master.

A 'For Sale' sign stood in the front yard. Maybe someone special would walk through its front door and see it not as it was, but as it had been, as it could be again. Maybe even today.

And as the house sat lonely under the blazing sun, a car pulled up and parked at its curb. A young man got out of the car and slapped another notice over the 'For Sale' sign. He stepped back to survey his handiwork.

'Sold.'

* * *

Sunset streaked in lines of purple and crimson over the horizon. It faded into streamers of rose and mauve before dying away into full dark.

Deep in the woods near Stone Creek, the giant emerged from the cave in the side of the hill. He stood, tall and still naked, and sniffed the air. His bare chest and upper arms were roadmaps of dried blood from the prior night's frenzied feeding, his hands reddish-brown. His animal intelligence knew there were things he must investigate. He didn't know exactly where he was but assumed he was still near Macon, Georgia, the city he'd chosen for his last and greatest victory. He didn't know what amount of time had passed since the hated white man snatched triumph from his waiting grasp, either, but from the foreign sounds floating through the dusk to his finely tuned sense of hearing, he assumed it had been an amount sufficient to afford great changes to the world as he'd known it.

He felt stirrings of the dark powers he'd first explored the prior night when he'd cast himself out into a whirling, swirling, disincorporated cloud that came together again into the solid form of his huge body by the power of his thoughts. Now, removed from the red mist of his urgent hunt for blood, he remembered the night of his defeat, his enemy's strength, the relentless attacks, no moment spared for the actual act of moving from one point to another. Now he understood.

He stood, upraised nostrils quivering to catch the scent of blood. He gave his body a mental push back into that swirling cloud of nothingness and disappeared into the thick trees. Every living wood creature went on high alert, fully aware of the new predator who appeared and disappeared silently with no warning.

The hours of the hunt flew by. He looked up at the moon, then back at the body of the coyote he was holding in his hands. He tossed the carcass casually into the pile of fur that only an hour before had roamed through the undergrowth in a large pack.

He laughed. His bloodlust lingered as a dull echo. He sensed that echo would never fully die away, no matter how much blood he guzzled. But for tonight, he'd had enough, which was as good as a feast. There were matters to be tended to, things to be considered.

He sent his swirling essence into the air and returned to his lair, where he sat in cogitation for some half-hour. The wood life, sensing the cessation of the active hunt, gradually resumed some measure of normality.

First, he needed to be sure he was still where he thought he was, somewhere on the fringes of the city. Then he needed to check how much time had truly passed in dark limbo. A very long time, he was sure. During the course of his hunt strange noises off in the distance reminded him of the rushing sound of a locomotive, but he knew that wasn't it, exactly. Things had changed. Considerably.

He needed an acolyte. Someone to introduce him to this new world. An acolyte to follow him blindly and serve him devotedly, do all things needful and necessary to be done to ensure his continued well-being.

Struck by a sudden idea, he got up and paced off the clearing in measured strides. Someone else had been here last night. Someone had uncovered the cave and pulled the rotting wood from his rib cage. He sniffed and came to point.

Two. There'd been two. One of the scents, though faint, still gave off the pleasing aroma of terror. The other scent, much stronger, was the scent of another predator leaving its spoor. Its strong smell of fear mingled with something else, something broadcasting simultaneous strength and weakness, flavored with a hint of madness. He smiled. Even a human should be able to track this spoor. And he was anything but.

Chapter Two

Just after dark, Justin Dinardo walked up to the door of Dennis Billings' big Tudor two-story in Country Hills Estates and rang the bell.

Joyce Billings opened the door and waved him in.

"He's in his room, Justin." She turned back towards the den to resume her interrupted phone conversation with Glynis Adams. "Been in a bad mood all day. See what you can do with him. God knows, nobody talks to their mother anymore!"

She resumed her phone conversation with Glynis about Tuesday's Bridge Club. It had never, nor would it ever, occur to her that Dennis never talked to her because she was always talking to someone else.

Justin's Nikes slapped the parquet floor of the foyer and slid into silence as he approached the carpeted stairs. He moved down the hall and knocked on the third door to the left. "I'm not hungry!" Dennis shouted.

"And I ain't your mother!" Justin snapped back. He glanced around the room, taking in the scattered books that lay haphazardly on the shelves of the desk's hutch, the clothes draped over the back of the chair, the rumpled spread covering the double bed. Something was different.

His eyes moved over the room. It looked the same, the room where they'd spent innumerable nights from the age of six upwards, just as they had in Justin's room in the house next door. So what was different?

Quiet. Too quiet. No blaring rock 'n' roll from the new state-of-the-art sound system.

"No sound, man?"

"No."

Dennis lay on his back on his bed, his hands behind his head. Justin glanced toward the shelves where the equipment should have been.

"Hey, what happened?"

The shelves were empty. Narrow strips of dusty wooden veneer formed frames for the polished rectangles where the sound equipment ought to be.

"I took it out to the Methodist Children's Home this morning."

"You did what?"

"I made a charitable donation for their rec room. Or wherever they want to put it. I don't care if they junk it."

"What the hell's wrong with you?"

Dennis sat up, swinging his legs off the bed. Almost eighteen, his long frame was shedding adolescent awkwardness. At six foot two, he towered over his mother. Almost a man's body, but the face underneath the fashionably cut sandy hair was still a boy's face, smooth and nondescript. Or it had been. Now, looking at Justin, the lines of his square jaw and the jut of his nose seemed stronger. His eyes held new wisdom. It was the face of a chrysalis, forecasting the emergence of the man.

"I'll tell you what's wrong with me. What we're doing makes me sick. And I'm not doing it anymore. I am *never* goin' back to that clearing, *never* goin' to sell an ounce of anything, ever again, not to anybody. And I'm never goin' to use anything I ever bought with any of that money, gave it all away. I won't have it in my room."

Justin glared at Dennis. His eyes narrowed and took on an obsidian gleam. He pursed his mouth and cooed sympathetically. "*Owww*, is the baby's wittle hands dirty?"

"Fuck you," Dennis said shortly. "And get the hell outta my room. Don't come back."

Justin was flabbergasted. This couldn't be Dennis Billings, who'd tagged along with all his whims since they were six years old. Dennis was a pain in the ass sometimes but he was handy to have around, no doubt about it. No one ever suspected that the duo could be involved in anything but clean fun and good living, mostly because of Dennis' all-American good looks. Justin needed that cover.

"Now listen, man, you're just freaked out about last night and I been thinking 'bout that. I think we just let our imaginations go crazy, you know?"

Dennis got up off the bed and advanced toward Justin.

"Doesn't matter what we saw. We saw it, and I'm not going back. And I told you to get the fuck outta my room."

Justin fell back. He'd never seen Dennis like this.

"You asshole! You limp-dick—"

"Not gonna work anymore, Justin. I don't care what you call me. Don't care what you think about me."

"You thing I'm goin' let you just walk away? From all that money?"

"Whatcha gonna do to stop me, Justin? Call the police?" Dennis laughed shortly. "'Cause you know what? I actually don't even care if you do. I just want out."

Justin turned and jerked the door open.

"You're going to regret crossing me, fucker! See if you don't!"

Justin stalked down the stairs. Dennis, falling heavily across his bed, heard the loud slam of the front door. *Good riddance.*

* * *

Justin Dinardo awoke with a start. The glow of the outside security lights streamed faintly into his room. A gigantic hand covered his mouth. His eyes widened.

His chest hurt from the sledgehammer force of his heartbeat, thumping wildly in sudden panic.

The face loomed over him. He stared into the round, ebony eyes. Hypnotic eyes. Powerful eyes. It was all so simple. All he had to do was follow those eyes and the world would fall at his feet. There was nothing to be scared of. The terror changed to instant adoration. Sensing the change, the owner of the hand removed it from Justin's mouth.

"Who—who are you?" Justin asked in wonder.

"My name be Cain." The voice rumbled low like distant thunder. "An' my color be sebben."

Chapter Three

Maria Elizabeth Knight came down the stairs of the big house on Orange Street and paused on the landing. She looked down at the crowd of well-wishers flowing across the floors of the new offices of Bishop & Knight, Attorneys at Law.

Her eye caught her partner, Jonathon Ralston Bishop III. They'd grown up together. He'd been her best friend from earliest childhood. Feeling her gaze, Johnny glanced up toward the stairs. He smiled and raised his hand and she waved and smiled back.

"No more hassles, no rule books, no more partners' dirty looks," Ria whispered to herself.

The house was meant to be hers. It had told her so the minute she'd set foot in it. This house had known life, heard the laughter of graceful ladies sipping iced tea in the parlor, the jokes of elegant, languid gentlemen sipping port in the drawing room, servants gossiping in the kitchens. Now, because of her and Johnny, it lived again.

Ria breathed in the smell of fresh paint, new carpet, furniture polish, the clean tang of lemon potpourri she'd scattered around the rooms. She'd had a hell of a time convincing Johnny, though. Finally, as ready as she was to leave the halls of the hundred year old firm where they practiced law as associates, he'd given in and conceded their combined trust funds would cover the renovations. The available space upstairs, converted into two separate apartments, obviated the need for separate mortgages or apartment leases.

She felt the house preen in its newfound elegance as she went down the stairs to join the guests.

* * *

It was almost three a.m. when the last of the crowd departed. Ria and Johnny stood in the middle of the foyer and surveyed the damage. Ria roused herself from the alcoholic haze. Empty bottles, dirty glasses, littered napkins, food trays holding only crumbs.

"Holy shit," she breathed.

"Don't worry 'bout it now," Johnny mumbled. He threw himself face forward onto one of the Victorian sofas of the reception room.

"I couldn't worry about it now if I had to," she admitted. "I'll help you up the stairs if you'll help me."

"No. Go 'way," he mumbled.

"You're going to stay here?"

"Damn straight."

"Oh, c'mon, Johnny! First official night in our new—"

She broke off at the snore. Out like a light. She thought about throwing herself onto the other sofa, but these sofas were for looks, not comfort. She painstakingly dragged herself up the stairs. She opened her door, determined to ignore the sofa and make it the bedroom. She froze.

"No," she whispered. This wasn't her new living room. This was a bedroom. A huge oriental rug covered the floor. A canopied four-poster bed, draped with blue velvet hangings, stood against one wall. A tall tiered mirror topped an old-fashioned dresser.

A young woman sat on the edge of the bed. Pale hair, almost pure gilt, streamed down her shoulders over the delicate lace of her pale blue negligee. Slightly tilted eyes emphasized the oval shape of her face. Her head shifted as a door opened. A smile lit her face.

"It was a lovely party, darlin', wasn't it?"

"Especially now that it's over." A tall man, lean and well-made, moved into view. He stripped off his shirt in lithe movements. He too, was blond, but of a ruddier hue. The golden brown tones of unstrained honey glowed in the lamplight.

"Paul, you are downright anti-social sometimes," she said with a pretty pout, as he dropped onto the bed beside her.

"Sometimes I just prefer my wife's company," he said, and pulled her into his arms.

"Sometimes I prefer my husband's company, but half of Macon pounds on the door and you go rushing out at one o'clock in the morning."

"Goes with the territory," he said.

"My mother told me not to marry a doctor."

"But think of the fringe benefits! I know all the right spots," he said, and nuzzled her neck.

Ria stood, trapped, an uninvited spectator to a very private moment in her own house. Her own bedroom, even. She backed out the door and closed it softly. She was drunk, that was it. She wasn't a hard drinker and she never drank very much. Tonight she'd overindulged in great excess. She loved this house and all through the renovations, she'd imagined it in its heyday. What better occupants could her imagination create than a young, handsome couple, madly in love? Her father was a doctor, hence the subconscious choice of the man's profession.

It was her imagination. Period. End of discussion.

She drew a deep breath and threw the door wide. Nothing. There was nothing there, nothing that wasn't supposed to be. She raced across the floor of the living room, reached the sanctuary of her own bedroom, closed the door, and locked it. In the morning, this would be amusing. Maybe.

She collapsed on top of the bed. Her thoughts spiraled upward out of her head in an ever-widening circle until the whole room spun and she sank gratefully down into darkness.

Justin Dinardo rode his dirt bike through the darkness, down the narrow path toward Cochran Short Route. He ran onto the blacktop and rode on for a mile and a half, where he pulled off into the overgrown lot of an old, rotting country store. He rode around the structure and opened the back of his waiting Tacoma pickup, lowering the long piece of 4x4 that he kept as a ramp for the dirt bike. It was an old routine for the small-time teenage drug dealer, retrieving stashed merchandise from buried deposits scattered throughout the woods of Stone Creek Swamp for resale.

Now it was performed with a new companion. Dennis Billings was history. The dirt bike safely stored, Justin got in behind the wheel and turned to the occupant of the passenger seat.

"Big pickup tonight," he said. "Gonna be a good profit."

"Dat's good."

Justin pulled the Tacoma out of its hiding spot and turned back to the highway.

"Cain?" His voice was low and respectful.

"Whut?"

"Where do you go? When you're not with me?"

"Dat ain't none of yo' business, boy. Yo' business doin' whut you told and bringin' in dat—profit." Cain chuckled to himself. After overcoming his amazement at finding more than a century had passed and the world as he knew it was gone forever, he'd settled back and enjoyed. And made plans.

"But don't you know? Don't you realize? What you could do? By now, I mean, it's been over a month, you could—"

"I gots my own reasons an' dey ain't none of yo's, boy. You watch yo' mouth."

"I wanta help you," Justin persisted cautiously. Wouldn't do to irritate Cain. "And I can't do that if you won't tell me what you want."

Cain gazed into the passing shadows as the Tacoma approached the entrance to I-16 and slowed. The things this world now held! He'd never have believed it. But whatever else it held, he knew it still held the man he sought, the man he wanted, the man he intended to find. Wherever he was. He'd use this fool, already the source of his spending money and creature comforts, to do it.

"I wants this town," he said. Justin shivered in anticipation, seeing himself at Cain's side, his trusted advisor. "It be mine, mine by right. Almos' had it one time and now ain't nuttin' goan stop me. But dere be somethin' I gots to tend to first."

"What's that?"

"Dere's a man I gots to find. Fancy white doctor, Devlin be his name. He the man whut put me in dat cave, whut stole dis town and all dat time away from me. I goan find him. And he goan pay."

"But it was so long ago—"

"An' I be sittin' right here in dis thing never thought about in my time. An' if I here, he here. Somewheres. An' dat's why I's waitin'."

"I don't understand."

Cain snorted. The fool. He was drunk with visions of himself in possession of Cain's marvelous power to fly disembodied through the air, to feast in the woods on hot and pumping blood, to cast his gaze into another's eyes and enslave a soul.

Cain wanted to take him. Just sitting next to him in the truck, Cain smelled the delectable aroma of human blood. No game animal would ever compete with that. Not now, though. If he did, he'd never be content to hunt the woods again. No, then he'd surge through the sprawling city streets in a frenzied, bloody orgasm advertising his presence to the world. His anonymity would be shot to shit.

Besides, to hunt humans indiscriminately created rivals. Rivals who would rise, fully renewed, possessing the same powers Cain was still exploring and mapping.

He didn't want rivals. He wanted slaves. When his time came round again, after he'd made his enemy sorry he'd ever been born, he'd be selective, feast fully and completely only on those poor-spirited souls he recognized as followers. All others, he'd drain to unconsciousness and then break their necks.

This fool? No. Too smart by half, far too much like Cain himself. He'd only semi-drain him. Then he'd snap his neck. Cain loved the sound of snapping bones. In the meantime, he'd grant his useful, adoring tool some small crumbs of satisfaction.

"Yo' time'll come, boy. After I find him. After he dead, finally and really dead, an' son, he goan be prayin' to die. Den you and me, we'll take dis town like it ain't never been took befo'. But till we find him, whut you want? Whut satisfy you?"

"I want Dennis Billings to lick the soles of my shoes," Justin said. "Right after I walk through dog shit."

Cain laughed. The fool talked his language.

"Well, I thinks we can manage dat, boy. Won't be no trouble a'tal. None a'tal."

Justin grinned. The pickup skipped lightly, carrying its cargo of madness down I-16. That cargo, caught in visions of grandeur to come, didn't notice.

Chapter Four

Six nights after the official housewarming and opening of Bishop & Knight, Attorneys at Law, Ria stepped out of her apartment and went downstairs to finish up work on the brief she'd spent most of the day drafting. She stood motionless in the office alcove.

"But I'm not drunk," she whispered in protest. The room no longer held their Victorian sofas or their secretary's desk, and certainly nothing as modern as a computer.

The sofas looked Victorian, but they weren't the ones recently purchased. The walls weren't light taupe, either. They were duck-egg blue.

The young woman sat on the sofa that really wasn't there. She looked just as lovely as she had in the resurrected bedroom in her blue negligee. Soft curls spilled out of an elegant chignon, glowing in the afternoon sun. She sat facing an older woman with a nose as sharp as a hacksaw. The younger vision held a box in her lap and lifted a white nightgown up out of the tissue.

"Well, it's just lovely, Mama," she declared. Charming, yes, but nothing like the blue negligee Ria'd seen in the bedroom. Safe bet Mama hadn't picked that number out.

"I thought it quite suitable," declared Mama. "Most tasteful, and I'm sure Paul will approve."

Devilish light danced in the slanted blue eyes.

"Well, actually, Mama, Paul prefers me when I'm not in a nightgown," she said, placing the gift back in the box and picking up her cup from the small table in front of the sofa.

For a moment, the meaning of that comment didn't register. Then it did.

"Chloe Duval Devlin! Have you no shame at all?"

"Well, he does." She laughed and shrugged. "Really, I prefer him the same way."

"Ah!" The tall, lean figure passed Ria as though she wasn't there. He strode over to the sofa and kissed Mama's cheek. "And how's my favorite mother-in-law today?"

Mama looked more than a bit flustered. "Leaving, actually, Paul. I was just leaving. Chloe, are you and Paul coming for Sunday supper?

"Certainly, Mama, we wouldn't miss it. Paul, will you walk Mama out?"

The vision named Paul escorted his mother-in-law to the door. He closed it firmly and made it back to the parlor. He burst into laughter.

"Chloe, you're a devil from hell! You almost gave your poor mother apoplexy!"

She rose and flung herself into his arms. "I can't help it if she doesn't know what she's missing," she said, and kissed her husband soundly. They didn't fade from sight. They just disappeared. One minute they were there, the next, gone. So was the afternoon light. It was night again.

Ria sat abruptly on one of their own Victorian sofas, miraculously visible again.

"Holy shit!" she breathed.

Ria had been fascinated for years by the paranormal. She'd poured over any library book she could find relating to the subject as a teenager. She culled her memory banks for information stored from those books. Ghosts, she recalled, were usually wavy mists, radiating a feeling of coldness. Theory held the coldness resulted when spirits drew warmth from their surroundings to acquire energy to materialize. She'd felt no coldness and the figures weren't misty. They weren't exactly solid, either. They were like three-dimensional projections, actors in a scene overlaid on current reality. They paid no attention whatsoever to her. She vaguely recalled a theory that claimed events imprinted themselves in their surroundings, that the proper catalyst made them replay like hitting the play button on a remote control. Could that be what was happening here?

Mama's shocked exclamation gave her a starting point. Chloe Duval Devlin. And the man was Paul. Paul Devlin. The first sighting told her he was a doctor. It was an old house. They had the property records. And the Washington Library had a very good genealogy section. These people were real. Or they had been. She'd find them.

She heard the key in the front door. Johnny.

"Hey," he said, pausing as he saw her sitting on the sofa. "Whatcha doing down here?"

"Just came down to work a while," she said.

"All work and no play makes Ria a dull girl. Want to hit downtown and do a little clubbing?"

"No, thanks, I don't think so."

"Want to come up to my place? Pop popcorn and watch a dirty movie?"

She laughed. "No, thanks. Actually, I don't think I'll work, either. I believe I'll go start that new book I picked up the other day."

"You're no fun at all."

"Providing your entertainment is not part of the partnership agreement," she said, and went upstairs.

She tossed and turned most of the night and finally, it was morning. She sped out the door and timed her arrival at the library to coincide with the opening of its doors.

Ria was a good researcher. She organized her attack, pulled reference volumes and began cross-indexing dates and names. Two hours after she began her search, she had them.

"Oh, no," she moaned softly to herself. "Oh, Chloe, no!"

The Devlin family arrived in Macon in the 1840s with roots trailing back to Stokes County, South Carolina. Paul wasn't the first doctor in the family, though he'd been the first to study in Edinburgh, Scotland. His father and grandfather were doctors, too. The Duval family went back in local history to the 1820s. Henry Duval was a prominent banker in town in the 1870s and 80s. Chloe's father, undoubtedly. Chloe was nineteen, Paul twenty-six when they married in 1883. She'd died in childbirth five years later, in 1888.

Ria felt bereaved herself. The girl deviling her mother was so alive and so in love. She moved down the pages, searching for further references to Paul.

There he was. After Chloe's death, he'd taken an "extended tour" of the western frontier and returned to Macon in a coffin. No details of death, but his body'd been brought home. Both Paul and Chloe were buried in Rose Arbor Cemetery.

Ria glared at the books as though they'd caused the tragedy. And she'd thought her house was such a happy house. *Shit.*

* * *

Having learned the final ending of the private movies the house played just for her, Ria half-expected them to cease. But no. They accelerated. On the Friday marking the end of their third official week in the house, she walked into the nook in the rear of the offices they used as the office mini-kitchen.

A short, plump black figure, her head dressed in a bright turban, stood in front of an old-fashioned stove. She bent to pull down the heavy iron door of the oven. Steam wafted out from behind it, and she turned her head suddenly toward the door.

"Joshua! You wipe yo' feet, boy! An' doan you dare slam dat door, you goan make my cake fall!"

"An' I know you goan take it out of my hide iff'n I do," he said. The vision named Joshua was a slender boy, sixteen or seventeen, his skin the color of *café au lait.*

"I sho' 'nuff is."

Johnny spoke behind Ria.

"Did you leave any coffee? I don't know how you ever get any sleep, much as you drink," he said, and moved to the coffee pot.

The tableau continued to play in front of her, as oblivious to Johnny's presence as to her own.

"Janie, Mist' Paul say tell you he goan be late tonight," Joshua said.

"Dat ain't no surprise," declared Janie. She turned away from the stove and back to her counter. She cut a slice of bread from a fresh loaf sitting on a clean white cloth and slathered it with butter. "Here, boy. Just got it out from de oven a few minutes ago. Doan know how you stays so little, much as you eat. Probably shrink to nuttin' did you slack off any."

Ria looked at Johnny. He sipped his coffee and stared unseeing at the two figures in front of them. "Got stuck with another new appointed criminal case this morning," he said. "God, I'll be glad when our five years are up and we can get off that list. You look a little funny. You alright?"

An African queen entered the kitchen. Her copper skin gleamed. She wore a wrapped turban on her head, too. On this woman, it served as the ultimate accessory of royalty, emphasizing the high cheekbones, the beautiful bone structure.

Janie continued her running commentary. "And Mist' Paul, I swear, dat man. Sadie, you needs to talk to dat boy! Ain't goan listen to you, neither, I knows dat, but you got more chance wid' him den anybody else do. Whut is it dis time? Sometimes I think doan nobody in this town, black nor white neither, stop to think dat man need time to eat and sleep hisself."

"Mist' Paul ain't no little boy, Janie, he doan need us to tell him how to tend his business." Sadie walked over to a cabinet and pulled out a glass.

Janie snorted. "Like dat ever stop you befo' from tellin' him whut to do! Sadie, you doan fool me none, woman. You raise dat boy, you all de time tellin' him whut to do!"

"Something must be wrong with yo' cars, den," said Sadie, "'cause now I save dat for when he really need it, doan waste my breath on things doan matter two hoots nor holler no way."

Ria laughed out loud. She couldn't help it.

"Ria? Earth to Ria Knight!" Johnny waved a hand in front of her face. "You all right?"

"I'm fine," Ria said. Confirmed then. Johnny didn't see a thing.

"Ria!" Their secretary Katie appeared in the door. "Eleven o'clock appointment's here!" She looked right through the trio talking somewhere in the past and moved over to the coffee pot to freshen her own cup. With regret, Ria walked out the door to meet with Mrs. Slatton and hear her tale of domestic woe. She'd have much preferred listening to that conversation from the past.

Chapter Five

Dennis Billings walked out the back door of his parents' house and headed in the direction of his Camaro, whistling as he walked. Freedom from Justin felt like being out of prison. What the hell had he been thinking? He'd never needed the money from that damn drug business, neither had Justin. Their folks were more than well-off and bought both of them anything they hinted they wanted. That drug deal scene was all Justin. For the thrills, Justin said. Some excitement. He'd always been the leader, Dennis the follower. Since they were six, for God's sakes! Thank God he'd come to his senses before they'd gotten busted!

During the past month, following his self-proclaimed emancipation from the influence of Justin Dinardo, Dennis rediscovered the advantages of independence. The biggest one was one Miss Lori Anne Denman. Even if she did beat the living shit out of him on the country club tennis courts. He and Lori were the new 'hot' couple and getting hotter by the day.

School started in two days, his senior year, and he intended to work his ass off. Sliding and free rides were over. Today, one of the last days of freedom, he and Lori were heading to the lake for a day of swimming and sunning.

His whistle cut off in mid-bar as he stared at the Camaro, sitting ungracefully on its four flat tires.

"Shit!"

He squatted by the right front tire and examined the valve stem. Leaky valves? On all four tires?

Justin's voice came over the hedge.

"Nice day for a drive, huh, buddy?"

* * *

On the second day of the new school year, the 3:15 bell resounded through the halls. Laughing, giggling teenagers poured in a floodtide out the doors. Dennis and Lori poured out with them, waving to friends across the parking lot. The school grounds echoed with good-natured insults, a light breeze tempered the heat, the sun was bright. In the air there was the mildest, faintest trace of a hint that autumn might come early to the south this year and possibly even consent to stay awahile.

Dennis shouted over the top of the Camaro's roof at Sean Whithers.

"You still drivin' that piece of shit, man? Thought you were goin' to do it a favor and shoot it!"

"Fuck you, Billings!" Sean shouted back. He was the proud owner of a red Mustang 5.0 five-speed. Most of the students old enough to drive had new or almost new sports cars. It was a rich, private school that catered to the children of professionals.

Dennis grinned and clicked unlock. They saw it at the same time.

Trash covered the seats and floorboards. The smell was overpowering. Miraculously, the leather upholstery and trim was still intact, but Dennis knew it wouldn't be the next time. This was just a little preview.

"But the doors were still locked!" Lori exclaimed. "How did anybody—why did anybody—I just don't get it!"

Dennis turned slowly around, searching over the parking lot for the figure he knew was watching. Justin stood by the hood of his green Tacoma and waited for Dennis to turn in his direction. Their eyes locked. Justin grinned and waved.

Dennis stood by the bank of lockers lining the hallway, waiting for Lori. The flat tires and trashed car had been the first volley in ongoing guerilla warfare, followed by gym shoes without laces, graffiti painted on his locker, pages torn from his calculus book. Minor league stuff, calculated to annoy and irritate. He'd confronted Justin head-on.

"Yeah? Whatcha goin' do about it, Dennis? Call the police? Be my guest."

Yeah, right. *You see, Officer, I know it's Justin, he's pissed at me 'cause I won't help him deal drugs anymore... .* Not a viable option. He was so engrossed in his thoughts he didn't notice Lori's approach until she swirled the combination of her locker.

"I swear!" Lori fussed mildly. "That woman! I've got enough English homework tonight to—"

Lori's face went greenish-yellow. Dennis almost gagged as the stench poured in waves from her open locker. He slammed the locker door shut before she started her high-pitched scream, but not before he saw the huge dead wharf-rat lying on top of her stack of books. Not before he saw the pile of disemboweled guts sitting in a steaming mass beside it.

He pulled Lori's head against his shoulder. He raised his head and looked over Lori's hair. Justin leaned against the wall, four lockers down, watching. He smiled.

Justin's hand moved to his jeans pocket, running his fingers lovingly across the material, caressing the scrim-shaw pocketknife he carried in violation of school regulations. Dennis got the message, all right, one he couldn't ignore. He needed help. And he knew where to go to get it.

While Dennis stared at Justin's hand caressing the hidden knife, Ria ambled through the well-kept grounds of Rose Arbor Cemetery, looking for the Devlin graves. Rose Arbor and neighboring Riverside Hills Cemetery were historic landmarks in the city, overlooking the banks of the Ocmulgee River. Tourists and locals visited frequently to walk the landscaped grounds dotted with groups of azalea bushes and tall, perfectly shaped cedars. Redbuds and dogwoods and marble benches rose among the diverse shapes of the tombstones. An occasional mausoleum mimicked a small Greek temple.

She found Chloe's grave by accident, her eyes caught by the lovely carving of the small statuette of the angel. She couldn't be reading the marker properly. Surely Paul and Chloe were buried side by side, under a double monument. She read the inscription again.

'Chloe Duval Devlin'. The letters, though blurred, were still legible. 'April 15, 1864—February 3, 1888.' Beneath it in smaller letters was inscribed, "Paul Everett Devlin IV". There was only one date. 'February 3, 1888.'

It made no sense. This was a double plot with one side vacant. She knew Paul's body had been shipped home. So why wasn't he lying beside Chloe?

She moved away from Chloe's grave and continued her ramble. Then she saw it. It was very large, as mausoleums go, probably the largest in the entire cemetery. It stood behind Chloe's grave. Close, yes, but why not regular burial beside the woman he'd so loved?

'Paul Everett Devin III.' The letters were sharper than the letters on Chloe's marker. The door was set under the roof's overhang, protected from the elements. 'July 21, 1858 – October 12, 1888.' There was no other inscription.

Ria stood puzzled for a few moments. Another group of visitors moved through the markers, calling to each other to come look at this or that. Ria shook her head and went back to her car. The couple's separation made no sense, and there was nothing she could do about it, but it bothered her. A lot.

* * *

Ria returned to the office. An unexpected visitor sat in the foyer, thumbing absently through the pages of a magazine.

"Dennis! What brings you here?"

There was genuine pleasure in the greeting. Ria's father practiced medicine with Dennis's father. Together the two men formed the professional medical group of Macon Neurology, P.C. Dennis had been Ria's favorite babysitting job back in her teens when Dennis had still needed a babysitter and she'd been his favorite and pretty much only babysitter. She loved him like a little brother, but he didn't fool her a bit. She knew damn well he was considerably smarter than his grades indicated and way too easygoing for his own good.

"I'm sorry I came down without calling, Ria."

"That's okay. You don't need to call to see me."

"Can I?"

"Can you what?"

"See you for a while. Ria, I need to talk."

"Sure," She headed to her office and hoped like hell this wasn't a professional call. Dennis radiated the nervous air of a kid in trouble.

She closed the door behind her.

"So. What kind of trouble are you in?"

"You never did beat around the bush."

"Do your parents know you're here?"

"No. I'm eighteen now, Ria, you don't have to tell 'em, do you?"

"Dennis, they're going to find out sooner or later, whether I tell 'em or not. Which I won't. Besides, you're over eighteen and you're consulting me in a professional capacity. So I couldn't tell 'em even if wanted to. Speeding ticket? DUI? Or possession, maybe?

"Jesus, Ria!"

"They're the most common ones. Which is it?"

"I haven't been arrested at all. But if I had been, I don't think it'd have been just for possession."

"Then what would it have been for?"

Dennis hesitated. He'd had a wild crush on Ria when he was a kid. Even at six and seven, he'd known she was major hot. But it wasn't just that. She was strong. Her self-confidence radiated out two feet in front of her. He'd never seen her in a situation where she didn't know what to do, not even the night he'd run that high fever while his parents were at a Country Club party. She'd taken his temperature and frowned. Then she'd dosed him with Tylenol and ordered him into a bathtub of warm water. By the time she'd run down his folks and gotten them back home, the thermometer read a mere 100 instead of 103. And she'd only been sixteen herself.

Shit. She was going to be so disappointed in him.

"Well?"

"I guess the charge'd be dealing. I guess."

"Dennis! You idiot!"

"I didn't think lawyers were supposed to give lectures."

"I've put you in the bathtub, boy! If all you want's a lawyer, you'll have to go somewhere else! If you want me, I'll lecture any time I feel like it! How in the *hell*— *why* in the hell did you get involved in something like— oh, wait! Let me guess! Justin Dinardo."

"You never did like Justin."

"Damn straight I've never liked that kid! There's something wrong there, Dennis, he's missing something! Did he ever pull the wings off flies and laugh when they tried to fly?"

Never could fool Ria. And he'd tried plenty. Now, looking at Justin with newly opened eyes, Dennis admitted he'd always known Justin was dangerous. Not because of size or athletic ability. Because Justin just wasn't *right*. And he'd been scared enough of him to allow Justin to control him. Dennis shuddered, envisioning Lori running down the halls from the school parking lot screaming, knife slashes pouring blood down her face. Not happening.

"Well, I'm waiting." Ria brought him out of the imaginary scene.

Dennis told her. Everything. Almost everything. He didn't tell her about the skeleton buried in the cave hill. She'd think he'd been using himself if he told her that.

"Maybe there's hope for you yet."

"What now? I know I was stupid, but Justin—I know you're right, Ria. He's got something missing somewhere. And I'm scared. But not for me, that rat in Lori's locker, and the look on his face when his hand moved to that knife in his pocket. And he's right next door to us. Suppose—"

"Suppose the house catches fire one night and your folks can't get out?"

Dennis nodded miserably.

"Wouldn't surprise me a lot."

"So what do we do?"

"Is he still selling?"

"Oh, yeah."

"You think he's still storing his stuff in the same spots?

"Probably."

"You know when he goes?"

"That varies."

"Could you figure out when he's going?"

"Why?"

"It's called turning state's evidence. You turn him over and you get immunity. Though we don't want him busted on a minor charge. He'll be home in six months, if he gets any jail time at all, right next door to you and your folks, if he goes up on a small possession charge. Even on a small selling charge. I want him for a big possession with intent to distribute. I'd like to catch him in a big sale, and the more drugs he's busted with, the bigger the charge, the longer the jail time. Especially since he's never been in trouble before and comes from a good family. We don't want to tap his hand with a ruler. He is already eighteen, isn't he?" she asked in sudden alarm, struck by the thought that Justin might still be a juvenile offender.

"Yeah. Yeah, he is."

"Well, thank God for small mercies."

"What do you think he'd get?"

"Well, that depends on what we can catch him with. And I'm not just going to tell you, I'm going to show you." Ria turned to her computer and tapped rapidly on the keyboard. "I assume y'all have some cocaine and crack stashed?"

"Oh, yeah."

"Of course, why did I ask? Schedule II. Here it is. Come look." Ria motioned him around to the screen. "Prison term of not less than five or more than twenty," she read aloud. "If we pin distribution on him. Same thing you'd be lookin' at if you were still fartin' around with him. You got that? Does that compute?"

"That much?"

"Dennis, that's for the first offense. A second conviction carries a life term. The law doesn't take drug traffic real lightly. But I doubt seriously he'd serve anywhere near that, no. So. You got it in your head now—real clear—I want it real clear, Dennis. That's what you've been flirtin' with. How's that make you feel, now that you're relatively sane again?"

"I guess I thought—"

"You thought it wouldn't be much worse than getting caught smoking a roach, right?

"Well, yeah. I guess."

"Welcome to the real world. How much did y'all keep stashed?"

"Ten, fifteen thousand dollars worth at the time, I guess. Sometimes more. We'd built up."

"In weight, Dennis, not dollars."

"Justin did all that, I never was any good with it."

Ria sighed. "Some dealer you are. Okay, was that your price or street value?"

"Our price."

"I guess to hell you had built up. That's a good chunk of street change."

"Do my folks have to know?"

"Dennis, you're not going to be able to put Justin out of action unless you're willing to testify, and trial testimony's public record. He's small time, and I don't know how much publicity it'll get, if any, or how well your folks read the newspapers or if the paper would carry anything about it at all. But you want to take the chance they'll find out about it that way, instead of from you? Don't kid yourself. In lots of ways, in our folks' social circle, Macon's still a real small town, and they'll find out. Probably sooner rather than later."

"But suppose I keep my mouth shut and he just gets busted? I mean, he could always just get busted, couldn't he?"

"Sure he could. He could screw up anytime. He could carve Lori's face before then, too, couldn't he?"

Dennis stood up and moved restlessly.

"Hey, probably I'm overreacting. I mean, he wouldn't really—"

"Dennis. He would. Really. Listen to me." She moved behind Dennis and put her hands on his shoulders. "I don't like Justin, I never have. Do you know why?"

"I never knew why but I knew you didn't."

"Then let me tell you a secret. Sometimes—" Ria broke off and searched for the right words. "Sometimes, I don't operate just on intellect, know what I mean? I don't mean I've got ESP or any shit like that, I just mean that sometimes, I get—I think people call 'em gut feelings. Everybody has 'em, but some folks seem to develop 'em a little more than others. I trust mine. If I get a real strong gut feeling, I go with it. I'm usually right. Like this house. It was a wreck, and everybody thought we'd lost our minds, but look at it now. Believe it or not, Dennis, when I walked in it the first time, I could hear it whispering 'buy me'."

"But I don't understand what that's got to do with Justin."

"Once or twice, your folks went out with Justin's folks and I sat with both of you, remember? Over at your house?"

"Yeah."

"And I never did it again. Told your mother I wasn't goin' to sit with Justin. Because Dennis, full-blown psychopaths don't just happen. They develop. Bit by bit. I could feel it. Coming out of him in waves. And he's been developing. From what you've told me, he's speeded up considerable in the last couple of months. Yeah, he'd carve Lori's face. Because he'd enjoy it. Now you tell me you don't know that, too."

Dennis bit his lip.

"Will you go with me?"

"To the District Attorney's Office? Hell, baby, I'm your lawyer. I'm going first. But to your parents? Un-huh. Time to put on your big boy panties and deal with it."

* * *

His parents were a lot worse than the District Attorney's Office. Ria relented somewhat and drove over to the Billings household immediately after Dennis' SOS.

Joyce Billings paced the family den, drink glass stained with lipstick in her hand. Don Billings, successful neurosurgeon who sliced and spliced without hesitation into the gray matter of living brain cells sat in his recliner and stared out the window.

Joyce Billings spewed her litany of insulted motherhood the moment Ria cleared the den door.

"Ria, do you know what Dennis has been telling us!"

"Of course I do. I'm his attorney."

37

"He's a child! You had no right not to tell us—"

"Excuse me, Mrs. Billings. This is Georgia, and he's over eighteen. I had an ethical obligation not to tell you. Besides, he told you himself."

"Oh, my God!" Joyce Billings moaned, and sank down on the couch. "How could you, Dennis? You have everything, you've always had everything. To do this to us! How could you? After all we've done for you, Dennis!"

Ria cut across the reproaches. "Mrs. Billings, you're not doing any good with all this. Dennis screwed up. He knows it. He's willing to do something about it, and I think you ought to be proud of him for taking responsibility like a man."

"What my bridge club is going to say—"

"Fuck your bridge club," said Don Billings suddenly.

"*What* did you say?"

"I said fuck your bridge club. If you'd ever paid any attention to him instead of playing bridge and shopping and doing lunch—"

"While you played golf and racketball and—"

"I fucked up, too. I admit it. Okay? Let's see what happens now. Ria?"

"Well, I talked to the DA's office and this is what they want to do. Dennis, did y'all just retrieve the stuff and make small sells? Or did you ever sell big? Maybe to another independent?"

"Yeah, we had some regulars. A couple of 'em."

"Really?"

"Yeah, to some guys who sell to the kids at the public high schools."

"I didn't realize you'd progressed to being middlemen."

"Just those few. There's one dude supplies the whole senior class at Bradley Central. That's his territory. We used to meet him out in the woods where we stash the stuff. Usually the first week of the month."

"Any particular night?"

"No. But I can watch. If I see Justin's truck leave, I can tell. He'll have the dirt bike in it."

"So cars and trucks don't take those trails?"

"Hell, no, not even a four-wheel drive. They're not wide enough."

"So when you call in, we need to have the stakeout ready to set up. Should be feasible, he has to drive a lot further than the drug squad does."

"Yeah."

"He'll see Dennis," Don Billings interjected.

"Dennis won't be there, all this is preliminary work. He'll need to go out with me and the drug squad and show them where to set up. Tomorrow afternoon."

"Then Justin won't know Dennis—"

"Sure he will. Justin's lots of things but stupid isn't one of 'em. And Dennis'll have to testify if he doesn't cop a plea."

"And he'll know it was me, anyway, I know that," Dennis interjected. "Ria, won't he get out on bail? Before trial?"

"Absolutely. But he'll be in enough trouble without adding any else like an harassment charge." She hoped.

* * *

Dennis and Ria took the drug squad of the Bibb County Sheriff's Department out the next afternoon. Dennis showed them the trial into the woods and pointed out the clearing. He glanced surreptitiously over his shoulder at the hillock holding the small cave. It was covered, thank God.

He pointed around the clearing.

"Here," he said, "and here, and here. All around here. I probably don't know all the spots anymore."

"This clearing's it?" one of the deputies asked.

"No, not quite. There's another one." Dennis moved over to a pile of brush and lifted it up, revealing another dirt trail through the trees. "This leads to another spot we cleared out, and there's some there,

39

too. I don't know which he'll use when he meets the dude that buys for Bradley Central. "

"Okay, let's check it out, too," said the Deputy. "We need to have both spots ready."

Dennis took them to the second site, about half a mile down the trail.

Ria pulled him away from the deputies. "Dennis! For God's sake! Did y'all have to use this spot?"

Three crumbling markers marked old graves from a private family cemetery, long forgotten. Once upon a time, the now-faint lettering almost invisible in the soft, disintegrating stone might have been a 'T', another possibly a 'J', another a probable 'D'. All else was hopeless.

"I didn't like it much," Dennis admitted. "Seemed disrespectful, somehow. But Justin said—"

"Damnit, Dennis! If Justin'd suddenly developed a passion for gang rape, would you have just gone along with that, too, for God's sakes?"

"I'm sorry," he muttered, and walked away.

Ria expelled another exasperated breath and moved to one of the deputies.

"These spots going to give you any special problems?"

"I don't think so. We'll be a lot closer to the place than Dennis's buddy Justin will be when he heads out. If he leaves from home, that is. And if Dennis sees him soon enough and calls us quick enough."

"Can't promise about the seeing part, but he'll damn sure be calling if he does."

* * *

The call came two nights later. Ria raced down to the Law Enforcement Center.

"Miss Knight, no offense, but we can't take civilians."

"Deputy Taylor, no offense, but I've got a personal interest here. Your informant's practically my baby brother. He messed up bad, he knows it. He's a good kid at the core. I need to be able to tell him I saw Justin go down. I can't ride with you, I know, but can I please, please, follow you?"

"We haven't forgotten to read anybody their rights in a long time, Miss Knight."

"I know you haven't." Ria put on a pitiful face and batted her eyes. Feminine weapons deployed by a master. "Please? I'll sign any release you want. I mean, lawyers are officers of the Court, I won't screw anything up."

"Oh, hell! But you stay back out of the way."

"Yes sir!"

From the background, Ria watched the spotlights hit the clearing.

"Sheriff! Freeze!"

Handcuffs clicked. "You have the right to an attorney. If you cannot afford an attorney, one will be appointed for you..."

Justin made one statement. Just one.

"You tell Dennis Billings he fucked up. Bad. And so did that bitch lawyer friend of his. Had to be her."

* * *

Cain paced the sleazy room in the sleazy hotel off Seventh Street. Something was wrong. Fool had gotten caught. He felt it. Throughout the course of his extensive career he'd been plagued with fools. And he'd thought this boy had possibilities. *Shiiiiiitttt*. Well, best check it out. And there were other fools out there. That never changed. He stood in the center of the room, raised his arms, relaxed his thoughts. He disappeared.

* * *

The antique hall clock, an office warming gift from her parents, signaled 1:00 a.m. as Ria trudged wearily into the foyer. A good night's work but damn, she was tired. She started up the steps and stopped. Joshua stood outside her office door holding a tray in his hands. He shifted it to balance it between his arm and his hip while he knocked.

"Leave me the hell alone!" Paul shouted from behind the door.

"Mist' Paul, you gots to come out sometime! You gots to eat!"

"I don't *gots* to do nothing, Josh! Now go away!"

"Mist' Paul—"

"Don't make me open this door and throw you down the hall!" The voice was rough and harsh and full of pain.

"Paul! I ain't gonna leave!"

Paul? What? Black servants in the 1880s didn't call their employers by their first names without the 'Mist' or 'Miss'. They just didn't.

Joshua knocked again and looked down both sides of the hall. Checking for listeners?

"You told me one time, you said, 'we'll take care of each other'. You remember that, Paul?"

Ria's mouth literally fell open as she watched from her spectator mode. Where had the distinctive black cadence gone?

"Well, I remember that. So I'm tellin' you now, I'm goin' to take care of you whether you want me to or not. You been in that room five straight days and nights, Paul! And I'm tellin' you, Doc Everett told Sadie you had 'til tomorrow noon to come outta there or he'll take the door down! You want your father to have to do that? Haul you out and clean you up like a baby?"

Joshua waited for a response that didn't come.

"Fine. You just stay there, then. And I'll stay right here. I ain't goin' nowhere!" Joshua sat down by the door and leaned his back against the wall. When the door opened, Paul Devlin's appearance matched his voice, exhausted and brimming with pain. His clothes were rumpled and stained, his eyes black under the sockets. Ria's heart twisted. Chloe was dead. For the first time, she regretted her private movies. She really didn't want to see this.

Paul stood in the doorway and glared down at Joshua. "Stubborn little bastard, aren't you?"

"Well," said Josh, speech still devoid of any black cadence, "I suppose that's fair enough. I am stubborn, and we both know I'm a bastard."

"Impudent, too."

"Door's open, though, ain't it?"

"Not for long. Go away. Tell Papa to leave me the hell alone, too."

Josh jumped to his feet and thrust his arm through the open door.

"No," he said. "Enough."

"Move your arm."

"No."

"I'll break it!"

"Go ahead, I'm real worried about it," said Josh.

"Stubborn bastard," Paul repeated.

"So you said. You need a bath. C'mon," Josh said, and pulled Paul's arm.

"Where?"

"Upstairs."

"I won't go back in that room. Not ever."

"Don't have to. We got plenty of rooms."

They disappeared. Ria resumed her weary trudge up the stairs, still mindboggled at Joshua's change of speech pattern, at the entire tone of the encounter. Unheard of in 1888. What was going on in this house?

Chapter Six

Three days later, Ria returned to the office, another appointed criminal case finished. The client wasn't thrilled with the plea bargain she'd negotiated., but the client's victim hadn't been thrilled by the twenty-two stitches closing the gash on his face inflicted by the broken liquor bottle either, so she wasn't terribly sympathetic. Johnny knocked perfunctorily on her door and came in to sit on her sofa.

"Took a message for you while you were out," he said. "You won't much like it."

"I won't?"

"Ted Dorry called from the DA's office. When you weren't in, he asked for me. Told him you were at the Courthouse, he musta' missed you."

"I guess so. What is it?"

"Justin Dinardo's skipped bail. He's gone."

Ria sat down heavily in her chair.

"Shit!"

"He's just a kid, Ria, he can't stay out of sight all that long."

"Did he take his truck?"

"Nope. Didn't take anything. They'll pick him up."

"Don't bet on it. I figure he's got a good bit of cash stashed."

"Yeah, but he's not going to stick around, Ria. Too risky. And for sure, too risky for him to try anything on Dennis. And you and I both know, he's a kid from a good family, first time he's ever been in trouble—"

"Yeah, but it's big trouble."

"I know, but the Judge wouldn't have thrown the book at him, Ria. He'd have let him off as light as possible. Fact of life." Johnny shrugged. "Now that he's skipped bail, if he ever slips up, that sort of alleviates the sympathy factor. You know?"

"Yeah," Ria sighed. "I guess."

"Well, nothing we can do about Justin. Had lunch?"

"Not hungry."

"I am."

"So go eat."

"I'm 'bout to go grab something and bring it back. What do you want? 'Cause I don't need a partner who's anorexic," Johnny said.

"Very funny." Ria's metabolism had been a running joke since childhood. She could out=eat any two men of her acquaintance and never gain an ounce.

"I'll split a sub with you. The foot-long one. With everything."

"Hell, no! I've never in my life eaten half a sub! Get me a whole one!"

* * *

Just when Ria began to think her private movie, having moved past Chloe's death, had played itself out, she woke to the sound of someone crying. No, that wasn't right, exactly. A man was crying. The sobs were rusty, as they so often were when men cried, as though the tears were wrenched from deep within, released under great protest.

She moved softly to her door. The bedroom she'd viewed the night of their housewarming was there, not her living room. Paul stood in front of Chloe's dresser, one of her negligees lifted to his face, muffling the sounds.

She walked over to him and put her hand on his shoulder. Her fingers passed right through the seemingly solid shoulder and he disappeared entirely.

45

* * *

Enough was enough. She didn't want to sit home and watch long-ago grief two nights in a row. Ria took herself to the mall. She needed crowds, lights, action. And besides, one of her favorite books had finally succumbed to years of thumbing and turned-down pages and totally disintegrated the other night when she'd picked it up, whole sections of pages parting company with the spine. For convenience, you couldn't beat an e-reader, but some books you just had to hold in your hands. She'd get a replacement and look over the new crop of novels.

Then maybe she'd hit the clothes racks at the fun stores and get a new outfit or two, something bright and fun that didn't look a bit like a lawyer. Grab dinner at one of the restaurants. Exactly what she wanted tonight. Crowds without interaction.

She stood near the back of Barnes & Nobles and glared up at one the higher shelves. It would be up there, of course. Hardly a current bestseller. She stood on tiptoe and stretched, but even at five foot eight she couldn't quite make it. And customers weren't supposed to climb the ladders and there wasn't a clerk in sight. She stretched again and succeeded in knocking a book off, but not the one she wanted.

"Damn," she muttered under her breath, bending to retrieve it.

The resonant voice sounded beside her.

"Here, let me help," it said. She started. That voice. Impossible. No way. Her eyes traveled slowly upward, taking in the well-cut tan Dockers, the long-sleeved denim shirt rolled casually up to reveal the lightly tanned forearms. They moved higher and settled on the face of the man beside her. No way.

"The one you want is always out of reach," the voice continued. Ria was staring, she knew she was. But the man she thought was there wasn't really there. In just a minute, her mind would clear itself out and replace the image she thought she was seeing with reality. But it was sure taking a hell of a long time for her mind to cooperate.

"Which one are you after? I'll be glad to get it for you."

"The—uh—" Ria stammered and stuttered, infuriated with herself. "I'm sorry, I'm not usually so muddled, but—have we met?" Oh, God. She sounded like a pickup in reverse.

He smiled. "No, I don't think so. I'm certain I'd remember."

"I—uh—" she stammered again and furiously told herself to get a grip. She pointed. "That hardback edition of the collected Shakespeare plays."

"Really?" he asked, surprise in his voice. "You read Shakespeare? For pleasure? Excuse me, that didn't come out right. It's just—he's not casual reading these days." He stretched his six-foot frame upward and pulled the volume down.

"No," she said, accepting the book. "I know he's not, it's just that he's soothing sometimes, when I'm real tired or irritated, the flow and rhythm and beauty of the words calm me down. My old copy fell apart a few weeks ago, I hated that. I grew up with it."

"Lots of humor in with the dark there, too. Always thought he'd get a real kick out of it if he could see how seriously the English professors take him. Personally, I think he just intended to tell a good story."

Ria laughed. She'd always thought the same.

The man wearing the impossible face held out his hand. "I'm Paul. Paul Everett." Ria's eyes widened. She froze in position, her mind repeating a name over and over again. Paul Everett Devlin, III. Then she shook her head slightly and held out her hand.

"Ria Knight," she said. "Are you from Macon, Mr. Everett?"

"Paul. No, I'm not from Macon. I'm—listen, did you want to look for anything else? I haven't eaten yet, and I was just about to grab something if you'd like to join me. I'm safe, I promise. 'Course, Jack the Ripper'd say the same thing."

Ria tried to make some sense of the kaleidoscopic jumble of thoughts and focused on the obvious. She'd lost her mind. Very simple. She was standing in a bookstore talking to empty space.

"I, uh—no! I mean yes! No, I wasn't going to look for anything else and yes, I'd like to join you."

He strode easily beside her back up to the cashier and slipped the volume of Shakespeare out of her hand, adding it to the two books he carried.

"Oh, no, that's so not—"

"It's not every day you run into somebody reads Shakespeare for pleasure. Consider it my support for the arts, why don't you?"

She stood aside and waited and as they walked out of the store, she stopped suddenly.

"Oh, that was stupid of me!"

"Pardon?"

"I ordered an out-of-stock book the other week and I meant to check on it tonight. I won't be a minute," she said, and dashed back to the counter.

"Excuse me," she said, homing in on the cashier who'd rung up Paul Everett's purchases. "That last man you checked out. What did he look like?"

The clerk stared. Customers. They were crazy and here was proof.

"Aren't you with him?"

"Well, yes, but what does he look like to you?"

"Like a model, actually."

"Yes, but what—"

"Blond hair, blue eyes. Tall, lean, great voice"

"He didn't pay with a card, did he?"

"Nope, used cash."

Shit. No way to confirm he'd really said his name was Paul Everett. Oh, well. At least she wasn't talking to thin air.

"Thank you," she said, and went back out. The clerk shrugged and returned to her duties. Customers. Crazy.

"Your book's not in?"

"No. Oh, well. Where do we eat?"

"You pick," he said, and spread his hand out towards the shops and stores lining the streets of the Mall designed to replicate the down-towns of the yesteryear.

"Mexican?"

"Any day of the week and twice on Sunday. Let's head down."

* * *

"So you're not from Macon?" she asked again when they settled in with their sandwiches.

"No." He shook open his napkin. "Actually, I'm in town on sort of a research trip."

"Research?"

"I'm on a leave of absence from a very small newspaper you never heard of. Sounds sort of self-important so I don't usually tell anybody but seeing as how you're a fan of fine literature, I'll tell you anyway. I'm working on—trying to work on—my first novel."

"Really? Here?"

"Yes, here. To be honest, I put my finger on a map of the south and it landed closer to here than anywhere else."

Ria laughed. "You're joking?"

"No. And you?"

"I'm an attorney."

"Now you're joking."

"No."

"You look way too young to be an established attorney."

"I said attorney, I didn't say established. Actually, I've been practicing a little over two years and a couple of months ago I went out on my own with a friend of mine. It's our office and home, we redid the second floor into two apartments. The first floor is Bishop & Knight, Attorneys at Law."

49

"You didn't get top billing?"

"Always start with the name that goes first in the phone book. Sound business practice. Johnny says we should have made up a silent partner. Aabco, Bishop & Knight. So folks thumbing through the phone book see our name first."

He laughed just like Paul Devlin laughed. Coincidence. Nothing else. Or maybe his people came from Macon after all and he just didn't know it. Maybe he was a Devlin descendant. She'd always heard everyone had a double.

"Johnny? Your partner's not another lady lawyer, then?"

"Not hardly. We go back a long way, friends from the cradle. Our mothers are best friends, we were sort of automatic brother and sister."

Ria caught the glint of metal on his finger. His wedding ring finger. She put down the tortilla chip she'd just dipped in salsa and stood up, calling herself a first-class idiot, letting herself get picked up by a married man in a bookstore just because he looked and sounded like her Paul.

"Thank you for the book, Mr. Everett. And for dinner."

"But you haven't finished! What—"

"And do be sure to give my regards to your wife. I hope she knows what a charming husband she has."

He glanced down at his hand.

"Oh, hell! Look, please sit down. My wife died several years ago. I've just never met anyone who ever gave me a reason to want to take her ring off."

Ria searched his face. Her radar wasn't usually wrong but it wasn't infallible either.

"That'd be a really shitty thing to say if it isn't true," Ria said, still standing.

"I'd be a complete scumbag. Lowest of the low. But it's true."

Ria sat back down. "Then I'm sorry. I overreacted."

"You believe me?"

"Yes." She sighed. "Does that prove I'm a gullible fool?"

"It proves you're a remarkable judge of character. Though of course, I'm sure—"

"That's what Jack the Ripper would say, too."

"Exactly," he said, and laughed.

"What newspaper do you work for that I've never heard of?"

"Mobile Reporter."

"Alabama boy."

"Guilty."

"What's your book about? Or do you talk about it? Mobile's full of history. Just as Southern as Macon, too, and a port city to boot. Why not stay there?"

"Too much chance of gettin' accused of airing other folks' dirty laundry. You know how people are, they'd swear and be damned I was malignin' family history. It's sort of an overlay of the past on the present. Or the present over the past. That type of thing. I'm researching Macon in the late 1800s right now."

"Our house was built then."

"Really?"

"Yes, 1883 I think was the date of the first deed."

"I'm sure it's beautiful."

"It is now. Looked like hell when we started."

"Macon's a great setting for that type of plot, you know. It's taken good care of so many of the older houses. And so much of downtown—some of the buildings still have the same use, did you know?"

"I know in general, but not really in specifics. Are you getting that deep with your research?"

"Oh, yes. I found some old maps. A lot of the old stores and government buildings, the firehouses. The churches, of course, the older residential sections. Those old downtown buildings—if they could only talk!"

Ria laughed. She wondered what he'd say if he knew hers did talk. Or at least it did to her.

"What?"

"Oh, just thinking."

"About?"

"That you should show me instead of tell me."

"Excuse me?"

"Show me. Your Macon. The Macon of your book." She stood up. "You through eatin'? Then let's ride downtown. Show me what it used to be."

He stared. "This is probably cutting my own throat, but you did just meet me, you know."

"I had dinner with you."

"In a crowded restaurant."

Ria shrugged. "You told me you were perfectly safe." She'd lost her mind, no doubt about it. But she'd eaten dinner with Paul Devlin's double. A double who claimed to know all about Paul Devlin's Macon.

"Well, to tell the truth, I left my car up at the Auto Service Center for an oil change, thought I'd get some errands out of the way, told them just to leave it out front when they closed."

"My car's sitting right in front of Barnes & Nobles. I'll bring you back."

He hesitated and then signaled their waitress. "Let me get the check."

* * *

She waited for his reaction when he saw her car. She loved her car. And hadn't met a man yet who didn't want to date her for it.

"*Woooooo!*" He gave a low whistle under his breath. "I thought you said you weren't an established attorney?"

"I'm not."

"Then you're independently wealthy."

"Not hardly. It's a classic, alright, but not a really out-of-sight classic like a '56 T-Bird or a Shelby."

"Still." Paul walked around it, stroking the finish of the '65 Mustang convertible. Candy apple red, black top and black interior. "It's beautiful."

"It was my Dad's, and I'm not sure how many transmissions and motors it's had," said Ria, unlocking the doors. "But he replaced the upholstery and top when he gave it to me after I graduated from law school. He really loved this car, he said it was an eary mid-life crisis present to himself."

They settled in. Ria turned the key and grinned. "Let's cruise. go down through the historic district, down Coleman Hill, and take Mulberry through Macon."

"You're driving." He settled back.

"And no cracks about my driving," Ria warned with mock sternness.

"Not a one."

She went out the back of the Mall to cross over to Vineville Avenue and thence down to College Street where she turned left and drove slowly past the old mansions and mini-mansions, still standing tall and stately. Most were renovated private homes or home-apartment combinations. Light spilled invitingly from the windows. She headed down Coleman Hill.

Paul gestured out the window. "Lots of these were here in the 1880s", he said, indicating huge Victorians and classic white-columned mansions. "The smaller ones weren't, they were built in the early 1900s."

On the right, the Hay House, a State historic trust, presided in Italian Renaissance splendor over the corner of Georgia Avenue and Spring Street. "The Hay House. That was the Johnston house originally, you know. They were—that is, I imagine they must have been so proud of it."

"Had to have been. You caught one of the tours yet? The inside of that place is unbelievable! Can't write about old Macon if you haven't seen it."

"Oh, yes, I've seen it. Know it well."

The city lights spread before them, sparkling like jewels. They ran down the double lanes of Mulberry Street, where inbound and outbound traffic were split by large islands of grassed park, with huge old Japanese magnolia trees and thickly massed azaleas.

"Mulberry Street Methodist and First Presbyterian," Paul said with pleasure, eyeing the old landmarks. "Think of the joys and sorrows those walls have seen."

"Makes you feel your mortality, doesn't it?" She continued to drive at a leisurely pace.

"Sol Hogue's Drug Store!" Paul exclaimed suddenly, pointing to the rows of multi-paned bay windows of a two-story edifice on the corner of Mulberry and Cotton, its complicated trim and scroll work now painstakingly painted in the deep antique green and royal purple signature colors of Lawrence Mayer's Florist. "Don't you just love all that complicated glass and scroll work?"

"Is that what it was then?"

"A drug store, yes. And I believe it was still a drug store well up into the 1980s or early 90s."

Ria laughed. "I'd almost forgotten. Young's Drugs. Daddy used to tell me about the hand-dipped milkshakes and how much he'd loved them when he was little."

They moved on through the light at Mulberry and Second.

"That was the Gas Light and Water Company," he said, pointing to the old buildings, now re-born as restaurants, printing shops, antique stores. "That was a lawyer's office, M. G. Baynes, I believe I recall. And that was a dentist, Dr. Barfield. And that," he said as he pointed, "was Berry & Flynn Tobacco Shop. They had a cherry blend that beat anything in London."

"Wow, it must have been something for the records to include that."

"Well, okay, that's from some of their ad advertisements in the old newspapers. Had a high opinion of themselves. Ah! The new Government Building!" he exclaimed, as they moved into the next block. "Which of course you know as the Federal

Courthouse, though it's not the same building, just the same spot. That was Kuhn's. Guns and knives and fishing tackle."

Ria turned onto Martin Luther King Boulevard, making a square and heading up Cherry Street.

"Fourth Street," Paul said, "in the old days. And then in the early 1900s it changed to Broadway. The original St. Joseph's was right there," he said, pointing.

"The Catholic church? Down here?"

"Un-huh."

She turned and headed down Cherry Street, Macon's main drag since its earliest beginnings. The roll call of the past continued.

"Jacques," he said, "grocers. Farquhar & Co., hardware. Straton's. That was a gun company. Gibian's. Grocery and tobacco. Coben's. Liquor and cigars. They imported some from Cuba you could steal for. Goodwyn & Small, drug store."

Ria looked at the buildings as he pointed and saw the past overlaid on the present. So Coben's liquor and cigars 'imported some from Cuba you could steal for', did they?

"Lieb's groceries," Paul continued. "Dr. Kenan's office. Hertz' Clothing. I—" He broke off suddenly and restarted the sentence. "If you can believe its ad, it was the only choice of Macon's professional men."

Ria turned at the top of Poplar Street and cut back down Cotton. The names just kept coming. "Bunk's. Books and stationers. Oliver & Holt. Grocers."

She settled into a slow and stately pace, dissecting the town into small squares and touring slowly along.

"Rogers & Winn, crackers and candy. Bone & Chappell, groceries. Cox and Corbin, liquor and groceries. O'Gorman's. Dry goods."

"Did Macon do anything but eat, Paul?"

"Oh, but think about it! To walk in a store and have the clerks call you by name, knowing that this cook's household preferred pork, and this one was shopping for beef, and little Ria Knight had a preference for lemon drops."

"It does sound nice."

"It was," he said, gazing out at the storefronts.

Was it now? She said nothing, moving out from the center of town, cutting down streets and continuing her squared pattern.

She turned back down to pick up Martin Luther and take the back road to Eisenhower Parkway.

"Hey!" Paul protested. "It's after dark! Please tell me you don't drive this route by yourself after dark?"

Ria laughed. No way to breed that protective instinct out of a southern man. And no, this absolutely wasn't a route for a lone woman to take after dark. Not now. Not in the present.

"No, I don't, I promise. Daddy and Johnny'd both have heart attacks. But since I'm not alone, and we're on this tour, I thought we'd pass the old streets."

Small juke joint style nightclubs sent flashy light into the darkness, blown bulbs obscuring part of their names. Crowds stood in front of liquor stores. The strange aroma indigent to this one particular area of the city crept into the car. An indefinable smell, not exactly greasy, not exactly dirty. A funky smell that existed nowhere else in town. They passed the remains of a Johnny V's Drive-In that had seen much better days.

"These streets," he said, gesturing to the short concrete posts which in daylight designated Ell Street, Hazel Street, Edge Street. "In the 1880s, this was middle-class Macon. Good working people, solid houses. Families. New babies. Hope. Those days are long-gone, though."

"That makes me feel very sad, Paul."

"Me, too," he said.

She turned right at the intersection with Eisenhower Parkway and headed back to the interstate entrance to I-75 back out to Riverside and the Mall, melancholy with memories of streets that used to be.

Had time suspended itself? Ria thought they'd been gone much longer than they had. They spoke simultaneously.

"How much longer—"

"I don't quite know long I'll—"

They laughed.

"Okay," Ria said. "You answered my question. You don't know how much longer you'll be in town."

"Not exactly. But if you'd like—"

"I would. Very much."

He grinned. "Suppose I'd been about to suggest a wild weekend at the Hilton?"

"Haven't had a Hilton here in a long time. You're a lot better with the past than you are with the present. And I was pretty sure you weren't going to suggest that. Yet."

"I bet you give your witnesses the devil."

"Haven't had that many trials yet, to tell the truth."

"I'll call you."

"I'm easy to find. No such thing as an unlisted attorney. Or an attorney without a business card." She reached into the door's side pocket and pulled one out, handing it to him.

He hesitated. Instead of leaning over and kissing her goodnight, he reached his hand out and picked up her own, bringing it to his lips. When he dropped it, the light reflected off his wedding ring, highlighting the etchings in the gold band. She pulled his hand back into the light.

"How unusual!" she said, peering through the shadows at the rolled scrollwork.

"My wife was an unusual woman. So are you." She dropped his hand.

"Paul!"

"Yes?"

"What was her name?"

"Her name?"

"Your wife."

He hesitated almost imperceptibly.

"Chloe. It's been a special evening, Ria."

"Yes. It was."

He got out of the car. "Go on and pull out now, so I can make sure you're headed home okay."

He stood, obviously going nowhere until she did. That southern chivalry again. She eased off the clutch and moved forward, back out toward Riverside.

While she drove, her mind moved in hyper-speed, processing the data compiled by the evening. Name, looks, voice, background. Knowledge of a city long past. A tobacco shop with a 'cherry blend that beat anything in London'. Another that imported Cuban cigars 'you could steal for'.

A skillful weaving of fact and fiction? Most successful liars incorporated as much truth as possible into their fabrications. Made for less confusion, wasn't as easy to get tripped up. When people found it expeditious to change their names, most often they dropped a surname, switched to a middle name, or tagged on a mother's maiden name.

She pulled into the two-car garage in the back of the house on Orange Street, formerly the carriage house. Sometimes she believed she could see waiting buggies, hear the soft snicker of a horse. She turned off the ignition. Time to have a long talk with herself.

"Okay, Ria," she whispered. "Admit it. You think he's Paul Devlin. Your Paul Devlin. Who comes to life and assumes solid form on the first full moon of October. Will you get a grip?"

She got out of the car and went inside. Had he found the secret of eternal youth? Did he still live and breathe and walk, telling smooth stories blending fact and falsehood? Why hadn't he said he was a doctor? Why wouldn't he have kept his training updated?

She went inside and up the steps, opening her apartment door. She automatically undressed and pulled on her robe. Then she walked to the living room, formerly the Devlin bedroom, and sat down on one of her sofas.

Paul Everett wasn't a ghost. Not the Paul she'd met at the bookstore, eaten dinner with, gone back in time with. He ate and drank and spent money. Modern money. And he was solid. She'd touched him. He'd kissed her hand. She picked up one of the sofa pillows and hugged it to her.

She'd lost her mind. End of story. She'd met a flesh and blood, living man. Who just coincidentally had almost the same name as the vision that haunted her house. And a deceased wife with the same name. How far could coincidence go?

He was out of the car, she thought. We were talking quietly, and I expected him to say her name was Chloe. I was primed for it. He said Cathy. Or Claire. Or Candice.

She got up and went into her room. She'd misunderstood, that was all. She'd place a phone call tomorrow, and confirm once and for all that a flesh and blood man named Paul Everett was on a leave of absence from the, what had he said? The Mobile Reporter. Then she'd make an appointment with a psychiatrist.

She clicked the lamp off and settled into her pillows. In her uneasy slumbers, she drove up and down the unpaved streets of 1888 Macon in her Mustang classic, passing horses standing with their reins wrapped casually around horse posts, teams of dray horses pulling delivery vans. The store names were painted on the front glass. A. B. Farquar, S. R. Jacques & Co., Coben's, Kuhns, Lieb's Fine Groceries. Paul Everett, dressed in tan Dockers and denim shirt, stood side by side with Paul Devlin, dressed in the tight britches and high-topped riding boots of 1888. Both men moved, just out of her reach, drawing her forward with gestures of their hands, pulling her back, back, back in time.

* * *

She didn't know how long she'd slept when the sounds woke her. Muffled sounds. Paul Devlin. Crying over Chloe's things. She got up and moved to the door, and there he was. He lifted a perfume bottle and held the stopper to his nose. The gesture caught her heart. How many nights had he cried for Chloe in this room?

She walked to his side. His hand moved. In the glow of the nightlights plugged around her living room, she caught the gleam of gold on his finger. His wedding ring.

She moved closer and touched his image. Again he disappeared at her touch. But not before she saw the rolled etchings engraved on the band of his ring.

Was he back? Had he ever been gone? She returned to her bed and tossed restlessly until dawn.

* * *

At 9:30 the next morning, Ria dialed a phone number. She'd already checked the internet. Mobile's newspaper was the Press-Register. It didn't have a Mobile Reporter. And a call to personnel verified that no reporter named Paul Everett worked for it. Or ever had.

She hung up. Well. If there was no verifiable living Paul Everett, his supposedly deceased double definitely had a verified address. Rose Arbor Cemetery. Today's schedule was hectic but her plans weren't daytime plans, anyway.

She went out of her office to their secretary's desk.

"Katie, would you do me a favor? Not professional. Girl stuff."

"Sure."

"If I'm in the office and I get a phone call from a Paul Everett, interrupt me."

Katie narrowed her eyes.

"I don't know the name. Out of state attorney? "

"Nope."

"Adjuster?"

"Nope."

Katie grinned. She gave Ria the devil about her social life, or lack of one.

"You don't say! Well, I certainly will interrupt you, don't worry about it."

"And if I'm not in—"

"Yeah?"

"Try to get a phone number."

"Why would I have to try? Most people leave phone numbers, Ria."

"Somehow, I don't think he will."

* * *

Ria moved through the day by rote, waiting for late afternoon. Finally, Katie turned off her computer and departed. Johnny closed his office door and attempted to lure her to the Rookery, flouncing out the door alone in good-natured exasperation when she refused. The house was hers.

She went upstairs and exchanged her tailored suit and high heels for jeans and Nikes. Then she ransacked the assortment of small tools, screws and nails her father had put together as things she might need around the house. She picked up a hammer, a small metal file, and her smallest flathead screwdriver and shoved them into a canvas tote. She checked her pocketbook and tossed her wallet, keys, and small metal nail file in after them. The nail file was smaller than the screwdriver. It might come in handy. She grabbed a flashlight from the shelf of her closet and tossed that in, too.

The sanctity of the Devlin mausoleum was toast. It either held a coffin wherein reposed the earthly remains of Dr. Paul Devlin or it didn't. And she was, by God, going to find out which.

* * *

She drove down Orange, turned left onto Walnut, onto College, and ran down the short stretch of hill to Riverside Drive. Operating on the theory that no one notices you if you act like you know what you're doing, she drove to the main entrance of Rose Arbor and rode slowly down the narrow lanes.

When she judged she was as out-of-sight as possible from Riverside Drive, she parked and got out, heading back toward the banks of the Ocmulgee and the Devlin mausoleum.

She glanced around. No one, thank God. And hopefully this close to dark, little possibility of anyone else showing up. She stood in front of the door and considered her attack. There was no padlock to file through. There was no lock panel, so there was no lock to pick. There was no friggin' handle. There was only the smooth seam of the door and a line of concrete against the marble. Shit. Just shit.

She stared thoughtfully. On closer inspection, the line of concrete wasn't so smooth. It was crumbling in spots. And with a tap here and there, and a nudge or two using the file as a chisel, it would crumble a lot more. She looked around again. Still alone. She pulled the hammer out of her bag and tapped carefully up and down the length of the door. A few crumbs of dust fell to the ground and she resisted the urge to tap harder, repeating her series of soft blows. A few more crumbs fell down and she pulled out the file and ran it up and down the length of the door. Particles fell to the ground with a shower of dust.

She bit back the surge of excitement, put her shoulder against the edge of the door, and pushed. She pushed harder, and then harder still. It gave the smallest fraction. She stopped and looked around yet again. Yeah, she was still the only insane person in the cemetery attempting to break into a hundred year old mausoleum. She took a deep breath, bit down on her lower lip, and shoved, almost falling through the door as it swung open.

She braced her hand against the side of one of the marble walls and straightened up to face the shadows. Almost but not yet twilight, the interior of the crypt was thick with darkness. She reached in the bag and located the flashlight by feel, pulled it out and turned it on.

Training the beam on the wall opposite her, she ran it over the books that stood, thick and crowded, on the shelves running from the floor to the roof. Next to the shelves stood a chest of drawers. On its top sat a silver brush and comb and a small silver picture frame. She walked to it and trained the flashlight on the picture. Chloe Devlin. What a surprise. *Not.* She turned the flash on the next wall, moving at right angles. A small wall table with a decanter, flanked by crystal goblets. The structure was big, unusually so for its purported purpose. She'd known that, but she hadn't expected such economy of design. Or any furnishings. A mausoleum designed for use. And not for any use such structures were intended, either.

She turned slowly, looking for the one furnishing that should be here. The light played along the shadows of the far wall. There it was. Mausoleums were intended to hold coffins. But not open coffins, wherein reposed bodies that could teach the embalmers of the Egyptian pharaohs a thing or two.

She moved closer. So. The old legends were wrong. Either that or, more likely, they were like Paul Everett's fabrications of the night before, skillful blends of fact and fiction.

He lay, not on his back with his arms crossed, but on his side, his hand curled under his cheek, an open book beside him, for all the world as though he'd fallen asleep. She ran the light over the interior again and saw shelves not seen on first glance, full of small modern conveniences of life. A battery radio and clock. Books, books and more books. Beside the coffin, a camping lantern.

She walked to him, hesitated, and stretched her hand out, placing her fingers lightly on his neck. No pulse point. She moved her hand in front of his nostrils. No breath, not even a faint one.

She turned the light on her watch. Quarter to seven on an early October evening, before the change back from Daylight Savings Time. Thirty minutes till sunset, maybe less. She needed to move her car. Because she was going to be here when sunset came. She was going to watch him wake.

The old legends rushed into her mind. The wicked teeth, the mesmerizing eyes, the insatiable thirst. And she was going to watch him rise? Hell, yeah.

She moved outside, holding the edge of the door, and then stopped, frustrated. The door had no outside handle. How to secure it? What if someone came by, saw it cracked open, and decided to investigate? Highly unlikely, but still. Not a risk she was entitled to take. She ran her hands over the outside door, feeling for a hidden catch, and then she felt it. There was a hollowed-out handhold. She pulled the door firmly closed and went back to her car. She didn't think any security patrols roamed the cemetery past sunset, but there was no reason to take the chance.

She got behind the wheel, driving back down Riverside Drive to the College Street intersection. A short section of College Street ran down a steep slope, right to the old back gates of Rose Arbor. No one traveling down Riverside in the dark would notice a car parked at the base of that slope in front of the gates.

She locked the doors and jumped lightly up on top of the long solid wall, hopped down and jogged back to the mausoleum.

She went inside and pulled the screwdriver out of her bag, inserting the handle between the door and the door jamb to allow herself enough of a handhold to get back out, just in case there was a hidden lock she didn't know about. She pushed the door closed and trained the flashlight first on the camping lantern. She turned the camping lantern on and turned the flashlight off. Then she pulled out the straight-backed chair from the small table and positioned it so she'd be the first object in his line of vision.

She sat. And waited.

The hands of the clock moved, the battery power measuring the minutes and seconds. Her gaze moved in a steady pattern: Paul's face, the clock, Paul's face. 7:00. 7:02. 7:05. 7:06, 7:07, 7:08....

He stirred and raised one arm over his head, stretching, just as she did when she woke. His eyes opened.

The silence lengthened. Then Ria spoke. The words weren't original but she thought them appropriate, all the same.

"Dr. Devlin, I presume?"

He sat up, throwing his long legs over and out of the satin that lined the coffin. He stood.

"How the hell did you find me?"

"Long story."

"I'd love to hear it."

"Not as much as I'd love to hear yours, buddy."

He laughed suddenly, the laugh that had so delighted her in the time they'd spent together the prior night.

"Did you know last night?"

"Let's say I had a real strong suspicion. Do we talk here? Or take a stroll?"

"You know, I most generally do a few things when I first get up. Change my shirt and brush my hair. You know, personal things like that."

"So change your shirt and brush your hair. I've seen a man's chest before," Ria assured him. *Including yours,* she thought, though she wasn't going to tell him that. Yet.

He threw up his hands in a gesture of surrender. "Or in other words, you're not going to let me out of your sight, are you?"

"Not for the next few hours, no."

"But I could, you know. Very easily. Get out of your sight."

"And why doesn't that surprise me? Because I'm all surprised out, you think? But it doesn't matter. Because I know where you are and I don't think it'd be real easy for you to move. And I will cheerfully haunt the holy hell out of you, just like you've haunted me."

"Excuse me?"

"Long story. Do your thing if you want to hear it."

He smiled and crossed to the chest of drawers. He pulled out a fresh shirt that smelled of April Fresh Downy. Ria closed her eyes and shook her head. His back was to her as he unbuttoned the shirt he was wearing. Her story was undoubtedly shorter than his. She might as well get it out of the way.

"I live in your house," she said. "On Orange Street."

He turned around, hand poised on the last button, and stared at her.

"My house, did you say?"

She scarcely heard him as she stared at his chest, the hard chest she'd seen before in the Devlin bedroom as he stripped his shirt off and tossed it aside. But it hadn't looked like this.

"Oh, my God, Paul!" She stood up and moved to him, her hand outstretched. She caught herself before her fingers traced the lines of scar tissue on the huge X forming the cross mark on his chest. They ran from his shoulders to his abdomen, intersecting above the navel. Never, never, had she seen cuts so deep, so wide, that had healed unstitched. She didn't know how they'd healed unstitched. Surely, anyone with cuts this bad would have—

"You bled to death. Didn't you?"

"Well, actually I did, but not from these. Though I would have."

"What happened?"

"Here, let me get changed. We'll go outside and talk."

He moved rapidly, yanking a fresh pullover shirt down over his head. He grabbed the silver hairbrush and ran it through his hair.

"Let's get you out of here," he said, and took her arm. He laughed as he bent over to retrieve the screwdriver pressed into service as a doorstop.

"Well, it seemed like a good idea at the time," she said.

"Very resourceful. That's you in a nutshell. Very resourceful. I—are you chilly? Breeze off the river has a lot of fall in it tonight."

"A little. I guess I wasn't thinking about being outside after dark."

"Wait a minute. And don't panic, I'm not running out on you. Be right back."

She expected him to reopen the door, but he didn't. He just disappeared. One minute he was there. The next, he was gone. And just as rapidly, he was back, with something over his arm and something else in his hand.

"How—what—how did you do that?"

"Thought you were all surprised out."

"Well, saying it and then seeing that—"

"I call it casting out. I just empty my mind and think about where I want to be, and there I am. Here, could you take these?"

She held out her hands and took the two wine goblets he held. He retained possession of the wine bottle and she saw a light jacket tossed over his arm.

"There's a spot I like very much down by the riverbanks. And I think this should keep you warm enough," he said, moving his arm slightly to indicate the jacket.

Ria looked down at the glasses in her hand. They had the feel of fine crystal. "How old are these?"

"I don't know exactly. They were my grandmother's."

Ria immediately slowed and began to feel for irregularities in the grass before she stepped. "I'm stumbling around in the dark carrying two hundred year old crystal?"

Paul laughed. "Grandmama'd be pleased to see them put to use."

"Don't you need a jacket or something?" Ria asked.

"No. I mean, I know it's getting a bit nippy. I know when it's cold and I know when it's hot. But the cold and the hot don't bother me. Here we are. Can you see?"

Paul stopped on a mound overlooking the Ocmulgee River. The lights of the city played over to their left, and directly in front of them, the lights of I-75 burned brightly. The headlights of the passing cars swept past them, moving rapidly.

"How beautiful!"

"Isn't it?" He sat the wine bottle down and reached for the glasses. Then he sat himself, bracing his back against the base of a marble statute that stood on the hill. He gestured for her to join him and draped his jacket over her shoulders, along with his arm. He pulled her gently back and settled her comfortably against his shoulder as if they'd known each other for years.

"And now," he said, "now that you're a captive, explain, please. Just how in the hell did you know a man named Paul Devlin ever existed? And why you're not screaming in terror to find out he still does."

She did, leaving nothing out. He sat in silence as she wound down her explanations.

"Well?" Ria asked, when she could stand the silence no longer. "Aren't you going to say anything?"

He sighed. Then he gave a soft laugh.

"And I thought my cover story was such a good one."

"Oh, but it was! I mean, it is! Nobody else would ever have doubted a thing you said. Nobody."

"Except you."

"Except me."

"You being the type of girl who watches dead people live and then goes to the library to look them up. You know, most sane people would've run out of the house screaming. What's the current phrase? Oh, yes! 'What planet are you from, anyway?'"

"Oh, you were easy to find. You just have to know where to look."

Paul shook his head. "You just don't get it, do you? You've been watching dead people live, Ria. And you never turned a hair. And tonight. It just didn't occur to you that it might not be the smartest thing in the world to sit there and watch me wake up? Knowing what I am?"

"Well, it's a little hard to be scared of a man you've watched cry over his wife's things. And anyway, I don't know what you are."

Paul raised one eyebrow. "You don't? C'mon, Ria Knight. Tell me another one."

"But I don't, not exactly," she protested. "I mean, I know what you seem to be, what you're closest to, but so many things don't fit. After all, you ate and drank and you never so much as glanced at my jugular vein—"

"Certainly I did. It's amazing, just like everything else about you."

"Paul."

"Sorry. You know, when I was in medical school— you said you knew from the old society registers that I studied in Scotland?"

He felt her nod against his shoulder.

"Well, since it was too far to come home to America during holidays, I used to 'holiday' in London. That's what the English call it, going on holiday. Lord, I loved London. Anyway, there was one type of little book they used to sell at the bookstalls called 'penny dreadfuls'. Forerunner of today's horror novels, you know, like Stephen King, Dean Koontz—"

"Robert Bloch, Clive Barker, John Saul and company. Of course. I'm addicted."

"You who read Shakespeare because it's soothing?"

"I am a lady of many and varied tastes and talents."

"You don't say," Paul said dryly. "Anyway, they were full of monsters. Werewolves and goblins and ghouls and vampires. I've thought of them often over the years, poor misbegotten creatures." He smiled slightly and continued. "There was a time, long ago, when I did stalk prey and guzzle blood."

He felt her start against him. "Oh, not for a long time. And not human, never—well, except for—no, I stand with that, never human. Not all creatures who walk upright on two legs are human, even if they look it. But the woods are full of prey."

"And you don't now?" Ria hesitated. "But if you are what you seem to be, don't you need it? Sometimes?"

"I did at first. But I learned to control that need. And I hunted less and less and finally, one night, I just decided I wouldn't. And if that decision did destroy me," he shrugged, "small loss to anyone. But it didn't."

"So all the old legends are like you. A curious blend of truth and fancy. The blood's an addiction and not a necessity?"

"Oh, it's a necessity. At first. But it can be overcome."

"But you eat and drink and cast reflections."

"You actually checked to see if I cast a reflection?"

"Well, *duh*. But that was more on the idea that you might be a ghost than a vampire. The eating and drinking were really messing me up on both those theories, though, I got to tell you."

Paul laughed. "Actually, I think that part of the legend, the no reflection part, came about because of the speed with which we can disappear."

Ria sat, struck by the word 'we'.

"Are there others? Like you?"

"Oh, I'm sure there must be, somewhere, or have been in the past. All the legends start from something. But the eating and drinking—I just do that 'cause it tastes good. I don't have to eat and in fact, sometimes I'll go for days without it. I just enjoy it. Especially the variety the world has now. Imagine, having ice anytime you want it! Which you've had all your life. The luxuries people take for granted now."

"What do you do for money?" Ria asked, a tad of hesitation in her voice. "I mean—"

"Well, life's been a great deal easier since they invented ATMs and the internet," he said, and grinned. "I used to have to bank by mail and that was really--inconvenient. And I've had some lucky hits on the stock market. Managed to get in very early with some *very* lucrative companies. And I do mean early."

Ria laughed. "As in you own a lot of original blue-chip stock?"

"Yes, ma'am."

Ria laughed. "I didn't see a computer anywhere."

"Well, I cheat a little on some things. I can get in the library anytime I want you know, and before the smartphone era, I'd use their computers. And I check out library books without a card, but nobody's ever objected. Had to slack off on buying 'em, place is getting crowded. You've no idea how many books have just appeared as donations on the library counters one morning over the years, hope they got used."

"You own original blue chip stock and you've got a smartphone. Dracula never had it so good."

He grinned and shifted and pulled it out of his pants pocket. "Right here. Latest version. I love gadgets."

"Where do you charge it?"

"I only use it for quick surfing, most of the time it's off. When it needs charging, I plug it in at the cemetery gatehouse before I, ah, turn in for the day, loose wall board up there I hide it behind, nobody's ever noticed."

"And what else do you cheat on?"

"Showers," he said without hesitation. "Hot showers are the single greatest invention of the Twentieth Century. Always an empty hotel room around somewhere. I sort of consider things like that Macon's compensation for past services I rendered the public a good while back. Nobody knows about it, of course. The past services I mean. And damn lucky for the town it doesn't."

"And that past service would be?"

"I guess you want to hear all the gruesome details?"

"Every last one."

Paul sighed and settled back against the stone he was using for a backrest.

"You live in my house and you've seen my family. So of course you know Joshua."

"Sure."

"Well, Joshua fell into some very bad company."

"And you decided to do something about it."

"I've always been a bit impulsive."

"You charged into the middle of something dangerous enough to turn you into this for a servant? A houseboy?"

Paul's laugh floated out over the Ocmulgee.

"I see the house didn't give up all the family secrets. Joshua wasn't my servant. Or my houseboy."

"Then what was he?"

"My brother."

Chapter Seven

The turbulent events of the summer of 1888 broke and swirled around a boy named Joshua Devlin; at least, insofar as the Devlin family was concerned. It was the hottest summer many Macon residents could recall, though fortunately for them, few of them had any idea of just how much hotter, metaphorically speaking, it almost was.

In that summer of 1888, Joshua was sixteen years old, a slender, handsome boy caught in the hormonal imbalance of adolescence. Back then even the medical doctors didn't understand the extreme physiological changes of puberty. Certainly Joshua didn't know his exuberant ups and his crashing downs were the common lot of all teenagers and nothing unusual at all.

He damn sure knew the structure of his entire world had shattered and re-formed when he was twelve years old, though. *That* he'd never forget. At seventeen, he still carried the scars of that personal reconstruction.

Roughly five foot eight inches in height, he was three inches shy of the five eleven he'd attain, probably 145 pounds in weight. He would never be heavy. His skin glowed with the creaminess of *café au lait*, milky brown. His eyes were large and lustrous, his features almost chiseled. His hair, while not straight, didn't have quite the same texture expected with his skin tone.

Joshua Devlin was a mulatto. Until he was twelve, he'd thought his mother died at his birth and Dr. Everett Devlin, the doctor in attendance, had taken him in and given him his last name. Everybody thought that, and nobody was surprised. Doc Everett was notorious for his gruff exterior and his soft heart.

He'd been a happy child. He didn't have a father, but he had Doc, who'd begun taking him on his medical rounds when Joshua was only six years old. In his earliest memories, he sat on shady back porches with his primer on his lap, watching Doc's horse and buggy. Anybody living in Doc's house was sure going to know how to read.

He didn't have a mother, but he had Sadie, the copper-skinned and regal mistress of Doc's household. Sadie wasn't one to engage in embraces and endearments, but his clothes were clean, his meals delicious and ample. In the midst of the childhood fevers of measles and chickenpox and scarlet fever, she was there with damp cloths, cool water, and freshly simmered broth.

Someone else lived in the Devlin household, a tall, golden boy whose name was Paul, the crown prince of the Devlin family. Joshua didn't know him well and interacted with him scarcely at all. Paul was fourteen years older than Joshua and couldn't be expected to lavish much attention on a child that much younger than himself, a household charity case at that, and Joshua didn't expect it. He just worshipped from afar.

When Joshua was four, this private god of his departed from home, reappearing only sporadically through the next four years. By the time Joshua was six, he knew Paul lived at some mysterious institution called Harvard. When Joshua was eight, even Paul's sporadic appearances ceased and he learned from conversations he overheard between Doc and some of Doc's friends—he didn't precisely eavesdrop, but after all, he wasn't deaf—that Paul was far, far away, over that vast expanse of water called an "ocean" which Joshua had never seen, in attendance at another school, one where he was learning to be a doctor, just like Doc. Joshua missed him, though he couldn't say why. The house just seemed more alive when Paul was home.

However, time passed as it does for all children, in a slow-moving pattern of endless days, changes marked mostly by the passage of the seasons. Days that revolved into endless weeks and moved into endless months and finally into endless years, and one day—one day Paul Devlin came home for good, and Joshua's world changed forever.

Joshua didn't listen on purpose. He'd approached the study door that evening as twilight came down over the streets of Macon for no other purpose than to tell Paul he'd finished rubbing down Cyclone, the big black stallion Doc had waiting for Paul on his return home.

Something in the tone of the voices he heard behind the door alerted him this wasn't an ordinary conversation. He put his head down low and concentrated and distinguished Doc's voice, Paul's voice, Sadie's voice.

"Didn't expect to have you come home, take over my practice, and get married all in the course of two weeks." Doc's tone was jocular, but there was something else, some note of unease that ran beneath the surface humor.

Paul laughed. "I haven't taken over your practice yet, Papa. And we're not quite married, either, you know."

"No, but you will be, very soon. That Chloe—once she makes up her mind about something, it's done. She says she don't want a long engagement, she won't have one. Bet you never thought when you were twelve and she was five and used to run away from her Mammy to follow you around—"

"She drove me crazy," admitted Paul. "And I've never believed in love at first sight, but when I saw her again—she's not five anymore, Papa."

"She sure isn't. You're well-matched, son. I'm real pleased."

"I'm glad." Paul's voice carried easily through the door.

"And with Henry already having Chloe's house built for her dowry—"

"Man of great foresight, my future father-in-law."

"Yes, well. Anyway, I'd like to furnish it for you."

"I appreciate that, Papa, but that's not necessary."

Joshua almost knocked to announce his presence. It was an ordinary conversation after all. Then Doc's next words snared his attention.

"I know it's not necessary, but I want to. And as far as your house staff goes—well, Sadie'd like to be your housekeeper, Paul."

"What!" Paul exclaimed. Behind the door, Joshua felt a shockwave hit him. Sadie was the North Star in Doc Everett's house. For her to leave it—that was about as likely as a snowstorm in the south in August.

"Sadie! You can't leave Papa, you run this house!"

"Last time I looked, Mist' Paul, I was free," said Sadie.

"And last time I looked, you've been my Mama since Mama died when I was eight! But Sadie, there's no reason to upset your life, Chloe and I can manage just fine, we'll set up our own house."

"Well, there's something else, son. I want young Joshua to move into your house with you, too."

What? Doc wanted him out of his house? Why? What had he done?

"Joshua? You've raised him!"

"Son, you can use him. He'd be a big help, lots of company, you're going to be out at night and working long hours—"

"He's a fine boy, Papa, but I'm not havin' you disrupt your whole household just for me!"

Joshua moved closer, making his ear a part of the door crack. Doc sighed.

"You just aren't goin' to make this easy, are you, son? You remember when Joshua came? Well, I know you don't remember, you were spending the summer in Charleston with your grandmother."

"Of course I remember. I was fourteen, not four."

"And I told you his mother was a street girl I'd found with no place to go, in no shape to survive childbirth?"

"So you took him. Of course you did. Papa, you've always practiced what you preached. No son ever had a better man to watch while he was growin' up."

Everett Devlin was ahead of his time. His gruff exterior notwithstanding, Everett Devlin's actions spoke of a humanity too rarely shown in the human race. Paul had grown up watching his father do what others only preached about.

Everett firmly believed no living human being had a right to own another, but he saw red whenever he heard or read the word 'emancipation'. Because of his profession, he understood firsthand the many problems faced by the newly freed slaves immediately after the Emancipation Proclamation and through the course of Reconstruction and beyond. They were children, turned suddenly loose and often just as helpless.

They hadn't been educated to deal with the responsibilities of freedom when invited to embrace its privileges. Doc frequently shook his head sadly when he left one of the black houses. He took a private vow to help whenever he could, however he could. It was a vow far beyond the Hippocratic Oath and one he'd kept for many years. It was as much a part of him as his salt and pepper hair, his round stomach, and his habit of expressing himself vigorously and loudly.

"I know you've always been your brother's keeper," Paul assured his father. "Raised me the same way. Papa, I'll always take care of our people. I'm my brother's keeper, too, couldn't get away from it if I tried."

"Yes, well," said Dr. Devlin slowly. "And some of them are more your brothers than others."

"Sir?"

"I lied."

"Sir?"

"You weren't in Charleston to visit your grandmother. You were in Charleston so you wouldn't be around to ask questions."

"About what?"

"Me, Mist' Paul," said Sadie softly. "'Bout why I weren't around either. I went off visitin' that summer, too. An' 'bout why yo' daddy was gone so much. Joshua's my son."

Lead settled in the pit of Joshua's stomach. He slumped against the wall. All this time and not a word to him, not a word!

"That doesn't make any sense, Sadie! Why the hell wouldn't you want him to know?"

"'Cause he'd ask who his daddy was."

"So tell him. Sadie, you can't tell me you don't know who his father is. I won't believe you."

"Oh, I knows, alright," she said.

"Then what—"

"Me," Dr. Devlin interjected abruptly. "Joshua's my son."

Joshua went numb. His world as he knew it was gone. And not a word, not in all these years. They must be so ashamed of him. Paul was, he could tell from the long, heavy silence. When he did speak, the disgust was tangible.

"Papa, how could you?"

"Boy, don't you take that tone with me! I wouldn't expect that out of you, Paul, lookin' at me like you think I fell to the depths of degradation, like I was too white to soil myself with Sadie!"

"Horseshit! Just horseshit! That's not it at all, goddamn it! Sadie's been my mother since I was eight years old! You think I think you're too good for her? She's too damn good for you, for this! All your rantin' and ragin' 'bout our responsibility to take care of our people, well you took care of her just *fine*, didn't you,

Papa? I don't know how I could have been so damn stupid, not to see! All these years, you've been using her! No chance for a husband, a family of her own!"

Sadie got up and moved to stand between the two raging Devlins. She tugged Paul's sleeve gently.

"Paul," she said softly. She'd raised this boy, she loved him as much as she loved her own boy. Because he was Everett Devlin's son, because of the child he'd been and the man he'd become. It was the first time in his life she'd ever addressed him without the obligatory 'Mist".

"Paul, don't talk to your daddy that way. I got a family. Your daddy and Joshua and you. We did the best we could, son. Might not have been good enough, but it was the best we could do."

Paul stood and stared at her for moment before he pulled her into his arms and hugged tightly.

"God, Sadie, how could you stand it all these years?"

"Her real name's Sadama, son," supplied Dr. Devlin. "Wish she'd use it, but she won't. Sadie sounds like a damn slave to me, always has. Let's sit down and talk about this, what do you say?"

Joshua remained where he was. He heard the words, but the meanings were beyond him.

"Sorry I yelled at you, Paul. You're just sayin' everything I've thought about myself for years now."

"Sorry I yelled at you, Papa. Not my place to judge."

"It's just—your mother'd been dead for four years and I was so lonely, Paul. And after Sadie—"

He broke off and smiled at Sadie. "You spoiled me, woman. Knew there'd never be anybody else but you. No question of remarriage to anyone 'suitable'." His tone put a bitter emphasis on the word. "God, I hate that word, suitable. I couldn't have Sadie, I didn't want anybody. Damn us all for hypocrites! You know, I'm sure some of my friends have speculations but they really don't care. Wouldn't even be surprised. Just how things are. But I wouldn't give a damn what anybody else thought. 'Cept for you. And Joshua. The two of you have to live in this town. See, Paul, I don't have to tell you—"

Sadie broke in. "A mulatto, he's neither one nor the other. Especially a boy. A girl woulda been easier, but a half-white boy, a half-white man, he doesn't fit anywhere. And since there was no way Joshua could ever live as a white man, he's had to live as a Negro."

Paul looked at her in puzzlement. Something was different. Her speech. The familiar rhythm and cadence and slurring of Negro speech was completely absent.

"Sadie, have you always been able to talk like this?"

"Yes," she said, with a smile. "Been with your daddy a long time."

"I've never heard you."

"I have to live as a Negro, too, Paul. And outside of this room, after tonight, you'll never hear it again. And you'll be 'Mist' Paul'. Forever."

"But Sadie, to raise the boy like this, without—and Papa, all your preachin' about education. You could have sent him to school, sent him North—"

"Paul, I've made sure he can read and write and cipher. But to do more until educated Negroes aren't freaks anymore, that would make him an outsider just as much as being half-white."

"And besides, the Yankees goan socialize with a nigger, Paul? Any more than the Collins up the street and the Thompsons on Washington or the Billings over on Orange goan do? Shoot, they worse den de folks down here!"

Sadie's voice slid without pause from educated white to upper echelon Negro and as she vented her ire at the system so completely entrapping her son, it moved on down into the funky street talk that was purely black.

"Why, dey scared of us, most of 'em! Actually scared, like dey think the black goan rub off iff'n dey touch us! We fine—we got lots o' rights—long as they don't have to socialize with us! North! Dat's de worse place in the *world* for an educated black man! 'Specially one dat's half white!"

Everett took over. "Paul, you're home now. I'm gettin' old, I'm tired, I'm cuttin' back. You can look after him, train him, teach him. You can teach him a lot. He's real good with animals, there's always a need for a good home-grown vet."

"I still don't want Sadie to leave you, Papa."

"Paul, I can run this house with my eyes closed. I'm still goan handle this house too, never intended anything different."

"And she comes and goes as she pleases, son. If she's not at your house, then you know where she is."

"*Whoooo*," sighed Paul softly, the breath whistling past his lips. "Yes, I guess I will. And Joshua doesn't know—"

"No. He doesn't know anything about it," said Dr. Devlin. Joshua broke out of shock and ran, heedless of the noise. They didn't want him. He'd never been anything but an embarrassment and his parents didn't want him. They never had and they didn't now, and they were giving him away, passing him on to Paul as though he were the slave boy he would have been twenty-five years before, available for purchase and resale. The noise of his running feet sounded harshly on the hardwood floors of the hall and startled the occupants of Everett's study.

"I don't think I'd make a bet on that," said Paul, and stood back up, moving rapidly to the door.

"Oh, God!" exclaimed Dr. Devlin. "I have to catch him, I have to explain!"

"No, Papa." Paul paused at the door and threw up his hand. "I don't think he's goin' to be real inclined to listen to you or Sadie right now. I'll go." And he ran down the hall, following his newly discovered brother.

Joshua's huddled figure crouched on the ground outside the backdoor. Paul put his hand on the boy's shoulder. He jerked violently away.

"Leave me be!" Joshua shouted, throwing off Paul's hand. "Just leave me be! All dese years dey lied to me! Tellin' me my mama was dead and dey didn't know my daddy! Dey let me think I's some trash dey found on de street!"

"Joshua, they didn't. They love you, they took care of you, they did the best they could."

"Well, it weren't good 'nuff!"

"Josh—"

"All dose nights, when I was little, when I laid 'wake and wondered 'bout my mama an' whut she like and was she lookin' down from heaven and watchin' over me, and it was Sadie, all de time, *all de time!*"

"But Josh, your mama was watching over you. All the time, just like she always watched over me."

"Mist' Paul, you do it? Like Doc say? You take me with you when you—"

"Of course I will. But let's get rid of the mister, alright?"

"No, suh. No, suh, we can't do dat." Josh raised his head. "I heard y'all, heard de whole thing. Shouldna' listened but I just couldn't walk away, and I guess dey was right. I got no place in any world but de one dey done made for me, and I'm mad, I can't help it, they coulda *tol'* me! But I can't live in dis world de same way do anybody knows I's Doc's son. And if I doan call you Mist', anybody hear me, dey think I's just an uppity nigger. No place in any world for an uppity nigger, Mist' Paul. No place a'tall. An' I won't be no trouble, I'll look after you, I'll take real good care of you, keep yo' horse groomed and yo' boots shined—"

Paul winced. He put both his hands on Josh's shoulders, and the boy turned around and threw himself into Paul's arms.

"What a world," Paul said softly as he held the boy. "What a goddamned mess! Don't worry, little brother. We'll take care of each other. We will. You'll see."

And as Joshua sobbed, he reached out and grabbed the lifeline offered by his brother in this sea of horrible and hurtful emotions. A new alliance, an alliance of brothers, one black, one white, an alliance that would last to the grave and beyond, forged itself in hot and scalding tears from the wreckage of the night.

Throughout that night, Paul tossed restlessly under his mosquito netting, Joshua's voice echoing in his ears. I won't be no trouble, I'll look after you, I'll take real good care of you, keep yo' horse groomed and yo' boots shined—

Paul cringed. His brother, carrying the same blood in his veins that he carried himself, spending his life grooming Paul's horse and shining Paul's boots? Fulfilling their father's highest expectations for him of becoming a home-trained horse vet?

No. Hell, no.

* * *

Paul had plans for his brother. But they'd require teamwork. After all, Paul was getting married. And if his bride had her way about it, which he was sure she would, he was getting married a lot sooner than his future mother-in-law thought suitable. It was time to talk with Chloe.

Paul drove the buggy over to the Duval household, picnic basket in the back. He didn't pull up into the driveway because he didn't want the chaperone Chloe's mother would insist on, even though they were engaged. They'd gotten very good at avoiding that in the few weeks he'd been home. Chloe waited for him out of view of the house, visions of a few lazy hours spent in his arms by the riverbank dancing in her head.

He jumped lightly down from the buggy to lift her up, retaking his own seat seconds later.

"God, you look good," he said, flicking the reins.

"You look strange," she commented, studying him carefully.

"I do?"

"You do. Like something's really on your mind. Haven't decided you want to stay a bachelor, have you?" she asked. She smiled as she said it. She'd felt him feel the lightning bolt that struck him from above his first night home at the small dinner party for twenty his father'd held in celebration of his homecoming. Her own lightning bolt she'd felt years ago in childhood, but she'd never forget its intensity.

Chloe laughed at his facial response. No verbal clarification needed.

"Then what on earth's the matter?"

Paul guided the horse forward, raising his hand in greeting to the pedestrians.

"Oh, Lord, that was Celia Davenport!" he exclaimed. "Your Mama's goin' to hear about this!"

"I don't care," said Chloe pertly and shrugged her shoulders. She hooked her arm underneath his to show how much she didn't care. "I'm almost a married lady. She can't lock me in my room. I know how to climb down the oak tree, done it plenty of times."

"Have you now?"

"I have. So what's the matter?"

"I guess I need to be sure you still want to marry me. After I tell you what I'm goin' to tell you."

"Lord, that sounds solemn!"

"Solemn subject."

Chloe studied this man she'd chosen when she was five and he was twelve. He hadn't appreciated his favored status at the time and in fact, had spent an inordinate amount of energy avoiding her attentions.

"You've seen the world, you don't want to stay in town, you want to go up North, or back to Europe. Fine with me, I don't give a damn."

"Chloe!" he exclaimed in mock horror. He loved her disregard of convention.

"Well, I don't. Whither thou goest, and all that. Is that the problem? Because you have been away a long time and I'll go anywhere with you, really."

"No, that's not it at all. Couldn't wait to get home and I never want to leave."

"Then what is it?"

Paul turned onto Wharf Street, taking the road out of the city limits proper towards a little secluded spot they knew down by the banks of the Ocmulgee.

"I have a brother," he said, and began to speak. By the time they'd reached their destination and spread the tablecloth on a grassy rise under the overhanging willows, Chloe knew as much as he did.

She spread the food, the bread and butter, the thick slices of roast beef and ham, the fried chicken legs, the bowl of potato salad, and filled their plates. She handed him his and settled into a pretty pose, her long skirt billowing off the cloth and onto the grass.

"I'm sorry," she said. "I know I'm missing something here, but what are you so upset about? It's not exactly like it's something that's never happened before, now is it?"

"And what would you know about it, Miss Worldly?"

"A lot," she said frankly. "You don't really think our mamas can always keep us in hot houses, do you? To tell the truth, you've been gone so much you wouldn't know, but there's always been talk about your father and Sadie. I've heard Mama and Papa. 'Course, they don't know that. Mama, she just can't stand not to see a man married, one night she was planning a party and carrying on about how Ella Tannen would be such a good match for Doc Everett now that she was out of mourning for her husband, and Papa just hollered and told her she shouldn't count on it 'cause that would interfere with Everett's brown sugar. I wish I could have seen it instead of just hear it. I bet Mama turned puce! Purely puce!" Chloe laughed in delight at the memory of her indomitable mother struck speechless.

"Thank you, darlin', that makes me feel so much better. Everybody in town knew about it but me!"

"I wouldn't go that far," said Chloe, nibbling daintily on a biscuit. "And I don't think I've ever heard anything about Joshua. Besides," she gave a pretty shrug, "everybody loves your papa. As long as he keeps it private, nobody's going to say anything about it. I mean, like I said, it's not like it's all that uncommon."

"No," Paul agreed, finally biting into a chicken leg. "But it makes me feel like I don't even know Papa, you know? He's so straight-forward, so honest, and they went to such lengths. Sent me to Charleston that summer, Sadie went off somewhere 'visiting', they said—"

He broke off as Chloe laughed.

"Overabundance of caution, if you ask me," she said.

"Why's that?"

"'Cause it involves Sadie. And if Sadie didn't want anybody to say anything, then they wouldn't. Well, the Negroes wouldn't, anyway. I guess the white folks might have been a problem but then, they don't pay that much attention when a darky housekeeper has a baby."

Chloe jumped from point to point a lot. Most folks thought she was scatterbrained. Paul knew better. She was so smart she frequently forgot her audience couldn't follow the darting quickness of her thoughts because she never had trouble following anybody else's, frequently before they knew where they were going themselves.

"Chloe, you did it again. You skipped something somewhere. I don't understand."

Her trilling laughter floated out under the willows.

"Darlin', you have been away from home for a long time. You just don't know all the ins and outs around town anymore, that's all."

"So tell me."

"Well, with the other Negroes, Sadie has considerable—power."

"Power?"

"Power," Chloe affirmed emphatically.

"What kind of power? How do you know about it?"

"Well, I have power of my own."

"I'm well aware."

"Not like that. I mean, I've got Betsy."

"Chloe—"

"My maid. Betsy."

"I know who Betsy is, I just don't know what that's got to with this."

"Well, Betsy's better than a telegraph. And she's a lot more than just my maid, she's my best friend. We practically grew up together, you know. She knows everything that goes on in town and she tells me. So I know just as much about what goes on in the Negro houses as they do. And a lot more about what goes on in the white houses than the other white folks do. Lord, I'm going to miss her!"

"Why? She isn't coming with you?"

Chloe sighed. "Oh, she went and fell in love. Not that I've got any room to talk. But she went all calf-eyed and moony over one of the Thorpes' tenants up at Bolingbroke and she's getting married and turning into a farmer's wife!"

Paul laughed at her woebegone expression. "I'm sorry, darlin'."

"So am I!" declared Chloe emphatically. Betsy was much better company than any of the white society girls of Chloe's acquaintance. And certainly far more experienced. She'd already lost a lot more than her heart to her young farmer and had shared with Chloe breathless descriptions of the franker joys of physical love. Sometimes as Chloe lay awake in the dark and counted the days until her wedding, she thought of Paul and imagined him already lying beside her. At such times, when her body raged in a fever that couldn't yet be slacked, she wished Betsy hadn't been quite so informative.

"But I still don't understand about Sadie—"

"Sadie knows mojos," Chloe stated baldly.

"Mojos?"

"Mojos. You know, magic and love potions and things like that. The other blacks have a lot of respect for her, but they're scared of her, too. None of them would dare cross her."

"I don't believe—"

"Believe it. I mean, she only uses good magic, but they're all pretty sure if they made her mad enough, she could pull out some black magic real fast, too."

Paul stared.

"Did I turn green?"

"Sadie just about raised me! She never misses a service at St. Barnabas, she hauls Joshua off every Sunday! She's better at Episcopal liturgy than I am, and you sit there and tell me she's the local witch woman?"

"Well," said Chloe, shrugging again. Facts were facts and not much changed them. "She is. Didn't know about her and your father, either, did you?"

"I'm beginning to think I don't know too much about anything!" he exclaimed, and examined the delicate contours of his future bride's features. "And not only do I not know any of this, you do! You know everything about everybody in town!"

"Not quite," she said modestly, "but I do try hard."

Paul dissolved into laughter and flung his plate aside, pulling her into his arms. Even the rigid confines of the foundation garments of 1883 didn't disguise the underlying softness. He pulled away, wondering suddenly if Chloe knew a lot more about a lot of things than he'd supposed. He certainly hoped so. He didn't know what the hell Chloe's mother'd told her about the physical side of marriage, but he was pretty sure it wasn't a recommendation. All the men in town were certain Henry Duval's male appendage had long since frozen off, considering what he had to stick it in.

"Chloe, do you know everything about everything? I mean, like marriage? Real marriage, a man and a woman, not just wedding cakes and white icing?"

"Not from personal experience," she said.

"Well, I hadn't supposed you did," he said with a grin.

"But Betsy does."

"Which information she has shared—"

"Betsy's very good with words."

"Ahhh!"

"And you'd better not disappoint me."

"Betsy, she seems to enjoy it, does she?"

"Enjoy it? My Lord, she thinks it's wonderful! Isn't it supposed to be?" she asked, sudden alarm in her voice.

"Well, yes, but sometimes, ladies seem to—"

"Betsy says it's the most wonderful feeling in the world, it's like when you have to go, I mean really, really go—"

"Go?"

"Paul, for heaven's sakes! You're a doctor. You know people use chamber pots!"

He roared.

"Anyway, she says that's the best she can describe it, it's like when you really, really have to go, but you can't right then, and then finally, when you do get to, that it feels like that, but even better."

"My God," said Paul in astonishment. Best description of human orgasm he'd ever heard.

"Is it like that?"

"I—yes. Yes, it is. And you go downtown tomorrow and pick out the very best wedding present you can think of for Betsy and tell 'em to charge it to me. Whatever you know she'd want, cost doesn't matter."

"That's very generous, darlin'! Are you sure?"

"Chloe, you have no idea of the wedding present she's just given me, explainin' things to you like that!"

She moved closer and leaned over, running her lips up his throat.

"Then why don't you go ahead and show me?" she whispered.

Paul pulled back, temptation roaring in his veins. Such a lovely spot, and the trees were thicker further back, and it was only three weeks, and what possible harm could it do? His gaze fell on her face, reflecting her every thought. Chloe would wear the glow of sexual satisfaction in a visible aura. It would transform her from a beautiful girl into an absolutely breathtaking woman, and the difference would be there, observable to all who knew what to look for.

Premature consummation would also subject his wife and any potential child to the tender mercies of the town matrons who kept track of all births and deaths and relentlessly backtracked the birthdate of all first children born to newly married couples. For a first child to make its appearance in the world nine months to the day from his parents' marriage was quite acceptable. For such child to make its appearance eight months and one week after his parent's marriage was not. He himself didn't care, but damned if they were going to snicker behind Chloe's back. It was only three weeks. Only. *Jesus.*

He pushed her gently away. "Back, girl!"

"Why not?" Her voice was plaintive, edging toward hurt.

"Because you show everything you think and feel on your face. I don't want anybody talkin' bad about you behind your back."

"I don't care."

"I care, because I love you. It's only three weeks, Chloe. Now move over a little and let me recover."

"From what? Are you in pain?"

"Yes, as a matter of fact, I am. But it won't last long. Now, is it alright with you if Joshua lives with us?

"Good Lord! Do you have to ask? Of course it's alright."

"But you see, it's not goin' to be the way or for the reason that Papa wants, so you might want to think about it a little harder."

"I don't understand."

"Chloe, I can't do what Papa wants! I can't just throw up my hands and say 'oh, well, too bad the Devlin blood's black this time', and turn him into a manservant and a horse vet. I can't do that!" He got up and began to pace the grass. "I mean, would you just look at me? Harvard and Edinburgh! And look at him! Same father, same blood. My brother's goin' to spend his life shining my boots? Like hell!"

"Paul. This is Macon. Georgia. Doc's right, he's not goin' to be invited to dinner no matter who his papa and brother are!"

"No, but damn it, Chloe! They could have done better than that. Papa didn't even educate him!"

"Now that's not true, Paul, be fair!" protested Chloe.

"Not the way he needs to be educated and not the way he can be educated. He's a smart boy, he can do anything if somebody'll give him the chance! He could be a doctor, Chloe! Horse vet, hell! And if Papa won't do it, I will!"

"But your father and Sadie—"

"They passed it to me."

"All right," she said quietly.

"I can teach him so much, and if you're willing to help me—he needs French. France is the best country for a black man and if you'll help with that—"

"I said all right!"

"You did?"

"I did."

"Oh. Sorry." He gazed at her quietly a moment and reached up to touch her cheek. "Thank you."

"As long as you don't make the same mistake your father did."

"Which is?"

“Joshua might have a few ideas about what he wants to do himself. Can you handle that? Paul Everett Devlin III?”

“I’m a lot like Papa, huh?”

“Oh, yes.”

“Well, most of the time that’s all right.”

Chapter Eight

The first class of Paul Devlin's private school went into session as soon as Paul and Chloe settled into the house on Orange after their wedding trip to Savannah. Joshua almost hyperventilated.

"Never goan do it! Never! An' you say you want Miss Chloe teach me to speak French? Mist' Paul, I can't even speak English like a white man do!"

"You can," declared Chloe emphatically. "You can. You just have to practice."

"I can't!"

"Josh Devlin," she declared, hands on her hip, 'doan you be tellin' me you can't do somethin'!" Both Joshua and Paul stood and stared at her as she slipped effortlessly into black speech. "On account o' you dang well *can* and I don't never wanta hear no different outta you! You hear me?"

Paul grinned and Joshua looked from one of the Devlins to the other as though they had both lost their minds.

"See?" Chloe dropped the inflection. "I can do it. Because I hear it. Every day. And if I can do something I hear every day—"

"So can you," finished Paul.

"*Uhhhh,*" Josh moaned softly. Within weeks, even his everyday speech began to change.

Paul and Chloe were thrilled. Sadie wasn't. Neither was Doc. He made an unannounced visit one morning and he and Sadie cornered Dr. Devlin the younger in his office.

"Son, now I know you mean well, but what you're doing—"

Sadie broke in. "Mist' Paul, you goan give dat boy ideas."

"I hope so, that's certainly my intention."

"Paul, now damn it, son! Sadie and I talked about this. All the time, all his life. And we know what's best for him!"

"Papa, with all due respect—"

"Now you listen here! I didn't ask you to take him with you so you could change every plan we ever made for him!" Everett Devlin's voice rose as his face took on the red tones generally exhibited in persons with high tempers and higher blood pressures. Paul didn't have high blood pressure and as things would turn out, never would, but on certain occasions, his temper flared in flames equal to his father's.

"No, you listen here! He's watched me while I've had everything and he's had nothing!"

"Nothing! That's a goddamn lie, Paul, that boy's always had—"

"*Nothing!* Not in comparison with *me*! Now you call *that* a goddamn lie!"

Everett stared at his son in defeat. Paul was right. He turned on his heel and walked out of the office. He never again raised a protest nor allowed Sadie to.

Throughout the next four years, the private school continued. During the days, Joshua trailed Paul as he moved around town, learning medicine by watching his brother practice it. Joshua didn't expect his adult life to be comparable to a white man's. Nor did he expect to ever again be truly part of the black man's world. He belonged fully in neither. That was all right, though, he was making his own world. But sometimes, oh, sometimes as he trailed after his brother, as he bent over his books in the evening, he heard the high-pitched lazy voices of his childhood friends. He followed their conversations and felt isolation.

"Hey! You, Silas! You see dat new maid over to de Crosby's house?"

"Yeah, I seen her. 'An seein' her be all you goan do, boy, no high-toned colored like dat goan be walkin' out with no coal-black nigger like you!"

He wasn't one of them anymore. Most times that was all right. Most times.

* * *

Paul and Chloe were a golden couple, not just in looks. Their marriage was the envy of the town. There was only one fly in Chloe's ointment. She wanted a child. Not because she felt incomplete or unfulfilled or as though she were only half a woman. Because it would be Paul's baby, part of him mixed with part of her, their private monument of partial immortality. Her disappointment grew with every month's evidence that no baby was coming.

"If you didn't worry about it so damn much, we might have better luck."

"But Paul! I want a baby!"

"Darlin', I am doin' absolutely the best I can. I have to sleep sometimes."

Finally, a few months past their fourth wedding anniversary, two months in a row had Chloe holding her breath. The third month, she started breathing again, knowing her child was finally on the way. Paul settled back and stared at her every chance he got. Chloe always glowed, but he didn't think he'd ever seen anything more beautiful than her carrying this child.

Doc Everett tried to be more professional.

"Are you goin' to deliver that baby yourself, son?"

"Of course I am. Why? Oh, I know. You don't trust me to deliver your grandchild. Is that it?" Paul grinned. His father's professional detachment didn't fool him one bit.

"Did you measure her pelvis? She's so small."

"Of course I did. What sort of fool you take me for? She's just fine, Papa, won't have a bit of trouble."

"But narrow women—"

95

"You know as well as I do outward appearances have nothing to do with interior pelvic span. She's fine."

"Well, if you're sure. But I want you to call me when labor starts. If you do run into trouble—doctors got no business tending their own when trouble starts unless they've got no choice about it. Too involved."

"And you're not? But all right, all right. I'll send for you."

When labor began in the small hours of the morning of February 3, Paul saw no reason to call his father from his warm bed merely to pass time while things progressed. Sadie'd remained at the Orange Street house for the last several weeks as the time approached and that was all the help he'd possibly require in the early stages of labor. Sadie'd seen a lot of things happen in childbirth, though. She made sure early in the morning that Joshua had Cyclone saddled and ready. Just in case.

In the end, when the sudden surge of blood burst from Chloe's body, it made no difference who was in attendance.

"Oh, my God! Sadie!" Sadie was already out the door calling for Joshua.

"Quick, son! Get to Doc, tell him de afterbirth's probably separated, move quick as he can!"

She slapped Cyclone's rump as Joshua settled into the waiting saddle. Boy and stallion flew down Orange and onto College Street in the gray February dawn and rushed around to the kitchen.

Everett was drinking coffee in the kitchen and feeling lonely while his cook sliced ham and cracked eggs into the well-seasoned cast-iron skillet. A man's children came first and he'd been the first to insist Sadie stay over with Paul and Chloe the last few weeks. But it'd been a sacrifice, that was no lie. He didn't sleep well without Sadie. And he missed Sadie's eggs, too. Louise's just weren't the same.

"Josh! Son! Is it Chloe?"

"Sadie said the afterbirth's probably separated, come quick as you can!" Unconsciously, Joshua's voice mimicked the underlying panic of Sadie's voice.

Everett's face turned ashen. He stood up, moving so rapidly his chair overturned.

"Time's real short, then. Let me take your horse, son. Grab one from the stable and follow me down. And dear God, please tell me you ain't ridin' Cyclone."

"Sorry," Joshua threw at his departing back. "I'm ridin' Cyclone."

He caught up with Doc in time to hear Everett's mumble a simultaneous curse and supplication. "Well, I couldn't get there any quicker, I don't guess. Long as the good Lord keeps the damn horse from killing me 'fore I do."

* * *

Sadie handled the chloroform cone as Paul steeled himself for the first incision. No time to wait on Everett. Why the hell hadn't he listened to his father, why hadn't he sent for him when the first pains hit? He lifted the tiny infant, blue-gray, from Chloe's womb as Everett walked in. A boy.

"Son?"

Paul didn't answer. Everett looked down at Chloe's still form. The grayness of death settled over the beautiful face as he watched. The face that had always glowed with life. Well. He could do nothing for Chloe. He could do nothing for his grandson. He took Paul's arm.

"C'mon, son. Let Sadie take you downstairs. I'll finish up here."

Paul shook off his father's hand, touching Chloe's cheek. His low moan, animalistic in intensity, vibrated in the air. Sadie had wrapped the baby's tiny body in a soft waiting blanket and placed him in the crook of his mother's arm. Paul stroked the soft skin of his son's face.

Then he turned on his heel and left the room. His footsteps, slow, steady, measured, measured his progress down the stairs and out into the first floor hall. Joshua, racing in through the front door, saw his brother's back, caught the close of his office door and then the turn of the key.

Everett closed the emergency caesarean incisions with as much care as he would have used on a living patient. Each stitch reminded him he'd never take this grandson fishing. He'd never see Chloe gracing the end of the dining room table again. Lord, Lord, death was a natural part of life and nobody knew it better than Everett Devlin. But its bitterness still tore savagely at his heart.

Joshua raced up the stairs and stopped abruptly at the open bedroom door.

"Paul's done locked himself in his office! Chloe's not—the baby's not—"

Everett sighed. "Just leave Paul alone, Josh. For right now, we'll just leave him alone."

And so the household did. All that day, all that night, and part of the next day. Everett finally knocked on the door.

"Son?"

"Go away."

"Son, you can't stay here forever, there's things has to be handled, decided."

"You do it."

Everett turned away and did so. He returned several hours later.

"Paul?"

"I said go away."

"Paul, we have to bury her, son."

"I told you to do it."

"It's set for tomorrow. You're not goin' to let her go to her grave without you, are you?" Everett cringed silently at the harshness of his words but didn't know how else to break through Paul's withdrawal.

"What time?"

"Eleven o'clock."

"I'll be ready. Now leave me alone."

At ten o'clock the next morning, Paul emerged from his office. He went silently up the steps, to another room, and readied himself for his wife's funeral. He'd never remember a word of the service. But he'd always remember the sound of the dirt as it hit the coffin.

"Ashes to ashes and dust to dust..."

He returned to his house, ignoring all hands, all hugs, all words offered in comfort. He locked himself in his office again, where he remained for the next three days.

Everett and Sadie debated endlessly.

"How long you gone let him do dis, Everett?"

"Oh, God, Sadie, he's hurting so bad. I just don't have the heart to keep pounding on the door."

"Goan starve hisself sick and drive hisself crazy. Everett, enough's enough. You doan do something, I will. An' doan you look at me like dat. He's my boy, too. I raised him just like I did Joshua."

Everett sighed. "Tomorrow, Sadie. Let's give him till sometime tomorrow."

"And if he doan come out, what then?"

"Then I guess I'll take the damn door down."

Sadie subsided. Joshua, who'd overheard from the hall, planned his stealth mission. He wasn't about to let his brother get hauled out of his office like a naughty child.

That night, Joshua took up sentry duty outside the door. Paul shouted and roared. Joshua threatened. And finally, Paul opened the door. Joshua led him upstairs.

"Won't go back in that room."

"Don't have to. We got plenty of others."

* * *

Paul slept deeply that night, emotionally and physically exhausted. Joshua sat by his bed and guarded his slumbers. The next morning, Joshua brought him piping hot coffee and newly baked biscuits slathered with butter and Paul began the long and painful process of living without Chloe.

He immersed himself in his work. He'd already taken over a great deal of Everett's huge practice, much of which was non-paying. That had always been irrelevant to Everett, and it certainly was to Paul. He was grateful for the volume of practice available to him. He moved in and took over more and more of his father's patients. Everett, content that his people were in good hands, better hands, he felt, than his own, given Paul's superior education and the vigor of his youth, sat back and abdicated more and more of his professional life to his son.

Sadie didn't like it. She didn't leave any doubt about her feelings, either, to Everett or to Paul.

"Boy goan kill hisself."

"He enjoys it, Sadie."

"No, he doan. He don't enjoy nothin' no more. Just uses it to fill his time."

"Same difference right now. Leave him be."

Finding no success with Everett, she turned her tongue on Paul.

"De Bible say 'physician, heal thyself', Mist' Paul. How you goan do dat when you tire yourself out so bad you catch de typhoid or something?"

"I'm fine, Sadie."

"You ain't. You ain't fine a'tall. You think deliverin' every baby in town goan bring yours back? Make Chloe live again?"

"Sadie, sometimes you're too smart for words."

"Paul. You listen to me." That got his attention all right. Sadie almost never omitted the 'Mist'. "I been yo' mama since you was eight years old. Didn' you say dat yo'self?"

"You know you have."

"Mamas knows. An' dis mama knows her boy's riding for a fall. You ain't made out of iron, son, you just think you is."

"Yes, ma'am," he said agreeably. "Now I got some calls over on Woolfolk Street if anybody needs me."

He strode away.

"Ridin' for a fall, boy! You hear me?"

He didn't pause in his stride and Sadie turned away, muttering under her breath. "Kill hisself. Pure-de-kill hisself!"

Formal lessons suspended in the Devlin household. Paul couldn't concentrate and had trouble staying still for longer than a few seconds at a time. Joshua mourned Chloe deeply. He didn't have the necessary concentration either. For the first time in four years, even though Joshua's days were still spent with Paul in a whirlwind of activity, his evenings were now free. Paul wouldn't let Joshua come with him on the evening emergencies. And there were a lot of evening emergencies now, since Paul made it clear to every doctor in Macon he'd take any night call anyone got.

"Why can't I go?" asked Joshua.

"Because you're a growing boy and you need your sleep."

"You don't?"

"I ain't grown any in a long time, Josh."

"Ain't what I meant and you know it."

"Break'll do you good, Josh, we'll start again this fall. Anyway, I probably been pushing too hard. Why don't you just read when I'm out in the evening? Reading's the best education you can get, anyway. And besides, you need some time off."

"Time off?"

"I worked you too hard, Josh. I didn't realize, but you never get out with any of your friends, you never court a girl. I been keeping you in here with your nose stuck in a book."

"Learned a lot, didn't I?" Josh asked proudly.

"Yes, and I'm real, real proud of you. But Josh, life's too short. God, it's too short. Summer's coming up, won't get dark 'til late. Go off with the other boys. Go fishin', go swimmin', go courtin'. For God's sake, just go! Go have some fun!"

Joshua didn't have the heart to tell his brother the truth. Which was, he didn't actually have any friends anymore. So as the lazy spring twilights lengthened into lazier summer twilights, he walked out the back door, onto the porch, and down the steps. He whistled as he walked as though he had a definite destination in mind. He maintained his purposeful stride until he was down the corner and out of sight.

The first few evenings he did this, he stuck a book under his shirt, out of Paul's view. He debated walking down to Doc's and claiming a corner to read in, but rejected the idea for several reasons.

In his own mind, he was still nothing but an inconvenient problem for Doc and Sadie. He wasn't comfortable in their presence. He still called them Doc and Sadie, just as he had before he'd known they were his parents, and he didn't ever plan to call them anything else. Lingering feelings of rejection were hard to overcome. Then, too, they'd ask why he was reading at the Devlin residence on College Street and not in his own room at the Devlin residence on Orange Street. Which meant he'd have to explain Paul had pretty much thrown him out of the house with orders to have fun with his friends which would mean explaining he didn't really have any friends to have fun with. He knew Doc and Sadie had always been scared to death his education would cut him off from both the white and black worlds, leaving him in limbo. And since it sort of had, wouldn't they just jump on that like a duck on a June bug?

None of this gave him a destination. The first few times he walked aimlessly and finally returned home after a suitable absence. But then one evening, as he headed down the street, he passed a group of three childhood cronies.

"Lord have mercy!" exclaimed Abe Ludlow, whose full and formal name was Abraham Emancipation Ludlow. "Josh! Yo' master don't need you wave a fan over him tonight?"

Joshua turned an icy stare on Abe, remembering the hot dusty mornings they'd sat in Doc's driveway shooting marbles. From his lips came the unbridled inflections of his childhood.

"You watch yo' mouth, nigger. Din' nobody ax yo' 'pinion."

"*Whooo!*" Eulises S. Jones chimed in. That was his name, Eulises S. His mother hadn't known what the S stood for, and she hadn't been sure of the spelling of 'Ulysses' either, but she wasn't going to pass up the elegance of the rolling syllables on a minor technicality.

"Watch it, Abe!" called Jeremiah Andrews. His mother quoted Bible verses every other breath. She blithely worked her way through the Old Testament whenever she needed to name a new child, usually every eleven to thirteen months. "He fixin' to get nasty!"

"No, I ain't!" declared Joshua. "Y'all are. Ain't done nuttin' to any one of y'all!"

"An you ain't done nuttin' wid us in so long we done forgot what yo' voice sound like!" exclaimed Abe. "Why you done forget where all us lives, boy? You too good or somethin'?"

Joshua stared at Abe. Could it be that simple? Had his friends ignored him only because they thought he was ignoring them?

"'Course I ain't. None of y'all wanted to have nuttin' to do with me."

"You ain't give us a chance, boy. Never see you no mo'. Everybody gots to work, but they don't do it all de damn time! What you do when you ain't workin'?"

"I been—Mist' Paul, he been teaching me—"

"Teachin' you what? You already knows how to read, don't you?"

"Sho."

"Den what else you need?"

"Dere's lots of things."

"Well, it ain't changed de way you talk, nigger. An' you still black."

Joshua wasn't brave enough to show them it had changed the way he talked. And he certainly couldn't dispute he was still black. He was more properly speaking brown, but he knew what Abe meant and didn't feel it expedient to get into an argument over semantics.

"Yep," he said finally. "I still is."

"An' you off yo' leash tonight?"

Joshua bridled at the implied insult to Paul, but felt it best to be agreeable. He nodded.

"Well! Wanna' mosey on with us a while?"

"Where you goin'?"

"Down to de river."

"Why come? You ain't got no fishin' pole."

"Ain't goan fish."

"Den whut?"

"You see iff'n you come. So is you comin' or is you ain't?"

Joshua stood for a moment, undecided. He didn't like walking blindly into situations he knew nothing about. Besides, something about his old friends seemed different. There was something furtive, secretive.

"Guess you ain't," said Abe with a shrug, and the boys started off.

Joshua stared after them. Of course they seemed different. He hadn't really talked to them in over four years, what did he expect? Probably they were just going skinny-dipping or maybe even meeting girls down by the riverbank. He called after them.

"Wait! I's comin'!"

He caught up with them, driving the final nail into the coffin his brother'd be sleeping in by fall. During the daylight hours, anyway.

* * *

"So why for we goin' to de river?" Josh asked again as they strolled briskly along towards Wharf Street.

"You see do we get dere. Got a meetin'."

"Meetin'? What kind of meetin'?"

"Boy, you just full up of questions, ain't you? Dat what all dat learnin' do for you?"

"I just—" Joshua started, but Jeremiah broke in.

"Damn, Abe! Act like it be some big secret or somethin'! Josh, you seen dat new feller whut started showin' up on Sunday at St. Barnabas?"

St. Barnabas was the black Episcopal church. It stood on the corner of Congress Street and Third Street and enjoyed a large attendance, consisting primarily of the house servants who worked in the big houses of the well-to-do streets.

Sadie'd hauled Joshua off to St. Barnabas every Sunday of his memory unless he was sick as sin. Sadie wasn't terribly social, though, and didn't linger after the sermon. So Joshua, confirmed member of the church though he was, really didn't know much about the church's social structure.

"Not really," he admitted.

"Boy! How you not notice him? Big man, coal black, shaved head?"

"I just—Sadie doan stay aroun' long after Brother Gorley finish. I just ain't noticed nobody like dat."

"Well, dat don't makc no never mind no how," Abe assured him. "He be real special."

"Special how? Whut his name?"

"His name be Cain," said Abe, almost reverently. "An he say—he say his color be sebben."

"He say whut?"

"His color be sebben."

105

"Dat don't make no sense a'tall. Colors ain't numbers."

Abe shook his head. "Can't 'splain. Can't 'splain nuttin' 'bout Cain. But you see. He—never mind. You see."

Josh hung slightly back. He didn't like the sound of this. He didn't understand his friends' fascination with a man who spoke in riddles. He almost turned around and headed back toward town and Abe, sensing his withdrawal, stopped dead in his tracks.

"Oh, go on! Don't know why I 'spected a white nigger like you to understan' a man like Cain! Go on back to yo' precious Mist' Paul!"

White nigger. That's what he was, alright. Abe's taunt hit the truth with a bullseye. What was all his work for? What good would his education do him or them if he lost touch with his own people, if they saw him as an outsider, a white nigger? And so he moved forward once again. Walking towards Wharf Street. Walking towards Paul's destiny.

* * *

Cain stood in a clearing among the willow trees lining the banks of the Ocmulgee just north of the town proper. He inspected his followers as they arrived. Mostly teenage boys with a smattering of teenage girls. He expected maybe twenty tonight. Not bad. He'd started with a mere handful and their ranks swelled with each gathering.

By next month the twenty would be thirty, forty, fifty. The pattern had held all the way from Mississippi to Alabama and over to Georgia. In the end, a private troop of devoted acolytes spread his gospel through ever swelling numbers, a gospel rooted in blood and nursed with hate. He looked back over his life's work and found it sweet. He smiled.

Where he came from, no one knew. He himself did not know. Sometimes he thought he had merely sprung, full-grown, from the depths of the deepest swamps, the darkest bayous, of Louisiana. No one remembers babyhood and early childhood consists of bright splashes of color highlighting fields of darkness stretching gradually into full memory, but Cain remembered no bright splashes.

When he thought about it, he realized his first memories were of hunger and wetness and cold nights on the waterfront stretching across New Orleans Harbor. He didn't think on them often, those memories of rummaging through refuse like a starved cat, barely tall enough to reach over the tops of the garbage barrels, his only means of sustenance.

But he survived. Many street urchins didn't. And he grew. Almost six feet tall in early adolescence, he soared past that to six foot six at the approximate age of sixteen, with massive shoulders to match his towering frame. He never knew his real age, or who his parents were or how he'd come to live on the streets. Of course, by that time, he'd had been working the docks, in one way or another, for the past ten or twelve years.

When he was roughly twelve, he made a great discovery. Sailors and dock workers drank. A lot. When they did, they stumbled out of the waterfront saloons and down into the alleys running beside them. Their skulls crushed easily when struck from the proper angle with the proper amount of force from the proper blunt instrument. He favored a length of iron pipe that held almost talismanic importance for him. They never offered any protest when he ransacked their pockets. It beat loading huge crates on and off shipboard to hell and back.

As his strength increased, he discovered their necks snapped almost as easily under the pressure of his huge hands as did their skulls under the iron pipe. He found the sound of snapping neck bone more melodious than the sound of cracking skulls. A true connoisseur, he was an artist at his work.

Everyone makes mistakes, though. Cain's mistake was Leo Salter. Leo looked just like every other drunken dock hand but he wasn't. The owner of a large plantation outside of Baton Rouge, he was on the hunt for a runaway wife. He'd been warned she was nothing but a little slut but he hadn't listened. Now she'd run away to New Orleans and taken up residence at one of the waterfront brothels. That made him madder than the initial desertion. If she wanted to be a whore, she could have at least joined a classy whorehouse. God knows, New Orleans had plenty.

Leo went undercover. He wandered the bars and brothels of the harbor. His clothes reeked of cheap whiskey, but his head was clear. He was going to kill the little tramp when he found her and didn't want sweet revenge blurred by an alcoholic haze. He wasn't a match for the huge hands pulling him into the alley, but he could and did make a lot of noise, enough noise to attract the attention of New Orlean's finest.

Leo wasn't dead, and there was no proof of the scores of murders Cain had committed in those alleys. Most of the murder victims hadn't been missed. Cain thus escaped the gallows. But Leo's testimony at Cain's trial sent Cain to a Louisiana prison camp in the depths of the snake and mosquito infested back bayous. His sentence was for thirty years.

For seven years, Cain survived the Cat-o'-Nine Tails, the periodic sweats in the hot box, and the muck and mud of the sugarcane fields. Then a moccasin bit the inmate attached to the other end of the chain manacled on Cain's ankle. When they unshackled the men to carry the screaming inmate back to base camp, Cain saw his chance. He took it. The chain itself was still attached to Cain's ankle but he didn't care. He ran. All the bullets fired at his fleeing back missed and Cain kept running.

He ran the rest of that afternoon and through that night, the baying of the bloodhounds ringing in his ears. The next morning, the officials shrugged, called in the dogs, and trotted back to the main prison camp. Odds were if the escaped prisoner hadn't been apprehended by now, he was dead from a snake bite or an encounter with a rouge bull 'gator. Even if he wasn't, he would be soon. A man didn't survive this bayou alone and unarmed. Not for long.

Cain didn't just survive. He entered his second gestation period. When he emerged from that swamp, he was reborn. His past life didn't matter anymore. In the depths of the deep swamps, in a ramshackle shack standing on poles to guard against rising rain water and nestled among the knotty cypress trees, he found his destiny.

Destiny comes in many shapes and sizes. This particular destiny stood perhaps five feet two inches tall, and appeared smaller due to the stoop of her shoulders. She was black, wizened, wrinkled, and quite insane. He never knew her name.

He'd driven his huge body until he could drive it no further, collapsing on a relatively dry rise of land. He hadn't heard the baying of the dogs at all that day and assumed he'd been left to perish in the swamps. He damn sure didn't plan to perish, but he had to rest. When he woke, a gnome-life figure with the face of a witchy woman was bending over him. She laughed softly to herself.

"Lookee what de swamp done sent me now," she chanted. "Jest lookee here."

He sat up quickly and pushed her away. He looked around and saw a piece of a shack, sitting on poles to avoid surges of rising water that would come with heavy rainfalls. His eyes bulged at the shack's decorations. Animal skulls. Ropes of bone. Amulets and crude figures, roughly human in shape, with slivers of bamboo thrust through them. They hung all around the porch.

"*Shiiiiiiiit!*" he exclaimed softly. "Whut I done landed myself in now?"

The old woman rocked back and forth on her heels. "Swamp sent you. Swamp sent you. You mine now."

"Swamp din' send you nuttin', old woman. An' I ain't nobody's." He got up and moved towards the house. The old woman trailed after him. He found a rusted saw and went to work on the manacle around his ankle. He ransacked the cupboards, shoving food into his mouth. Time to go. Old woman was crazy as a bedbug.

"You cain't leave," she said.

"Like hell I cain't."

She cackled, an eerie sound that echoed through the swamp. She held up a crude figure, similar in shape to those hanging on the porch, wrapped in a rag torn from the shirt he was wearing. Producing a short length of rusted chain, she wrapped it around the legs of the figure, still cackling. Cain snorted in derision and made to leave. Then he bellowed in rage.

"Take dat off! *Woman! You crazy!* I say take dat off!"

The more he bellowed, the more she cackled. He couldn't move. He literally, figuratively couldn't move.

"You mine, boy! Sent to serve me! You say so!"

"No!"

"You say so!" she ordered, pulling the chain tighter. Feeling the circulation in his legs cut off, his eyes widened in amazement.

"All right!" he roared. "All right. Stop it! Take it off!"

She took it off and transferred one bird-like hand to the head of the figure. She smiled and squeezed. Cain's eyes bulged. He felt his head imploding. He screamed.

"Learn to mind yo' betters, boy?"

"Yes! Yes! Stop it!"

"Dat's better," she said. She released the pressure and Cain settled down for several weeks of virtual slavery.

Never one to miss an opportunity, Cain studied the old woman. He assumed an attitude of placid obedience while he studied her bones and figures and skulls. She gave him drinks made from swamp plants, mushrooms and fungi growing on the trunks of the overhanging trees. The drinks left him floating in clouds of color. She handed him home-rolled cigarettes with an aroma different from ordinary tobacco. And the effect was *damn* sure different. The world expanded and there was nothing, nothing, he couldn't do. If he ever decided to. Somehow the energy for action deserted him. During one spell of lucidity, he realized the smoke and the drinks were sapping him of his will to leave, deterring him in his quest for future greatness.

He moderated their use considerably, disposing of his rations when the old woman wasn't looking. He cajoled her to initiate him into the rituals of the crude figures, the bones and skulls.

One night, she took his hand and held it in front of the flickering firelight. She inspected it closely.

"When you born, boy?"

"Doan know."

"No idea a'tall?"

"Naw."

"Dat too bad. Can't know yo' full power less'n you know de stars dat rule you."

"Nuttin', nobody, rule me."

"I rule you, boy. Be you needin' any reminder?"

"Naw." Cain wasn't ready to take on the old woman and he knew it.

"But you got power, all right. Strong power. Dark power."

"What sort of power?"

"Power what ken make you—boy, is you de sebbenth son of a sebbenth son?"

Cain laughed. "Got no idea in hell, ol' woman."

"Ain't seen none to beat you. 'Cept me, o'course." She cackled, the cackle that made his skin prickle.

"Ken you teach me? Whut you do?"

"Why I want do dat? So's you can match power with me?"

"So's I can help you. Ain't dat whut you said? Dat I was sent? Why come, if you not goan show me whut you do?"

Cain didn't know what the old woman actually did and he didn't think she did either, but he didn't doubt whatever it was, it packed a hell of a punch. When he learned her secrets, he'd be unstoppable.

She sat and cogitated a moment. "I think on it," she finally allowed.

And so Cain entered into an intense study of things best left undisturbed. Three months later, when he judged he'd learned all she had to teach, he strangled her in her sleep and headed out of the bayou. "Don't never pay to be too sure of yourself, ol' woman," he muttered. He never looked back.

He was that most dangerous of men, a man of charismatic power holding secrets he didn't understand and certainly didn't respect, not exactly a charlatan but assuredly not a seer. Only two things mattered to him, his pleasure and his gain. As he moved out of the Louisiana swamps, over and up into the farmlands of middle Mississippi, he conceived his master plan. He stopped to try it out in a small township called Tonka Creek. It worked admirably. Like a charm.

* * *

Tonka Creek was too small to have any central system of authority but far enough away from the next large town to prevent passers-through from noticing any marked changes in its population. It was perfect.

Cain's only formal schooling came from that strange bayou college wherein his wizened, wrinkled professor presided over a class of one, but he was a natural psychologist. He recognized in religion a formidable tool, a means to ease his way into the fabric of community life gradually, drawing the population into his talons, into his control. By the time he gave his first demonstration of power, real power, his targets were so hypnotized they felt no revulsion for the rituals calling forth that power. By that time, they begged for it.

Tonka Creek was perfect for another reason. It didn't have a resident preacher. Among the white population, various townsmen assumed the pulpit made by draping a cloth over the counter of the General Store every Sunday and painted pictures of hell-fire and damnation.

The Negroes convened in different homes each Sabbath, but followed the same practice of rotating ministry. Cain hired himself out to one of the white farmers who was a cut above a sharecropper and exchanged his great strength in the fields for his daily keep and a bed in the barn. In the evenings, he applied himself to gaining the acceptance of the local Negroes.

He attended the black services for several Sundays before he made his first move. Then he volunteered to preach.

He brought the house down. Within a month, he was the exclusive speaker at the black Sunday services. Within two months, he'd moved those services down to the banks of Tonka Creek.

"God made dis world," he expounded. "De whole world His house. How much mo' He like de' sound of worship out in His biggest house den in four walls of wood?"

The population considered this and found it good.

"Every day God's day," Cain proclaimed. "Not just Sundays. We labor long durin' de days, to earn our bread with de sweat of our brows, and dat's right, dat's proper, 'cause man walked out of Eden under his own power, too stupid to pay attention to de words of de Lord, but we got our nights, doan we? Can't we give him a night or two to raise our voices in praise down by de beauty of dese woods and creeks he done give us?"

The population considered this and found it admirable.

"Christ broke bread wid his followers," Cain preached, "An' shared de wine. We do de same, but we doan do it often 'nuff. What we got do we not got each other and Christ's love?"

"Yeah, Lord!" chanted Cain's congregation. "Praise God!"

They loved the wafers Cain provided for the partaking of Christ's bread. Smoking was a tool of the devil, everybody knew that, but thanks to his deceased professor, Cain knew there was an amazing plant with leaves that could be rolled and smoked or dried and crumbled into baked goods.

They became downright attached to the drinks Cain passed down their ranks, the ones he distilled from certain mushrooms and growths of wood fungi. The world expanded in bright and wondrous colors. Occasionally, one of their ranks rose and shouted of great dangers, of huge, segmented worms crawling down trees, rivers rising and swirling with blood, strange beasts standing on their hind legs that tore and rendered sinners asunder. The congregation loved these visions of Armageddon. God would smite the world and only the blessed would be spared.

Cain sat back and smiled. One night he brought two newborn calves to the creek banks. Sheep would have been better, symbolically speaking, but sheep weren't that common in the flat Mississippi farmlands. He stood at the head of the congregation, putty in his hands, already drunk from his special Communion. He shouted for attention.

"Christ say, 'I be de light of the world, de blood of de lamb!' How we tell Him we understan' Him doan we drink His blood?" A machete of wicked proportions flashed, slitting the calves' throats. Specially picked acolytes caught the brightly spurting blood in waiting vessels and passed it down the ranks.

Most of the congregation grabbed the crude goblets passing down the rows and drank with the fervor of new converts. A few of them glanced at this new Communion with horror, passing the goblets to their neighbors quickly. One or two of them even dared to rise and leave. Cain marked these people in his memory.

In the early hours of the morning, fire bloomed in three separate houses. No one ever rose and departed one of Cain's services again.

The evening gatherings increased in frequency. Cain began to appear bare-chested, his great shoulders draped with necklaces and amulets of bone.

"I be Cain!" he proclaimed. "'An all us knows de story of Cain, how Cain tilled de earth and made his offerin' to God! An' God turn his face away from him to Abel, de keeper of sheep. He like Abel's offering, but Cain, de sweat of his brow, it not be good 'nuff. 'An when Cain rose up in righteousness and slew Abel, de Lord laid de blame on Cain, never seein' nor carin' dat he'd done turned his light from him. He make his mark on Cain and sent him out to de world, and dat mark, it set Cain and all his peoples apart from de rest of de world. An' dat mark, it be blackness!"

Cain didn't know if this interpretation of the Biblical mark branding Cain was accurate, but since it suited his purposes perfectly, he didn't care.

"We carry dat mark, and we de ones suffer for it, when all de time, it be God's fault! God's I say! What we done to make us de slaves of de white man? You say we ain't slaves no mo' but I tell you, we is! Jest' de same as it wuz when we in chains. An' whose fault be dat? Ours? I tell you truly! It be God's ! De white man's God, him what done turn his face away from us. But dat doan matter no mo'! Do it? I say, do it?"

"'Doan matter!" chanted Cain's followers. "Doan matter no mo'!"

"No! It doan matter 'cause dey be other gods! I say to you, dere be other gods, darker and mo' powerful den any God made in de white man's image, and dose gods, dey be de ones whut can make us strong!"

"Strong!" chanted the crowd, hypnotized by powerful homemade hallucinogens, drunk on the scent of the blood rising from the slaughtered calves, enthralled by the power of Cain's gospel. Their lot in life was preordained, set upon them by a vengeful god who'd looked askance at the offerings made by the original Cain. Nothing they did would ever be good enough for a white man's god. They wondered why they'd never seen that before, why they'd never realized there were other gods, better gods, gods who recognized their worthiness.

"An' dese gods, what we need to do? What they want? How we show 'em we worthy o' dere notice?"

"Blood!" chanted the crowd. "De power be blood!"

"De power be blood!" affirmed Cain. "An' de power be in us! In each one of us! In de men, when de sight of a woman turn us hard and powerful, when we take a woman and ram our way into her, when we plant our seed! In de women, in dere dark and secret center, dat can drain de strength out of de strongest man and leave him limp as last year's cornstalk, weak and gaspin' to catch his breath! In de strength dat make new flesh and blood from man's power when it meets woman's! De white man's god, he say dat power bad when it used without his leave. We gots to hide dat power an' not never use it without his say so! Do dat be right? Dat de greatest power whut we has be hid under cover of sheets and blankets? Dat we's got to have his permission—I say his permission! To be men and women like de smallest child not be allowed to wander from his yard without his mama's leave?"

"No!" roared the crowd. "Dat not be right! Dat not be right a'tall!"

"Den let's show de white man's god our power!" roared Cain, and so they did. The crowd shed their clothes and writhed and rolled in frenzied couplings, dizzy from the unexpected freedom of sexual release. The sounds of animal rutting filled the night. No one retained enough clarity of vision to inspect the closest available partner. Brother took sister, father took daughter, best friend took best friend's wife. Cain stood back. He smiled. It was good. It was very good.

In the next week, Cain moved the saga of Tonka Creek to its ultimate conclusion. He stood before his acolytes, waving his representative figures fashioned from dried corn shucks.

"An' who profits from us? From us who wuz cast down by de white man's god to be forever without his favor? To wander de earth wid de mark of Cain on our face? I ask you? Who?"

"De white man!" chanted the crowd. "De white man!"

"An' now, my brothers and sisters, now dat I done showed you de true way, de true light, de true power, de true gods! I say now, what you goan do 'bout it? Is you goan stay, livin' in yo' shacks and scrounging de' white man's field for yo' bread? Is you? I say, is you?"

"No! No mo'! No mo'!"

"An' how you gone escape, my peoples? Does you know?"

"Tell us! Tell us!"

"Wid dese!" roared Cain. He held the corn shuck figures draped in rags scavenged from local clotheslines. "Wid dese!"

Cain bent and twisted the limbs of the figures into contortions no real limbs of flesh and blood could assume.

"Dey at yo' mercy, my peoples! Go! Go and reap de harvest I done sown for you!"

The people raced out into the night to the outlying farms of the white farmers. When they arrived at their destinations, they watched in wonder while the white oppressors rolled and writhed in agony, limbs contorted and broken, blood spilling onto the floors.

Cain appeared, moving his way through the crowd.

"I say reap de harvest, my peoples! *Reap yo' harvest!*"

They poured through the houses, using handy knives, heavy furniture, their bare hands. Torches flew through the air and a great and terrible burning filled the night. When morning came, Tonka Creek held only black and smoldering remains and a confused and baffled group of Negroes. They looked around in wonderment, bewildered at the smoking carnage. Their nerve ends screamed as the residues of Cain's communion offerings slowly dissipated form their systems.

"My, my," Cain mused, as he put as many miles as possible between him and the great wonders he'd wrought. His pockets were stuffed with all the ready cash he could carry, scavenged from the houses of blacks and whites alike.

"Ain't dey goan be hurting when dey figures out dey can't make dat stuff by demselves!"

A trace of the mad cackle of his bayou professor echoed in his laughter. "Dey need some when de white folkses come into town from Twin City. Yea, Lord, dey need some den!" He regretted he wouldn't be around to watch the hangings.

* * *

In the days that followed, tension hung heavy over the middle Mississippi flatlands. The whites started at every footfall, expecting a bloodbath around every corner. The blacks walked in terror, afraid some innocent action would be misinterpreted and bring white vengeance down around their heads. And while the Mississippi flatlands trembled, the instrument of Tonka Creek's destruction passed over the Mississippi border into Alabama.

Cain thought hard on how to obtain the best bang from the lessons learned during the seven months he'd spent in Tonka Creek. Appearances were everything. Folks were fascinated by mysteries. So how to make himself even more mysterious? He remembered the great and glowing colors that bloomed in the wake of his homemade potions. Colors had power. Numbers had power, too. Like seven. He'd waited seven long years for deliverance from the cane fields of that Louisiana prison camp. Cane fields. Damn, that was funny just by itself right there. He'd taken Tonka Creek in seven months. In his ears, his mad bayou professor asked over and over, *be you de sebbenth son of a sebbenth son, boy?*

He walked up to a little backwoods Alabama black church. Seven Cedars Baptist. It stood right outside Seven Cedars, Alabama. He laughed. *Be you de sebbenth son of a sebbenth son, boy?* Well, maybe he was, maybe he wasn't. Sounded good, though. He went inside to join the ongoing service. Within a month, he'd collected a group of ten or so of the black community's finest young men. He met with them down by the banks of Seven Cedar Creek.

"My name be Cain," he announced. "An' my color be sebben."

* * *

Reverend Jackson Dennard was a pain in Cain's posterior that had to go. Brother Dennard kept a weather eye out on the congregation of Seven Cedars. He bounced jauntily in and out of his flock's homes in his spare time, a habit Cain found most annoying. Within a few weeks, Reverend Dennard found himself gripped with a low and unrelenting fever. It wasn't bad enough to drop him in his tracks, but it tired him out. He spent his spare time in bed, attempting to fight off the low heat turning his bones to ground glass.

Reverend Dennard unwillingly became the first permanent member of Cain's entourage after his flock dismembered him down in the circle of oak trees down

119

in the deep woods behind his church, Cain's first human sacrifice. He found it an exhilarating experience and promised himself he would repeat it whenever possible. He strung a fine length of chain through the hole he bored in the top of the meticulously cleaned skull and hung it from the limb of one of the sweet gum trees standing as outpost for the meeting place.

He didn't do it often, but this was a special occasion. So Cain drank from his own potions and invoked his dark gods in a special ceremony. Misshapen creatures, bat-like of body and demonic of face, flew out of nowhere, swooping and swirling above the congregation. One of them settled on top of Reverend Dennard's skull and melted itself down over it. An eerie blue light glowed from the bone and red sparked from the eye sockets.

"Our sentry!" roared Cain. "De disbelievers, dey serve us yet, to deliver dere warning do any of our enemies draw nigh!"

Seven Cedars fell in seven months. Cain looked back on his work, pausing now and then in his flight to turn and savor the flames flickering behind him. His pockets were full, his expertise increasing. Reverend Dennard's skull rested in his saddlebag. Sentries were very handy. In fact, he'd need more. Bigger things were coming.

* * *

He rode south, towards the Alabama Gulf coast, and nine months later he rode away from the smoldering ruins of Tarper, heading northeast towards the Chattanooga River and the Georgia border. Three more skulls joined Reverend Dennard's in his saddlebags, one to face each direction. Two of these belonged to white men who'd dared walk among shadows where white men weren't meant to walk.

He stopped briefly in a valley on the Alabama-Georgia border. He considered briefly and regretfully shook his head. Too close. He needed to go much further into Georgia, into the interior. Did he want another small town, a mid-sized target, a small city?

He shrugged. *What the hell?* He wandered into a general store and asked for a map of Georgia. He closed his eyes and placed his finger on the map. When he opened them, his finger was almost squarely in the center of the state.

"Suh!" Cain motioned the store clerk over. Reading wasn't one of the subjects studied with the mad bayou professor. "Whut dis town be?"

"Macon," the clerk advised.

Macon. Cain frowned. One of the larger cities in the state. Centrally located. A railroad depot of considerable traffic. Was he ready? For something that big? But hell, it was a rich little city. There'd be many Negro servants serving many well-to-do white families, large farms spreading out from the city limits. And the Ocmulgee River. Cain was very partial to creeks and rivers.

He laughed. Oh, why not? Why the hell not?

He rode out of that Alabama valley astride the finest horse he'd ever ridden. He turned his face east. In early February, 1888, he rode into Macon, Georgia. He spent several days touring, passing the time of day with the Negro inhabitants, and before the week was out, he knew where he needed to be on Sabbath next. St. Barnabas.

It wouldn't be easy, but it was doable. And he needed a challenge, challenges kept folks on their toes. Of course, Reverend Gorley, he was a big problem. Reverend Gorley was much better educated than the unfortunate Reverend Dennard. Had a whole lot of personal charisma himself, too. But it could be done. Oh, yes, it could be done.

* * *

Cain moved slower in Macon. Bigger town, more sophisticated audience. He hadn't even held one of his special Communions yet. So far, nothing had gone on at the river meetings that couldn't take place in full public view. Reverend Gorley'd been having headaches from hell, but that was the extent of Cain's preparations so far. But tonight he'd brought some of those wafers and drinks his prior congregations loved so much. Time to step things up a notch or three.

Joshua's friends settled him down beside them in the semi-circle gathered around the campfire. Cain strode to the center of the group and took the stage. His eyes checked the attendants. Three newcomers. Good, that was good. Slow and steady. The summer was young.

"My brothers and sisters," he began. "I be pleased to see y'all tonight, out in de beauty of God's world, not all cramped up and hid from his sight in de walls of de church. Now y'all knows how I value de church, but surely He loves to hear our voices raised in praise out in His great and beautiful world."

"Amen! Amen!"

"So c'mon! Raise our voices in praise of His great works!"

The gathering dusk filled with low and melodious voices blending in simple harmony. When the last notes had died away, Cain raised a bottle.

"Christ broke bread with His disciples. He shared de wine, and 'fore He went to his Glory, He told 'em, dis is my body. Dis is my blood."

"Praise de Lord!"

"An' we share His body and His blood, we do dat to dis day, and brothers and sisters, we find such love and happiness here together by dis riverbank, could dere be a better place to join with Christ? So, brothers and sisters, it please me greatly do you do dat now, here with me."

"Praise God!"

The young people eagerly passed his Communion wine and specially baked wafers down their ranks. Cain grinned as their eyes widened, as the world expanded in their vision, as the great and glowing colors bloomed. He'd never get tired of watching this. It signaled the beginning of his rule.

Cain spoke steadily, his deep voice soft and melodious, but he knew his words didn't really matter. Right now, nobody here either knew or cared what he said. They were floating, floating, on clouds of crimson and purple, soaring over the riverbanks.

Joshua rode a huge white stallion towards the newly risen moon. Somewhere in the back of his mind, he knew he should be scared shitless. The effort just wasn't worth the trouble. He urged his phantom mount higher. He heard Cain's voice, soothing and soft, but it was only meaningless noise. It seemed he'd only arrived at the riverbank when Abe pulled his arm and hauled him to his feet. He was mildly resentful of the interruption. He'd passed the moon and was on his way to the stars.

"Time to go, Josh."

"Already! We just got here."

Abe laughed. "Dat's de way it seem when you listen to Cain. Tol' you. But tonight, I doan rightly know just why, tonight it do seem different someway."

"Sho' 'nuff," concurred Eulises. "Cain be cut from a different cloth, dat's for sho'. Do you be wantin' to speak with him, Josh? You ain't rightly met him yet."

"Well, we fix dat right now," said Cain. He appeared soundless at the boys' side. "You ain't joined us 'fore now, has you, son?"

"No, suh." Now that he'd come down from the night sky, Joshua's senses were beginning to clear. He knew the polite thing to do was introduce himself. Right now he wasn't sure he wanted to.

Cain saw returning clarity in the boy's eyes. Have to watch this boy. His eyes gleamed with intelligence.

"Well, I be real pleased you did, son. Real pleased. And glad to have you back. Anytime. De fellowship of our brothers and sisters. Be dere anything finer in dis great world?"

"No, suh," said Josh, beginning to back away. "I thanks you for lettin' us come. Abe, ain't it time we headed back?"

"Probably so. My mama, she goan likely tear me up bein' out dis late," he said, evidencing little concern over the prospect. Up until Cain's arrival, the thought of his mother's wrath made him cower like a six year old.

The boys turned and headed back up to the boundaries of Wharf Street.

Cain stared thoughtfully after them. That boy. He'd noticed him before, at St. Barnabas. Cain called out to one of his remaining followers.

"Silas!"

"Yes, suh?" Silas didn't precisely stand at attention but it was a close thing.

"Dat boy, de one come with Abe and Eulises and Jeremiah. He ain't come 'fore now."

"Naw, suh."

"Who he be? Whut his name?"

Silas looked after the departing group.

"Oh, him. Dat be Josh Devlin. Surprised to see him here."

"Why dat?"

"Josh, he got mighty uppity last few years. Like he ain't got time for none of us no mo'."

"How so?"

"He, well, Doc Everett, dat's Doc Everett Devlin, he raise Josh since he a baby. Josh's Mama, she come off de street and she die havin' Josh. Doc Everett, he take him in. Doc like dat, didn't surprise nobody. But back four, five year ago, Doc Everett's son, Mist' Paul, he come home from someplace foreign where he in school. An' Josh, he go to live with him. He a doctor, too. An' dat do be all Josh seem to care about now, taggin' after Mist' Paul. Like I say, I surprised to see him here."

"Sho' nuff," mused Cain. "Now, ain't dat interestin'?"

Cain walked away. When he was far enough removed from any of his followers, he laughed. *Doc Everett, he take him in. Doc like dat.* Sure Doc was like that. The boy's nose was sharp, his skin creamy brown. His lips, though full, couldn't be called large. Either the older Devlin'd been having some fun or the younger Devlin'd been getting educated. Because that boy was half-white. And a Devlin, for certain sure. Foundling, hell.

So. Could he use this? Cain already knew both Dr. Devlins, father and son, had a lot of influence in the black community. Cain always did his homework. And it did appear that whichever Devlin had fathered the boy, Joshua was important to the Devlin family. Oh, yes. Cain could use this. He didn't know exactly how, not right at the moment, but he'd know when the time came.

* * *

Joshua never slept late. The next morning, he woke only because Paul was shaking his shoulder. Hard. "Josh! Time to get moving! What's the matter, late night? You out with some sweet young thing last night? Knew I wasn't giving you enough free time, why didn't you ever say anything?"

"*Unnnnn,*" intoned Josh, and tried to settle back in his pillow.

"Hey, wait a minute! You feel alright? Something wrong?"

"I'm fine. Give me a minute, will ya?"

"Sure?"

"Sure I'm sure. Can't anybody sleep late once in a while in this house?"

"No. Don't have time for it. Janie's got hotcakes for breakfast."

"Not hungry."

"What? Thought you weren't sick?"

"Not sick. Just not hungry. Up in a minute."

"Better be. Got lots of rounds to make this morning."

Joshua threw back his covers in irritation when Paul left the room. He felt nervy, itchy, scratchy, unsettled in his skin. A body couldn't even get any decent sleep around here. He realized suddenly he was annoyed with Paul. Not for waking him up. For being Paul. What on earth was the matter with him?

All at once Joshua remembered his moonlight ride across the heavens and shivered. He wasn't sure if he shivered in apprehension or in anticipation.

"Josh! I'm goin' to eat your stack of hotcakes if you ain't out here in two minutes flat!"

Joshua fought a sudden, inexplicable urge to yell back, "Just shut the hell up!" He'd never felt like that before in his life.

"Comin'!" he yelled back.

* * *

Joshua fought intense irritation all day. It moved under his skin, swarming like ants every time he heard Paul's voice. It had something to do with that great phantom horse he'd ridden across the face of the moon last night. That night ride hadn't been normal and he knew it. It shouldn't be repeated. He knew nothing about Cain, where he came from or why. And he knew he shouldn't go back to the riverbank.

But what an adventure! And being with his own people again! Who would ever understand him better?

He strolled out of the house around 7:00 p.m. that evening, mind made up. He was never going back to that riverbank. No way, no how. Nothing would make him change his mind.

Abe and Eulises and Jeremiah passed by the house. They paused and lifted their hands in greeting. They hadn't done that since they'd all been twelve years old.

"You comin'?"

Joshua hesitated for only a heartbeat. He went.

Chapter Nine

Sadie noticed the changes first. Even Doc didn't realize the pain it had cost Sadie to raise Joshua without acknowledging him as her son, and no mother ever guarded a child with more care. She knew him. Inside and out.

The changes were small at first. Josh paced restlessly throughout the house. His eyes, which had always viewed the world with wonder, were dull and lifeless, as though they'd turned inward. Now it seemed nothing gave him any pleasure. His voice lost expression. His sense of humor, uncannily similar to his brother's, went into hibernation. Most of all, she noticed a certain flash in Joshua's eye when anybody even spoke to him. When that flash seemed to edge past irritation and over into anger, she consulted Paul.

"Mist' Paul, you notice anything different 'bout Josh lately?"

"He's growing up."

"Dat ain't it. Since he been goin' out with his friends in de evenings, he different."

"God, Sadie, I pushed him too hard. I didn't realize. He needed some time to himself."

"He full of hisself, he ill as a goat, and he ain't eating right."

Paul grinned.

"Well, whut? Doan jest grin at me like a monkey!"

"He's in love."

"He whut?"

"He's in love. Face it, Sadie, he's almost a man."

"You know dat for sho'?"

"*Welllll*," Paul drawled out the word. Of course he'd noticed the changes but he'd been a seventeen year old boy himself. He was pretty sure all of Josh's symptoms would be instantly cured by a good roll in the hay, but he valued his own hide enough not to say such to Sadie.

"He hasn't come right out and said so, but I know, just the same."

"He in love, he tell you 'bout it, Paul. He tell you everything. Dat ain't it."

"No, he wouldn't. When you're seventeen, nothing's ever happened to anybody else but you, so nobody else understands. This is one thing that's real private, Sadie. He wouldn't tell me."

"*Humph!*" snorted Sadie. "Well, it ain't goan stay private too much longer do he keep flashin' dat look. You know de one I mean?"

Paul laughed. "Yeah, I know. Caught it a time or two myself, but Sadie, he was such a good child. He's been such a good boy. Growing up's not easy and it's been especially hard for him."

"I knows dat."

"He's never given a speck of trouble so he's entitled to be a little difficult every now and then. Don't you think?"

"*Humph!*" Sadie snorted again. "Little difficult be one thing. He's just about crossed dat line over into a pure-de-pain in the behind!"

Paul hooted.

"An' he cross it any further, I'm goan give him a pain in the behind! You hush up dat laughin', I mean it."

"I know you do, Sadie, don't doubt it for a minute." Paul assumed a straight face and went about his business.

Joshua was in love all right. Paul was right about that. But he wouldn't be cured by anything as simple as a good roll in the hay. He was in love with those wafers and potions Cain dispensed at his special Communions. And the strength of those wafers and potions increased dramatically as Cain eased his sermons away from brotherhood and love, toward rage and blood and the service of his own dark gods.

Sometimes during brief periods of clarity, Joshua felt waves of terror. The dark things flitting at the edge of his consciousness—they couldn't be real. He hadn't drunk the blood of slaughtered newborn calves. He hadn't really slung any of the young girls at the riverbank to the ground and rutted like a wild animal. Had he? No, of course not. Those things happened only in the dream world. Every world held darkness somewhere.

Cain began to dispense little cloth bags to his faithful, small tidbits to "tide them over" from one service to the next. And so for Joshua, the periods of lucidity when he realized he wasn't ever completely lucid for very long anymore began to disappear entirely. A tidbit here and there throughout the day took care of that.

The tidbits took care of Joshua's lifelong habit of catlike neatness, too. Even as a child, he'd been precise, his play toys placed, not merely strewn across his room. Sadie opened the door to his room one morning when he was running an errand for Paul. The bed covers were thrown aside, clothes scattered over its foot and spilling onto the floor. His books, his proudest possessions, lay helter-skelter in heaps.

Sadie tightened her lips. This was too much. She didn't care what Paul said. She'd get this room in order and then she'd get Joshua in order.

"Too big for his britches," she muttered, picking up the scattered clothes. "Won't stand for it. Don't care what Mist' Paul say. Tan his hide for him, I will! The idea! The very idea! Of leaving dis room like dis!"

She folded and straightened, sniffing the clothes to see if they needed to be laundered. She shook a pair of pants. Encrusted mud fell off the legs and onto her clean floor.

No question where these pants were going and she plunged her hands into the pockets to check their contents before consigning them to the laundry hampers. Her hand closed on a small cloth bag.

What on earth? She plunged her fingers into the small sack. Her blood ran cold as she examined the contents. She broke open the small, hard wafers and sniffed. Small, dried mushrooms. Seeds. With a pungent odor. Not too many folks would have a clue what they were. Sadie did. Holding the bag tight, she walked out of the room and closed the door firmly behind her, heading to the room she used on the infrequent occasions when she spent the night at the Orange Street house. She sat down on the bed and squeezed her eyes shut.

"Oh, Joshua!" she moaned. "Son, whut you done got into now? Whut?"

* * *

The front door slammed. Joshua. Paul had sent him down to Sol Hogue's Drug Store for quinine.

"Oh, good!" Paul met him in the hall. "Now we can start rounds. Needed this for Jimbo James, those malaria fevers are coming and going and I know he needs some more—"

"Doan got none." Joshua walked past Paul toward the kitchen.

"You don't—you didn't get any? Why not?"

"Doc Hogue say he out."

"You out of grammar this morning too, it seems. But Josh, you knew I needed this. Didn't you go down to Goodwyn's to see if they had any?"

"You didn't say to."

"I didn't say—Josh, what's wrong with you, boy? I shouldn't have to tell you—"

Josh whirled to face Paul. Watching from the stair landing, Sadie almost stepped back from the rage in his expression.

"Ain't yo' *boy!* An' I ain't yo' *slave!* Doan you call me *boy!*"

Paul grabbed his arm and jerked. "You hold it! You hold it right there! You got no call to talk to me like that! Sadie calls *me* boy!"

Josh's expression changed to murderous wrath. Sadie shot down the stairs, intent on getting between them. Josh moved faster. He broke Paul's grip and raced back down the hall towards the front door.

Sadie grabbed Paul's arm as he started after him.

"Paul, please! Please, right now, jest let him go! We gots to talk, son!"

"The hell I will!" exclaimed Paul, impatiently shaking off Sadie's hand. Too late. Joshua was already out the door. Paul turned back to Sadie.

"Sadie, what the hell? You were right and I was wrong and I'm goin' to find him and bring him back so you can put that pain on his behind you were talking about. 'Cause if I do it right now, I'm goin' to put some serious *hurt* on him!"

Sadie thrust the bag in front of Paul.

"I found dis. In his pants pocket when I wuz straightening his room. You looked in his room lately?"

"No."

"Come," said Sadie.

Paul looked around in astonishment. "We got a boarder I don't know about? Josh has never—"

Sadie shook the bag again. "You know what dis is?"

Paul took the bag and opened it. He shrugged.

"Some dried mushrooms. Seeds of some kind." He picked up one of the wafers. "Some sort of hard cookie? What?"

"It's poison, Mist' Paul. Pure-de-poison. Not too many folks know whut dis is, whut it do. It fill yo' head with color and sights of wonder, sapps yo' will, put you in somebody else's power. Make you do and think and feel whatever dat somebody else tell you to do and think and feel. An' sometimes, sometimes, de bright colors, de pretty dreams, dey twist and turn into snakes dat fill you up and send you screamin', runnin' and beggin' for mercy."

From nowhere, he heard Chloe's voice on the banks of the Ocmulgee. *Sadie has power. Sadie knows mojos.*

"How do you know about things like this?"

Sadie sighed. "Might be we ought to go in your office and sit a spell."

"Might be."

* * *

They settled down on Paul's big leather couch.

"So," said Paul. "Tell me."

"While I talk, you forget I'm Sadie, Sadie like you knows me. An' doan take no insult, 'cause right now I ain't speakin' as yo' hired help."

"Sadie! I had enough of that horseshit out of Josh. You're not hired help, you're family. You're my Mama, for God's sakes!"

She continued as though he hadn't spoken. "Or as yo' daddy's woman. Yo' daddy, he tol' you my real name one time. You 'member?"

"Sadama. Wished you'd used it, Sadie. It suits you a lot better."

"I made a choice a long time ago. To live in dis world de way I do. I had a chance at another world, an' my sister, she do live in dat world."

"I didn't know you had a sister, Sadie."

"Lord, Mist' Paul. Got sebben of 'em."

"Seven? Your mama must have had her hands full."

"My Mama, she a great lady. She work all her life, she work hard, and my Daddy did, too, and dey done dere best for all of us, but my Mama, she didn't jest live in dis world. She have power, Mist' Paul. Now, I knows you goan laugh, but she have de sight. She could see things, things dat move just beyond de veil of this world. See, what you doan know, not too many men, black or white neither knows, is this world, it be ringed

133

with worlds on worlds. Dey shift, dey overlap, and some of dose worlds be real dark, full of evil and danger, and some of 'em, dey be real bright and beautiful."

Sadie paused to look at Paul's face and gauge the effect of her words. Satisfied, she continued.

"An' some folks can pass back and forth whenever dey want to. An' dey can use de powers of dose worlds in dis one. I doan know jest why or what it is dey have dat let's 'em do it. But whut I do knows is whatever dat thing is, it doan care whether the body dat gots it be good or bad. An' whether the body dat gots it be good or bad, dat whut makes dere power good or bad. 'Cause a bad person, be dat person black or white or man or woman, dey goan use dat power bad, and a good person, dey goan do great wonders wid it. Do you see a'tall whut I'm saying?"

The Paul educated in Edinburgh where the religion of rationalism ruled laughed at Sadie's earnest explanations. The Paul who'd moved in and out of the black sub-culture around him since earliest boyhood didn't laugh. That Paul leaned forward in anticipation and shouted, *"Finally! I knew sooner or later somebody'd tell me the truth!"*

"And your Mama, she could do this? And you, too?"

"Yes. No. Well, my Mama, she could do it some. She was a sebbenth daughter, the sebbenth girlchild of my Grandmama. Numbers, dey have dere own powers and sebben, it be a real powerful number. So yes, my Mama could do more den lots of folks could. But she didn't never use dat power for no badness and truth be tol', she didn't use it no more den she could help. I think it scare her. An' dat's good, Mist' Paul, dat's real good, 'cause if you doan use it right, if you doan knows 'xactly whut you doing, bad things can happen. Real bad things. Things can cross over to us dat weren't never 'sposed to be in dis world."

"And you?"

"I gots, almost all my sisters, gots de sight a little. Sometimes, we knows things we shouldn't know. I tol' you once, I was a mama and mamas jest knows?"

Paul nodded.

"Well, dat's true and all mamas gots de sight a little do it come to dere young'uns, but whut we gots goes a little beyond dat. But I knows my limits, an' what I got, it jest enough to be dangerous. 'Cause I can't control it real good. Doan know 'xactly why I can see some things and not others, and I never know 'xactly when it'll happen. So I don't fool around with it."

"At all?"

"No. Some folks whut remember my mama, dey think I do, and dey come to me sometimes and ask my help with something. An' if I feel comfortable wid it, like a young girl want a man to notice her, den I give 'em a potion I tell 'em'll get his attenion. But whut I really gives 'em is spring water. See, if dey think de man's goan notice 'em, den dey pretty demselves up, they flutter dere eyelashes, and de man, he come over and starts to talking. An' dey think the potion's working, so dey talk back, and 'fore you know it, dey done got dere man."

Paul laughed. "Sadie, that's brilliant!"

"No, it ain't. Ain't a'tall. Jest human nature. An' whut with yo' daddy and Josh, I din' want nobody speculatin' nor payin' too much 'ttention to me. So I act sort of mysterious and doan never get too involved wid church folks and all, and dey think it's cause I's too busy wid my potions and such, an' so dey doan get close 'nuff to be no trouble."

"But Sadie, if you don't fool around with any of that, then how do you know what the stuff in that bag is?"

"Like I say, almost all my sisters got de sight. But my twin sister, she be truly blessed. Or cursed. I reckon it all depends on how you look at it. You goan laugh at me?"

Paul shook his head.

"She de sebbenth daughter of a sebbenth daughter. An' her power be wondrous to behold. She couldn't no mo' run away from it den a newborn baby can walk."

"Your twin sister?"

Sadie nodded. 'She born first. She the sebbenth daughter. I the eighth. An' I tell you truly, Paul, I done spent my life thanking God for dat, so's I doan have to worry 'bout controlling dat power."

"Sadie, let me ask you something. You're tellin' me about other worlds, darkness and light, strange powers. But you thank God. So if you believe in the other, then do you believe—"

"In God?"

Paul nodded.

"Why, sho'ly I do. Dere's only one God, Mist' Paul. But see, whut I knows is, dere's good, and dere's evil. An' dere's spirits dat be good and evil. An' de good things, all de good things, dey part of God. God's jest a tad more complicated den all de preachers make out. He got his nose in lots more business den dey think. An' dere's a lot more evil out dere, a lot mo', den dey want to think 'bout. Dat's all."

"Fascinating," Paul muttered under this breath. "Absolutely fascinating!"

"Whut?"

"Nothing. And your sister?"

"Her name be Tamara. She spent her life learnin' how to use dat power. She ain't got time for dis world, for a man or chill'uns of her own. She serve de light, de goodness, and in dat service, she know, has to know, how to recognize de evil."

"Why haven't I ever met her? Josh hasn't either, unless you're playin' favorites there, takin' him to visit and not me. He's never mentioned her."

"Josh doan know her, same reason you doan. She tell me not to bring you out wid me when you wuz little, she say it ain't time, and when Josh born, she say it ain't time for her to see him neither. Never understood dat, but I don't argue. I doan sees her all dat much, but I go out sometimes. We not jest sisters, we twins. When I needs her, I goes. If she need me, I knows it, and I go. She doan live in town. She live way out in the country, down in de woods. Almos' in de swamps. Dat's so she can find the things she need—"

"Like these?" Paul raised the bag he was still holding.

"Lik' dat. Dey doan necessarily have to be put to a bad use, she can use 'em in other things, good things. Lik' I say, all depends on de person using 'em. An' she live out by Stone Creek, where de woods start to slide into de swamps."

Stone Creek. Five or so miles outside the city. In a carriage, about an hour out, an hour back, give or take a bit.

"How does she live?"

"Folks take care of her. She take care of dem, dey take care of her. Problem too big for me, I send 'em to her. Iff'n I think dey deserve dat kind of help, dat is."

"But if these things," Paul shook the bag again. "If these things can be good—"

"Wherever Josh got these, dey ain't good, Paul. 'Way he's been actin', I knew soon as I seen 'em whut he been doing. He been goin' out at night wid boys he ain't had nuttin' to do wid since he twelve years old."

"How do you know that? I mean, I told him to go out with his friends, have some fun."

"Ain't got no real friends, Mist' Paul. Ain't had in a long time. He doan think I knows dat, but I do. De other boys, dey think he put on airs since he been spendin' all his time wid you."

"You mean, I set him apart. Made him different. Just like you said I would. I didn't know. Sadie, why didn't you tell me?"

"'Cause I wuz wrong 'bout dat. An' you wuz right. An' Josh, he a Devlin, jest like his Daddy and his brother, an' ain't nobody ought to try and keep a Devlin out of books. Jest took me a while to see it, dat's all."

"And now?"

"Now, Mist' Paul, whoever Josh and dose boys he hanging out wid, dey done got in deep. Too deep. Somebody new in town, somebody knows whut dese can do." Sadie reached over and took the bag. "An' doan care. Dese not be ground up, nor mixed with anything else, dey be full strength. Person whut passin' dis stuff out, dey doan care 'bout nuttin' but spreading dere own power."

"How do you know it's somebody new?"

"Gots to be. 'Cause dere ain't nobody in dis town goan cross Tamara's path. Dis her town. An' whoever passin' dis out, dey doan know nobody like Tamara's aroun' or dey wouldn't be doin' it. Nobody dare. An' he mighty lucky, too. Dat she ain't stumbled 'cross him yet."

"You think it's a man?"

"Doan really know. Could be either one. I gots to talk to my sister."

Paul glanced at the clock. It was just past ten in the morning.

"I'll hitch up the buggy. Go tell Janie to tell any afternoon patients I might not be back till 4:00 or 5:00, maybe later."

"You doan got to go wid me."

"Yes, I do."

"Everett needs to know."

"No. Please don't, Sadie."

Sadie sighed. "Thought so."

"Thought what?"

"Everett ain't well. Is he?"

Paul hesitated. "I wouldn't say he's not well. I'd say I don't like the way his face gets red when he gets the least bit upset. Or the way he breathes when he walks fast. Don't let's tell Papa yet."

"Well. Up to you, son. Best be getting' started."

* * *

Paul turned at Sadie's direction and headed down the path winding into the woods edging Stone Creek. He halfway expected a ramshackle hut, dark and overshadowed by huge trees, its owner draped in flowing, ragged tatters of black, bent and stooped.

The path ended in a sunny clearing. In its center stood a neat white cottage with a stone chimney. Flowerbeds glowed with color and neatly-trimmed shrubs hugged the walls. A covered well, the walls constructed from the same stone sported by the chimney, stood off to the side.

Paul laughed.

"Whut?"

"Not what I expected."

"What'd you 'spect?"

"Tell you the truth, Sadie, I'm not real sure."

"Pull de buggy over dere. Hit her flowerbeds, she goan yell. Hope she didn't go to too much trouble for dinner."

"Dinner?"

"Getting' on toward noon. She goan 'spect us to eat 'wid her."

"She don't know we're coming!"

"Yeah, you keep right on thinkin' dat, son. She know." The door of the cottage opened as Paul handed Sadie down from the buggy. Tamara strode toward them with the same regal bearing, the same copper-colored skin, the same type of turban on her head. Sadie's double. Identical twins.

"So you be Everett's oldest boy!" she exclaimed, and held out her hand. Paul took it and felt a flood of warmth run from her hand to his. The warmth seemed curiously alive, as though Tamara, by her touch, sent part of herself out into him, exploring his thoughts, his soul.

"Got biscuits rising in de oven," she said, "an' new honey. Joe Turner robbed a hive yesterday down in de swamp and brought me a quart jar. Hope ham alright wid you. Thought 'bout a chicken, but didn't figger I had 'nuff time. You sendin' out streaks of worry like lightnin', woman. Whut's bad 'nuff to worry you so you got to bring Paul out here?"

She took Sadie's arm and began to walk towards the cottage door.

Paul hurried to catch up with the sisters. "I hope you're not upset with Sadie for bringin' me, I don't mean to intrude."

Tamara laughed. A good laugh, a joyous laugh.

"Shoot, boy! Jest 'cause you ain't never met me doan mean I ain't never met you! You nor Joshua neither. Knows you both. Watched you grow up. Sadie think it time to bring you here, it be time. You mo' den welcome."

Tamara settled them at a wooden table. Its surface gleamed with years of use and polish.

"First thing first," Tamara said, bustling around her stove. "Let's us eat some dinner. Folks got to take care of dere bodies do dey 'spect dere bodies to take care of dem. Ain't dat right, Paul?"

"Yes ma'am."

"An' whut you gots to tell me be real worrisome. Worse than worrisome, I feel darkness. Evil. Can't eat right wid evil flowing through de room in our words. So for right now, let's us jest take care of dese biscuits."

They passed a pleasant half-hour at Tamara's table as they worked their way through the fried ham and new potatoes, the mounds of biscuits. Tamara produced a big blackberry cobbler when the last biscuit sopped the last of the meat juice off the plates. Sadie visibly began to relax. Paul felt the waves of comfort flowing out from one sister to the other.

And when Tamara judged the time right, she gathered the dishes off the table and transferred them over to the stone sink that stood by the cast iron stove. She sat back down.

"Tell me," she said.

Paul pulled the cloth bag out of his pocket and handed it back to Sadie. This was part of her world. It wasn't his. Not yet.

She took it from him but didn't give it to Tamara.

"Josh, he seem to start changin' 'bout two months back. I'd place it 'round mid-May, wouldn't you say, Paul?"

"Oh, I don't think it was that far back."

"Yes. Yes, it was. Little things at first, things you wouldn't have paid no never mind to. 'Sides, you jest now lately been paying mind to things other than sick folks yourself."

Paul smiled slightly. Hadn't ever fooled Sadie in his life.

"An' it bother me, but at first, I think, well, he done growed up on me. Might be he done found a girl takes his fancy. But de changes, dey doan seem to be dat kind. He absentminded alright, and he doan pay much 'ttention to things less'n you jest 'bout knock him up side de head, but it weren't happy woolgatherin' de way it is when a body in love. An de look in his eye when you interrupt him at somethin', my Lord! I shoulda knowed sooner. If'n I'd talked to him den, or followed him, or—"

"An' if a bullfrog had wings," said Tamara solemnly, "he wouldn't have bumped his hiney when he jumped off'n de lily pad. Can't help shoulda done now."

"No," agreed Sadie, finally handing her sister the bag. "An' dis morning, Josh's room be a pure-de-wreck. An' he doan never leave no room like dat. So when I go in to pick up, madder den a wet hen, I find dis."

Tamara opened the bag and looked in. When she raised her head, her eyes flashed.

"Somebody in my town? Be passin' dis stuff out an' I doan know 'bout it? I doan believe it! Doan believe I been sittin' back here all happy and sassy, I shoulda been checkin', I ain't been tendin' to my business!"

"If a bullfrog had wings—" said Paul.

"Doan' be turnin' my own words 'gainst me, boy."

"*Boy* seems to be a dangerous word today," said Paul. "I called Josh boy this morning and he blew sky-high and stormed out of the house. And if Sadie hadn't just found that bag and stopped me, I'd have hauled him back and blistered his hind-end."

"He been takin' dis stuff, he doan know whut he sayin', Paul. Doan hardly know whut he doin'."

"So Sadie tells me."

"Tamara, can you feel him? Whoever give dis to Josh? An' if Josh has it, he been hangin' out wid a crowd of boys at night, Josh ain't goan be de only one whut has dis stuff."

Sadie broke off as Tamara stood up, holding the bag in her hand.

"Let's us see." She walked to the canisters that sat on the kitchen counters and scooped up a handful of flour and a handful of cornmeal. She knelt in front of the fireplace, her moving hands pouring out designs on the floor.

"Sadie, what the hell is she—"

"Quiet. She got to concentrate. Dey be veves."

"They be what?"

"Veves. Dey concentrate de power, call the sweet spirits. Now hush up."

Tamara finished her designs. She closed her eyes and started a low, melodious chant. Mingled French and English. Older words, lilting words. The vision of a large grassy plain filled Paul's brain, a vision of an African pampas. He didn't know how he knew, but he did. The room filled with scent. Heliotrope, lemon verbena, cloves, sandalwood.

"Sadie?" Paul murmured.

"Hush up," she responded in a bare whisper. "Dey talkin' to her."

"Who?"

"Hush up!"

Tamara ceased her chant. A frown furrowed her brow. She sat for a space of time that might have been a minute, or five, or ten. Paul felt as though he were in the trance with her. Without warning the scent changed. The stench of ordure, the sulfuric smell of rotten eggs. Tamara dropped the bag as though its touch burned her skin.

Sadie rushed to her sister.

"What the hell?" Paul had an idea he'd be asking that a lot over the next days.

Tamara pushed off Sadie's hand and rose to her feet. She pulled a canister of homemade potpourri from a cabinet and walked around the room, scattering handfuls in small, strategically placed dishes. The smell of apples and spice fought to repel the awful stench. She sat back down at the table.

If a black person could be said to look pale, she did. Her skin looked lifeless.

"Ain't been tendin' my business," she said. "Sittin' back here, restin' on my haunches, forgettin' dat de light got to be guarded. I done let evil get a foothold here."

"A bokor?" asked Sadie.

"A what?" asked Paul, certain he'd be told to 'hush up' again, but no.

"You 'member what I said 'bout de worlds dat surround this one?"

He nodded.

"Well, dose worlds and dis one, dey have dere own spirits. Dey be de Loa."

"Sadie, you told me you believed in one god."

"An' I do. All de goodness, the total of it, and all de sweet spirits, de sweet Loa, dey be God's. But He's got different parts, all the goodness put together. An' de devil, de way most folks see him, is all de badness put together. But de dark and de light, dey both got dere own spirits. An' de spirits of goodness be the spirits of the Rada. An' de badness be de powers of de Dark, the Congo or the Petro, de bitter Loas. Now, I tol' you, folks what have de power can use 'em either bad or good?"

Paul nodded.

"Folks whut use dere powers for the de dark, they be bokors. An' folk whut use dere powers for de light, dey be houngans if dey men, mambos if dey women."

"Like Tamara."

"Yes."

"So whoever's in town—"

"Is a bokor," said Tamara. "But not 'xactly."

"Whut you mean, 'not 'xactly'?" asked Sadie.

"I saw a man, a dark man. He black as coal, but dat ain't why he dark. He big, one of de biggest I ever seen, an' dats a gift from de dark side, but he both more and less den a bokor."

"I doan understand."

"I doan neither, yet, not 'xactly. But he ain't a bokor 'cause he choose to be. Not one whut takes his power and sharpens it on purpose, devotin' his life to studyin' de bitter Loa. He do know some of de rituals of power, and he use 'em, but he doan understan' 'em. He use 'em lik' a little chile doan know how to read yet still can say his 'a-b-c's.'"

"But if he doan know, den where de power come from?"

"Doan know. He doan neither. It jest be dere. Might be de stars set in jest de right place when he born. Or somethin' else real powerful. Might be a sebbenth son of a sebbenth son hisself. Or both. Or neither one or somethin' else. But whut matters is, he de most dangerous man I believe I ever knowed about. 'Cause he thinks he using de powers of darkness. But really, dey usin' him. An' he ain't really doin' all de things he think he is. Dey lettin' him do 'em 'cause dey knows he doan know whut he doin'. Ain't goan hold back, and dey might can get control. An' he doan know 'nuff to send 'em back."

"Who?" asked Paul. He knew, without pausing for thought, that nothing Sadie or Tamara said was a direct contradiction of Christianity. There existed a heaven, a hell, and earth. And an all-powerful God who was good and a Satan who was evil. Sadie and Tamara believed exactly that. They just broke the components down into further subparts.

"De dark Loa. Dey waitin', dey hopin', to send dere own dark angels out."

Sadie's complexion looked like dark parchment, almost lifeless.

"Can you stop him?"

Tamara ran her tongue slowly around her dry lips.

"Sadie, I doan know!" she said. "I jest doan know!"

Sadie moaned. "My sweet Jesus! Whut we goan do? Whut can we do?"

"Let's get back to town," Paul said, rising suddenly.

"Why?"

"Because I need to talk to Bobby Ryles."

"De Chief of Police?"

"Yes."

"Why?"

"Maybe this man's been somewhere else before. Maybe news of some strange happenings is beginning to come over the wires. Maybe even news of some strange happenings here in town. And we have to find Josh, get him straightened out. He ought to be able to tell us something."

"How we goan straighten Josh out?" Sadie asked, facing her greatest fear.

"Hogtie him, if we have to. He ain't going back out. To wherever he goes."

"Dat stuff, it be real powerful, Paul," advised Tamara. "Even when a body ain't had none for a while, a long while, it can kick up again and fill dere head up wid sights. Visions. Some good. And some whut can make a body scream aloud and beg for mercy."

"Then the sooner he stops taking the stuff, the sooner we'll know the damage. Let's get back to town, Sadie."

Tamara hesitated. She knew far more than she'd shared with her sister. The gods, her powerful gods of light, had spoken to her on the scent of flowers filling the room as she conversed with her veve.

"'Fore you leave, Paul, might be you and me might wander down in the woods a spell."

Sadie's eyes filled with alarm.

"Tamara? Why?"

"Oh, hush up, Sadie. First time I had a chance to meet yo' boy, doan grudge me a few minutes alone wid him, now do you?"

* * *

Tamara led him out into the woods and down a small path. She stopped at a carved wooden bench under a gigantic water oak.

"Let's us sit a spell, son."

Paul sat. "You saw more than you wanted Sadie to hear. Didn't you?"

"Well, now, might be dat's why I thought you and me ought to have dis talk. Give me yo' hand, son."

"What?"

"Yo' hand. Give me yo' hand."

She reached out and turned it palm upward, leaned close, and traced several lines with the tip of her finger. Finally, she sat back. And said nothing.

Paul broke the silence.

"I wish I thought you weren't sayin' anything because there's nothing there tells you anything. But I don't think that's the reason you ain't talkin'."

Tamara gave a half-hearted smile. "You a caution, boy. I's just tryin' to think how to 'splain it, dat's all. See here, I can't help you as much as I want to. I's goan have to sort of sit myself back and advise. My power's not goan stop dis man, not all by itself."

"Why not? You tellin' me your gods of Light ain't more powerful than the gods of Dark?"

"No, I ain't. Ain't tellin' you dat a'tall. I'm tellin' you I ain't de one dey goan use to stop dis man. Dey mo' powerful, sho' nuff. Doan you be thinkin' else wise, good always goan be stronger, but boy, it always goan be a struggle. An' in dis struggle, ain't me goan be dere soldier. It be you."

"Me?"

"You. An' I's goan help you jest as much as I possibly can, doan fret yourself none 'bout dat. An' dere's things I can do, things goan help protect you, but I can't do most of it. You have to. An' dere's not one thing I can do whut goan change dat. Wish dere was."

Paul dispassionately noted the ripples of sunlight that splashed through the leaves. This was pretty country. He wished he'd brought Chloe into the country more often.

Finally, he spoke.

"Will I win?"

"Yes." Tamara responded with no hesitation.

Paul lifted his hand and turned Tamara's face to look into her eyes. He trusted this woman. In fact, he already loved her, as though the love he felt for Sadie spread over onto this duplicate face. He smiled. She was telling the truth. Just not all of it.

"Will I live to know it?"

"Oh, yes, son. Oh, yes. You got a long life 'head of you, boy."

Paul smiled again. He wondered how enjoyable his long life would be. He pressed Tamara no further. He'd get his brother out of this mess and right now, that was good enough.

"All right," he said, dropping his hand from her face and standing up. "I best be getting back to town."

"When you find Joshua, you do jest like you say. You hogtie him, do you has to."

* * *

Tamara stood in her sunny yard and watched them drive off. Her heart ached. Long ago, she'd made a choice. She'd refused to meet her sister's sons—and in Sadie's heart, Paul was as much her son as Joshua—as youngsters. She'd always known, somewhere deep in her heart. She'd known something dark and evil would stalk them. When that time came round, she'd need a clear head. She didn't need her objectivity hampered by memories of them running into her arms with welcoming hugs or scenes of them playing in her yard cluttering her head. She'd have to be strong. For them. For all of them.

"Lord, my God," she breathed softly. Tamara had no conflict with the concept of God. He merely used many sources to work His will. "I knows dis is how it gonna' be. But why? Why? Did you have to pick one of our boys to be yo' dark angel?"

* * *

Paul and Sadie rode back to town in silence, each deep within their own thoughts. Dark thoughts, smoky clouds swirling in gathering turmoil.

Long life ahead of you, boy....

Almost but not quite, he understood. He didn't want to understand. If he did, he might leave everything and everyone and run. Run like the demons of hell were snapping at his ankles.

He didn't recall ever in his life running away from anything. He straightened his shoulders. What would happen would happen. He'd survive. Tamara said so. And he thought that might not be a good thing. But he'd deal with later—later.

* * *

Sadie sat in silence and stole glances at Paul's profile, memorizing the straight, proud nose, the curving lips, the finely drawn bones.

Something bad was coming. She felt it. Somehow taking Paul to Tamara had—not caused it, exactly, but drawn it closer, made it irrevocable. A mother could not, should not, choose between her children. Sadie would sacrifice herself in a heartbeat to save either of her sons. Deep in her aching heart, she knew she didn't have that choice. Whatever was coming, it didn't want her. It wanted her boys.

"Paul?"

"Yes, Sadie?"

"I love you, son."

Paul smiled. Sadie wasn't free with words of affection. She expressed her love in more concrete ways. Closets full of clean clothes, the swift mending of a favorite shirt, chocolate cake at the end of the meal, tall glasses of cool tea offered in the heat of summer. Chiding words of criticism and warm glances of approval.

"I know. I love you, too."

"I know."

Paul smiled. And, having said all that was really important, they arrived back home.

Chapter Ten

Paul's afternoon didn't go as he'd hoped. Several patients waited for him when they arrived home and by the time he'd finished his afternoon hours, it was too late to make the trip downtown to City Hall to speak with Bobby Ryles, Macon's Chief of Police.

Paul stood in thought and walked to the front windows, glancing up and down the streets. No sign of Joshua. He went in search of Sadie and found her standing on a chair attacking the shelves of books in the library with a damp dust cloth.

"You did those last week," he said behind her.

She started in surprise and almost lost her balance. He moved forward, caught her waist and steadied her. Then he offered her his hand and she stepped down.

"I know," she said. "But I gots to stay busy and these take a lot of time."

"Sadie, you said you'd seen him with some of the other boys. Who?"

"You goan go look?"

"Don't know what else to do."

"Please be careful, son."

"Sadie, Josh is in trouble, not me."

"I seen him wid Abe Ludlow t'other evening. An' Eulises Jones. Think dey was with Jeremiah Andrews, too."

"See where they were heading?"

"Just down de street. Could have been goin' anywhere."

"Down the street which way? Toward town?"

"No, son. Toward the river."

"Good a place as any, I guess," said Paul, and headed out the door.

She closed her eyes and sank down into the chair.

"*Sadie!*" Paul's roar echoed back down the hall. Heart in her throat, she raced down the short corridor. In the front door, Paul bent over Joshua, slumped against the door frame with his back against the wall of the house. His legs were drawn tightly against his chest, his head bent against his knees. He was hugging himself and moaning.

"Josh?" Paul spoke in a low voice, shaking his brother's shoulders gently. "Josh, it's me, it's Paul. C'mon, let go," he urged. He tried to push the boy's arms down and coax him to stand up.

"*Unnnnn.*" The moans continued. Josh's arms stayed wrapped tightly around himself.

"Josh, please, it's Paul, now let go!"

Josh threw back his head. His eyes widened. A scream of pure terror gushed from his mouth.

"Oh, hell!" Paul exclaimed. "Sadie, I got to get him inside!"

"*Nooooooo*! Can't touch it! It burns! *It burns*! Get away from me! *Get away*! I want Paul, but I can't go home! *I can't go home! Get awayyyy!*"

Josh finally loosened his arms and kicked his legs out, flailing wildly at some vision dancing in his sight alone. Paul got one arm under Josh's shoulders, the other under his legs, and scooped his brother, still flailing and kicking, up in his arms. He strode rapidly towards Josh's room.

He realized in only a few moments there was no way he could keep Johusa on the bed short of tying or drugging him.

"Sadie! Get me something, a sheet, maybe. Tear it in strips! Hurry!"

Sadie ran to the kitchen and pulled open a cabinet where she kept cleaning supplies. She grabbed a sheet she'd culled from the laundry as ready to be cut into future cleaning cloths. Not taking the time to locate the scissors, she ran back towards Joshua's room, tearing at the hem with her teeth. Her lean hands, strong from years of household service, finally won the battle with the cloth and it shredded with a noisy rip.

"I can't let go of him! You have to do it! Loop it over his hands first and tie it to the bedpost!"

Sadie barely managed. Joshua's wildly thrashing arms almost defeated both her and Paul. Josh moaned, the moans interspersed with screams. "It's coming! *Oh God, it's coming*! Jesus, it's so *big*!"

When she had one arm secured, Paul turned loose with one of his hands and grabbed for the next strip, slipping the cloth over Josh's wrist and securing the other end to the bedpost. Working together, they finished the job and stood back, breathing in short gasps. Joshua's strength was astonishing and it had taken both of them to manage.

"Go get me the laudanum, Sadie!"

"On top of *this?* Paul, you don't know what that'll do!"

"I know he's going into convulsions in about two more seconds if I don't! Now get it!"

Sadie got it.

"Hold his head still!" Paul commanded, and Sadie managed, barely, to keep Josh's head still and his mouth open as Paul slipped the spoon home. He threw the liquid down quickly and shoved Josh's mouth shut before he spewed the narcotic out, holding it shut with one hand while he gently rubbed Josh's throat with the other until the throat muscles worked. He waited for the drug to take effect, wondering if it would work at all. He knew he dared give the boy no more. Finally, the moans slowed. Josh shuddered. His head fell to one side and his eyes closed. Quiet.

"Thank God!" Paul sat heavily on the bed.

"Amen!" Sadie sank down into the armchair that stood by the bed.

"Well, son? What now?"

"The boys you've seen him with. Do you see them regularly? Any certain time? Any certain day?"

"I've only noticed 'em occasionally but den I ain't really been lookin'. Sometimes Josh head out on his own, but the times I seen 'em, look to me like dey was coming by to get him. Seems like it was about 7:00."

"Go stay in the parlor and watch. And if you see 'em, come get me."

"Why?"

"'Cause if Josh don't come out, they ain't goin' to walk up and knock for him. Not if they're all in this. And I want to see where they go."

"You goan follow 'em?"

"That's the idea. 'Less you got a better one."

"Well, I do," Sadie declared. "I most certainly do. I'll follow 'em."

"Like hell you will," he retorted. "We don't know what you'd be following them to and I ain't about to let you walk by yourself straight into God knows what."

"Like hell I won't," she spat back.

"Pardon?" Paul asked in masculine surprise.

"I said, like hell I won't. Smooth yo' ruffled feathers down and think a minute. 'Spose you gone and Josh comes to. Suppose he quiet. What I 'sposed to do? Untie him? And if he has another spell, I'm goan be able to keep him still by myself? Suppose he wake up jest like he was? I'm goan judge whut to give him? If I'm 'sposed to give him anything? You got to stay with Josh, Paul. You got to."

Goddamn it. She was right.

"Then you stay in, too. Hell with it. You ain't traipsing off by yourself!"

"I be careful."

"We don't know what the hell you have to be careful of!"

"Oh, hush up! Dey find out Josh ain't coming back out, they stop passin' by and we lose the chance to follow 'em."

She got up and headed out of the room.

"Sadie! I said *no!*" He got up and followed her.

She turned on her heel and faced him, hands on hips.

"Boy, I don't recall I asked yo' permission!"

Suddenly Paul was eleven years old again, climbing back in his upstairs bedroom window in the wee hours of the morning after a moonlit skinny-dipping swim with Tom Benson and Billy Jenkins. His heart had dropped to his stomach when he'd made his successful entry and viewed the long dark shadow on his floor. He'd raised his eyes slowly, following the line of the shadow resolving itself into the long lines of Sadie's body. Just so had her hands been positioned on her hips. Just so had her face borne the same implacable look of inevitability.

He made one last effort.

"Please?"

"Paul, I gots to, son. Surely you see that?"

He moved forward and pulled her into a swift hug.

"If you see them, call me when you leave."

Sadie nodded, her head against his chest.

"And for God's sakes, *be careful.*"

* * *

Sadie paced restlessly in front of the windows, checking the mantle clock every two minutes or so. Occasionally she thrust her hand into her deep skirt pocket, the one where she'd secreted the largest kitchen knife she could easily conceal. Paul wanted her to take his pistol but she overrode his protests with the reminder a pistol had to be reloaded. She didn't intend to be seen and she certainly had no intention of becoming a captive, but if such event did come to pass, she knew she could do more damage with a knife.

She looked at the clock again. It was ten minutes past seven. The boys weren't coming. Just when she was ready to admit this opportunity was lost, she saw them.

They walked steadily past the house, glancing at the porch. Their pace slowed. When they reached the fence gate, they stopped entirely and engaged in swift conversation. Finally, they moved on.

Sadie held her breath and waited for them to pass from sight. She slipped out the door and angled down the yard, cursing the fences that separated the yards of the houses from the sidewalks. There was no way she could maneuver under cover of the shrubbery. She hung back and did something she tried never to do. She loosened her control of the portion of her brain that sometimes showed her scenes her eyes couldn't see, trying to keep the boys in sight even out of sight.

They headed down Orange, cut across a few side streets and angled toward Wharf Street, toward the river and out of town. Sadie paused, holding her side and cursing her advancing years. It was hell to get older. She heard voices off in the distance and hung back further. She peered through the deep tree shadows in the swiftly falling haze that wasn't so much darkness yet as grayness. A clearing loomed ahead. She crept closer, judging her distance, and finally settled at a spot she judged safe, some yards back from the full clearing. She caught her breath.

A giant stood in the center of the clearing. A big man, dear God, so big! He towered over his subjects in full regalia, amulets of gold and necklaces of bone draped over his massive shoulders. He'd had no need for pretense for the last month past. A circle of fires leapt and danced. Sadie gave a quick count. Seven fires. Greased with fat, the giant gleamed in the firelight. The oppressive heat of the humid day hung heavy in the air, intensified by the glowing coals of the red flames.

Sadie recognized him immediately. St. Barnabas' charismatic newest member. Several of her friends, some widowed, some married, had been swooning over this man since his arrival. His black velvet voice, so at odds with his thickly muscled body, almost had them in physical combat as they fought for his attention at church suppers with heaping platters of fried chicken and fresh vegetables, the thickest pieces of pound cake, bowls of cobbler filled with dumplings.

He always smiled, she recalled, accepting these offerings as his due, as though he conveyed great privilege to the ladies in allowing them to admire his rippling shoulders. She hadn't liked him. No concrete reason, she just hadn't, and so had avoided any contact with him.

Now he motioned to one of his acolytes, who hurried forth with a tiny newborn calf. He pulled a machete from the leather scabbard at his side and raised it high, swirling it in swishing patterns over his head. Liquid firelight caught the blade and poured red rain back over the crowd.

"Blood!" he shouted. "'De power be *blood*!" The machete descended in a wicked flash, decapitating the calf. Blood gushed from the stump and flooded into the basins held by his chosen lieutenants. Their hands ran with gore as the basins filled.

Sadie closed her eyes and swayed. Hell. This clearing was an outpost of Hell.

"An' de power be in *us*! My peoples! Be you ready to show de white god yo' power?"

Shirts and dresses fell like rain. Sadie couldn't distinguish many features in the mass of frenzied bodies writhing in the murky light of the glowing fires. Enough. She refused to stand and witness this degradation, people she'd known all their lives parodying Christian rites, reducing the highest expression of love between a man and woman to this bestial behavior.

Moving as soundlessly as possible, she headed out of the woods, back toward Wharf Street. A tug on the hem of her skirt sent her heart into her throat. She swirled around, her hand grabbing the handle of the knife, but there was no one there. She glanced down. Her skirt had caught on a tree root. She gave a shaky sigh of relief and bent to loosen it, but it was caught firmly. She yanked, and the material ripped free.

She burst through the front door and hurried down the hall. Paul sat in the arm chair, keeping watch over his brother, just as Joshua'd guarded Paul's sleep the night he'd finally emerged from his office, three days after Chloe's burial.

"His name be Cain," she said.

* * *

Cain stood by the riverbank for a moment and watched his flock depart. Close. He was getting so close. He strode confidently through the darkest shadows on his way back to his rented room. A glimmer of something light caught his eye. He bent and plucked the scrap of cloth from the tree root. Someone had caught their clothing on the root and torn it as they passed.

He frowned. None of his acolytes took this path. He knew the direction each took, both in approach and in departure. He cursed. Laxness. He hadn't posted his sentries, those grisly skulls that guarded his secret rituals. He needed to rectify that. Immediately. Tomorrow night he'd hang them and hold the special ceremony investing them with their guardian spirits.

He laughed and tucked the scrap of cloth into his pocket. Maybe he'd play with the intruder for awhile.

* * *

"You know him?" Paul pulled Sadie over to the armchair and made her sit. She trembled, both from reaction and the unaccustomed stress she'd inflicted on her body in the past hours. "Here, don't try and talk yet. You need some brandy."

Paul walked quickly to his study and returned in a few moments with a crystal decanter and glass.

"Hate dis stuff."

157

"You need it. Now drink."

She shuddered as the fiery liquid passed down her throat. She handed the glass back to Paul.

"You know him?" he repeated.

"Yes. And no. He at one of the Sunday services at St. Barnabas 'bout, let me think. First time I seen him was back in February. Big man, Lord, he's big. Coal black. His head is shaved but dat doan make him look nothing but even mo' fierce. But it's a fierce dat's hid inside his heart, on de outside, he the most politest man you'd ever hope to meet. Got most of de ladies, married ones, too, 'bout to swoon when he notices 'em."

"Is he always there?"

"Always. Never misses a Sunday. An' probably doan miss much in between, but I doan know 'bout dat, you know I doan fool with all that social foolishness."

"So Isaiah Gorley could maybe tell me where he lives."

"I doan know. From whut I seen, he doan come to church to pay much mind to Brother Gorley, he come to strut before de ladies. An' de young folk, yeah, I ain't put it together before but dey hang all over him. An' when I think back on it, doan think Isaiah like dat too much, but it's a church, what he goan say 'bout it? He doan like a member takin' up time wid de young peoples?"

Paul sank down on the bed by Joshua. "Sadie, Isaiah was in here today."

"I know dat, I seen him. Must be somethin' if Nona can get him in de office."

"He's been having headaches, he says. Well, Nona says, Isaiah tried to play it down."

Sadie snorted. "Men all alike, weren't for dere women, dey doan got 'nuff sense to come in out of de rain. Nona only reason he come at all."

"Yeah, I know. But when I pushed, he admitted it. They're real bad, real sudden, real strange. Worried me, can't pinpoint any reason. Thought about a brain tumor, to tell the truth, from his description, but his eyes look just fine. Sadie, that smell, the one that came out of nowhere in Tamara's cottage?"

Sadie nodded.

"He says, right before they hit, the headaches? That he smells something real bad."

"Well," said Sadie. "I guess we knows whut dat is."

"Could he do that?"

"If he be whut Tamara say, he can do dat."

"Is he? What Tamara says?"

"I think he even worse."

"How so? What did he do?"

Sadie bit her lip.

"Sadie? What did he do?"

"What did who do?" Everett stood in the doorway. He wasn't a happy man. "Knocked the damn door down, you didn't hear me? What's the matter with Josh?" Everett came swiftly into the room. "Why the hell is he tied down?"

"Papa, calm down." Everett's complexion edged from the florid red Paul found alarming enough towards purple.

"Calm down, hell, I get back from a call, it's later'n hell, Sadie ain't home, ain't sent word she's goan be late or why—woman, you know better than that! Scared me to death, thought you'd gotten run over by a runaway buggy or attacked on the way home! Neither of you hear me pounding the damn door, I walk in and find Joshua tied to the goddamn bed—"

Paul grabbed his father's arms. "Papa, sit down and *shut up!*"

"What the hell did you just say to me?!"

"Shut up, Everett!" Sadie exclaimed. "Just shut up! Or we ain't goan tell you nothing! You understan' me?"

Everett's face finished turning purple, but the shock of Sadie's attack on top of Paul's won. He sat down.

"I'm listenin'," he said.

An hour's explanation later, Everett's complexion was so pale it seemed to have never held any color at all. He leaned over and stroked Joshua's forehead.

"Sweet, sweet Jesus," he said.

"You believe us?" asked Paul.

"Son, I tell you true. I wouldn't believe a word of it coming from anybody else. But it's you and Sadie, so yes, I believe. Question is, what are we goin' to do about it?" Then a touch of his old fire surfaced. "And why the hell did you let Sadie follow the boys to the riverbank alone?"

"Think I could have stopped her, do you?"

"Well," he admitted. "No."

"Good. I'm only human."

"Two of you ain't goan get nothin' done by sittin' dere insultin' me."

"Ain't an insult, Sadie, just the truth," said Everett. And time for him to admit some other truths. He was getting old. His years hadn't aged him but his profession had. His heart wasn't all it should be. The shadow of an apoplectic seizure stood close to his side. He knew it, and he knew Paul knew it, too.

Now, his family and his chosen people were under attack from this human who walked inhuman paths, and what could he do about it? Damn little. Any extreme extra exertion would likely kill him and Paul and Sadie sure didn't need anything else to worry about right now, especially him. Both of them were exhausted too, they needed rest. He sighed.

"Son," he began, and Paul cut him off.

"Papa, I know what you're going to say, but you are *not—*"

"Paul," said Everett wearily. "Your turn. You just shut up for a minute. Now, I know you think I'm an old fool too busy takin' care of other folks to admit what's happenin' to me. And I don't want to admit it but I know. I'm old. This is a young man's fight. It's your fight. I know that. But what I can do is, I can sit with Joshua tonight. You and Sadie got a busy day tomorrow. Need your sleep. And I'll keep your office hours for you tomorrow afternoon so you can be out doing whatever it is needs doin'. Probably all I'm good for. Ain't much, God knows. Hell, I hate getting old!"

Paul looked at his father. Everett had never been a tall man, but he'd always been robust. Now his frame seemed shrunken. When had his hair begun to thin so, when had his hands acquired those tell-tale spots of brown? Where was his Papa, the man who, if he wasn't always right, was wrong at the top of his voice, the man who occupied such a special spot, the king of the town's medical profession? That man had just abdicated, passing his mantle of self-assumed responsibility to his successor. The king was dead. Long live the king. Tears pricked behind Paul's eyes.

"Thank you, Papa."

* * *

In his rented room in the boarding house near the railroad tracks on Seventh Street, Cain toyed delicately with the crude doll he'd formed from the corn shucks he always kept handy. The piece of cloth he'd plucked from the woods draped its form. What to do, what to do?

Fire, now. Fire was good. These figures burned like, why they burned like dried corn shucks. Cain chuckled to himself. He'd taken care of a few busybodies in such fashion back in Tarper, including one who'd dared refuse the communion of blood. A mistake no one else made, not after the fiery spectacle that discriminating but unfortunate soul offered to the town when he'd burst into flames walking down the street the next morning.

His hands ran lightly down the limbs of the figure. He could take this leg, now, and pull it out in a ninety degree angle, opposite the one nature intended it to go. Or this arm. Or both.

He dropped his hand and caressed the head. He almost tightened his fingers. Then he laughed suddenly and dropped the figure back to the tabletop. If he killed the intruder now, they wouldn't be back. And Cain wanted them to come back. Oh my, yes. With friends. You could never have enough sentries.

* * *

Joshua roused in the darkness of the early morning hours. It took several moments to realize he was tied to the bed. His eyes roamed around the grayness and settled on a slouched figure sitting in the armchair next to his bed. Paul?

He didn't feel well, not at all. His arms and legs were full of ground glass grating in his joints, his head stuffed with un-ginned cotton. His stomach churned and rumbled and threatened to revolt. But that wasn't the worst of it. As fuzzy as his brain felt, it was far clearer than it had been in much longer than Joshua cared to think about. He heard Cain's voice roaring in his ears. He saw the shoulder muscles rippling in the blood shadows of the flames. He saw fire glinting off the wicked, downward slash of the machete flying home, smelled the hot, metallic scent of blood.

This morning. He'd done something awful. What? And what had he said to Paul? What had he done? He didn't remember. He remembered the past weeks, Paul's voice sending swarms of ants crawling over his skin. Irritation over nothing, irritation which had rapidly turned to anger and then transmuted itself by some mysterious alchemy to rage and then past rage, to blinding fury. Finally, this morning, to murderous wrath. Had he hurt Paul? He didn't know. He'd wanted to kill him.

Maybe he had. He was tied to his bed. But he'd be in jail, wouldn't he? A tree limb's shadow shifted on the wall and became a nest of writhing snakes. He'd seen snakes all day, scaly creatures from the pages of

162

Bullfinch's Mythology. But the creatures Joshua'd seen made the two-headed Hydra laughable, the Cyclops no worse than a child's stuffed animal. Right now Joshua could look on the face of Medusa with no effect. He'd stared at visions much worse than Medusa all day.

"Paul?" Joshua called softly. The figure started, shook its head. As the man moved, Josh knew this wasn't the elegant shadow his brother threw.

"Son?"

"Doc?"

"Hang on, boy, let me light this lamp down low here and get a look at you."

"Don't!"

"*Ssssh*. Don't take on, now. Just want to check your eyes, get you some water."

A match hissed. Shadows jumped to gargantuan proportions as the lamplight flared, and then tapered slowly down to normal size as Everett adjusted the flame. Everett gently lifted Joshua's eyelids.

"Well. Bloodshot, but all things considered, guess you'll do. What's your name, son?"

"My name?"

"You ain't had a real good day, son. Humor the old man. What's your name?"

"Joshua."

"Joshua what?"

"Joshua Devlin."

"What's my name?"

"Doc."

"My real name."

"Everett. Everett Devlin. Doc, where's Paul?"

"Sleeping. He's had a right tiresome day himself."

"Is he—is he alright?"

"'Course he is."

"What did I do? He don't want to see me. Does he?"

"*Whoaaa,* son. Here, sip this water." Everett held the glass to his lips.

Joshua drank. "What did I do?" he repeated. "Something awful, I know it was, did I hurt Paul? Or Sadie?"

"No!" said Everett forcefully. "You didn't hurt anybody. But somebody sho' 'nuff tried to hurt you. Now, I sat with you tonight so your brother and mother could get some rest. They been busy today, trying to figure all this out. Be surprised what they've come up with. And they goin' to be busier tomorrow, trying to see what's the best way to handle this mare's nest."

"Ain't no best way, Doc. I got to tell 'em—"

"You can tell 'em tomorrow, son. For tonight, you look to be recovering nicely and tomorrow, what you can tell us, that'll be a big help. You think your brother's mad at you, don't you, son?"

"He should be," Joshua said bitterly.

"Well, he ain't. Nobody is. Not your mother, not your brother, not me. And everything's goin' to be just fine."

"No, it ain't. World's full of monsters, Doc."

"Well, ain't no monsters in this room, son. Just your ol' Papa. You ain't never called me that, and I understand why. But in my heart, son, I've always been your papa. And papas, they keep the monsters away. So you lie back. Tell you what, I'm goin' take these things off."

Everett loosened the cloth bonds and slipped them off Josh's wrists.

"We didn't like it, but we didn't know how long it'd take you to come back to us and we couldn't chance you hurting yourself. Now, you just go back to sleep and in the morning, things'll be a lot better."

Joshua lay back. He didn't think things would be a bit better in the morning, but it would do no good to argue. And Paul was alright. Joshua began to fall back towards sleep but visions of his monsters crept forward from the back shadows of his eyes.

He glanced over at the chair. "Papa?" he murmured.

Everett's heart flipped in his chest. Joshua'd never called him Papa. Everett hadn't believed he ever would.

"What, son?"

"The monsters. They are real."

"Well," said Everett, "they ain't coming past this papa this night."

Chapter Eleven

Paul strode briskly out the front door the next morning. First, he'd make the house calls he hadn't made yesterday morning. His afternoon was free, since his father was taking his afternoon patients.

Joshua was weak but clear-headed. After tea and dry toast, the boy wept in shame as he spoke of the blood sacrifices, the sex orgies. He'd held nothing back, and Paul was a man on a mission. He was taking that son-of-a-bitch down. Paul halted abruptly. Bobby Ryles, Macon's Chief of Police, dismounted at the gate and looped his horse's reins over the wrought-iron fence.

Apprehension swelled in Paul's stomach. He'd certainly planned to meet with the man that afternoon, but he didn't like it that the Chief coming to him. Bobby Ryles liked his position of authority. He didn't move around Macon's streets himself very often. His visit signaled a sure sign of something wrong somewhere.

"'Morning, Paul," called the Chief, heading up the walk. "Glad I caught you."

"You're out early this morning, Chief." Paul strode easily forward to meet him, holding out his hand.

"Yeah, well, probably out chasing smoke clouds but what the hell? Got to earn my money somehow. You got a minute or two 'fore you head out? See you already about to start your rounds."

"Certainly. Let's sit on the porch. Or would you like to come in and have a cup of coffee?" Paul didn't want him in the house. Suppose Joshua had a sudden relapse and started screaming warnings of monsters?

No choice, though. Southern hospitality made the invitation mandatory.

"Oh, no, no," disclaimed the Chief, dropping easily into one of the front porch rocking chairs. "Thanks, but I've already had my limit for the day. Where's your boy?"

"My boy?"

"Your nigger. Joshua, ain't that his name? Don't usually see you go out without him."

Paul bit his lip. "He isn't feeling well today."

"Don't want to go out in the heat, probably. Either that or he's got a stomachache from raidin' somebody's watermelon patch."

"What can I do for you this morning, Chief?"

Chief Ryles settled back and rocked comfortably. "Love these rocking chairs," he said. "Ain't a front porch without one. Tell the truth, Paul, I ain't sure you can do anything for me. But I thought, Paul Devlin. Now, if any white man in Macon has an ear in Niggertown, it's him."

"I'm sorry, I don't understand."

"Well, see, we've been getting some pretty disturbing reports over the telegraph lately. Took a while to get to us, but they're spreadin' on down the line."

"What sort of reports?"

"Been havin' a lot of trouble with the niggers lately in Mississippi and Alabama. Just one incident wouldn't have made it over here but damned if these things don't seem to have a pattern."

"Mississippi and Alabama are pretty far away, Chief."

"Yeah, they are. They are at that. And it don't seem widespread, these things happening a good distance apart, but damned if they ain't unusual. Seems like whole damn towns been going up in flames. That's after most of the white folks already been butchered. And I mean butchered. Like cows."

The low wave of apprehension in Paul's stomach moved up into his chest.

"Where?"

"Well, first one was just this little farm community over in Mississippi. Name of Tonka Creek. It was bad. I mean, it was damn bad. So the neighboring town sort of sent out an alert for folks to be on the lookout for trouble. And the same thing happened over in Alabama 'bout seven months later. Little place called Seven Cedars. And then again in another little spot. Tarper, Alabama down on the gulf coast. And see here, the thing is, these places are too far apart for it to be just a general wave of nigger trouble. More like maybe there's some troublemaker moving around. See what I mean?"

Paul saw, all right.

"Macon's a long way from Alabama, Chief."

"It is," the Chief agreed. "But see here, the thing is, I've had the damnedest reports lately. And not just me, either, Hank Eason's 'bout to pull his hair out."

Hank Eason was the Sheriff of Bibb County, the law enforcement official charged with overseeing the peace of the sprawling mid-Georgia county.

"How so?"

"Livestock's been disappearing. At first, it was just one or two incidents, but lately? Hank, his farmers 'bout to drive him crazy. Somebody's been raiding their herds."

"Always been cattle thieves," Paul observed.

"That's so. But usually, folks that steal stock want it 'cause they're hungry, like vagrants on the move and all, or they want it to resell. And to do that, they got to herd 'em out of the area. And to herd cattle, they got to be big enough to walk a good distance. These boys, they're losing all their new calves. Now don't that beat all?"

"Well, it's odd. But I don't see what that's got to do with these other things," lied Paul, who saw the connection very clearly.

"Thing is, Paul, there was one or two survivors from Seven Cedars. Folks out of town that night, visitin' relations. And there were three from Tarper. Tarper was the biggest. Now, damned if those folks don't say pretty much the same thing happened over there. And they also say the local niggers, they changed a good bit in the month or so before the big blood baths. Seems like they started, well, disappearing at night. Nobody knows 'xactly where to. And they also say—hindsight being the best sight, like my Granny used to say—they also say seems like they recollect a new nigger being in town. Big man, real big. Who seemed to have just a deal of influence with the locals."

Paul felt a sudden uplift of his spirits. Cain wasn't as smart as he thought he was, not as careful. Maybe he could just dump this in Bobby Ryles' lap and the whole thing could be over and done with.

"What sort of influence, Chief?"

"Let's put it this way. There's been a considerable amount of hanging over Mississippi and Alabama way. Guess you can imagine. But not one of them niggers, not one, even about to have his neck stretched, will breathe a word about that man. 'Cept one of 'em. And all he said was, he'd rather face the white man's god than the dark ones. Fancy that."

Paul fancied that with no trouble.

"So's the way we tend to figure it, this upstart nigger's pulling out some of that jungle horseshit, you know, the spells and the mojos and such. Fits right in with the missing livestock. Sacrifices and all. You can take the nigger out of the jungle, but you can't take the jungle out of the nigger. Hell, can't tell me you ain't got niggers go straight from your office to the damn root doctor, Paul. I swear, sometimes I don't know why you bother."

"I'm sure you don't," said Paul. He regretted the sarcasm immediately, but it was lost on Chief Ryles.

"Anyway, since we been having such a sudden incidence of missing stock, Hank and I just thought we might oughta do some checking. And you know what? I've had a couple of hysterical mamas the past couple of weeks. Seems like their boys all of a sudden ain't coming home when they're supposed to. And just in talking with folks here and there, seems like a lot of folks been noticing a change in the niggers. 'Course, at first, they just shrugged it off but putting all this together—"

"Yes, Chief, puttin' it all together, why are you talkin' to me?"

"'Cause, Paul, like I said. Any white man in town knows the heartbeat of Niggertown, it's you. And the way I figure it, if this troublemaker has ended up here—and really, I think all of this is probably just coincidence, after all, Macon? Surely ain't no rogue crazy enough to take on this big a town, but just say he has. Then I'd guess he's holding meetings somewhere. Not in town, 'course, out in the woods someplace. Anybody wants to make blood sacrifices and God knows what all else, town ain't the place to do it. And if I could find out where—if, mind you, there's anything to find—well, I could just nip this thing right in the bud. And if you got wind of any such goings on, then you could let me know. Know you ain't heard nothing yet, you'da told me."

Paul whipped several scenarios through his brain at the speed of light. If he told Chief Ryles where to find the circle by the river, there'd be a big crowd. And people might get hurt. But if he gave the Chief Cain's identity and location, that might work.

"Suppose I do some digging, Chief. And I get wind of some stranger in town might fit in with all this. If I can find out where he is for you, you could bring him right down to the station, couldn't you? No need to put a crowd of folks in trouble."

"*Wellll*," the Chief drawled. "I could, I 'spose. But I don't really think that'd do much good. What I'd like to do is follow this joree out to one of those meetings and catch him in the act. Wouldn't have no evidence otherwise."

"You really care about evidence, do you, Bobby"?"

"Well, no, but got to observe the protocol, don't you know?"

"But if it's out in the country, that's not your—"

"Oh, Hank and me, we don't pay much mind to that jurisdictional horseshit. We figure all the folks our responsibility. He'll be right there with me."

"Oh. I see. But Chief, any man that's capable of something like you've described, suppose he—what's the phrase? Resists arrest?"

Chief Ryles smiled. Like a predator. Like a lean and hungry gray wolf.

"Now wouldn't that be just my luck?"

"But if he has a following, people he's using because they're scared of him, they could get hurt, too."

"With any luck, Paul, they'll rush right to his defense. And we can take care of the whole lot of 'em at one time. Save everybody a lot of time and trouble, don't you think?"

"Or even if they don't. Come rushin' to his defense. That's what you mean, isn't it?"

"Damn, Paul, I misjudged you. Didn't think you had it in you. Yeah, that's what I mean."

"I see," said Paul.

"So if you should hear of any strange doins' on the grapevine, you just trot on in and we'll get this wrapped right up."

"I'll be sure you hear about anything you need to know, Chief."

Because what the Chief needed to know and what he wanted to know were two entirely different matters. And what he wanted to know, he wouldn't be hearing from Paul Devlin.

The Chief rose and strolled leisurely back to his horse. Paul headed back out to attend his house-bound patients. At least one thing Paul intended to do that afternoon was out of the way. And at least one thing was crystal clear. Going to the law wasn't an option. Paul was on his own.

* * *

Paul made Reverend Isaiah Gorley the last call of his rounds. Nona Gorley pulled Paul inside the trim little house that stood near St. Barnabas on Congress Street.

"We jest finishin' up dinner, Mist' Paul, you stopped to eat yet? No, you ain't," she said, answering her own question as she directed him to the table. "But you in de right place, I been puttin' up vegetables. Din' bother to fix no meat but I's got plenty of butterbeans and corn. Look at dis okree, ain't seen none better in I doan know when. And de 'maters dis year! Red as fire engines."

Paul's stomach rumbled at the aromas wafting from the back of the house. He took the plate piled high with the bountiful plenty of the Southern summer and sighed in contentment.

"Isaiah, don't know how you keep from being big as a barn, way Nona cooks."

"Dat's a blessin' from de Lord, Mist' Paul, and dat's de truth. None of my folks run to fat."

Reverend Gorley leaned back in his chair and sipped from his tea glass, watching Paul eat.

"Ain't dat I ain't glad to see you, Mist' Paul, doan take no 'ffense, but why you 'cide to stop in?"

"Oh, I just thought it couldn't hurt to take another look at your eyes, Isaiah. You know me, can't leave nothing alone."

"You worry too much. Jest saw me yestid'y and I doan think my eyes goan show much more today den dey did den. Dat's a little mo' caution den even you usually show. Doan you think?" Reverend Gorley raised his eyebrow with the question.

Paul laughed. "Alright, alright, you caught me. I do want to keep an eye on you, Isaiah, but that ain't why

I'm here now. I got somethin' I need to talk to you about."

"Well, we both here. Talk."

Paul finished off the last of his buttered cornbread stick and pushed his plate back.

"Nona, that was wonderful."

"You best say so," she declared, picking up the plate.

"Isaiah, Sadie tells me a new man came into St. Barnabas end of the winter. Says his name is Cain."

Reverend Gorley's mouth tightened. "Dat's so," he said.

"What do you know about him?"

"Know we doan need him in our church!" declared Nona Gorley in a firm voice.

"Nona, now dat's not a Christian thing to say. Church belong to everybody."

"Doan you try and fool me, Isaiah Gorley! Lived wid you for thirty years, birthed and raised yo' five chillun! You can't stand de man!"

"Ain't required to like everybody, woman, but it be our Christian duty to love 'em anyway. Can't turn nobody out of my church and still call myself a man of God."

"*Ummmp!*" snorted Nona. She turned on her heel and departed to her kitchen, muttering under her breath about the stupidity of men in general and her man in particular.

"Nona doan like him," said Isaiah with a grin.

"Neither does Sadie," said Paul. "Do you?"

Reverend Gorley frowned. "No. I doan. Dat's de pure-de-truth and I can't 'xactly say why. I hopes it's not 'cause I be jealous. See, de young folks, dey always comes to me wid dere problems. I been real proud of dat over the years, real proud. An' dere's always been fo' or five young ones hangin' 'roun de house any given time, even after ours growed up and gone. But de past few months, dey seem to be hangin' 'roun dis Cain fellow an' it got my nose out of joint. But dat's a failin' in me, hurts my pride which we ain't 'sposed to have an excess of anyway, you know, ain't his fault."

Paul leaned forward, placing his elbows on the table. "Oh, yes, it is. It is his fault. Isaiah, I have to tell you about this man. He has faults you can't even imagine."

Some time later when Paul finished, Isaiah sat quietly.

"Isaiah?"

"He usin' my chilluns."

"Yes."

"Joshua goan be alright?"

"I think so. I hope so."

"Lord, my God, the trials he sends his people! Now, I gots to tell you, I doan hold wid all dat soothsaying and such, but I do know dere's folk what do. An' de Bible, it do speak of demons though in my 'sperience, mos' demons, dey mo' rightly got another name, an' dat name, it be an evil man. An' no matter whut, we got us an evil man now, sho' 'nuff. Whut you want me to do, Mist' Paul?"

"Do you know where this man stays, Isaiah?"

"Doan' know nuttin' 'bout him. Seem like he take care I doan. So whut's we goan do?"

Paul still didn't know. Not exactly. He felt himself edging towards an irrevocable decision he still wasn't ready to make. Not quite. Not just yet.

"Isaiah, Sadie saw 'em. And I think I have to. Maybe his power isn't quite as absolute as we think. Maybe if I can watch, I can figure something out."

"I'm goin' wid you den."

"I don't know if you should, Isaiah. I know you don't hold with soothsaying and all that, but those headaches, the smells you say you smell? I smelled something like that in Tamara's cottage. If Cain has some means of causing your headaches, it might mean—"

"He have some sort of control over me?"

Paul nodded.

"Might be. But whut we knows for sho' is, he got control over my peoples. I'm goin' wid you."

Paul looked at Isaiah. A man of simple dignity, simple goodness.

"Alright. Come to my house. We'll leave from there. Right at dark fall."

* * *

"Doan like dis," muttered Sadie while they all waited for Isaiah in the front parlor. She'd made that abundantly clear throughout the enitre afternoon.

"Sadie, I don't know what else to do!" exclaimed Paul, edging close to exasperation.

"You could tell de Chief."

"No, I can't. He'd massacre them, Sadie. Everybody. Everybody there."

"But neither one of *my* boys would be dere!"

"Sadie, you don't mean that!"

"I *do* mean dat! *I do*! By what right, what justice, do dis land in yo' lap?"

"Tamara said—"

"Doan give a *damn* what Tamara say! You *my* boy! Ain't I done spent nights sittin' by yo' bed when you little, when you runnin' fevers? Ain't I kept yo' clothes clean and yo' stomach full ever since you tiny? Ain't I miss you dose years you gone up North and in Scotland, readin' yo' letters to yo' daddy over and over, prayin' every night you stay safe? Ain't I grieved and cried for you de days and nights after I watch you bury Chloe? *Well? Ain't I?*" Then Sadie did the unthinkable. She dissolved into tears.

Paul pulled her into his arms and stood, holding her for a moment. In a two-day span, he'd seen his brother reduced to mindless terror, watched his father's irrevocable change to an old man. Now he watched the woman who'd raised him as her own, in his mind, his Mama, lose control. He'd never imagined

175

he'd see that. Not ever. Oh, yes. This son of a bitch was going *down.*

A knock sounded on the door.

"That'll be Isaiah."

"Doan go, son. Please doan go."

"You went, and you came back home."

"Tonight's different. I feel it. Please doan go."

Paul kissed her forehead. He looked over at his brother. "Joshua!"

"Yes, Paul?"

"You're in charge here. You take care of Mama and Papa. You hear?"

Paul walked out the door.

* * *

Sadie's ground work gave Paul a huge advantage tonight. They knew where they were going. They waited for full dark and rode their horses swiftly toward the river. Tethering the horses, they moved soundlessly into the woods toward the river banks.

Paul's hand slipped down to check the side holster cradling the Colt .45 that usually resided in a locked drawer in his office desk. Paul only took it with him during late night emergencies to the outskirts of the city. Even then, he sometimes forgot it. This was his town, these were his people. It seldom crossed his mind he could meet with danger.

Tonight, though, danger hung heavy in the air. No longer abstract, it had shape and form. Paul had spent the hours between his return home and Isaiah's arrival in his office chair, deep in thought, examining the situation first from one angle and then from the other. And he knew what he had to do.

Cain was an abnormality. A rogue, a murderer, a butcher. He'd killed and burned with great pleasure in the past. He planned to do the same here. Then he'd move on and do it again. Again. And again. Until someone stopped him. There was one man on earth

176

with sufficient knowledge and information to do that without unleashing a full-scale massacre. Paul Devlin. And there was only one way to do it.

He intended to place a .45 bullet squarely through Cain's brain, coldly, with good aim and absolute calculation. No warning. He'd have only one chance. He hadn't shared his intentions with Isaiah Gorley, man of God. It was his alone, this decision to serve as executor, and the burden of it sat heavy on his heart.

They crept closer. Paul's blood froze as he heard the voices, reverberating back and forth in the trees. These were the people, the friends, he took care of? The people who always greeted him with warm smiles and genuine pleasure?

"Blood! Blood! De power be blood!"

The chant rose to crescendo and cut off abruptly when Cain rose to assume his position as Master of Ceremonies. The two intruders reached a hiding spot and crouched in observation. Beads of sweat popped up on Isaiah's forehead.

"Our enemies!" shouted Cain. "Dey be searching for us!"

"*No!*"

"*Yes*, I say! Yes, forever and always, de truth have enemies searchin' for it! De white man and his white god, dey always lookin' for ways to keep you from de truth! But dey can't do it! No, de truth, *our truth*, it give us ways! I say it give us ways to protect ourselves!"

"Yes, yes!"

"An' it use de enemies demselves to do it!" Cain grabbed the rough sheet covering a crude table. His sentries. Cain lifted two of the four skulls high.

"Sweet Jesus Christ!" Paul hissed. Isaiah was speechless.

Cain chanted, garbled and twisted words and phrases breathing darkness. Paul knew Tamara would die before she'd utter this chant.

His hand gripped the butt of the pistol. One chance. He'd get only one chance. Isaiah's eyes widened at the sight of the weapon.

"There's no other way, Isaiah," Paul whispered. "Leave if you have to."

"No other way," Isaiah whispered back. "I's staying."

Cain fell to his knees while he chanted, encircled and shielded by his followers. Far in the distance, lightning flashed. Horrendous cracks of thunder shook the ground as Cain called forth the denizens Sadie claimed could pass back and forth between the worlds that ringed this world.

Isaiah grabbed Paul's arm in a grip of iron and pointed. Two winged shapes, bat-like of body and demonic of face, with razor-edged teeth and great, glowing golden eyes, swooped low out of nowhere and settled on the skulls Cain held aloft in his huge hands. Its brethren rained forth with the lightning cracks, as though an invisible door opened with each flash. Two others settled on the skulls sitting on the crude table.

"No," Paul whispered, trying to deny the sight that had unfolded in front of him.

"Mist' Paul, I be mighty afeard it be yes."

The chosen denizens settled on the skulls, folded their wings. Sending forth clouds of hissing steam, they melted into the white bone of the skulls. The crowd swayed in ecstasy.

In seconds, the perched creatures were gone. The skulls glowed with an eerie blue light, highlighted by the red embers flashing in the empty eye sockets.

"*Our sentries*!" Cain roared. He stood erect and rotated the skulls he held in his hands, sending their light out into the shadows surrounding the clearing.

Deep in those shadows, while the light streamed from the skull, coming ever nearer to their hiding place, Paul steadied the pistol and wished like hell he'd spent more time perfecting his marksmanship.

* * *

Sadie paced the parlor, wringing her hands. She wanted to moan, she wanted to scream. She wanted to tear her hair and heap curses on the force that insisted on involving her boys in this nightmare.

Joshua lay on the couch, propped up by its pillows. Everett sat in one of the big wing-backed chairs. He envied Sadie her freedom to pace. He remained stationary by a supreme effort of will, determined not to let himself fly into a useless rage that might precipitate a stroke or heart attack.

The knock on the door split the tension in the room, shattering Sadie's raw and bleeding nerve endings. Everett rose to his feet.

"Everett, you go out tonight to tend any sick folks, I's never goan forgive you! Not never!" she spat, as he crossed the floor.

"Woman, I wouldn't leave you tonight to tend the damn president," he said, and opened the door. He stared at the entity standing on the porch and then turned his head quickly to stare back into the room at Sadie. Then he looked back at the visitor again. He'd known Sadie had a twin, but he'd never met her. Sadie rushed up and pulled Tamara into the hall.

"Whut on earth you doin' here?"

"Doan know. I jest know I need to be here."

"Oh, God! Whatever's happenin', it goan happen *tonight*?!"

"Sadie, I doan know. I jest—"

"Well, why doan you know? You always know! Know for everybody else, you can't know for yo' own family? All you can do is lay this on my boy and not give him no help?"

"Sadie." Everett laid his hand on her shoulder. "You know it ain't Tamara's fault."

Sadie's face crumbled. She turned blindly and Everett pulled her into his arms, murmuring softly against her ear.

179

"Don't, honey," he said. It was the first endearment he'd ever uttered to her in the presence of others. "Don't. He'll be home."

***

Paul had Cain in his sights, a perfect shot lined up to hit his target's brain dead center. As though the nightmare creations from beyond the door sensed Cain's eminent danger, they swarmed, swooping and swirling in front of him simultaneously with the gun's roar. One of them absorbed the bullet flying home to its target between Cain's eyes. It gave a high-pitched squeal of rage. The reddened hole where the bullet entered healed over almost instaneously.

Isaiah shouted in disbelief. Paul fired the smoking gun instinctively, expending all remaining bullets. The deadly swarm intercepted every shot.

"*Spies!*" roared Cain. "*Go, my peoples!* Bring me de spies of our enemies!"

"Run, Isaiah! Run!"

The swarm of demons swooped in front of them, hissing and squealing, slowing their speed, blocking their path, obscuring their vision. Paul and Isaiah, with no words passing between them, turned at the same time to face the mob. There was no way out. Frenzied hands, fueled by the extra strength of the drugs, dragged them back to the clearing.

"Well, well, well," laughed Cain. "White man, you walkin' where you got *noooo* business to walk. Know dat?"

"You peoples done lost yo' *minds*?" Isaiah spewed forth, attempting to reach the members of a congregation no longer his.

Cain casually lifted his hand and backhanded the Reverend so hard he spit blood.

"Nobody interested in whut you got to say, ol' man. Not no mo'." Cain didn't shift his eyes from Paul. "You dat doctor, ain't you? Devlin. De do-gooder. You

Joshua's Daddy? Anybody wid one eye and half-sense know dat boy half-white. Fact is, now dat I see you, you even favor some. Notice he ain't here tonight."

Paul stared back at Cain.

"Ax'd you a question, white man."

Paul stared. Cain laughed. Then he backhanded Isaiah again, so hard Paul feared the older man's neck had cracked.

"I say, I ax'd you a question, white man." Cain lifted his hand toward Isaiah again.

"He's my brother."

"An' ain't nobody never noticed, has dey? I swear, stupid as all dese niggers be, ain't no wonder de white man runnin' all over 'em." Cain stood and gazed thoughtfully at his captives. A small smile danced on his lips. "So Josh done gone runnin' to his big brother, has he? Doan much like dat, white man. Doan nobody run 'way from me, not once dey mine."

Paul stared straight back at Cain, refusing to lower his eyes.

"An' doan no man, 'specially no *white man!*" Cain spat the words out as though they were spoiled meat. "No *white man* goan walk away from dis circle." He threw his head back from his mighty shoulders and laughed. "You and yo' brother, you mighty tight wid each other, ain't you?"

Paul didn't answer. Cain lazily raised his hand towards again. Isaiah could take few more of Cain's blows.

"Yes," Paul said, and elaborated no further.

"'Course, I knew dat already, way everybody talk 'bout how he always trailin' after you. An' you jest come a runnin' you find out he been keepin' my company. Dat boy, he do take a little mo' pushin' den most do. Once or twice dere, I wondered myself how he keep walkin', much as I had to feed him. Still, you right handy, showin' up right now. I believe, yeah, I do believe, you do real well. Had me somethin' special planned to kick off things in dis town, ain't never tried it 'fore, and yeah, you do real *fiiiinnnne.*"

Cain laughed again. "An' yo' brother, I doan want him to miss de fun. An' I sho' can't let him tell our secrets and think he get away wid it. My peoples wouldn't like it. Too bad. Dat boy real bright. Mighta even had a future. Coulda taught him a lot. Not many folkses got 'nuff sense. Let's us see, now. You here, and he ain't. So I jest take a wild guess he sittin' in dat fine house of yo's on that fancy street while his big brother take care of de bad man. Dat be right?"

Paul, damned if he did and equally damned if he didn't, didn't wait for Cain to raise his hand in Isaiah's direction.

"No," he said, knowing full well Cain knew exactly where Joshua was.

"Damn, white men bad liars. Well, dat doan matter right now. I want him here." He pointed to Isaiah and motioned to two of his older, and therefore, stronger, acolytes, Levi Thompson and Jake Milton.

"Take him," he said. "Middle of de circle."

"Jake, I pulled you through scarlet fever last winter!" Paul shouted. "My papa saved your leg when that wagon overturned on you two years ago, Levi! Isaiah baptized both of you!"

Cain's fist lashed out. In the first stunned seconds after its impact with his flesh, Paul was sure his jaw was broken.

"I say, *take him!*"

Levi and Jake grabbed Isaiah's arms and pulled him forward.

"*No!*"

Isaiah turned his head and spoke over his shoulder to be certain Paul heard him.

"Mist' Paul, you can't do nuttin'. You a mighty fine man, son, been proud to know you."

"Isaiah!"

"*Shiiiiiiittt,* white man! He in better shape den you. Leastways his be quick."

* * *

Shadows hung heavy in the corners of the parlor. Tension, thick as Janie's stew, vibrated in the air. Suddenly the night filled with the echoing laughter of Cain's First Lieutenant. A dull thud sounded on the floor as he lobbed Cain's calling card through the open window. It bounced and then lay still. Isaiah Gorley's bloody head.

Sadie rushed to Everett and bracketed his cheeks in her palms.

"Doan you dare!" she ordered. "Doan you dare give in and start rantin' and ravin'! You have a fallin' down fit now, I ain't *never* goan forgive you!"

Everett raised his own hands and encircled Sadie's wrists.

"I won't," he promised. "Let go, honey. I won't."

Sadie wasn't convinced but he'd reacted much better than she'd hoped. Taking him at his word, she moved toward her sister.

"We goin' after my boy," she said.

"*Mama!*" Josh yelled behind her. He tore off the sofa and rushed to his father. Everett, on his knees in the center of the floor near Isaiah's head, gripped his chest with one hand. His face poured sweat and turned blue.

"Oh, my God," moaned Sadie, kneeling beside him. "You lied to me, Everett, you said you wouldn't! You ain't never lied to me before!"

"Did not," he managed to gasp. "Ain't having a stroke, it's my heart."

"Joshua, go get Doc Cabot!" commanded Sadie.

"No!" Tamara moved forward.

"Doan you tell me—"

"Ain't got time to argue wid you, woman! Now, you *listen* to me!" Tamara grabbed a throw rug. She knelt and lifted Isaiah's head gently, placed it on the rug and wrapped the sides.

183

"Doan' mean no disrespect, I know he understand," she said. "Sadie, you go get dat other doctor. Now. We's got to clean dis—Joshua!" she called, but Joshua was already on his way back from the kitchen, a cleaning bucket and strips of old sheeting in his hands. He wanted to gag, he wanted to throw up, but he knew it was important Dr. Cabot not see this.

"I've got it," he said.

"Good boy." She turned back to her sister. "Now, Sadie, go! We get dis cleaned up, me and Josh goin' after Paul. You hurry dere and you hurry back!"

"Everett be by hisself!"

"Don't matter," Everett panted. "Listen to her. Go."

"I done lost one boy, I don't want Josh near—"

"You ain't lost him yet. I needs Joshua, Sadie. Everett need you," Tamara, down on her knees, helped Joshua wipe up the bloody gore. "Now, *go*!"

Sadie turned and ran.

* * *

Bloody cleaning chores completed, Tamara hurried to the door. Josh hung back. His nervous system, now denied Cain's soothing concoctions for close to forty-eight hours, screamed with rage. In a fever to get to Paul, he found it almost impossible to leave his father alone on the floor, blue-faced and covered in sweat.

"Papa," he said softly. Tamara took his arm and gently pulled.

Everett gasped instructions and pointed shakily to the door.

"Son, ain't nothing ... you can do ... here. Find your ... brother."

Tamara pulled Joshua out the door.

"Oh, my God," the boy moaned. "I did this. All of this. Oh, God, what have I done?"

"Son, you ain't got time to stop and feel sorry for yo'self and I ain't got time to soothe you down. Get in

184

de wagon!" she commanded, striding swiftly to her small buckboard which waited beyond the wrought iron fence.

"Horses faster," Josh said. "I can saddle real quick—"

"No. Might need de wagon. He prob'ly can't ride."

"'Cause he dead," Josh spoke quietly into the night, in the lilting, flowing, hybrid speech pattern habitually employed by his mother, which, like Joshua, was neither wholly black nor wholly white.

"We doan know dat."

"What you think."

"No, it ain't. Ain't a'tall. Paul's alive yet. Cain's waitin' on you."

"Me?"

"Why else you think he send Isaiah's head? Wants you to know he got 'em. Wants you dere to watch."

Hope surged in Joshua's heart. Until he realized he'd left the house with absolutely no weapon. It was the first time he'd even thought of it.

"Go back!" he shouted.

"Ain't got time."

"I ain't got no gun! No knife, no nuttin'! Go back! If he's waitin' on me, we got time!"

"Guns and knives ain't goan do nuttin', boy, nuttin'! An' Cain ain't de one to worry 'bout. He 'bout to start somethin' he can't handle. An' when he do, he ain't goan be able to wait on you!"

"Then Paul's a dead man."

"No, he ain't," said Tamara, flicking the reins and urging her horses forward down Wharf Street. "He jest goan wish he was."

* * *

Cain paced the clearing impatiently. He paused occasionally to lash out with his huge hands and deliver a neck-snapping blow to Paul's head. He was ready, damn it, ready. Paul, stripped of his shirt, was lashed

185

bare-chested to a sturdy stake implanted firmly in the center of the circle.

Cain paused in his long strides and struck again.

"Well, where is he, white man? *Where*?"

"Told you he wasn't at my house." Paul ground the words out between his swollen, bleeding lips.

"*He wuz! I know he wuz*! He jest doan give a damn! Dat's it, white man! You done give yo' life for a boy doan give a fuckin' *damn* 'bout yours! How dat feel? *Shiiiittt*, maybe dat boy better den I thought! Mo' like me den you, after all!"

Cain paced the clearing again.

"*Shiiiitttt!!* Dat's enough! De gods, *dey hungry*!"

He pulled the knife from the scabbard belted around his waist.

Cain's roar of rage trembled on the night air. Tamara and Joshua rushed toward the riverbank on foot. There was no path for the wagon. The crowd chanted, covering the sounds of the underbrush and snapping twigs.

"Too late," Josh moaned.

"Shut up and move!" commanded Tamara. She pushed harder and gained a clear view of the circle.

Blood ran down Paul's chin, the product of his own gnashing teeth as Cain's knife twisted slowly and deeply while Cain drew it lingeringly, almost lovingly, over the skin. Blood poured from two deep, wide cuts forming an X across Paul's chest, running from each shoulder down to his belt buckle. Cain thrust his hands into the blood, held them high, and chanted.

Tamara burst into the clearing, Joshua at her heels, knowing what she'd see, what was coming. She'd seen it written on Paul's hand, preordained, immutable, unstoppable. One last, desperate hope remained to circumvent destiny. If she could just prevent Cain from cracking the door about to burst open—too late to save Paul entirely, he'd bleed to death before they got back to town. But he'd prefer that to the alternative.

"You fool!" she shouted. "You doan know whut you doin', man! Stop!"

Cain turned. About to unleash power such as the world had never seen, and a *woman* dared interfere? Oh, no. He didn't think so.

"*Take 'em!*" he shouted. A lightning bolt struck directly at Cain's feet, knocking him down.

Tamara groaned. Too late. The air filled with electric current flowing from the flashing lightning. The door cracked and opened to the worlds on worlds that ring this world. The air changed. It hissed, it burned, it smoldered.

Cain's followers fell back. Their retreat turned into a blind stampede fleeing toward town and the sanctuary of the city streets. Toward sanity.

It appeared from nowhere. One moment, nothing. The next, nightmare incarnate. It. Cain's eyes widened. He back-propelled his body along the ground with his hands, scrambling back from the clearing.

It was huge, ten feet or more in height. The thing from beyond the door stomped the ground of the clearing and screamed, composite of all predators on earth. Visions of a lion's mane, a wolf's fur, a monkey's face, a lizard's feet, raced across Joshua's sight. His eyes settled on alligator-like teeth ringing an open mouth.

Cain's eyes bulged. The old woman hadn't told him nightmares moved behind the gates. He didn't need anyone to tell him there was no way he could send this one back.

The creature eyed the humans. It growled and turned. It smelled blood, lovely blood. Hot. Rich. Heavy. What luck! The doors so seldom cracked into this dimension, the creature's favorite hunting ground, so full of blood. Bright red blood that ran like wine down its thirsty throat, not the anemic liquid flowing in the creatures it usually fed on.

The blood scent was maddening. Where was it? Fresh, hot. The aroma pulsated in the open air. It turned in a searching pattern and roared in triumph. Its lizard-like hands grabbed Paul's arms and pulled the post itself completely out of the ground. It held Paul high in the air above it and lapped the flowing blood from the cross cuts on Paul's chest.

The surface blood only whetted the creature's appetite. It wanted hot blood, blood heated by pumping organs. It opened its mouth and fastened its razor-edged teeth into Paul's neck directly over the jugular vein, tearing and gnawing. Joshua charged forward and leaped onto the creature's back, pounding with his fists as Paul's scream reverberated over the clearing and down to the river.

Tamara fell to her knees and began to chant. Her face poured sweat, her eyes reddened and leaked blood as she begged God and the Loa of the Rada, the sweet spirits of the Light, to send the invader back to the worlds where it belonged. She chanted harder, feeling the Rada battling with the blood drinker, child from the outer reaches of the planes of darkness.

Feeling the attack, the creature dropped Paul's body to the ground. Joshua slipped from its back and ran to his brother, clawing and pulling at the binding rope. The invader turned to Tamara and her relentless chants. Abruptly, a monstrous bolt of lightning split the air. The Blood Drinker disappeared.

Tamara collapsed. Joshua gathered Paul into his arms and stared into the open blue eyes.

"Paul! Paul, talk to me! Please, please, *please* talk to me!" He raised his hand and slapped Paul's check, he shook his shoulders furiously. He moved his hand down to the ravaged flesh scored by the fangs of the Blood Drinker. He raised his hand slowly and moaned. No blood. He touched the open wounds on Paul's chest. No blood. No blood in his brother's body. Not even a trace.

He raised his head and stared at Cain, still crouched frozen on the ground.

Cain stared back but he didn't see Joshua. He saw nothing but the Blood Drinker, the monster, the visitor from the furtherest planes of darkness.

Joshua cradled Paul's body and rocked him back and forth while silent tears ran down his cheeks. Then he spoke, not loudly, but very clearly, the spaces measured between each word.

"I'm going to kill you, Cain. No matter where you run."

Cain's eyes shifted. The he stood. And abruptly, he broke and ran into the woods.

"*No matter where you run!*" Joshua shouted after him. The words echoed after Cain, running harder than he'd ever run when he departed the Louisiana cane fields. He ran and ran and kept on running.

Chapter Twelve

Tamara's moans of returning consciousness filtered into Joshua's private descent into Hell. He glanced over and saw her twitch. He looked down at his brother. There was nothing he could do for Paul. After all, he'd killed him. He gently laid Paul's long form on the ground, taking special care not to jar his head, and moved over to his aunt.

"Tamara?" He lifted her head and gently stroked her cheek.

Tamara stirred again and opened her eyes.

"It's gone," she said. Not a question. Otherwise, neither of them would be here. The creature's appetite was insatiable.

"Yes."

"We got to get him back. My house be best. De root cellar."

Joshua stared. His aunt was crazy. That was all there was to it. She'd dabbled in spells and potions and incantations her entire life and this final confrontation with – It – had just sent her right 'round the bend.

"No," he said. "We takin' him home. Papa might be dead already, you know Mama's half out of her mind. But however bad it is to know, it's worse to wonder. We takin' him home."

Tamara laughed shortly and pushed herself up to a sitting position.

"Boy, I done tol' you, I ain't got time to argue wid you tonight! Yo' brother ain't dead. Not 'xactly. Where be Cain?"

"He ran off into the woods. I told him I was goin' to kill him, no matter where he ran. I mean it. Doan know how and doan know where, but—"

"An' you will," his aunt assured him. "You and Paul. Together. You will."

Joshua's frayed nerve endings snapped.

"Stop saying that!" he shouted. "Paul is dead! There is no blood in his body! You do not live without blood!"

Tamara pulled the boy into her arms, rocking him as he sobbed, just as he'd rocked back and forth with Paul.

"Son. Much as you seen tonight, you doan trust me?"

"No. You talkin' foolishness. My brother's dead. I killed him."

"Blood Drinkers doan kill, son. Not 'xactly. Dere do be dose whut say dey give eternal life."

Joshua raised his head. "Blood Drinkers? Is that what that thing—"

"Well, I doan know 'xactly what its name actually is. Whut I knows is dat dis world, son, it be ringed with worlds on worlds." Tamara's voice was low, soothing, speaking almost the words her sister had spoken to Paul a mere day before.

"'Dey shift, dey overlap. Some of 'em be real dark, full of evil and danger. Some of 'em, dey be real bright and beautiful. An' sometimes, folks whut doan know whut dey doin', dey can make things happ'n whut wasn't never 'sposed to happ'n. An' things can cross over from 'dem other worlds to dis one."

Joshua shuddered. "Bad things. Real bad things."

"Well, now, dat all depends. Sho', dat Blood Drinker be a real bad thing here. But it ain't bad in and of itself. It made to live in a certain world, and in dat world, it have its own purpose. Over here, well, weren't meant to be over here. But it weren't de thing's fault. It be de fault of de one whut called it. Humans, son, dey be some of de only creatures in all 'dese worlds whut can choose whether dey be good or evil. An' some folks, de ones whut has mo' power den others, what dey choose, it upset de balance."

"Like you and Cain?" he asked.

She nodded. "Like me and Cain."

"Couldn't you have turned the Blood Drinker on Cain?"

"Wish I could have, son. Dat's de human in me. I want Cain to hurt, jest lik' you do. But I was askin' de' Light for help and when you serve de Light, you gots to think about the good of all folks. You start trying' to use dat power for dark things, like revenge, den you turn de good to evil an' it blow up in yo' face lik' a firecracker. Know what would'a happened had I tried to turn it on Cain?"

Joshua shook his head.

"Well, I woulda been thinkin' 'bout me. 'Bout yo' Mama, who I love mo' den any other person still livin' on dis earth. 'Bout Paul an' 'bout you. Jest met y'all but I been lovin' you both for years, boy, all yo' lives. You best believe it. An' revenge. An' to keep dat thing here to get Cain, well, if I'd waited too much longer to try and send it back, I mighta not been able to. An' it woulda been loose, son. Loose in dis town. An' dat woulda been my fault. You see whut I'm sayin'?"

"Have there been others?"

"Blood Drinkers?"

Josh nodded.

"Yeah. Sometime de doors 'tween de worlds, dey crack all by dere lonesomes and things slip back and forth. Doan happen often, an' when it do, seem like somethin', some balance, doan let de doors stay open long. An' when dey close, all de things dat slipped through get sucked back where dey 'sposed to be. But dere's been Blood Drinkers through before. An' dey've left behind folk like Paul."

Joshua's eyes widened. Paul's collection of penny-dreadfuls from London. The monsters. Werewoves, ghouls and ghosts. And—

"No," Joshua whispered. "No. Please no."

"You see, doan you, son?"

"He isn't. Those stories aren't real, they're just stories, they're *not real!*"

"Son, most stories start from somewhere."

"And the stories—the vampire stories—they come from the Blood Drinkers?"

Tamara nodded.

"They sleep by day and rise by night, and—oh God! He'd rather be dead, Tamara!"

"Son," she said gently. "Dere's some things jest cain't be changed. I know. I tried."

"I won't let my brother live like that! He's so good, Tamara, he's the best man in the world! He won't be able to stand it!"

"But son, dat's whut I been tryin' to 'splain. Humans got de choice. An' Paul still part human. Dat Blood Drinker, he jest is. He do whut he have to do, whut his nature tell him to do. But not humans. I have power. Cain have power. We both chooses to be whut we are, whut we do wid it. An' Paul, dis give him power, Josh, power like few men ever have in dis world. De power to stop Cain. With your help. Paul goan make his own choice. An' we both knows. We knows dat wid Paul, the powers of darkness now be servants of de Light."

"But—but *blood!* Won't he want, won't he need—"

"We goan help him. You and me. An' yo' Mama. Tonight, Isaiah dead. An' Paul makin' de change. From life to something dat ain't life like we know it, but it ain't death neither. Tomorrow night, son, dat's for Cain."

"You intend for Paul—"

"Ain't my intention. It jest how things goan be."

Joshua protested. "But in the stories, vampires, their victims rise! Cain'll be like Paul, he won't be dead!"

"Has to have time for de change, son. An' dat's where you come in. Now, you goan help me wid yo' brother?"

"Mama and Papa—"

"I gots to think 'bout Paul first. An' I needs to get him to my house. Dat's where he gots to wake up."

* * *

Joshua led Paul's great black stallion, Cyclone, back to the clearing. The horse hesitated as it approached the circle of blood, smelling the horror from another dimension. He reared on his muscled back legs and vented his protests in loud screams that split the night.

"Ain't goan do it, Tamara! This horse just ain't goan do it!"

"Gots to. We can't carry him all de way to de wagon." Tamara walked up to the horse and placed her hands firmly on either side of the great head. The huge dark eyes rolled. She breathed gently into his straining nostrils and gradually, Cyclone calmed down.

"How did you do that?"

"Doan matter how. He'll do it. He tol' me he would. Help me."

The two of them heaved Paul's body over the saddle and began the first leg of the nightmare journey.

When they made it to the wagon Tamara settled an old blanket across Paul's body, making certain he was fully covered. The second leg of the nightmare ended at the little white cottage on the edges of Stone Creek Swamp.

Tamara pulled the wagon up close to the house. She jumped down and quickly pulled open the wooden doors set into the stone foundations of the cottage.

"Wait!" she ordered. She descended the stairs cautiously. Lantern light flared from the aperture. Tamara emerged.

"Here. Dis de darkest, safest place we gots."

Together, they brought Paul's body down the stairs and laid it on a makeshift bed of blankets lying ready.

"Hoped I wouldn't need 'em." She sighed. "But I got ready. Jest in case."

She dipped a soft cloth into the basin of water standing ready and gently washed Paul's battered face. She cleansed the gaping cuts on his chest, the huge wound on his throat. Joshua watched, totally numb and grateful for it. Otherwise, he'd have cried until all the moisture in his own body drained out of him in tears.

Tamara covered Paul again with the softest of the blankets and turned the edge neatly back across his chest.

She turned to Joshua.

"So, boy. You be alright while I gone?"

"Gone? Where you goin'?"

"Back to town. Got to get to yo' mama."

Tamara's eyes were red, lined with capillaries broken in the intensity of her chant. Her skin was lackluster, tinged with grayness. Paul was six feet tall and weighed 185 pounds. In death, that weight was— well, dead weight. Joshua was exhausted. He didn't know how his aunt was still standing.

"You can't. You 'bout to fall down in your tracks."

"Gots to. Sadie be out of her mind. You know dat."

"I'll go. You stay and rest."

Tamara laughed shortly. "Ought to look at yo'self, boy. Still ain't got yo' strength back from Cain's poison. You never make it. I rest later. You stay wid Paul. Gots to change my team out, you rub 'em down and get 'em settled after I leave. After dat, you go lay yo'self on my bed and sleep, you hear? I be back."

She turned and ascended the steps, closing the cellar doors tightly after Joshua's exit. Together they changed the team and Tamara settled onto the seat and shook the reins.

"One mo' time, sweet Lord, get me dere one mo' time tonight! Now, boy," she leaned over to Joshua. "Mind you keep dem doors closed tight. Doan crack 'em, doan look, doan need to let in no mo' light den can be hepped come daylight. You goan likely wake 'fore we get back. But you doan go back down into dat cellar without yo' Mama and me. You hear?"

He nodded. She flicked the reins and he listened to the creak of the wagon wheels winding toward town until they died away completely and left only the night sounds of the woods.

* * *

Back at the house on Orange Street, Dr. Cabot had come and gone.

"Nothing I can do that you can't, Sadie," he'd said. He looked at Sadie with some sympathy. Everett's contemporaries were pretty sure Sadie wasn't just the Devlins' housekeeper but such an arrangement wasn't unusual. And everyone conceded Everett handled the situation with great discretion. "This one was, well, anything like this is bad, but it could have been a lot worse. Another one will be. But if we can keep him quiet, maybe there won't be a next one. Lestways 'til he's got some of his strength back. Where'd you say Paul was?"

"He had a 'mergency. Up toward Bolingbroke way. Said he might not be back tonight."

"Well." Dave Cabot glanced back from the hall into the bedroom. "Maybe I ought to stay."

"No!" exclaimed Sadie, and modified her tone at the expression on Dr. Cabot's face. "I mean, I been in a doctor's house a long time, Doc Cabot. Either he goan sleep or he goan have another one, ain't dat right?"

"Pretty much, yeah."

"An' do he have another one, ain't nothing you goan be able to do about it, is dere?"

"No. I'm sorry."

"Then you go on back home. I watch him."

Dr. Cabot left, knowing Sadie would, indeed, watch closely.

196

Now Sadie paced. She'd paced all night. Her present path moved from the back bedroom where Everett lay and the front windows, keeping watch for Tamara's return. Right now it seemed nothing had ever existed except this path between the back bedroom and the front windows and nothing else would ever exist again. As she paced, she chanted, a chant not so much a supplication as a demand for her sons to return with her sister.

She peered for the thousandth time from the sheer curtains draping the front windows, expecting to see nothing but the yard. It took a moment to realize her sister was actually climbing wearily down from the wagon seat. Tamara stopped and rested her head for a moment across the rough boards of the wagon.

Sadie flew out the door and down the walk. She stopped dead in her tracks, eyes rapidly scanning the wagon.

"My boys. You ain't brought neither one of 'em back."

"Dey at my house. Joshua wore plum' out. Hope he sleepin'."

"Paul?"

"He sleepin', too, Sadie. But it be a different sleep."

Sleeping. A different sleep. Sadie looked at her twin. She hadn't known any human, this exhausted, could still function.

"Come in de house." Sadie took Tamara's sister's arm. "Lean on me. You needs it."

"Everett?"

"He restin'. Look lik' he goan beat dis one."

The sisters walked inside. Sadie settled her twin on the sofa and brought her steaming, strong, sweet tea and as the wee hours of morning turned into daybreak, the two of them, with hot tears and steely determination, decided matters waiting for decisions.

* * *

Cain watched sunrise from the railings of the covered bridge spanning the Ocmulgee River down below Fifth Street. After fleeing the clearing with Joshua's determined shout ringing in his ears, he'd raced through the woods, back to the civilization of Wharf Street, back to the streets of the city proper. He'd wandered those streets all night and now barely remembered his wanderings.

For years, he'd perched precariously on the borderlands between sanity and lunacy. A megalomaniac of great power, secure in his strength, confident of his special gifts. It was inconceivable he could be less than the supreme being he envisioned himself to be. In his mind, the huge figure of the nightmarish thing he'd called forth shrank and modified until it was nothing but a larger version of the creatures that created his sentries.

A trick of the shadows, that was it. That was all. And his followers, his acolytes, had dared to break and run from the illusions. Intolerable. Unacceptable. Tonight at the clearing they'd feel his wrath. They'd never dare desert him again. It didn't cross his mind his following was no more, that no one would ever come to the clearing again, no matter how badly their nerve endings screamed for the artificial nirvana his concoctions dispensed. Of course they'd be there. And they'd be so *sorry* they'd abandoned him.

Cain threw back his head and laughed, startling the pigeons nesting in the rafters of the covered bridge. Rest. He needed rest. He turned and headed back to his rooming house, a great wolf returning to his lair. He'd sleep the daylight hours through and this evening he'd rise, refreshed. His followers, the cowards, and their city, would feel his righteous wrath.

Early morning travelers on their way to work fell back from his huge shadow as he passed, sensing darkness in the strange light glaring from his eyes. Cain no longer perched on the borders of sanity and lunacy.

He'd passed that border, never to return. He was totally, hopelessly, irrevocably insane.

* * *

Tamara slept. Everett rested as comfortably as possible in the back bedroom of the house on Orange Street under Janie's supervision. He was clinging steadfastly to Tamara's explanation—Paul wasn't dead, he was merely changed. Sadie didn't think the full consequences of Paul's change had made an impression on Everett yet but since he was coping with the situation far better than she'd hoped, she was grateful for any small crumb falling her way.

While those loved ones rested, Sadie implemented the first of the tasks she and Tamara had determined must be done. She knocked on Nona Gorley's door. Nona came up behind her, almost startling her into a faint.

"Isaiah, he made me spend de night wid our oldest girl. Say he doan want me here alone." Nona sank down to her top step. "Ain't never worried 'bout me spending de night alone, never, not in thirty year, do he need to be out with sick folks and such. But dis time, he be right, didn't he? Dey ain't coming back. Is dey?"

"Nona, I's so sorry. An' I can't tell you everything—"

"I heard 'em. Whilst I was in the kitchen. Talkin' 'bout dat man. Dat debil spawn, whut he done?"

"He goan pay, Nona. Isaiah, he goan be foun' behind de church. Sorta, anyway," Sadie explained. "An' de police, dey goan think some crazy person did it. An' dey ain't never goan find out who. But he goan pay. Doan you worry none over dat."

Nona sat. For a minute, Sadie was afraid the shock was too great. Then Nona spoke, her voice strong. "'Vengeance is mine, sayeth the Lord.' Dat's whut Isaiah say. But I ain't near as good as Isaiah. Mist' Paul?"

199

"He ain't never goan come home again neither, Nona. But his body ain't never goan be found."

"Is it over?"

"Not yet. But it will be. Tonight. I promise you, Nona. I promise."

* * *

Back at the cottage, Joshua woke on Tamara's bed. It was mid-afternoon by the light streaming in through the windows. The Blood Drinker had stalked his dreams. Paul. What changes were going on, down there in the cellar Tamara had forbidden him to enter without her? And did he dare slip through the cellar doors to see?

Mind you keep dem doors closed tight. Doan crack 'em, doan look, doan need to let in no mo' light den can be hepped come daylight... you doan go back down into dat cellar....

Did he dare disobey? If intruding light might hurt his brother, he shouldn't risk it. If she was worried about any potential danger to Joshua, Joshua didn't give a damn. And he'd move quickly and crack the door the bare minimum.

He slipped into the cellar through the barest crack possible. He moved slowly, feet leaden, across the hard-packed dirt floor. His brother lay in exactly the same position they'd settled him in last night. But something was different. His bruised face was unmarked. The huge cuts on his chest were—was he seeing things? No. The huge cuts were closing as he watched, changing into white, ropey scar tissue. And the gaping tears on his throat were completely closed. Closed as though they'd never been. Without a single marring scar.

* * *

200

Sadie returned to the Orange Street house after her sorrowful visit to Nona and the two sisters made the journey, yet again, to Tamara's cottage. They arrived near four o'clock in the afternoon. Joshua sat, carved of stone, at Tamara's table.

Sadie hugged him, pulling him hard against her body. He didn't return the hug. "I killed him, Mama. I killed Paul. But I'm goan kill Cain, too. Tamara promised."

Sadie looked over Joshua's head toward her sister.

"You and Paul, Josh. You and Paul together. Yes, I promise."

"I went in the cellar when I woke up. I was real careful. No light got in. And they're gone. All gone." said Josh.

"What, son?"

"The marks. His face. The bruises. Now his face is clear. The cuts, Cain cut him so bad, Mama, and now they're just old scars. All white and raised, like the one on my leg where I fell on Miz Bennett's picket fence when I was little. And his neck, where the Blood Drinker, where it—it's gone. It's just gone. Ain't even no scar. Nothing."

"Sadie." Tamara's voice broke into the blackness of Sadie's thoughts. "Let Josh sit. Won't be dat much longer 'til dark fall. Got things to do."

"You all right, son?" Sadie asked.

"Ain't never goan be alright again," Joshua stated flatly. No. It wouldn't. There being nothing to say to that, Sadie dropped her arms and followed her sister out.

* * *

The three of them sat in the cellar in lantern light vigil by Paul while twilight edged down over the lingering colors of sunset.

"What's goan happen?" Joshua asked. "When?"

"Time gettin' close, boy. Real close. We jest have to watch, can't really judge without no windows. But soon, now. Real soon.

Heaviness hung in the air. Joshua saw the blanket stir and moved closer, leaning over Paul's body.

"Josh, doan do dat! Goan take him a minute or two, he ain't goan know whut he doin'!"

Paul's eyes flew open. His hand raised and flashed upward. He caught Joshua by the throat and pulled him down. Joshua stared at his brother's mouth, at the sharp fangs replacing the incisors. He offered no resistance. If Paul needed Joshua's blood, it was his and welcome.

Tamara and Sadie, moving as one, grabbed Joshua's arms from either side and pulled.

"Paul! No!"

He loosened his grip enough for them to pull Joshua away. Tamara's feet scarcely touched the floor as she flew to the supplies waiting at the ready. Her flock of chickens was sorely depleted.

Paul sat up. He threw the blanket back, his coordination jerky, and tried to rise. A man regaining consciousness after a severe illness.

"Hurts." His voice mimicked the rough growl of an animal. "Thirsty. So *thirsty*!" He moved forward.

Tamara lifted the glass jar in her hands in offering.

"Den drink!" she said.

Paul stared at its ruby-red contents. Lantern light reflected off the glass in jewel-like points of color. His mouth twisted into revulsion and then, snarling in anticipation and despair, he grabbed it and raised it high. Like a man lost in the desert for three days, he drained it dry.

Joshua moaned as drops of blood ran from the corners of his brother's lips. He'd done this. The night he'd first trailed Abe and Eulises down to the river bank. His fault. All his fault.

Paul lowered the jar, his movements more coordinated, almost as though he were a piece of rusted machinery needing oil.

"More?" Half question. Half demand.

Tamara took the empty jar from his hands and replaced it with another. Paul drained it too, and shook his head as though to clear it.

"Where? What?" His voice, still gruff, sounded almost normal.

"My house, son. My root cellar."

"I'm not—I shouldn't be—it hurts, Tamara."

"I know, son. I know."

"Is there any more?"

"Yes. But not here, not right now."

"Then—"

"You knows, boy. You knows."

Paul straightened and glanced down, noticing for the first time he was shirtless. He stared at the raised scars on his chest and ran his finger lightly over their long length.

He raised his head. "Impossible." His hand moved to his neck, searching for the gaping wound he knew should be on this throat.

"Dat's gone, son. De Blood Drinker leave its own healing power behind."

"But my chest—"

"Dey was already dere 'fore de Blood Drinker. Cain did dat. You 'member? So dey heal too, but not clean."

Tamara moved to the table standing in the center of the room and shook out one of Paul's shirts Sadie brought with them. She handed it to him.

Paul's blue eyes flashed, visible in the darkness.

"I remember," he said. His voice was cold as New England in the depths of winter. He took the shirt and slipped his arms into the sleeves. Tamara moved closer and fastened the buttons for him.

"You feel him, son? You know where he be?"

Paul shook his head.

"But you can. You can do you try."

Paul withdrew into himself. His eyes focused on the far wall. He stood utterly still.

"The river bank. He's back at the river bank. And tonight I can kill him. Can't I?"

Tamara nodded.

"That thing. It changed me."

Tamara nodded.

"For how long?"

Tamara bit her lip.

"For how long?"

"Forever, son. Forever."

Paul threw back his head and laughed. A laugh made of icicles, sharp and cold as the ones that had ringed the gingerbread fretwork of the front porch during last January's ice storm. Joshua shivered.

Paul looked at his brother and smiled. "Don't worry, little brother. Nothing lasts forever. But we'll discuss that later. Won't we, Tamara?"

"Paul—"

"Later. You and I, we'll talk later. But for now, there's Cain. I need a horse."

Tamara shook her head. "No, son. You don't."

"Then how?" he asked.

"Close yo' eyes, son. Close yo' eyes and turn 'em inward and see whut wonders can you work now."

He stood still and closed his eyes. He opened them and smiled.

"It's that easy?"

"Is for you."

"And afterwards?"

"Leave dat to us. We be followin' behind to pick up de trash."

Paul laughed again, more human this time, almost the mirthful laugh of a child enjoying a great jest.

He raised his arms high. His body wavered in misty lines, one moment solid, then the barest trace of fog. After a few seconds of indecision, he was gone.

"My sweet Jesus," whispered Sadie. "My boy. My poor boy."

"Sadie, we got to move. Bet my teams know de way to town all by dere lonesomes by now."

"Tamara, he ain't goan live like dis. When he say you and he goan talk, you know whut he goan want—"

"Whut we wants and whut we gets ain't always de same thing. Now, we gots to move. Like I say. Dere's trash goan need picking up."

* * *

Cain strode the river bank. His bare chest gleamed with oil. Amulets of gold and necklaces of bone draped his neck and shoulders. He paced in growing fury. Alone.

"Cowards!" he muttered under his breath. "'De fools! De stupid fools dare turn dere backs on me!" He stopped suddenly in mid-stride.

"*Where are you?*" he shouted, his voice echoing back into the trees. "*Where are you, fools?*"

They would pay. The whole town would pay. He swayed in concentration, moving among the seven fires burning in the clearing.

"Sebben. My color be sebben. Color be sebben ... sebben ... sebben...."

He knelt before the skulls of his grisly sentries, their glowing eyes powered by the demons imbuing them with sight. His demons. He'd call them forth, yes, and all their brethren, and send them streaming through the town, darting though open windows. Feasting till they burst.

He reached down and lifted two skulls high, one in each of his huge hands

"Last chance, *fools*!" he shouted. "*Where are you?*"

"*Here I am.*" And almost instantly, from the opposite side of the clearing, the words repeated. "*And here. And here.*" Shifting, ever-moving. "*Here ... and here ... and here.*" The voice, human, held silvery overtones of inhumanity

205

Cain twirled around in circles, following the voice. A voice he recognized. Except he didn't. Because it was impossible. Wasn't it?

"*White man!*" he shouted. "Dat you?"

"And here ... and here ... and here ... here ... here...."

Cain swirled in a dizzying circle as the voice catcalled, moving, floating, seemingly coming from all directions at once.

"Come out! Show yo'self! Like a man!"

The taunting ceased, replaced by laughter floating in the air from everywhere at once. The laughter stopped. Echoes bounced back from river.

A tall figure materialized directly in front of Cain. It smiled a terrible smile and curled its lips. Four incisors, honed to razor sharpness, gleamed in the mingled moonlight and fire glow.

"But I'm not a man, Cain. Not anymore. You took care of that."

Paul advanced toward him and Cain fell back, fear rising from the lower reaches of his stomach. It moved up his spine, accelerated and raced upward, leaving his body almost numb. This man was dead, executed by his demons. Dead! But wait! If dead, he belonged to the regions of darkness Cain ruled. Confidence rekindled. He could control this being. He halted his retreat and stood tall.

"You can't do nothin', *white man!* I *made* you! I *control* you! You does whut *I* says you do!"

"You keep right on thinkin' that." Paul smiled. His arm flashed out and caught Cain by the throat. His hand squeezed. Cain's eyes bulged under the pressure.

Cain curled his fists, raining blows on Paul's head and face. But Paul's head didn't snap back. His lips didn't split. He loosened the pressure on Cain's neck a bit, allowing a trace of air to flow back into his windpipe.

"Who *are* you?" Cain croaked. "*What* are you?"

"You don't know?" Paul released Cain's throat, immediately grabbing both his arms. He threw him across the clearing like a sack of feed. The impact of landing knocked the breath from his lungs. He tried to suck in enough wind to stand and fight.

From nowhere, Paul fell on him again, hauling his bulk off the ground as though it weighed nothing. He tossed him into the middle of the clearing. Cain's right arm landed in the center fire. His left arm twisted and bent beneath his great weight with a snapping sound. Cain screamed. He jerked away from the flames, trying to shift his body, his right arm a running river of agony. Fire fed on flesh.

Paul reached down and grabbed the charred skin, jerking and twisting. Bone snapped again as he hauled Cain free of the flames and loomed over him, wicked incisors coming closer, closer.

"No! No!"

Cain felt the blood leaving his vessels, draining from the valves of his heart, the pit of his stomach, the chambers of his lungs, the smallest capillaries of his body. As it left, it burned, burned with an intensity so hot it was ice cold. Finally, the clearing held only dying moans and the wet, sucking sounds of Paul's mouth.

Paul floated, then soared with an exultation unlike any he'd ever experienced. He felt the power of hot blood as it rushed throughout his body. Sated, he dropped Cain's bulk to the ground like an apple core and laughed. He laughed and laughed until the laughter turned to sobs. He raised his hands and wiped the blood from his lips.

He looked down at his hands, at the bloodstains gleaming black under the moon, and rushed to the banks of the river, down to the water. He leaned over and gazed into the slow-moving eddies of the river. Moonlight glazed the water, turning it to a shimmering mirror.

He stared at his reflection and curled his lips, showed his teeth. His hand flashed down, breaking the surface of the water. He cupped his hand and scooped water to his mouth, scrubbing viciously.

He was still perched on the river's edge when his clean-up crew arrived at the scene to pick up the trash, engaged in an endless, repetitive cycle. Hand to river water, river water to mouth, scrubbing and scrubbing as though his lips would never be clean again.

The cycle broke when Tamara reached down and gently shook his shoulder.

"Son?"

He hadn't heard their approach and wondered how he'd missed it. The world around him buzzed with noise. He could hear the heartbeat of the wood creatures crouched in the furthermost shadows.

"You all right, son?" Sadie reached out a tentative hand.

Paul laughed. "I'm not ever goin' to be all right again. Your trash is in the clearing, Tamara."

"So I seen. How'd it feel, boy?"

"Oh, God, it felt good! So good. And I'm so scared, Tamara, never been this scared in my life! What if I can't—but I can't, I know I can't. I can't live without blood now. Can I?"

Tamara pursed her lips and sent out a thin whistle.

"Boy, dere's blood, and den dere's blood. Up to you to pick yo' prey. I doan got no doubts 'bout yo' choice. Do you?"

Paul didn't answer. Seconds before, he'd been sated, full of Cain's blood. He hadn't thought he'd ever, ever, look at blood again. And now, so soon, his senses remembered the thrill, the exultation, the power. He smelled the blood all around him, the richness of it as it flowed through Joshua, through Sadie, through Tamara.

"I have to leave! I have to hunt!" He backed away and raised his arms.

"Paul!" Sadie grabbed his hand. "Son, you don't know where you goin'! What to do 'fore day breaks—"

"Yes, I do. I go back to the root cellar. Don't I?"

"Dat's right, boy. An' you see dat you be dere."

"You can't just let him go, Tamara! He doan understand!"

"He got to reach his own understandin'. You hunt, boy. An' you come home. We talk tomorrow night. Ain't nuttin' so bad as you think. Let go his hand, Sadie."

Sadie stepped back. Paul raised his arms, wavered in and out a few times, and disappeared.

"How could you do that?" Sadie turned on her sister in a spasm of rage. "How you jest let him go like dat?"

"How you think I stop him, woman? Now, he's done his part. Let's us do ours. Josh, go back to de wagon and unhitch one of de horses. We gots to load de trash."

"And what we do with him now we got him?" It was the first time Joshua had spoken since leaving Tamara's house.

"I shows you, boy. I shows you."

* * *

While the clean-up crew collected the trash and began the final weary trudge to Tamara's little cottage by the edge of Stone Creek Swamp, Paul roamed the woods surrounding the Ocmulgee River, ranging from side to side. His nose and ears, tuned to animal perception, followed the smell and night noises of the wood creatures. Raccoons and possums, rabbits and deer. No quarry too small or too large.

He stalked and captured, bit and tore. And drank. And drank. And drank. At the conclusion of each stalking hunt, he swore—no more. God, no more. But then his nose caught the rich smell of hot, pumping blood in the distance and he cast out again and again.

Finally, some new instinct alerted him to check the horizon. Darkness was lifting. Day was leaving night. If he didn't seek the shelter of Tamara's root cellar, would he simply cease to exist? Or lie in agony as the sun seared into him until night fell again?

He didn't know. He knew he never wanted to live through another night, but he didn't know what, if anything, would destroy him. Better to seek shelter, rise again as dusk descended, consult Tamara. She'd help him. She had to. For the last time that endless night, he cast himself into the wind.

* * *

Tamara led her weary troupe to their final destination. The small cave loomed out of the face of the low-rising hillock where Stone Creek Woods slid into Stone Creek Swamp. Tamara had first found it by accident several months before on one of her forages for herbs and plants, almost entirely closed by rocks. The rocks had loosened and tumbled down when she pulled at some vines and darkness had loomed beyond. The cave walls were dark and dank, partly stone, mostly dirt. For no reason, other than she'd frequently found that the most seemingly useless things sometimes had great uses, she'd returned later and fully uncovered the entrance, piling the rocks to one side for possible future use.

The cave's time had come. Forever and all time, Cain's unhallowed crypt.

The three of them pulled and grappled and finally, Cain's huge bulk lay inside the damp and dripping walls of the cave. They backed out and collapsed in front of the entrance while they watched the approach of dawn.

"Paul," said Sadie. "Tamara, whut if he don't come back?"

"He'll come," she replied. "Got no choice. Won't know whut else to do. He'll be lying in his bed, waitin' on us, when we gets back."

"Tamara, we gots to set him free."

"Right now, we gots to finish what we's started, sister."

"How?" asked Joshua. "You did all this—"

210

"Boy, I didn't do nuttin'."

"No," he agreed. "I guess you didn't. But you saw Paul. If *he's* like that, when Cain rises there'll be no stopping him. These rocks ain't goin' hold him back. Paul just raises his arms and leaves."

"Dere's ways, Josh. Didn't I promise? You and Paul. Paul's done his part. Yo' turn."

"My turn?"

"No!" exclaimed Sadie. "I do it. Or you do it. Why Josh got to be involved anymo'?"

"'Cause he *needs* to, Sadie. 'Cause it be his *right*, and I ain't goan let you takes it away from him."

"How?" the boy asked again.

"Only one sho' way to stop one of de Blood Drinker's chilluns. De heart. An' de head. You take a nice, sturdy stake. An' you pounds it through de heart. An' den you cuts off de head and throws it in runnin' water."

"Then what are we waitin' for? Why'd we bring him all the way back here?"

"Not now, son. Wouldn't do no good right now. He's like Paul was. Ain't really dead, but he ain't really alive, neither. Gots to be after de change. Nuttin' hurt 'em while dey changes, 'cause dey jest keep healin' dereselves."

"Not even sunlight? You said Paul had to be in the dark."

"Sunlight slow it down. It doan stop it. An' I doan wants nobody else stumblin' 'cross his body. I wants dis to be sho'. Doan you?"

"Then what do we do?"

"We wait. An' at dusk, Josh, jest before he wakes all de way up, when you sees his eyelids start to flutter, you takes dat stake, and you pounds it through his heart. You leave it dere. Long as it stays in place, he never rise no 'mo. An' den you cut off de head an' you throws it in Stone Creek. An' you cover de cave so nobody and nuttin' ever let light on dis man's bones again. Can you do dis, son? I gives you dis, it yo' right, but iff'n you doan think you can—"

"I can," said Joshua. "I can."

Sadie shuddered. The hard steel in his voice rocked her to the core. Her boys, her gentle boys. Healers, both of them. It was in their blood. Now Paul hunted the woods, a night predator like no other. And Joshua. Ready to pound a stake through Cain's heart. Anxious for it.

"My boys," she moaned. "My beautiful, beautiful boys!"

Tamara touched her sister's arm. "We gots to get back to de cottage. Check on Paul. Rest ourselves. I give you somethin' hep you sleep."

"Ain't no help. De spirits turned on us. God done turned on us. Ain't no help."

"'Dere's reasons we doan always understan'."

"They be awful reasons and God ain't got no right to do dis to my boys!"

"Joshua!" Tamara commanded. "Hep me wid yo' mama!"

Tamara took one arm, Joshua took other. Sadie mumbled ceaselessly all the way to the cottage. "No right, no right. No right a'tall."

* * *

Paul lay on his bed of blankets in the dark of the root cellar, his white shirt covered in dried and drying blood. Tamara reclosed the doors, fastened them securely and led her sister and nephew inside. She coaxed a tincture down Sadie's throat and led her to her bed. Sadie's protesting mumbles slowed and she slipped down into healing sleep.

Tamara turned to face her nephew. "Well, boy? You needs anything to eat?"

"God, no. I never want to eat again."

"Den rest. You want some of de stuff I give—"

"No. I never want to take anything like that, not ever again."

"Well," she said. "Den you lay down 'side yo' mama and sleep."

"Your bed. You need to rest, too."

"I will." She took his arm and led him to the other side of the bed. "I will, but you lay down. You gots to head back to de cave. Want you to start no later 'den four o'clock."

"Ain't you coming, too?"

"No. I ain't. I gots to be here for Paul. Cain be yours now. Jest lik' I promised. I ax' you 'gin, boy. Can you do this thing?"

"I can do it."

"I knows you can. Now rest."

She moved to her stove and put a kettle on to boil. Before her soothing cup of chamomile tea was properly brewed, she saw the boy join his mother in slumber. Good.

She sat down in her rocking chair and rocked, sipping her tea, feeling its warmth pour new strength into her weary bones. Through the day, moving in and out of light dosing sleep, she guarded the slumbers of the three people she loved most in the world.

* * *

Joshua woke naturally, sometime around two o'clock in the afternoon. Tamara made him eat and packed a croaker sack with tools he'd need to complete his evening's work. She watched him start out into the woods, knowing whatever was still left of boy would not return from this supreme rite of passage into manhood.

Sadie still slept and Tamara was glad. She'd feared for her sister's sanity more than once in the past hours. She moved out into her yard, harvesting the remainder of her chickens. She didn't want Paul to cast out immediately and hunt. She wanted him to stay, talk, listen. Come to terms with destiny.

Joshua followed the path into the woods, turning at the marker of the ancient sweet gum tree coated with resiny gum. He moved swiftly and reached the cave well before twilight. He sat down to wait.

The sun sank low, nearing the tops of the trees. When it neared the edge of the west, he moved inside the cave and dropped to his knees beside Cain's body. He pulled his tools from the croaker sack. Long, thick wooden stake, sharpened to the point of an ancient, deadly spear. Sturdy mallet to hammer the stake home. The burn marks on Cain's arm were now raised whelps of white scar tissue, startling against the black of his ebony skin.

So Cain had healed. The transformation was almost complete. Time to get ready. There was no way to tell the exact position of the sun in the dimness of the cave and Joshua had no intention of being surprised. He positioned the stake directly over Cain's heart. Paul's anatomy lessons made that easy. His lip actually lifted in a half-smile at the thought. Poetic judgment.

He was ready. The first flutter of his eyelids, Tamara'd said. There. Was that it? It was. Joshua swung the mallet, restraining the force of the blow. He wanted the stake to penetrate, not fully impale. A geyser of red gushed upward, covering the stake and the mallet and Joshua's hand. As the eyes opened fully and settled on his face, Joshua saw what he'd been waiting for. The light of recognition. Cain's hand moved upward, fluttering around the stake, attempting to pull it out. Joshua raised the mallet high again.

"Told you I'd kill you, Cain! *No matter where you ran!*"

The mallet slammed down, through the body and into the floor of the cave itself. A great scream, inhuman, roared across the woods and moved on further, filling the deepest reaches of the swamp. Night fishermen, tending their trot lines along the creek, stopped dead in their tracks and shivered. The night noises of the frogs and crickets ceased. No hoot-owl or whippoorwill sent forth its distinctive call. Even the swamp snakes, just beginning to creep forth on their nightly forages, ceased to slither. The heartbeat of the woods and swamp stopped. It took a remarkably long time for it to resume.

Joshua leaned over Cain and stared into the dead eyes. He dropped the mallet and held up his dripping hands. It was done. It was over.

He turned his head and vomited, retching again and again until the dry heaves sent up a flood of foul-tasting bile. He shuddered and wiped his face, not pausing to collect the croaker sack. He sat a moment in the clear night air and wiped sweat from his forehead. When his stomach settled from a continuous roll to an occasional spasm, he started shifting the rocks, piling them over the cave's entrance until it was covered.

Then he sat down and cried, his tears a scalding apology to his brother.

He was done. Tamara's last instruction wasn't even a faint memory in the nauseating mix of rage and blood and vomit of the last hour. Cain's head remained attached to his shoulders.

* * *

Paul woke the second night of his new life cycle and ripped off his shirt, stiff and scratchy with dried blood. He rushed to the basin and water pitcher Tamara'd left for him and washed. And washed. He dressed in the fresh clothes lying by the basin. Neither the soap and water nor the clothes erased the feel and smell of blood. He never wanted to see blood again.

Except he did. The new driving instinct rose in gushing waves and threatened to drown him. Enough. This had to end. He started for the door and remembered he had no need of doors. He raised his arms and re-materialized in the main living area of the cottage. The smell of pumping blood assaulted his nostrils. He stayed back, away from the women.

"Son." Tamara glanced over his immaculate clothes and nodded in approval. "Thought you'd want some privacy when you woke dis night."

She offered the glass jar waiting ready. His tongue could taste the contents, even as his mind screamed his revolt at the need for it.

"No," he said. "We have to talk. You can't do this to me. End it. Please. There has to be a way."

She shook her head sorrowfully.

"Can't do dat, son."

"You can't? Or you won't?"

"Both."

In Paul's newly transformed state, the temper inherited from his father erupted like a volcano. He grabbed her arms and shook her like a terrier worrying a rat.

"You will!"

"Paul!" Sadie rushed forward and grabbed his arms. Realizing what he'd done, what he could have done, he dropped Tamara's arms and backed away.

"You see? Don't you see? *Look at me!* Do you know what I could do to you?"

Tamara rubbed her arms, feeling bruises already forming.

"Son, dis happ'n for a reason. Weren't my choice. An' ain't my choice to end it for you, neither. Would if I could."

"What'd you do to Cain? Something, I know. You'd never let him rise."

"Yo' brother be tendin' to dat."

"How?"

Tamara shook her head and Sadie answered.

"You takes a stake, a stake made out of sturdy wood, and you drives it through de heart."

"You sent Joshua to do that?"

"Be his right," pronounced Tamara.

"Well, what about *my* rights? It's done, it's *over!* Now *you let me go!*"

Tamara shook her head.

"Cain be over, son. But yo' new life, dat jest be startin'."

"What the *hell* do you *mean*?" Paul advanced on her again, menace in every step. "This ain't enough? What the *hell* else do your almighty spirits of the Light want?"

"You, boy. An' dey got you."

"No, dey doan." Sadie stood and advanced on her sister. "Dey doan. He right. He done 'nuff. His choice. An' do he say he wants to be free, I do it. My boys done 'nuff."

"Woman, look at you! You jest about at de end of yo' last thread already. Think you can do dat to yo' boy and stay sane?"

"Dat doan matter. I do whut my boys need."

"Paul, she can't do dat and survive. She think she doin' you a service, but she ain't. 'Cause dat ain't yo' destiny."

Paul paced the room, carefully staying away from Tamara lest his anger explode over her again.

"Then what is, goddamn it? *What is?* Give me a reason I can't sharpen my own stake! You think after the last two nights I'd hesitate to fall on it myself?"

"Oh, God, son!" Tamara moved forward and grabbed his arms, her face a mask of horror. "Doan you even think such! Doan you think it, you hear me?"

"Better than this. Anything is."

"No, it ain't. Son, de' world, it be ringed with worlds—"

"Worlds on worlds. So you keep saying. No more, Tamara. I can't take anymore!"

"You think you jest tuck yo' tail and run? Prob'ly you even thinks Chloe be waitin' on you. Well, she won't be, boy. Dey a special world for folks whut takes it on dereselves to try and run away from fate in dis one.

It be dark and lonesome, full of cold winds and dreary lands where dem folks wander, never bein' in dis world nor no 'nother one. An' dey wander all alone, never meetin' even no other wandering spirit. You think dis bad, boy? You try dat! Try it for all eternity!"

Paul crossed to her fireplace and sat heavily on the hearth. He dropped his head. No way out.

"Well, they just got it all covered, don't they? Your precious spirits of the Light."

"Son, I tol' you. Dey not mine. Dey be parts of God, de one God. Sometimes it seems lik', an' I doan know why, de Light, it got to use de powers of darkness to fight de dark. "Dat's what you did, you a child of de Light dat walks now wid de powers of darkness. An' you not through yet. It be on yo' hand, de first time you come see me. You 'member, I look at yo' hand?"

Paul nodded.

Tamara sat next to him and picked up his palm, tracing lines with the tip of her finger.

"See here? Dat be yo' life line. An' look here." She pointed to a spot on that line. "It doan stop, 'xactly, but it start to run under de skin, not on top, and it run on down." Her finger traced the path. "It run all down here, and circle back 'round yo' thumb. Yo' path ain't walked yet, boy. You gots a long, long ways to go. You is God's own dark angel, son, and you ain't goan be free 'til he say you is."

She offered him the glass jar again. "Dere's blood and den dere's blood. You can do dis, son. You walk yo' own path. A path of light an' dark."

Paul raised his head and stared at the jar. Then he reached out and took it from her. He shuddered. "To long life," he said. "Convey my appreciation to the spirits, Tamara." He drained it.

Joshua burst through the door.

"It's done. Over. God, Paul, my fault, all my fault."

Paul's body screamed to be out, to be on the hunt, but he was still human enough to feel the agony pouring out of his brother's soul.

For the first time since his own transformation, he touched Joshua. Controlling the new instinct to feed on hot and flowing blood, he pulled him into his arms and hugged him as hard as he'd hugged that long-ago night when Joshua's world had crashed around him and he'd sobbed on the backporch steps.

Paul looked over at Tamara and stared into her eyes. She stared back.

"You want him to carry dat, too, Paul? To wake every day knowing whut he done to Cain wuz done to you? To dream ever' night of you havin' a stake poundin' through yo' heart?"

Paul held Joshua for a few more moments. Then he pushed him gently away. He spread his arms and like a child with a new and dreadful toy, he cast himself into the dark.

Chapter Thirteen

Paul sat in silence. He'd talked himself out through the night, sharing that summer of 1888 with Ria. Reliving it. Something he hadn't done in all the long years of his existence. Then again, no living human except Ria Knight had ever tracked him to his mausoleum, watched him rise, and demanded all the details. He savored the warmth of her body through her jacket as she sat with his arms around her. An empty wine bottle and his grandmother's old crystal goblets stood beside them. From the look of the sky, he'd talked himself out none too soon.

Something wet dropped onto his hand. He raised it slightly, feeling the liquid run over the skin. He smiled and shifted her to one side to gain a view of her face.

"And what are these?" he asked, watching tears stream silently out of her eyes.

"You know very well what they are. God, how did you do it? And still stay sane?"

He shrugged. "Because I had to. Ria, it's almost dawn. You said you barely slept last night and now you've been up all night again."

"Won't kill me. I've done it before."

"And you haven't eaten a damn thing tonight, either." He eased her out of his arms. "Wait here."

"What—" she started. She stopped when she realized she was talking to thin air. She sat and watched the sky. How long till dawn? She watched the pre-dawn traffic speed north toward Atlanta and south towards Savannah. The cars and trucks seemed intrusive, out of place. She felt she'd been transported to 1888 and had been there for a very long time. She still hadn't come completely back.

"Here." Paul spoke quietly behind her and she started. Then she sniffed and smiled. Fresh coffee and fast food breakfast biscuits. She catapulted back into her own year.

"Sausage or steak?" Paul asked, digging into the bags.

She laughed.

"What?"

"You," she said. "Voodoo and bokors and mambos. Tamara and Cain and Blood Drinkers. Sausage or steak."

He grinned. "And you need to hurry up and decide, 'cause darlin', I'm goin' have to excuse myself in a red-hot hurry in about—" he glanced up at the sky, "twenty minutes, now."

"Steak."

He handed her the wrapped biscuit and flipped the lid of his coffee cup, drinking quickly. She did the same and almost spewed the liquid back out.

"Damn! That's hot!"

"Well, yes."

"You're drinkin' it like water!"

"I told you, hot and cold don't bother me too much."

They sat and ate in silence for a few minutes.

"Good cover story, you gettin' killed out west. The body shipped back home."

"Papa. He did himself proud. I always thought so."

"So he did recover?"

"He had a few more years."

"And Joshua?"

"We sent him north that winter. Boarding school in Boston."

"Why do you still use the mausoleum? I mean, wouldn't a house or an apartment be more comfortable?"

"Too dangerous. Neighbors, you know, unless you're way out in the country and even then, you have repair people, utility workers. Somebody, sometime, would notice they never saw me in the daytime. Not just seldom, but never. Besides, this is sort of home now."

"I guess so."

"I did toy with the idea of getting rid of the coffin, getting a regular bed or at least a mattress, but somehow I never got around to it."

Ria laughed. "It's a perverted sense of humor, and you know it!"

"Well, yes. Yes, it is."

They sat in silence again, both of them watching the sky.

"Paul? What now? You're not goin' to just disappear, are you? Never see me again?"

"I should."

"I don't see why."

"Don't you? You've known me for two days and you've lost two nights' sleep already. Real normal lifestyle there. Very healthy."

"There's a reason I saw you, your past in the Orange Street house. So I'd know you when I did see you. I was *meant* to, Paul."

"C'mon. I'll walk you to your car. I don't have long." He stood and offered his hand. They moved back up the hill, through the old markers.

Paul stopped at the short wall and spotted her car in front of the gate guarding a back entrance to the cemetery, the least observable place Ria could think of to park.

"Dangerous place to park all night, don't you think?"

"Didn't want to leave it in the cemetery grounds. I don't think any patrol cars tour through it at night but I wasn't sure."

Ria started to jump up on the ledge and Paul stopped her.

"Wait."

He lifted her up easily and sat her on her perch.

"Now hold on." He disappeared and reappeared almost instantaneously on the outside of the wall and held his hands up to her.

"I got to admit, that does take some getting used to."

Paul smiled.

"Now, get on home," he said. "I have to get back. Maybe five minute to sunrise."

"Paul, wait! You never answered me. Will you come? Tonight? My house? I mean your house? "

"Ria, you've got to sleep."

"I'll take a nap this afternoon, I don't have much on the calendar today. And I'll sleep some tonight. I promise. You'd have called me again if I hadn't found you, wouldn't you?"

"Yes," he admitted. "Knowing I shouldn't, I'd have called you. But then I was a man passing through town who'd be leaving in a month or so. There's no point in even trying to pretend tonight hasn't changed things and you know it."

"Don't kid yourself, buddy. If I'd never known Paul Devlin existed, Paul Everett would *never* have been a casual thing for me, not after the first sentence or two in that book store. And you know it. You felt it too, I know you did. Now, will you come?"

"I don't know. I'll have to think about it."

"Oh! That thing about having to be invited—"

"Is pretty much a crock, actually. I can go anywhere. As long as I know where I'm going. I can't just decide to show up somewhere if I have no idea how to get there."

"Then you shouldn't have any problems. It's your house, after all."

"I'll think about it."

That was the best she was going to get, and she knew it. This might be the last time she'd see him. She moved into his arms and raised her face. He kissed her forehead.

She pulled his head down and gently grazed his lips with her own.

"No, don't."

He was afraid to kiss, frightened of the sharpness of his incisors.

"You won't hurt me, Paul. You know you won't." She raised her face again and he did kiss her, gently at first and then, gaining confidence, more deeply.

The old legends raced through her mind. The wicked incisors, the fetid odor of the vampire's mouth. He tasted of new coffee and fresh biscuits, the hot, sage spice of sausage. The trace smell-taste reminded her of sunup, country mornings, open pastures. Paul hadn't seen sunrise in over a hundred years. He'd never see it again. And the sun was close.

"Go," she said. "Tonight. Please."

"No promises."

"There'd be lots of fringe benefits. I'd let you use my shower and you wouldn't have to borrow empty hotel rooms anymore," she offered.

He laughed. "That is an advantage I hadn't considered," he said thoughtfully. Then he grinned and disappeared.

* * *

Paul materialized directly in front of the small chest. His wife Chloe, the love of his human life, smiled at him from her picture. He lifted it and smiled back. Then he frowned. Ria Knight. Lord God, what to do, what to do?

Of course he'd known she was different the minute he'd seen her. Chloe'd been a lightning bolt from above when he'd come home from medical school in Edinburgh, Scotland. Ria? Growling thunder, building to the crescendo of a sonic boom with every moment he spent in her company. And now she'd tracked him, by God, with unerring instinct and steely determination.

All he could offer were hours of darkness. Ria needed sunlight, a man to court her over open picnic baskets in sunny meadows, exchange vows with her under a garden bower. Instead, she'd met him.

He'd made his own peace with destiny. Good books, an occasional good meal, just for the sheer pleasure of the taste of it, a night spent in the back of a dark theater watching the huge screen, or mingling with the crowds at the malls. He poured over medical journals and hovered invisibly in the emergency rooms and corridors of the local hospitals, still practicing pseudo-medicine of a sort. He'd made himself forget what life was like with ... *the one*. He'd come to terms with who and what he was.

And now another woman was ... *the one*. Her fascination wouldn't last, it couldn't. Sometime, somewhere in the future, she'd meet a man to walk beside her in the sunlight. If that didn't happen, before he ruined her life completely, he'd erase himself from her memory. Very easily. The mesmerizing stare of the vampire wasn't legend. It was truth.

But for a little while, a few weeks, a few months, even a year, maybe, couldn't he have—whatever he could have? He looked at Chloe again and raised his head. His senses warned him as energy drained away. Sunrise.

He gently tugged off the ring Chloe'd placed on his finger over a hundred years ago and laid it on the chest beside her picture. With his last remaining strength of night, he fell onto the satin of his coffin. He slept.

* * *

Ria moved through the day mechanically and took a nap during the three open hours on her afternoon calendar. She watched night approach through her windows and paced the length of her living room. Would he come? And if he did, what then?

* * *

Paul rose with the early moon and swung his legs out of the coffin. He moved to the chest of drawers and stared at Chloe's picture. He changed into fresh clothes. Then he picked up his wedding ring and put it back on his finger. He couldn't share Ria's life for any time, no matter how short. Insanity to think so.

He gave himself a mental push and materialized on the banks of the river where he'd relived the summer of 1888 with Ria and watched the cars pass by on the interstate.

* * *

In neighboring, more modern Riverside Hills Cemetery, another entity possessed of Paul Devlin's powers also woke.

No fool, Cain recognized the safety inherent in taking up residence in a cemetery mausoleum. It was much nicer than the cave he'd accidently been resurrected in out by Stone Creek Swamp. A lot dryer, too. The folks who'd spread the legends about the dampness of the tomb should try a stint in a swamp cave. However, he didn't have the advantage of a specially designed structure complete with secret living quarters such as Paul Devlin had. Then again, he had no need for books or radios and wasn't particular about changing his clothes all that frequently. He'd simply materialized within the walls of one of the larger mausoleums and ripped the top off the coffin containing the earthly remains of Nathan Wilkerson, 1892-1956. Those remains now sprawled unceremoniously on the concrete slab floor. Ethel Wilkerson, who'd never in her life known any man except her husband, still slept comfortably in her own

226

coffin. She'd have been horrified to know she was sharing her bedroom with another man.

Cain yawned. His stomach didn't rumble exactly; rather, his whole body vibrated with the new hunger that had overtaken him immediately in this second life. Blood hunger. Time to hunt. He cast out into the dark, intending to cross the river to the woods. Something different. What? He stopped flight and hovered a moment. Something else. A moving life form, human in shape. Cain turned his swirling essence to the right, moving over the grounds of Riverside Hills and out across the boundaries of Rose Arbor. He hovered over the seated figure gazing out over the river at the vehicles passing by on I-75.

Cain had difficulty pulling himself together again, quite literally, in his excitement but finally managed. He materialized behind some cedar trees several hundred feet to the figure's left. Could it possibly be? The man who'd banished him to that dark cave all those years ago? Though he hadn't been just a man then and wasn't just a man now, no more than Cain was. No mere man could ever have defeated Cain at the peak of his power all those years ago. Then Paul moved his head, giving a clear silhouette of his profile. His hair gleamed, mingled gold and silver, under the moonbeams.

Him. It was him. Cain smiled. The dark gods were with him.

* * *

Ria paced restlessly across her living room floor. She'd paced for hours. It was almost midnight. He wasn't coming. She could go to him, of course. But she wouldn't. If any man, ever, had earned the right to his own peace, it was Paul Devlin. She'd never see him again. She didn't even feel the tears running down her cheeks.

* * *

Paul sat quietly by the river. His thoughts moved as restlessly as Ria's feet. If he hadn't been re-living the feel of Ria's head against his shoulder, maybe he'd have sensed the dark presence watching and waiting with the patience of a giant snake. But maybe not.

He rose abruptly and walked swiftly back to his own mausoleum, disappearing behind the door. Cain strained his senses and felt Paul's swirling essence emerge from the structure's roof and turn toward town. He followed and hovered outside over a big house on one of the city's older streets. The enemy was within.

* * *

Paul stood in the glow of the nightlight in Ria's living room. The mantle clock sounded one a.m. in soft chimes. He glanced around the room, his vision needing no extra lighting. The room looked just like her. Full of rich, soft color. Shelves of books ran from floor to ceiling on one whole wall. Feminine but not frilly, elegant but not sparse. He breathed in her scent. Lemony. Like sunlight. The open door led to the bedroom. He walked over on cat's feet and stood in the doorframe, watching her sleep.

She moved in and out of restless dreams, tossing and turning. She hadn't wanted to sleep but the last two nights had finally caught up to her. She'd realized by midnight he wasn't coming. She gave in to her drooping eyelids and sought her bed. Maybe in sleep she'd forget she'd found the man who'd haunted her these past months. And that she'd lost him after two nights.

He moved forward and stood beside the bed. Her hair pooled in dark shadows over the pillowslip and her eyelids fluttered. Dream sleep, he thought, and hoped her dreams were happy. He wanted to touch her but he didn't.

228

He'd spent the entire night swinging like a pendulum from one resolution to the other. He was back on the opposite side of the swinging arc that had finally sent him flying to her through the night. He backed away, both relieved and disappointed she slept. Her eyes flew open. She spoke as he began the process of disincorporation.

"I thought you weren't coming."

He halted the process and moved a step closer.

"I didn't think I was, either."

"But you did."

She sat up and without thinking, raised her hand and ran her fingers through her sleep-tousled hair. The strands flowed like liquid darkness in the shadows.

"Yes. I did."

She reached and took his hand in both of hers. He let the gentle pressure of the tug pull him nearer. On the wall, his shadow followed him. Ria's fingers caressed his hand and her lips curved in a slight smile as they moved over his fingers.

"Your ring's gone," she said softly.

"Someone gave me a reason to take it off."

The shadow of her arms raised toward him. The shadow of his arms moved downward.

Shadows and bodies merged.

The bricks and boards of the house smiled as it listened. The rhythms of love, the whispers and low laughter and sighs of lovers had been gone too long from these rooms. And now the master of the house was home.

Outside, above the roof, Cain swirled and caught the sounds. He swooped closer and passed through the ceiling, hovering in the corner of the bedroom. His old nemesis had a new love. Oh, the dark gods were *so* good! Cain laughed to himself, endless possibilities running swiftly through his brain. Retribution wouldn't be swift. But it would be terrible.

The first few nights were theirs alone. Neither had any need for the outside world. They talked and laughed and watched old movies. They touched and kissed and made love, and when Ria succumbed to human limitations and fell asleep in his arms, Paul held her and watched as she slept. Ria sensed his great restraint when he held her.

"I don't break, you know," she said, lying on her side against him with her head on his shoulder and his muscled thigh clasped tightly between her own.

"I could break you, Ria. I could break you into pieces without even trying. And all it'd take to do it is to forget for just a second that I can."

She never commented on his gentleness again. She just savored his hard muscles and the strength of his body, eternally that of a thirty year old man at the height of his physical perfection. A body conditioned by hours in the saddle and miles of walking. A body that perpetually wore the light tan of a summer more than a century gone.

"Paul?"

"Um?"

"When we do start to go out, when you start to meet my friends, are you Paul Everett or Paul Devlin?"

"Everett."

"Why? There's absolutely no chance there's anybody around now that'd remember the name."

"I'm used to it. And besides, Paul Devlin's dead. Part of him died with Chloe and most of the rest died in August of 1888. And what little bit was left died—"

He broke off abruptly.

"You never ate anything tonight," he said lightly. "Let's raid the kitchen. Aren't you hungry?"

"The rest of him died when?"

"A long time ago. Let's see what's in your refrigerator, if anything is. Don't you ever cook?"

"Not if I can help it," Ria said, but she swung off the bed and slipped on her robe.

They often put together simple meals in Ria's newly remodeled kitchen. When she didn't have a necessary ingredient, which was pretty often, Paul would sigh in mock exasperation and disappear, returning in ten or twenty minutes from one of the local stores.

Handy as that skill was, a thought occurred to Ria.

"You don't know how to drive, do you?"

"I couldn't figure out how to add a garage to the mausoleum."

"Smartass. Would you like to learn? You never know when it might come in handy."

"I'd love to."

They spent hours on the back country highways that stretched across Bibb and Jones Counties, moving south to Twiggs County and north up to Monroe County, and west over into Houston County. In just a few nights, Paul handled the classic Mustang's gears as easily as he'd handled his high-strung black stallion, Cyclone.

October headed into November and the holiday season neared. It was time to move out as a couple into Ria's circle of friends.

"And how are you goin' to explain me?" Paul asked.

"Same way you explained yourself to me. You're a reporter taking a sabbatical to write a book. Even though the Mobile Reporter doesn't exist. Mobile's paper is the Press-Register, so you might wanta make a mental note."

"You knew that the first night we met?"

"Nope. But I looked it up to check your cover story the next day. And to see if they had a reporter named Paul Everett. Guess what? They didn't."

"And the moral to that story is, always check your facts before you talk to a lawyer."

"And don't you forget it. You're actually nervous, aren't you?"

"Been a long time since I've seen the same group of people on a regular basis. Suppose they notice—something?"

"Like I'm madly in love? That'll surprise some folks, yeah. Think they had a pool going on when I'd fall for a guy, actually. Most folks were bettin' on when hell froze over."

Paul didn't need to worry. His southern charm hadn't faded over the years. He wowed them all, up to and including Johnny Bishop, Ria's life-long best friend, virtual brother, law partner and co-owner of the house who had his own apartment across from Ria's. Maybe, if Paul hadn't been in love for the first time in over a century, he'd have noticed the fluttering presence tracking them most evenings. Maybe, if Ria hadn't been in love for the first time in her life, her legally trained brain would have noticed the old clunker following behind them on other evenings. But they were and they didn't.

By the second week of November Paul had met almost everyone of importance in Ria's life. With one notable exception.

"I think I've met about everybody you know, darlin'. 'Cept your parents. You ashamed of me, or do I smell bad, or do you just not get along with 'em?"

Ria laughed.

"Well, you do get embarrassing when you start drooling over people's necks the way you do."

"I haven't done that since Halloween!" He curled his lips and his incisors, never noticeable unless he chose to show them, gleamed sharply.

Ria goosed him in the side.

"Cut that out!"

"So why don't you want me to meet your parents?"

"It's not that I don't want you to meet them, it's just—well, my parents are weird for parents."

"Good weird or bad weird?"

"Oh, good weird, definitely."

"Well, that explains it."

"No, what I mean is, they don't hover over me very much, they don't plan their activities around me, they don't issue notices for command performances. Daddy believes you do as much harm or good to a child as you're going to do by the time a kid's 12, you need to stop trying by the time they're 18, and you need to let 'em go if you want to keep 'em. And Daddy's schedule's real hectic and Mom's real social and has lots of clubs and volunteer stuff so when I see them it's usually for lunch and not usually together. You're sort of not available to do lunch, you know."

"True. What's your father do, anyway? You've never said. Is he an attorney, too?"

"Oh, God forbid! He's way too blunt for that, he'd stay in contempt of court all the time. No, he's a doctor. I never told you that?"

"No, you didn't. Then I've probably seen him somewhere, I used to hang around in the hospitals a good bit before I got the free shower offer."

"I swear, you love that shower more than me."

"No way, darlin', but there's no point in not taking advantage of—Knight!" Paul broke off suddenly as realization dawned. "Charlie Knight?"

"Yeah, that's my Daddy. "

"Of course. Damn, you look a lot like him."

"So I'm told. Often. You've seen him then?"

"God, yes. Neurosurgeon. Gets called in a lot for emergency head traumas, car accidents, things that can't wait for morning or I wouldn't get to see."

"That's my daddy, all right. I take it you're a fan of his technique?"

"Past that. He's past good, he's brilliant. What I'd have given to be able to do what he does."

"If you'd had the current training, you could've. Lots of that is just modern science, you know. And equipment."

"Not all of it. He's a natural. He's a healer. He was born to be a doctor."

"Seems I've heard that said about him a time or two, yeah. Okay, I'll call Mom but for God's sakes don't tell him you're a groupie. Be sort of hard to explain how you've been watching."

* * *

Ria never got a chance to call her mother. She and Paul ran into her Dad's practice partner and his wife, Don and Joyce Billings, while in the movie line at AmStar Theaters. Ria could actually feel Joyce running her eyes up and down Paul's long frame.

"Well, I waited too long on that one," she whispered to Paul as they settled into their seats.

"What?"

"Joyce Billings is probably texting Mom a blow-by-blow description of you up to and including the shade of your hair and an estimate of your height and weight as we speak."

"Then why don't we step out of the movie and go drop by your parents now?"

"Are you kiddin' me? I've been waiting for this movie to hit the screens! I'll call her in the morning, nothing's goin' to change the fact Joyce saw you before she did, no reason to deprive her of this opportunity to fuss at me. It'll be fine, lean back and enjoy."

* * *

She was just about to punch in her mother's speed dial number the next morning when Liz Knight knocked perfunctorily on her office door and sat down with a frown.

"Really, Ria!" she exclaimed, settling herself into one of Ria's client chairs. "I don't expect you to give me a copy of your social calendar but it would have been nice to meet your new boyfriend before Joyce Billings did, of all people!"

No love was lost between the wives of the two doctors who formed Macon Neurology, P.C. Liz Knight was as classy as a Rolls Royce, Joyce Billings as ostentatious as a pink Cadillac with chrome wheels. The two just didn't mix well.

Ria groaned. "I'm sorry about Joyce, Mom, really. I was just callin' you now."

"But not sorry for not telling me about this new development in your love life, I don't suppose?" Liz raised her eyebrow but smiled.

"You and Daddy stay so busy, Mom. I just hadn't gotten around to introducing you yet. You didn't have to rush down here to call me on the carpet, either, you could have called."

"I did not rush down to call you on the carpet," her mother sniffed. "I happen to have an early morning Executive Board Meeting of the Friends of the Library so I just stopped in to ask you why everybody in town, including Joyce Billings, has met your new boyfriend except Daddy and me."

"Oh, c'mon, Mom! Everybody in town hasn't met him."

"Well, according to Joyce, you've been an item for the past three months and just can't keep your hands off each other."

"Joyce says? You've never believed one word Joyce Billings ever said and you're starting now? You make it sound like we were making love on one of the movie chairs, Miss I-fell-head-over-heels-in-love-with a man 15 years older than me and married him in two months!" Her mother and father's story was legendary in the annals of family history. Both of Ria's maternal grandparents had nearly had heart attacks.

Her mother laughed. "Well, making love wouldn't be terribly uncomfortable in the new reclining movie chairs, maybe Daddy and I should give it a shot. And yes, I'd do it all over again, too! And anyway, he was a doctor! Thought your grandmother was really goin' to explode when I reminded her she always wanted her girls to marry *doctors!*"

"Thanks, Mom, I could have gone all day without that image in my head! You're not upset, you've just been messin' with me, haven't you?"

"Mostly. You know Daddy and I have always respected your privacy. Most of the time, anyway. But we'd really like to meet him."

"How 'bout I bring him to dinner tonight? Y'all goin' to be home?"

"Great. What should I fix?"

"Like it matters? You've never cooked a bad meal in your life! Why do you think all the kids were always at our house when I was in high school?"

"Because you were a popular girl, of course!"

"*Duh.* That and your pizza. And burgers. And fries. And Buffalo wings."

"Not any of that for an introductory dinner, though. I'll stop in and get a nice roast to slow-cook all afternoon. That'll work. Almost late, darlin', got to go! See you tonight!" Her mother bounced up and out. Ria called after her.

"Mom!"

"What, sweetie?"

"I want to be just like you when I grow up."

"Try real hard not to grow up, baby. Daddy and I never have. Being grown-up's not near as much fun."

* * *

Ria made certain to be showered and dressed before Paul arrived. They'd never make it on time if he found her in the shower. She was inserting her earrings when she saw him behind her in the mirror.

"Good *eveennning*." He kissed the top of her head. "I take it we're going out?"

"Good *eveennning*, Bela Lugosi. How nice of you to visit. If you want a shower, make it quick."

"Not as much fun without you. Do I smell?"

236

"Like the crypt."

"And where are we so obviously going?"

"My folks. Command performance."

"Thought you didn't have command performances."

"Yeah, well, Joyce Billings, the lady we ran into last night—"

"Of course. Was your Mom upset you hadn't told her?"

"Mom thoroughly enjoyed the opportunity to mess with me a little bit and no, she really wasn't upset. But she does want to meet you and I figured tonight was as good as any. So if you do want to shower and change, hurry up." A good portion of Paul's wardrobe now resided in Ria's closet.

"Do I really smell?"

"Like April Fresh Downy. Your clothes always did, even before you started washing them here. Always loved that about you, a vampire that stops to think about fabric softener."

"Then hand me my most masculine smelling aftershave and I'll be right with you."

* * *

Ria pulled up in her parents' driveway at precisely seven p.m.

"Ready?"

"As I'll ever be. My experience with parents—"

"I've seen your mother-in-law," Ria said. "The house playbacks before I met you, remember? Anything's a step up."

Charles Knight threw the door open while they were still walking up and pulled her into an exuberant hug.

"Your mother was pretty put out with you, young lady!" He offered his hand to Paul. "Pleased to meet you, young man. Charlie Knight."

Paul shook.

237

"Paul Everett, Dr. Knight. I apologize for not insisting that Ria introduce us sooner. We didn't mean to cause a fuss."

"Oh, Liz enjoys fussin'. C'mon in the house." Dr. Knight knew this was no casual relationship. Ria could feel it. They'd always had a sixth sense between them.

"Okay, Liz, they're here. Come inspect!"

Liz bustled out of her kitchen, cheeks flushed from the heat of the oven. Liz had aged well, which is to say, scarcely at all, and occasionally strangers took the mother and daughter for sisters.

"So this is where you get your good looks!"

Ria grinned. Paul had learned the art of social byplay in a more gracious era.

"Well, thank you, Paul," said Ria's father. "I appreciate that."

Liz punched his shoulder. Ria looked like both her parents but her coloring did make her resemblance to her father more pronounced.

"And your sense of humor," said Paul, and Charles Knight laughed.

"Call it what it is, Paul. You mean her warped sense of humor. And that's gotten her into a lot of trouble over the years, too, right along with her father," Liz said. "Dinner's on the table."

"Smells great, Mom," Ria said, and moved toward the dining room. "C'mon, Paul."

Dr. Knight's cell phone rang as they sat down.

"You aren't on call are you, Charlie?" Liz's tone left no doubt she considered that a statement, not a question.

"Not officially," he said. "'Scuse me a minute, folks." He went out into the hall and came back in short order.

"Liz, throw some slices of roast in a couple of those biscuits for me please, so I can eat on the way." He leaned over Ria's chair and kissed the top of her head. "Sorry to do this, baby, but—"

"Duty calls. What's up, Daddy?"

"Charlie, tonight?" Liz protested.

"I know, but that was Kyle Herrington on the phone, car crash just came in, six year old with massive head trauma, can't wait, we got to move."

"There are other neurosurgeons in this town, you know."

Even while protesting, Liz moved around the table, splitting biscuits and filling them with thick slices of roast.

"But they aren't Daddy. If I was six years old and lying there, you'd want—"

"I know, I know!"

"Sorry to miss the get-together, Paul."

"There'll be other times, Dr. Knight."

Paul looked longingly after him as he left. Ria knew he missed his own past interrupted dinners.

"Paul, I'm sorry this happened the first time we get to meet you," Liz apologized.

"I think it's wonderful. To know you're going out into the night to save a child's life, save her mind, knowing you have the skill to do that."

Ria slipped her hand surreptitiously under the table and rested in on his knee in sympathy, feeling Paul's envy.

They finished dinner and Paul spent the next two hours wooing Ria's mother while she showed him Ria's childhood through the family albums.

"You ought to be illegal," she observed, as they drove back to the Orange Street house. "And why on earth did Mom think you'd want to look at my old baby pictures?"

"Because I did. Great night, darlin'. I had fun. Didn't you?"

"Yeah. Yeah, I did."

Chapter Fourteen

Ria woke abruptly. A ringing phone, shrill and insistent. She glanced at the pillow beside her. Paul was gone but the pillow still showed the indention of his head. Past sunrise, then, but not by much. She looked at the alarm clock as she grabbed the phone. Seven a.m. On a Saturday morning. Have mercy. She fumbled the receiver when she picked it up.

"Oh hell! I woke you up, didn't I, baby?"

Ria sat straight up.

"Daddy, what's the matter? Did you lose your little girl?" Dr. Knight was a professional. Professionals had to maintain detachment. Her father sucked at it, though. When he lost a patient, especially a child, it took him awhile to get his balance back. Time with Ria always seemed to help the balance return and had since her earliest memories.

"No, I didn't. Got a long way to go, but I think she'll be just fine."

"Oh, I'm so glad."

"Yeah, me too. And since your mother's just left to drive up to Atlanta and go shopping with your Aunt Margaret, God help us all, I thought I'd see if you'd like to have breakfast with your old man."

"You've been up all night?"

"Goes with the territory, baby."

"Then come straight here and I'll fix you breakfast."

"I don't want to intrude."

"Daddy! You don't intrude."

"Listen, you know what I mean. I'm not blind and I'm not stupid. So if you've still got a house guest from last night, I don't want to make either of you uncomfortable. I won't come over and I don't want you hauling him up and shoving him out the door on my account. Must be tireder than I thought, should've thought of it before I called but I just didn't."

"Paul's not here, Daddy, really. So c'mon over."

"You're sure?"

"Positive."

"Be there in a few."

Ria pulled on her favorite robe and went to her kitchen. She plugged the waffle iron in to heat, and mixed a batch of batter. She heard a low buzz and her father's voice came over the intercom system they'd installed during the remodeling process as the easiest way to handle visitors since the law offices were downstairs.

"Baby?"

"Come on up, Daddy."

She hit the release button for the front door lock and went out to the stairs to meet him. He came inside and stopped. Immediately. Ria heard voices. Paul's, mingled with Joshua's. *Shit.* The house was in replay mode. It hadn't done that since she'd met Paul. Then she remembered nobody could see the replays but her, so it was nothing to worry about. She started down the steps.

"Hi, Daddy!" She kissed his cheek and tugged at his arm.

He stared at her office door. She knew it was closed, but it was open in the playback. Paul stood in the frame, wearing the high-topped boots and tight-legged britches of the 1880s.

"Josh! I need you to run down to the drugstore. Try Hogue's first. They don't have it, check at Goodwyn's. Give 'em this."

"Yes, suh."

"Tell him I got somebody waitin'."

Ria looked at her father. His eyes widened, his mouth opened a bit. *Oh, dear God.* No one else ever saw the replays. He couldn't be seeing anything. Could he? The sooner she got him upstairs, the better.

"We're having waffles," she said, and tugged his arm again. He shook his head slightly and she held her breath. If he really was seeing Paul and Joshua, if he asked, how on earth was she going to explain? He moved with her and went on upstairs.

"I'm so glad you called me," she said, leading him into the kitchen.

"Sorry I woke you this morning, baby."

"That's all right. Don't see enough of you," Ria said, pouring the batter and closing the lid.

"No, we don't, busy professionals that we are and all. Even when we try, something always seems to happen. Sorry 'bout last night too, sugar."

"Don't be silly."

"So since your mother's gone, I thought maybe this morning'd be a good chance to visit. You know, just you and me."

The light went out on the waffle iron and Ria deftly transferred the golden waffle to a plate and sat it in front of her father next to the syrup and butter.

"You've improved, baby," said her father approvingly, as he took a bite of his waffle. "These taste like your mother's."

"It's the buttermilk. Paul taught me. He was horrified I was using plain two percent milk. So what's up?"

"Oh, I thought maybe we'd chat about family history. 'Bout me, your mother, your family. When you start to realize your little girl's big enough to start her own family, makes you think about such things. Don't know why I never thought about it before, guess it's 'cause I've never seen you look at anybody the way you look at Paul."

Ria poured the batter for her own waffle before turning around.

"I don't think there's much I don't know about you and Mom, Daddy."

"Now that's the conceit of the young if ever I heard it. We were around a good while 'fore you were ever thought about, you know."

"Well, yes, I guess so."

"And I guess you do know all about your mother's family. But you don't know beans about mine, now do you?"

Ria turned around to check the waffle light.

"No, now that you mention it, I don't guess I do. You've never told me much except that you worked a lot of your own way through college and medical school. It's like as far as you're concerned, your life started with Mom."

"To a certain extent it did. My background didn't exactly jive with your mother's. Sometimes I think your mother and me are living proof of fate. No other explanation. Me being fifteen years older than her and not movin' in her social circles at all, well, it's just a miracle we ever met. You know?"

"I knew you weren't from one of the old rich families like Mom's. So what? Never bothered Mom. Sure as heck never bothered me."

"Yeah, but did you ever wonder?"

"Yes sir. I even asked you about it a few times when I was little but you never answered. Sidetracked me, in fact. It's the only time in my life I ever remember you doing that. So I dropped it."

Ria opened the iron, placed her own waffle on a plate and joined her father at the small table.

"So why are you talking about it now?"

"Well, maybe I think it's time you knew about it."

"Wait a minute. The time's never come before? Because you've never thought I was serious about anybody and now you do? Does insanity run in your family, or some congenital birth defect, or something you think I need to know if I'm planning a family? Because I have to tell you, we're not at that stage yet. And is that why I'm an only child? Always wondered about that."

Ria spoke lightly as she reached for the syrup, but her heart squeezed. There'd never be a family with Paul Devlin, no matter how much she wanted one. And nothing could change that.

"Heredity's a funny thing. Some folks think you look like your mother, and most of 'em think you look like me. And you do. But nobody didn't know her would ever realize just how much you look like my mother."

"I do?"

"Oh, yes. Coloring and all."

"But my coloring's like yours." Ria loved her dramatic coloring. It gave her that exotic air she cultivated shamelessly. Her father looked like a descendant of Spanish hidalgos. Probably what first caught her mother's eye. It sure as hell would've caught Ria's.

"Yeah, it is. I'm sorry you never knew your grandmother, Ria. She was—well, I am what I am because of her. Very determined lady. 'You'll be somebody, Charlie. No matter what I have to do to make sure of it. I'm not my mother,' she'd say. 'You come first. No matter what I have to do, you come first.' She didn't like her own mother too much, always felt she let her down, that she could have done better by her, but circumstances being what they were, I don't sit in judgment. Not on my mother, not on my grandmother. 'Cause for sure, my grandmother rowed a hard row."

Ria put down her fork. Some revelation of great magnitude was coming. She felt it. She sat and waited.

"See," he continued, "my mother, she was alone in the world. Used what she had to get by in it. And what she mostly had was looks. Beautiful woman, my mother. Missed her time. In another place, another era, she'd have been a rich woman. Didn't do too badly as it was, but in say, the late 1800s, early 1900s, New Orleans, she'd have been a legend."

Ria stared. Her grandmother used what she had. Her looks. New Orleans. Late 1800s. Images of the

French Quarter, exclusive houses catering to gentlemen of means.

"Daddy—"

"Even the name, you see. I don't really know what my father's name was. Don't know who he was. If she knew, she never told me. Knight's an example of that warped sense of humor seems to run down the line from me to you. She thought it made a perfect stage name, as it were, seeing as how she was a lady of the—"

"Night." Ria finished softly. "Daddy, you are joking?"

"Baby, you don't joke about your mama being a prostitute."

Ria said nothing. She couldn't. She was too busy imagining the scene taking place within the walls of the huge Stanton two story mansion off Ingleside Avenue if her maternal grandfather had ever heard this story.

"Now, in my mother's defense," continued Dr. Knight, "women have used their bodies to survive for years. Lots of times, they had no choice about it. I sort of have a sympathetic view, you know. And I never saw that much difference between all the arranged marriages the so-called good families used to set up and prostitution. Now, my mother, she had the looks to marry money. And even in this day and age, you got girlfriends fell conveniently in love with money, don't you?"

Ria nodded.

"And my mother, I guess she'd have done the same if she could have, but she had this other little thing to deal with too. Made that a little difficult. Back then, anyway, wouldn't have been that big a deal now."

Ria's thoughts spun in a circle. New Orleans. The French Quarter. The dark and exotic Creole culture, the Quadroon Balls.

"Daddy—"

"Her mother was white, her father a mulatto. I don't know much about that, I don't think she did either. Or if she did, she preferred to forget it. Her mother worked in the textile mills, which means she was an old, old woman at a very young age and died way before she shoulda. My mother watched what it did to her, and she'd have done—well, I guess she did do—whatever she had to do to stay out of them. And to keep me out of them. I was a late life baby, you see, I'm sure she was as careful as she could be considering the times and circumstances, she never intended to have a child. She was real honest with me about that, when I was old enough for her to be, of course. Said when she knew she was pregnant in her forties that it had to be meant, that I was a gift from God. She always called me that. And she was determined that her professional life wasn't goin' to touch me, or any ancient family history come back to haunt me. So 'bout all I know about that family history is that her father, that would be my grandfather, was real well-educated, all things considered. A preacher, in fact. Ran sort of a mission church. And he met my grandmother when she ran away from her husband, which event shortened his life considerable. 'Pears her husband didn't take real kindly to a 'nigger' giving his wife sanctuary. This being round about the turn of the century, you know, guess maybe you can figure the rest of it out."

"Oh, my God," said Ria softly. The walls of the Stanton family home her mother grew up in wouldn't still be standing if her grandparents had any idea. "Mom knows all this though?"

"Hell, yes, all of it. Think I'd marry somebody wondering if they'd leave me if they knew where I came from? Though we had a mutual agreement might be best her side of the family didn't know any it. I didn't give a damn who knew personally, still don't, but they're your mother's people, she loves them. No sense looking for trouble."

"No sense at all. And surely you don't think Paul would care?"

"Not in the slightest. I liked him, baby. Liked him a lot."

"So why'd you decide, after all this time, to tell me now?"

"Well, I wouldn't have. Probably wouldn't have thought about it. It really doesn't have a lot of immediate significance to me, you know. And then I met Paul."

"And we just agreed it wouldn't matter two hoots in hell to him."

"Oh, I know! I just thought he'd find it real interestin'. Didn't your mother tell me he's a writer?"

"Yes, but I don't see what that's got to do with anything."

"And he's from out of town, right?"

"Yes, sir. Mobile."

"But I'd take a big bet his family's from here. Some of it, anyway."

"No, sir. They weren't."

"Sure about that?"

"He is. I asked him."

"Well, maybe he just hasn't stumbled on it yet. Lots of folks don't know much family history anymore. And if he didn't know the name, I don't reckon he'd connect."

"What are you talking about?"

"Knocked me for a loop when I first saw him. You notice me staring?"

"Well, yeah, but I thought you were just inspecting. Knocked you for a loop how?"

"'Cause just last week your mother got in one of her moods and was sorting out the old picture albums. You know, the *real* old pictures. Pretty much all of 'em from her family, of course, and it's been so long since I looked at 'em, I wouldn't have remembered or noticed—and anyway, I don't have but a couple and one of 'em is a group shot, what'd they call 'em? The tintype pictures, you know what I mean. Has a man in it named Paul Devlin. He was a doctor in town, back in the late 1800s. And I swear, your Paul is his exact double. So much so, I'd have sworn the minute I saw him he just had to have family connections somewhere."

Ria's eyes widened.

"And you have this picture why? Of this, who'd you say, Dr. Devlin? How do you know his name?"

"Because." Dr. Knight reached inside his jacket and pulled something out before he continued.

"Like I said, your mother'd just been reworking the real old pictures last week. And she had the albums out when I got home, guess she was showing Paul your baby pictures. Didn't get to the real old ones, I don't guess. Good thing, probably. Like I said, I don't know much about my mother's people and what she knew, she didn't like to talk about it. But she always saved this. Said it meant a lot to my grandmother, it was the only picture she had of my mother's father. I told you, Knight's a misnomer. Just a stage name. The name my mother grew up with was Devlin."

He held out his hand, showing an old, old photograph. Ria looked at the pictured group, the beautiful young woman, the laughing young man, the solemn younger boy. An unconventional grouping for the time period and she knew the date, just as she knew the people in the group.

"My grandfather as a young boy. I told you, remember? He was very well-educated for the time period and his coloring. His half-brother made sure of it. 'Bout the only thing I do know about my mother's family. That her father's name was Joshua Devlin and his half-brother's name was Paul."

Dr. Knight watched Ria closely. "Now, at first, when I saw your young man last night, I just thought, fancy that. Coincidence is really the damnedest thing. Boy has to be a Devlin descendant from somewhere down the white side of the line. This picture's real old and faded out some but the resemblance is just downright uncanny, don't you think? And I thought, seein' as how your mother said he was doing research for a novel, you both might get a real kick out of this."

Ria struggled to regain her equilibrium. She tried to speak but her voice stuck in her throat. She cleared it and tried again.

"Daddy, that's really thoughtful of you," she finally said, holding out her hand for the picture. "Can I keep this to show him tonight?"

"*Unh, unh, unh!*" said her father, holding the picture out of her reach. "Not so fast. Like I said, I really just thought y'all would get a kick out of it. But things have changed a little bit."

"They have? How?" Ria asked, remembering with sinking heart her father's face as he stared at Paul and Joshua before climbing her stairs. *Doomed,* she thought to herself. *I'm doomed.*

"Don't get cute, Ria. Just explain to me why, when I walk in your door I see Paul, who ain't supposed to be here in the first place, dressed in clothes nobody's worn in years, talkin' to the boy in this picture, who just happens to be my grandfather. *In exactly the same voice.*"

Doomed, she thought again. *We're doomed.* She didn't remember the last time she'd tried to lie to her father, mostly because it never worked. He always knew she was lying. It never occurred to her before that all fathers didn't know when their children were lying. For the first time, knowing now the blood of Joshua, of Sadie, of Tamara of the wondrous powers and the second sight flowed in their veins, she wondered if she and her father were somehow mentally linked.

"Sometimes the house, it—well, it shows things."

"You don't say. But why is it showing them?"

"The house used to be his. Dr. Devlin's, I mean. I looked it up."

"Oh, I see. Guess that explains why you acted like you'd never heard the name before. Johnny see stuff, too?"

"Good God, no!"

"Didn't think so. That kid could never even sit through a horror movie. How long you been seein' 'em?"

"Since right after we moved in."

"Passin' strange you meeting up with your Paul Everett right after moving into this house. Isn't it?"

"Yes, isn't it?" Ria agreed brightly.

"Ria, I said don't get cute. Talk to me, girl."

She bit her lip. "I can't."

"Think you might could later? After you talk to a certain individual, maybe?"

"Maybe."

"And when do you think that might be?"

"Tonight."

"You got your cell phone in your robe pocket. Know you do, always have it with you. You could call him."

"No. I can't."

"You can't, huh? Well, ain't that interestin'?" he asked thoughtfully. "I'll be home this evening, barring any emergencies. And your mother's spending the night in Atlanta with Aunt Margaret, why in God's name I don't know. I'd be real pleased to get a call." Dr. Knight stood up and headed for the door.

"Can I keep the picture, please?"

Dr. Knight handed it to her.

"Grab a nap if you can, Daddy," Ria said as she took it and kissed him good-by. "I'm not makin' any promises but it might be a real long night."

"But are you all right?"

"Top of the world. I promise."

"Well, that's what's important, after all," he said. "Do your best for the old man, though, might die of curiosity before too much longer." He threw his last words over his shoulder as he walked out.

* * *

Ria stood for a moment after her father left, her thoughts spinning wildly off into many-faceted tangents. The first thing to sort out was the relationship.

If Joshua was her father's grandfather, then he was her great-grandfather, and Paul would be her father's great-uncle, thereby making him her great-great uncle. No, that wasn't right, exactly, Paul and Joshua were half-brothers, so Paul would be her great-great half-uncle.

She sighed in relief. The Biblical taboos against incest were deeply ingrained and the thought was unsettling, but there were two generations between herself and Paul and it was a half-blood relationship at that, spanning over a century. Besides, nowhere else but in European nobility had families intermarried in modern times to a greater degree than the families of the American South. Marriages between varying degrees of cousins were commonplace up until World War II and still not unheard of. And besides, the real danger was to any offspring and might as well face it, a human and a vampire just weren't going to be parents.

Would he let her bring her father into this? How would he feel about it? She knew how she felt about it. Suddenly hopeful. Her father was way past being a good doctor. He was brilliant. And why not? He was the fourth doctor in five generations of Devlins. It was in his blood. He was born to be a doctor. And he knew lots of other brilliant doctors. Maybe, if Paul actually talked to him, there was something, some tests to run that could shed some light on Paul's medical condition without making him the center of a medical circus. She didn't dare hope for a cure, but maybe the condition could at least be mitigated.

She moved over to one of the couches and sat down, grabbed a pillow and hugged it to her. Paul had never told her what happened to Joshua and she'd never asked. But now he was her blood, her past. How had that blood, that mulatto blend of black and white, come to mingle with other white blood, trickling down through the years to its final repository in her veins?

But her father wouldn't be able to follow the continuation of the story without knowing the first part, always supposing Paul would even tell them the rest of the story. And the first part was long and complicated enough. She looked over at her laptop. If nothing else, putting that story into written form would keep her mind focused for the rest of the day until she could talk to Paul.

Still in her robe, she walked over to her desk, sat and raised the cover of the laptop. She was still there when daylight passed into dark.

* * *

She jumped when Paul's arms came around her from the back.

"Sorry. Thought you were used to me by now."

"Is it dark already?"

Fatigue showed under her eyes as she turned around. Ria supposed she'd gotten up and visited the bathroom occasionally, but she didn't remember. She knew she hadn't stopped to eat. Her neck and back muscles were screaming and her hands ached.

"Yes, it's dark. What's the matter? You got a case so hot you had to work on it all day? I take it you'd rather stay in tonight?"

Ria looked down at herself in surprise.

"Oh, Lord! I didn't even think—I never dressed."

"I don't mind."

"Don't joke," she said. She picked up the picture that was turned face down on her desk and stood up. "I've got something to show you."

"What?"

"This," she said, handing it to him. "Daddy brought it to me this morning. It's a picture of my great-grandfather."

Paul's eyes fixed on the group and widened. All color drained from his face. He reached out and took it from her.

"It's what?"

"It's a picture of my great-grandfather," Ria repeated. She'd expected an intense reaction, but not quite this intense. "Daddy brought it to me this morning."

Paul turned and sat down heavily on the couch. "Your what?" he asked again, and Ria, suddenly realizing the origin of that anxious look, roared.

"Oh, good God, Paul! Not you! Joshua!"

His breath expelled in audible relief and she roared again.

"Paul, you couldn't have possibly thought—you can't tell me you ever cheated on Chloe! I won't believe you!"

"Ria, I didn't marry Chloe until I was twenty-five!"

Still laughing, she sat down beside him and hugged him hard. She'd needed the comic relief.

"Sorry I gave you a heart attack. Even though it doesn't really beat."

"And so you should be," he said. He sat up straighter and inspected the portrait again. "But Joshua? I don't know if that's any better and I really don't know how—". He broke off and stared at her. "Oh. My. God." he exclaimed slowly.

"What?"

"I don't know why I never noticed, well, of course, I didn't see her but once or twice, but still—your eyes are dark and hers were blue, you're a lot taller and your complexion's darker—but your hair, your face, the shape of your mouth. Jesus, you're the spittin' image of Serena Wentworth! And I've been making love to my brother's—"

"*Whoa!* I knew you were goin' to freak on me! Your half-brother's great granddaughter. I already worked it all out. Big deal. Whoopee shit. Lots of time and lots of blood between the two of us, Paul. We're not even as close as second and third cousins, and you know down here they intermarried all the time! It doesn't change us. It just intensifies us. So straighten it up or I won't let you use my shower anymore and you'll have to go back to empty hotel rooms."

Paul gave a half-smile. "Well, some conveniences I'm willing to do without. And some I'm not."

"Thanks. My love life saved by a shower."

"I wasn't talking about the shower," he said, pulling her into his arms. "And I guess genetically speaking, we're probably just as distant as second or even third cousins. You say your father brought this to you?"

"Oh, yeah," Ria said, relaxing against him. "We had a real enlightening discussion."

"How enlightening?"

"Not that enlightening. Not yet, anyway. But Paul, please. We need to tell him."

"Ria—"

"No, just listen to me!" And Ria recounted her breakfast with her father.

"Oh, God! I should have checked on her, especially when I found out she didn't take the money, but I was so—"

Paul broke off and Ria didn't ask for explanations. He needed time to sort this out.

"My God! I let my brother's daughter—oh shit! Papa and Sadie's granddaughter! Grow up and run a whore house! They'd kill me!"

"Hate to tell you this, babe, but you're already dead. Technically speaking, that is."

"Oh, my God!"

In Paul's time, there'd been no greater shame to a good family than professional gamblers and whores. Give their druthers, they'd probably rather claim a murderer as family.

"Paul, it's done. A long time ago. You didn't know Joshua had a child, did you?"

"No. God, no. Don't you think I'd have made sure she was taken care of?"

"Of course you would. But you didn't know. And we're not talking about a child, actually, Paul, we're talking about my grandmother who was already in her grave before I was born. She made her way in life the best she could with what she had and I don't care if she was a prostitute, she loved my Daddy and I promise you, I know from this morning—he loved her and he never lacked for anything a child needed. And besides, if anything had been different, Daddy wouldn't be Daddy, and I wouldn't be me! I wouldn't even be here, I'd be somebody else altogether and I seriously doubt that anybody else could have tracked down the real Paul Devlin so you wouldn't be here, either. Well, not on this sofa, anyway."

"And you'd be better off if you'd never seen me."

"Don't say that!"

"Why not? It's the truth!"

"It's a crock of shit!" Ria exploded. "And I think we're having our first fight."

"We can't tell your father."

"Why not? You don't think he's entitled to know what happened to his own grandfather? What about me?"

"We can't tell your father about Joshua without telling him about me! And I'm sure he'll just be delighted to know his daughter's involved with a livin' dead man. I mean, I know if it were my daughter, I'd just be thrilled to death!"

"He already knows something's going on, Paul! I told you, he saw you! You and Joshua. There's your blood connection. Nobody but me and now Daddy has ever seen the house replay anything. He deserves to know. And besides, Paul, Daddy's a *doctor*! Do you understand what I'm tellin' you? And he knows other doctors, and maybe they could—"

"Put me in the middle of a research three-ring circus! And what do you think they'd find, Ria? *'Oh, it's just a little virus, we'll knock it right out'*!"

"Well, suppose that is all it is?"

"Ria, grow up! This is not a fairytale! Something like this, my whole genetic structure's mutated! Why do you think I've tried so hard to keep up? So I can hang a shingle on the door of the mausoleum? And the more research advances, the more certain it is—my whole DNA pattern's shot to shit!"

"They engineer the genetic structure now. Didn't you read that part?"

"No. They *play* with the DNA structure and they don't really know what they're doin' or the long-term consequences of it. They can't reconstruct one!"

"How the hell do you know?"

"They'd have a field day with me."

"Daddy wouldn't let that happen. He wouldn't bring in anybody who'd—"

"Ria! *No!*"

"His best friend from medical school is one of the head honchos at the Atlanta Center for Disease Control. Ever hear of the place?"

"One more time, Ria. This is not a fairytale."

"Suppose it could be? Sunlight, open pastures, picnics, rainbows. Makin' love in the daytime. With me. For the rest of our natural lives. I'm not worth the risk?"

Paul sighed heavily.

"You don't fight fair."

"I'm a lawyer, get used to it."

"I don't know if I can stand to tell it again," he finally said.

"You don't have to. I've spent all day telling it for you." Ria got up and walked over to her desk, picking up a thick sheaf of paper. "It's right here. The first part. And the rest of it, about Joshua, well, you'll have to tell me that."

"I absolutely *can't*, I won't, tell that story twice. I'll tell you and your father together. After your father reads this."

"Don't you want to look at it first? See what I said?"

"No. Call your father and then get dressed. I'll wait for you in the car. We'll go out or something while we wait for him to read it."

"Feel like a movie?"

"No. Something quiet. I just want to sit. Now call your father." He kissed the top of her head and dematerialized.

He answered on the first ring. It was probably the shortest conversation she'd ever had with her father in her life.

"Want to come over?"

"Be there in ten minutes," he said, and hung up. Her intercom buzzed in nine minutes flat.

"I'm glad I didn't get a call to bail you out of jail on a speedin' charge," she said dryly, as he walked in. She'd barely finished her quick shower and pulled on her jeans.

"I'm a doctor, remember? Medical emergency."

"Right."

"You by yourself?"

"Paul's waiting for me in the car. We'll be back in a few hours. After you've had a chance to read this." She picked up the thick stack and handed it to him. "Make yourself at home. Got some light beer in the refrigerator but you're probably going to want something stronger. I'll call you before we come back."

Dr. Knight flipped the folder open and glanced at the typed sheets.

"Paul's novel?"

"It's not a novel. It's his story but every word's true, so help me God. I started where I met him so you could sort of meet him with me. You read fast and it's not medical jargon so you ought to move along pretty quick. I'll see you in a couple of hours.

She walked out and Dr. Knight moved to an armchair and adjusted the lamp.

"Where to?" she asked Paul, getting into the car.

"I could not possibly care less."

"Well, this looks to be a real fun evening," she said, shifting into reverse and backing out of the garage.

* * *

257

The evening wasn't as bad as Ria feared. They ended up at a local seafood restaurant and ran into Dennis Billings and his girlfriend Lori in the lobby. Ria made the introductions, pleased at the chance meeting. She expected great things from him, now that he'd declared independence from Justin Dinardo. Justin was still out there, though, no one had seen him since he'd skipped bail. His disappearance worried her. Justin was dangerous. Dennis, however, was a different person, finally fulfilling the promise of the little boy who was the closest thing to a little brother she'd ever had. And Paul, who'd helped raise his little brother Joshua, had forgotten how much he enjoyed the company of teenagers.

"I'm so pleased to meet you, Miss Knight," Lori confided breathlessly when they were all seated. "Dennis talks about you so much."

"Thank you, Lori, but my name's Ria."

"Dennis, tell her," Lori prodded.

"Tell her what?"

"Men!" Lori exclaimed in exasperation, and Ria smiled. "Dennis made the honor roll last week, Ria."

"Dennis! I'm so proud!"

Dennis shrugged.

"I'm not. No excuse for not doing it before."

"Better late than never."

"But not good enough for what I want. I'll make up for it in college, though. But I might need to bug you to help me, Ria. Like you taught me mythology when I was little, remember?"

"Your favorite was always Hercules. So what great mission have you picked in life?"

"I want to go to law school. So I can help somebody like you helped me. And I'm goin' to make it through, too."

"Damn straight you will," Ria affirmed, feeling the stirrings of an emotion she recognized as surprisingly maternal. "By the time you get through, Johnny and I might even be able to afford an associate."

She called her father before pulling out of the parking lot.

"Should we come home?"

"Give me another hour."

"So you can have the men in white coats waiting for us?"

"Give me another hour."

"Yes, sir."

She clicked her phone closed and turned to Paul.

"Damn, I know he's finished. Must be rereading some of it." She shrugged. "Let's cruise a while then."

They drove slowly through the dark streets of Macon. An old, ragged car held together by threads of rust followed them, hanging two or three cars back. At the wheel of that car, stolen from the backstreets off Martin Luther King Boulevard, Justin Dinardo whistled cheerfully.

"Boy, shut up dat noise!" his companion ordered.

Justin complied immediately.

"Sorry," he offered. "It's just, I can't believe how lucky this is. I mean, you want him, I want her." No fool, Justin knew who'd masterminded traitor Dennis turning state's evidence. And Cain had certainly been descriptive regarding what he'd like to do to the man.

"Slow down some," Cain ordered. "Gettin' too close." Cain kept an eye on them frequently by hovering invisibly, of course, but he had to get some use of his new acolyte. In the main, Justin performed very well. Cain was satisfied with him and anyway, it wasn't like he'd had a lot of choices to pick from. Besides, that constant hovering took a lot of concentration.

"They ain't paying any attention."

"I say slow down. Ain't like we doan know where to find 'em."

"When?"

"When whut?"

"When are we going to find them?"

"Soon now. Real soon."

* * *

Finally, Ria pulled back into her garage.

"Well, it's now or never." She slammed the car door. "I wonder if he's made arrangements to check us into the psychiatric hospital yet."

Dr. Knight watched stone-faced from the couch as they walked in.

"Prove it," he said shortly.

Paul disappeared. Completely. Then he reappeared on the other side of the room and disappeared again. He materialized directly in front of Dr. Knight.

"Jesus Christ," Dr. Knight said flatly.

"No, I'm afraid he didn't have much to do with this," Paul said dryly.

"Well, all right, let's have the rest of it. I've always wondered how my granddaddy managed to get himself killed by an irate white man. And Ria?"

"Yes, Daddy?"

"You're right. I want something a hell of a lot stronger than beer. Fix me a drink, please."

She mixed drinks for everyone and settled onto her other couch facing her father. Paul paced restlessly around the room. She patted the seat beside her.

"Paul?"

He sat down and took her hand.

"I don't know how to start. How to begin. So much of it, you see, I don't even know firsthand, just from Sadie and Joshua. 'Cause I wasn't ever around in the daytime. And after all this time, it hurts like it happened yesterday. I just can't—how to—you have no idea how much I loved my brother."

"I think that's pretty obvious from the first part,"
Dr. Knight observed.

"No, not really, that doesn't even begin to explain
it. Because over the years, when he was a man, our
relationship changed. Completely. He didn't need me
anymore, not really, but I needed him. He was my
connection, you see. With normal life. He was my best
friend. He lived the rest of his life trying to atone for
that summer of 1888. And no man was *ever* more truly
his brother's keeper."

Chapter Fifteen

Joshua Devlin had begun the summer of 1888 as a boy but had emerged as a man. What doesn't kill us makes us stronger and the young man striding briskly across the grounds of Rose Arbor Cemetery in the summer dusk of June 18, 1892 was a strong man.

His skin still glowed with the creaminess of *café au lait*. His eyes were still large and lustrous. He was still a mulatto, a mixture of his white father, Dr. Everett Devlin, and his black mother, Sadie. In his maturity, he'd finally realized how absolutely beyond remarkable both his parents were. The resentment of his youth for his mixed heritage and the confusing social limbo it cast him into had long passed. His height stopped an inch short of six feet, and his slender frame had expanded and filled out with manhood. Still, he'd never be heavy. His name was Joshua Devlin, and he was home. He increased his stride and laughed suddenly at the stray thought wandering across his mind.

A nigger in a cemetery at sunset! What would the white folks say?

The intense formal education his brother had begun upon his return from medical school in Scotland was now well-supplemented by the four years Joshua had spent in Boston. At this point in his life, even his thought patterns followed white idiom and he had to make a conscious effort to shift back into the flowing, hybrid lilt between white and black speech used by his mother. For a few days, at least. Until his personal master plan could be implemented.

He approached the doors of the large marble structure, so much larger than any other that stood in the bounds of the cemetery, and glanced swiftly around. No one. He opened the door and stepped in. He frowned.

The top of the coffin was open. Again. Paul didn't appreciate the protective covering the casket offered. Well, no matter. He was home for good now. He'd take care of his brother whether Paul wanted him to or not.

Paul's hand twitched and Joshua moved closer.

"Joshua!"

Paul stood and pulled his little brother into a bear hug.

"Oh, it's good to be home, Paul!"

"I remember the feeling. At least you're not heading out for school again like I did, all the way to Europe."

"Hell, no! I'm scared to leave you alone that long! Did you close that casket lid *one time* since I been gone?"

"C'mon, let's get out of here," said Paul. "No, I didn't and I don't intend to, and I thought new preachers watched their language." He'd never tried to explain how suffocating it felt to wake under the closed lid. How dark darkness could be. Joshua carried enough guilt. No reason to inflict any more.

"Then I guess I'll just trot out here every day at dawn and close it myself! Paul, show a little sense! What if somebody opened the mausoleum?"

"Now, this might surprise you, little brother, but in Rose Arbor not too many folks come knocking on the doors demanding entrance."

"Really? From what I heard, folks just dying to get in," Joshua quipped. Paul laughed at the bad joke.

The brothers headed to the riverbank to sit and talk.

"You disappointed in me?" Joshua asked.

"Josh!"

"Well, all that work, all that time. I know you expected to get another doctor out of the effort. So did Papa, by the end."

"All that effort, as you call it, was to make sure you could make the life you wanted for yourself, little brother. I didn't have any expectations for me. Hope I never made you think I did."

Joshua did just fine exerting pressure on himself, any outside pressure would have been wasted. In his months away from home, Joshua struggled with nightmares. Something good had to come from Cain's reign of blood and hate, but he couldn't see what. Cain possessed abnormal power, power enabling him to mold his followers into slaves. There were many men, though, who held petty power, and Joshua, now always on the alert, spotted them everywhere. They moved through the poorer, uneducated classes, ensnaring both black and white, taking their money with promises of great changes, easy lives, luxuries such as the rich folks enjoyed. People were easily led, and usually to the slaughter.

But what if? An idea germinated in Joshua's fertile mind from seeds sown years before by Everett Devlin. There was power in education. Many confidence men, possessing not a tenth of Cain's charisma, used the trappings of religion to hook their marks. Cain had been the ultimate master, of course, using homemade drugs to bind his followers close so they barely noticed the shift in his preaching from love to hate, accepted the blood sacrifices as natural, the sexual orgies as their right. But suppose a different sort of confidence man, one seeking a higher goal, used religion as his hook to pull his catch closer and closer to the greatest good of all? Education.

Joshua examined the idea from every angle. He wasn't and never would be conventionally religious. No one who'd plunged headfirst into the worlds on worlds that ringed this world at seventeen could be. His mother's twin Tamara, powerful Mambo, priestess of the Sweet Loa of the Rata, champion of the Light— she'd made a believer out of him. Without her, Cain might have won.

Still, like his mother and his Aunt Tamara, he had no trouble at all with the concept of God. There was good and there was evil. There was God and there was Satan. They were merely made up of many parts.

Joshua didn't think his private theology would endear him to any church's congregation but in this case, what they didn't know wouldn't hurt them. He could use a church as a base. And from that base, he'd move outward and onward.

The church could have a shelter, a place for those to go who had nowhere else to turn. That shelter could have a school. And that school could teach. And with those teachings, the people, his people and their future generations, would never follow false prophets like Cain again.

Joshua walked the streets of Boston in the evenings. He stood in the slums and watched the immigrants. He met the second generation Irish refugees from the potato famines and heard their stories of the signs greeting their parents: *No Irish need apply.*

He moved into the streets where Italy's accents echoed from the corners and mixed and mingled with the accents of Spain and Germany and Russia. He watched the lines of workers move in and out of the sweat shops. During his visits home, he moved around the streets of Macon. He watched the textile workers empty out of the mills. He saw the children, black and white, pour out the doors and disappear. To where? Despair and hopelessness had no geographical boundaries.

The whites weren't the only race with prejudices. Joshua knew that for a fact. The black population where he would, of necessity, build his base, looked down their noses on the 'po white trash' that formed the bottom of the pyramid in Southern society just as much as did the whites.

I'd rather live next to a decent nigger than po' white trash any day of the week. How many times in his life had he heard white folks say that? Too many to count. He couldn't do everything at once. But he could make a start. And in his church, in his shelter, no one's color made him an outcast. No child would ever be turned away. Not even if they were plaid.

But he had to start somewhere. Where? Three months before he came home for good, he got a letter from his mother. Joshua'd been raised in St. Barnabas Episcopal Church. St. Barnabas hadn't been fortunate in its ministers after Isaiah Gorley's unfortunate and unexplained demise in the summer of 1888, that unsung hero and true man of God who'd died trying to help Paul end Cain's rule. The church was looking for a new minister. Again.

Joshua wrote letters and made inquiry. When he stepped off the train that June day in 1892, he was the new minister of St. Barnabas. He could almost see Isaiah smile.

He returned from his musings and spoke to his brother.

"First sermon's Sunday. Sunday night."

"Sunday night? You forget about Sunday morning?"

"'Course not. But my first Sunday's special. The morning's going to be a big homecoming type picnic. You don't go to too many morning picnics. The sermon's Sunday night. In case you wanta sort of— hang around? Over in a corner?"

Paul laughed. "You've come a long way, little brother."

"Not as far as I intend to go. Does Mama seem, well, different, to you, Paul?"

Sadie'd never fully recovered from the successive shocks of that summer, but she'd pulled herself back together for three reasons. Paul needed her, Joshua needed her, and Everett needed her. Everett needed her no more. He'd suffered one more heart attack in the months following Paul's transformation and a third one the prior October. He hadn't recovered from the third one, and now lay beside his first and only legal wife, Paul's mother, in Rose Arbor.

Paul hesitated in his reply. He worried about Sadie a good deal. But Joshua was home for good now. And he was the mainspring that would keep Sadie going.

"She's had a hard time adjusting to Papa's being gone," he said finally. "But I think you coming home for good ought to pull her over the hump."

"Paul, I'd like to sell the house."

Sadie now occupied the Devlin family home on College Street alone and had since Everett's death. Town gossip soared into the stratosphere over the terms of Everett's Will. That house belonged to Sadie for as long as she wanted to occupy it. After that, it belonged to the foundling Everett took in off the street and gave his name to so many years ago. Joshua Devlin. Everybody knew Everett Devlin'd been downright peculiar when it came to the blacks anyway. More than a few folks suspected for years Sadie wasn't just the housekeeper and Joshua hadn't been a foundling. They actually appreciated the obvious confirmation of those suspicions evidenced by Everett's Will.

"Won't bother me any but I don't think Mama's goin' be too pleased."

Seeing as how Sadie was the only actual mother Paul really remembered, he'd decided long ago it was stupid not to call her what she was, and she was as much his mama as she was Joshua's.

"There's no hurry, naturally. It's just, I'd like to buy a house—or build one—a big one, nearer the Church."

"Big enough for your shelter."

"Yes."

"I wouldn't tell her about it just yet, Josh. I'm sure it'll work out."

The brothers sat a while longer and finally parted, planning to meet shortly within the walls of the College Street house. Sadie took a lot of reassurance. She never slept well unless she inspected her boys, singly or together. Sadie's peace of mind died during Cain's reign, another of his casualties.

* * *

Sunday night, Paul hovered, invisible, in the corner of St. Barnabas' main sanctuary. He watched with pride as Joshua strode to the pulpit.

Joshua greeted the congregation with the practiced ease of a minister with years more experience than he actually had, but then, Joshua'd learned from the best. Or the worst. He guessed it all depended on your point of view. And Cain could damn sure work a crowd, even without the aid of his hallucinogens.

"My people!" he called in greeting. He raised his hand high. "The proverbial prodigal son has come home!"

"Praise the Lord!" The congregation responded with less than its usual enthusiasm. There was something different about their new minister tonight. He didn't sound like he'd sounded when he moved among them during the morning social gathering. He didn't even walk the same way. Damned if he didn't look and sound white.

"I see y'all looking at me a little funny," he continued, resting his hands against the podium. His speech was more casual, but it was still white.

"Wouldn't be 'cause you notice I'm speaking a little different, would it?"

The congregation shifted uneasily. In her seat on the front pew, Sadie went rigid. What was the boy thinking?

"'Cause I am. You know why? I want to illustrate for you the text of tonight's sermon. Know what that is? 'Course you don't, I ain't told you yet."

That did elicit a small chuckle from the crowd.

"Well, tonight, people, we're going to talk about the most important thing in this world. The truth. Now, we

268

all know about truth. Know the truth and it will set you free! And the truth is, I've spent years, not just the years up north, but years before that, getting something that always leads to the truth. It's called an education. This is the way I talk. Most of the time. And I can't stand before you tonight and talk about the truth and tell you a lie just by the way I speak. Especially not when I want to get rid of a lie that's cast its shadow across this congregation for the past four years."

Many of the people sitting in the pews had attended Cain's services. They'd fled in terror before the sight of the Blood Drinker. They knew who they were, and they knew Joshua knew who they were. The members of the congregation who hadn't been part of Cain's entourage weren't exactly ignorant, either. Something that big didn't have a prayer's chance in hell of staying secret.

"Do I need to tell you what lie I'm talking about?" asked Joshua, his tone still conversational. "I doubt it. But just in case, I'll tell you anyway."

He moved in front of the pulpit and dropped the cloak of casualness.

"I'm talking about *Cain!* How long has it been since any of you thought of him? You, Abe, or you, Eulises?" He moved around the pews. "Or you, Silas, or you, Jeremiah? Not long, I hope. I hope you think about him a lot. All of you. The ones of you who know first-hand what I'm talking about and the ones who only know from the stories. And folks, if you only know from stories, you don't know how lucky you are! 'Cause I know about him first hand. Like you do John, and you do, Betsy, and you do, Clara! And I think about him a lot! And how he used us, and how we listened to his *lies* because we weren't strong in the *truth*! We followed false gods because they offered us things we didn't have, pleasures we couldn't imagine. And what did it cost us?"

Joshua dropped his hands and lowered his voice. "It cost us our integrity, our pride, our self-respect.

Who among you have been proud of yourselves since that summer? *Who*? Not me. 'Cause it cost us even more than that. Is there anyone sitting in this room, anyone, who doesn't know how Isaiah Gorley *really* died?"

The crowd hung its head in collective shame. No one in that sanctuary didn't know that Cain had beheaded Isaiah and lobbed his head through Paul's front windows, even though his murder was still an unsolved and forgotten question mark on the white police records.

"I didn't think so," said Joshua. "But Isaiah didn't come to that riverbank alone. Did he?"

The crowd looked up again. They remembered Paul Devlin, but they never spoke his name.

"No, he didn't. He came with a white man. A man who tended your cuts and broke your fevers and in the end, *died* delivering you from Cain's prison. That man and his father, between them, they gave me my name and made me who I am. His name was Paul Devlin. Is there anyone here who doesn't remember that?"

Another murmur went through the crowd.

"Of course not," said Joshua. "And none of you know exactly how *he* died, do you? None of you know *because you broke and you ran*. Finally, you ran, away from Cain and his false gods. And you left Paul Devlin behind. He went down to that riverbank to free you from Cain! And he did, people, he did. Make no mistake about that. He did. And you know what that cost him? *His life*. Is there anyone here doesn't feel a debt for that? I hope not."

Joshua surveyed the crowd, judging its mood.

"I told you this was about the truth and it is. You can't move forward till you leave the past behind and you can't leave the past owing old debts. And there's a way you can pay that debt. To Isaiah Gorley and to Paul Devlin. You can make sure that the *truth* is the most important thing in your lives and in your children's lives. Sometimes, it's hard, oh, Lord, it's *hard*, to judge the difference between truth and lies. But there is one thing that will always help you judge. It's called education. I want to build this church, people!"

Joshua began to pace again, moving into the free-flowing rhythm of worship his congregation expected.

"I want to build this church to a church Isaiah Gorley would be proud of! *Are you with me?*"

"Yes, Lord!"

"Will you *help* me?"

"Yes, Lord!"

"Will you *help me* move this church *out?* Out into the streets, to be the source of light and truth for all the folks that have anywhere else to turn?"

"Praise de Lord!"

"That's right!" exclaimed Joshua, moving freely now with the swaying rhythm of the crowd. "And to praise the Lord we have to *know* Him! And we have to teach our children to *know* Him! *We have to teach our children the truth!*"

"Amen! Amen!"

"And more than that, we have to *educate* our children so they can *judge* the truth, *see* the truth, for themselves!"

"Yes, Lord!"

Joshua, breathing heavily, stood in front of the altar. Mission accomplished, groundwork laid. The rest would follow as the day followed night.

"It's good to be home, people," he said.

* * *

Paul materialized within the walls of the College Street house and waited for his brother's return. He expected to wait for a while. Judging from the crowd's enthusiasm, it'd take Joshua some time to clear the church out. Paul turned his head as the door opened.

"You, little brother, are a dangerous man."

"Well," said Joshua with a sigh, as he helped Sadie slip off her summer shawl. "Personally, I prefer not to

271

use all that swaying and chanting but I got to say, it gets their attention."

"You hesh up, both of you!" said Sadie. "I wuz 'bout to bust, I's so proud."

"You're a con artist, Joshua," said Paul, "a con artist with a cause."

"Damn right. All good preachers are. So what do you think?"

"I think I'm so proud I could bust. Isaiah would be too."

"Well, that's who it's for. You and Isaiah."

* * *

Had Joshua attempted to further the cause of education for education's own sake, protests would have swelled. *"I ken sign my name an' count my money an' dat was good 'nuff for my daddy an' it be good 'nuff fo' me."* That's what the congregation would've said. Now all of his plans proceeded with the express approval of the church, its members, and the Holy Ghost. All of this was for a cause, a reason. For the church. Jesus was looking down and smiling. Josh didn't feel a bit guilty, either. He figured Jesus *was* looking down and smiling.

The executor and trustee of Everett's Will sold the house on College Street. Everett's attorney had never met this Executor. P. J. Devlin was a distant cousin who resided in, of all places, Boston, but every family had a cross to bear and it was no wonder the Devlins hadn't advertised their connection to Yankee relatives. Lawyer Young repressed a shudder.

Of course, Lawyer Young didn't know P. J. Devlin occupied not one body, but two, or that the initials P. J. consolidated the personages of Paul Devlin, supposedly deceased, and Joshua Devlin. Fortunately, the "J" portion of the entity had school friends in Boston accommodating enough to re-mail P. J.'s instructions to Lawyer Young from Boston.

272

As Paul expected, Sadie bounced back with
astonishing vigor. With both her boys in easy reach, she
gloried in organizing the new house-shelter specially
designed and constructed near St. Barnabas on
Congress Street. She fussed and clucked over Joshua
while helping oversee the day-to-day administration of
the combination school-shelter and the ever-
increasing numbers of the needy passing through the
doors of that shelter, christened Gorley House in honor
of Isaiah Gorley.

A dozen or so children, black and while, walked out
of the textile mills and didn't return, becoming the first
permanent residents of the shelter. Sadie's heart
warmed as she watched these children revert to being
children, at least a little bit, but the mixture of black
and white skin worried her. So did Joshua's steadfast
and absolute refusal to use black dialect when in white
company.

"One day dose chillun goan land you in trouble,
son."

"Mama, for God's sake! Nobody knows or cares
about any of these children. Nobody else wants 'em!"

"Dat doan matter none do it come to de white
folks' 'ttenion you raisin' 'em all together. But dat doan
worry me near as much as de way you talk."

"You can talk just like me. You just don't do it very
much anymore."

"I doan wear every necklace and broach I own at de
same time, neither," Sadie pronounced. "Ain't
necessary to show 'em off just 'cause I got 'em."

"Mama, I can't preach education, education,
education and talk like I don't have one! I have to show
everybody talking properly isn't anything to be
ashamed of!"

"But you doan have to do it in front of white folks!
Dey think you an uppity nigger. An' boy, shouldn't be
no need for me to tell you what happens to uppity
niggers!"

"I don't make any trouble. I mind my own business. I don't preach insurrection and riot. I just take care of folks nobody else wants and try to teach our own people things nobody else will."

"An' de way you talk goan get you in trouble while you do it!"

"*Unnhhh!*" Joshua threw up his hands and gave up the argument. He wasn't oblivious to the hard truth at the core of Sadie's observations and he really was careful around the white folks. Not careful enough for Sadie, though.

The nineteenth century moved closer to its merger with the twentieth century and the streets of Macon changed. Pavement appeared where horses formerly trod upon hard-packed earth. A few horseless carriages wound down the roads with noisy motors and blatting horns. A new contraption installed in some of the businesses and more elite residences of the town let folks talk to others through wires and cables.

Life was easier for Paul with Joshua home. He visited with Joshua and Sadie almost every night, and watched Joshua's dreams mature at breakneck speed, mostly because of the funds available to P. J. Devlin. Sadie's sister Tamara, the pivotal force spearheading the battle against Cain, had been right all those years ago back at the beginning. He'd learned to control the new, disturbing urges surging through his body.

Still, on occasion the lust for blood and urge to hunt hit him so strongly he couldn't ignore it. When it did, he roamed the woods with the scent of blood in his nostrils. At those times he again stalked and captured, bit and tore. And drank. And drank. And drank.

After those nights, he always cast himself into the dark and materialized at Tamara's little cottage near Stone Creek Swamp.

"I thought it be 'bout time for my best boy to come vistin'!" she always exclaimed.

She always had some fresh-baked treat waiting for him. Blackberry cobbler when blackberries were in season, peach cobbler, pound cake, or biscuits and wild honey. He didn't need the food but he relished the taste. It linked him somehow to normality.

In the mid-portion of 1909, he observed a gray tinge creeping into Tamara's complexion, followed quickly by undeniable weight loss. She brushed his concerns aside.

"Boy, I done lived a good life. Ain't got no regrets. Well, I've always grieved I couldn't change things for you, but 'cept for dat, it's been a good life. Sho' ain't goan start tryin' to change nuttin' now. What happens, son, it happen. Ain't no use to waste time an' energy tryin' to change it."

Tamara knew, as surely as Dr. Paul Devlin knew. Her body harbored a malignant invader. She was dying.

"Tamara, let me bring you something. You're hurtin', don't try to deny it."

She threw back her head and laughed.

"Where you goan get it, boy?"

"I ain't above a little breakin' and enterin' in Sol Hogue's drug store. Not for you and not for this."

Tamara smiled. "I 'preciate it, son, but I doan need it. Gots my own little remedies scattered around. An' you de best one. You reckon maybe you might could stop in a trifle mo' often?"

Paul didn't think any of Tamara's remedies approached the strength of morphine but he knew she wouldn't want to live in befuddled fog. He visited almost nightly and waited for the inevitable.

"You likes it out here, doan you son?" she asked one night. "In de country."

"Very much."

"Dis yours, you know. When I gone. Yo' own refuge. Dat marble house in de cemetery in de daytime, dat's safer, no ways 'round dat, but dis is yours. For yo' nights."

Pain stabbed Paul's heart. Nights without Tamara. He didn't even want to think about it. She'd been his anchor through those first dark nights. He spoke in a light tone. "Makes me feel like a rich man, Tamara. A city house and a country house. 'Cept mine's a daytime house and a nighttime house."

"You lik' dat?"

"I like that."

* * *

By January of 1910, Gorley House, both its shelter and orphanage, were firmly established. Quietly and without fanfare, it filled a vital community need. Neither black nor white Macon had any problems with who or what was filling that need. It was just one less thing for the city to worry about. Then in the late hours of a February night in 1910, somebody knocked on the shelter's doors and everything changed. Forever.

Joshua and Sadie, comfortably ensconced by the iron stove, sipped coffee from steaming mugs. Outside, the wind howled, making sure everyone knew just how bitter the night was. A hesitant knock sounded on the door, so softly Joshua wasn't sure it was anything but the wind.

"Was that the door?"

"Lord, I hope not. Bad night, an' I think all de beds full."

"If that's a knock, we'll have to find someplace. It's freezing out there." He opened the door. He had to drop his gaze from eye level to see her.

She was very small, no more than five foot two or three. She hugged a big cloak to her tightly, shivering in its folds. Joshua looked into dark blue eyes. Strands of black hair had escaped their confining bun and hung, limply now, around her face. Exhaustion and illness tinted a naturally fair complexion to ghostly white.

"I—" The caller stopped and attempted to clear the croak from her voice. Bad sore throat there, Joshua knew. He hadn't pursued any formal medical education

276

but he hadn't forgotten his early training, either. If he had lived in one of the small towns on the western frontier, he'd probably have ended up serving as town doctor.

"It's late, I know," the caller spoke again. "I'm sorry, but I heard, someone told me—I don't have anywhere else to go," she finished, and simply stood.

Joshua took her arm and pulled her inside.

"You do now," he said, and led her to the stove.

"I—thank you," she said. "I won't bother you for long." Her eyes rolled upward and she pitched forward to the floor.

"Mama!" Sadie was already there, blankets in hand.

"Trouble," she muttered. "Bad trouble."

"Mama, ain't got time for that now. Help me get this wet cloak off her. God, she's burning up!" He shifted her slight body to remove the clinging folds of damp cloth. "Lord, she don't weigh nothing! There's nothing to her!"

The last clinging folds fell away. Joshua stared down in dismay.

"Yeah, dere is," said Sadie in a resigned tone. Nothing she could say or do would make Joshua get this woman out of the house anytime soon.

"Dere sho'ly is," she repeated. She looked down at the woman's swollen stomach, huge with child.

"Trouble," she repeated. "Bad trouble."

* * *

Between the two of them, they got her to Sadie's room. Joshua collected his medical supplies while Sadie shifted her from her clothes into a clean, dry nightgown. He checked her forehead again as she lay back semi-conscious against the white pillowslips.

"Well?" asked Sadie.

"Bad fever. Well, we'll just have to do the best we can right now." He inserted the ear pieces of one of

Paul's stethoscopes in his ears and bent over her. "Thank God. No pneumonia, I don't think, at least not yet. It goes into pneumonia, that'll probably finish her." He laid the first of many wet cloths against her forehead. "And thank God we've got aspirin now, or we'd be brewing a lot of cherry bark. We do have some, don't we?"

"I'm sorry," the woman muttered, "didn't want to be so much trouble."

"Everything's fine. See if you can sleep."

She did, and by the next afternoon, the new miracle drug that changed the medical world in 1899 had broken her fever. By that night, she could sip clear broth. Joshua decided it was question and answer time.

His shelter was open to anyone in need, and it was obvious this woman was in bad need. However, he did have rules. Individuals on the run from the law weren't welcome. This woman was on the run from something, he and Sadie were in agreement on that. Not from the law, though, he didn't think. Then from what?

"So." He sat down in the armchair by the side of the bed. "You feel like having a little talk?"

She hesitated. No, she didn't feel like having a talk, little or otherwise, but one couldn't just barge into another's home, even it was common street knowledge that home was a shelter, with no explanations.

"Yes, of course."

"My name's Joshua," he said. "Joshua Devlin."

"Yes, I know. I heard, when I was on the streets. They told me Reverend Devlin always helped, never turned anyone away. And I can't tell you how much I appreciate all you've done."

He nodded.

"It's what I do. Don't use the Reverend much, though. You know, when somebody introduces themselves, the person they introduce themselves to usually do the same."

She gave a shaky laugh. "Yes, of course, what you must think! My name's Se-Sally. Sally Ferris."

"Is it now, Miss Se-Sally?" he asked, lifting his eyebrow. "Let's start over. My name's Joshua Devlin. What's yours?"

She closed her eyes.

"I'm usually better than that. The fever must have me off balance."

"Probably. I'm waiting."

"I'm not in any trouble," she said firmly.

"Then you got a strange definition of trouble, ma'am."

"I mean, I'm not—I haven't done anything wrong."

Joshua considered. Some men were born gentlemen and he was one of them. His early rearing and education reinforced his natural inclination toward chivalry and he didn't enjoy browbeating this young woman, alone, sick and near term. Still, he had a responsibility to those who depended on the shelter.

"Look, ma'am. I help people, or I try to. It's what I do, a decision I made a long time ago. But I can't help if I don't know what the problem is. You say you've heard about me. Then surely you know you can trust me?"

She hesitated, very much off-balance. Joshua Devlin wasn't at all what she'd expected. And his speech. She was a native Southerner, born and bred. Contrary to anything the rest of America thought, the white Southerner, more than any other American, interacted with the Negro on a personal level that would've astounded a resident of any other section of the country.

But this man. He sounded white. And his mannerisms, the way he moved. She hadn't hesitated to seek shelter here, mostly because she figured it was the last place the man looking for her would look. She'd expected Reverend Devlin to be well aware he was a Negro and as such, hadn't expected him to question any story she, obviously white and obviously a lady, cared to spin. She was a lot younger than he'd expected, too, mid-thirties at the most. She looked more closely and wondered how she'd missed it. He was a mulatto.

And extremely well-educated. Polite and concerned, but not deferential. And he wouldn't appreciate being lied to, even supposing she could lie to him successfully. She didn't think she could. Not to this man. Might as well not try. She had nothing to lose.

"My name's Serena Wentworth," she said. "My husband's David Wentworth. Of the Greenville, South Carolina Wentworths. And if you try and send me back to him, I'll throw myself in the nearest river, see if I don't."

Well, that damn sure had the ring of truth about it. Joshua nodded.

"I see. Well, the Greenville, South Carolina Wentworths don't throw a lot of weight around down here in Macon, Georgia. But I take it they throw a lot in Greenville, South Carolina."

She made no response.

"And I further take it that Mr. David Wentworth is not a pleasant individual to live with. Seein' as how you're on the run, at least eight months pregnant, sick as hell and looking for shelter with the niggers."

"I—please don't—it's not—he hurts me," she finished simply. "In ways—I don't want to talk about it."

"Oh, I get the general idea."

Mr. David Wentworth must go far beyond the bounds of accepted husbandly rights and privileges to send a pregnant woman running with such determination.

"How long you been runnin'?"

"Five months."

"That long?" Joshua cocked his head. "He must be a *real* unpleasant individual. And you must be a real determined lady. Wouldn't think you could make it that long or this far."

"I ran out of money."

"Safe to say he's lookin' for you?"

"No. Yes. Not exactly. Me, I mean. He's looking for the baby. His *son*."

"Ahhhh. One of those."

"Yes."

It wasn't technically a criminal offense for a woman to run away from her husband but it was troublesome, just the same.

"What are you going to do with me?"

"Oh, I think the first order of business is for you to have that baby. Don't you?"

She gave a shaky laugh. "I can't tell you how ready I am for that to happen."

"I think you should use Serena. Always easier to stick as close to the truth as possible and you might forget to answer to Sally. Lots of folks wouldn't notice but believe me, my Mama would. And she wouldn't be too fond of the idea of an irate Daddy lookin' for his baby around these parts."

"I'll leave as soon as I can, I promise."

"But I don't think it'd be a good idea to spread the Wentworth name around. Is Ferris your maiden name?"

"No. It just popped in my head."

"What is? Your maiden name? Like I said, keep as close to the truth as you can, less chance to slip up."

"Foxton."

"Well, Mrs. Serena Foxton, welcome to Gorley House. Now, about your husband. I take it you'd be just as pleased to be a widow?"

"Yes, but I'm not that lucky."

"Then right now, just to get us through this, let's just pretend you are. Welcome to widowhood."

Joshua rose and got to the doorway before he turned back.

"Oh, there's just one thing."

"Anything!"

"If you're goin' make a slip, for God's sake, *don't* do it around Mama."

"That would be Sadie, wouldn't it?"

"Yeah."

"I'll be careful. You're—" she paused and then continued, "very unusual. Aren't you?"

"You mean for a nigger?" He smiled.

"For a minister. You don't talk like one and you thought that story up so fast."

"I had an unusual upbringing. We'll talk later. Get some rest."

* * *

Sadie wasn't happy. She didn't think Serena was a widow, either. This woman was on the run. And you did not run from dead husbands, you ran from live ones. Rich, unpleasant live ones, if the clothes Serena Foxton, or whatever her name was, wore were any indication. Those clothes might be worn out but they'd originally been good quality and very expensive. No point in even trying to argue with Joshua, though. No way he was going to turn her out while she was carrying that child.

Serena donned a fluffy cotton robe and began moving carefully and slowly around. Most especially, she watched Joshua. By keeping her eyes and ears open, she pieced together his background. Well, at least she pieced together the background Joshua'd put out for public consumption, which wasn't exactly his true one.

Always proper, she was "Miss Serena" and "ma'am". For the first time in her life, mostly because of his speech and his striking good looks, skin color played no part in her opinion of another. He wasn't 'a good-looking man for a Negro' nor did he 'show a lot of sense for a Negro.' He was simply a good-looking man. Period. And a highly intelligent one. Period. Though damn near any man of any color would be, compared to the one she was running from.

"Miss Serena," he said one evening, "I think we need to consider what we're goin' to do when that baby decides to come."

282

"I told you, I'll leave just as soon as I possibly can."

"No. I mean what we're going to do when it decides to actually come. I don't want to scare you, ma'am, but you've had a hard time. You didn't have much strength left to start with and that fever took what little you had left. I think you're goin' to need a doctor, not just a midwife. I'd feel a lot better if you had one, I know that."

"*No!* Please, no! There may be fliers out, notices! I can't take the chance!"

"Now, Miss Serena—"

"You can't tell me your Mama's not a good midwife, I know better. I've heard things."

"Yeah, but she's not a doctor and she's getting' on up there, doesn't get much practice."

"You've done it, too. Delivered babies. I told you, I've talked to the people in the shelter, I know you've done it!"

"Whoa!" Joshua kept a firm grip on reality, no matter how much Sadie worried he didn't. In this town, he was a Negro. A Negro *man*. Serena Foxton was a lady. A *white* lady. Maybe if they were stranded somewhere together fifty miles from any other available help, society might overlook that. Maybe. In the city limits of Macon, Georgia? Not a chance in hell, he would immediately revert back to "uppity nigger" status in the eyes of the town. "I can't do that," he said.

"Why not?"

"Miss Serena, I call certain facts to your attention. You're white. I'm black. Delivering a baby involves a certain amount of—bare skin. And if the town found out a black man delivered a white baby—"

"I don't care. And nobody else would have to know. Let them think Sadie did it."

He stared at her.

"You honestly don't, do you?"

"Do I what?"

"Care."

"I trust you. You're the only man since Papa died that's cared what happens to me. I want you to bring my baby. No doctor. Please."

"*Unnhhh!*" Joshua moaned. He didn't want to upset her. He'd just have to cross that bridge when he came to it.

He crossed it the next night. Labor was long and hard. When the time came for transition from labor to delivery, transition didn't.

"Son, we got to get a doctor. Dat baby goan need forceps. I can't do dat, and neither can you."

"*No!*"

"Girl, you hesh up!" Sadie commanded. "Doan know whut you sayin'! Dat baby ain't goan survive dis, even if you do! Not without mo' help den me and Joshua can give!"

Serena grabbed Joshua's hand.

"*Then let me die!* I'd rather die than risk goin' back!"

Sadie shook her head.

"I knew it," she said. "I jest knew it."

Joshua bit his lip.

"I can get you a doctor," he said slowly. "One that won't say anything."

"Son! Whut you thinkin'?

"But you have to promise, you have to swear to me—you'll never, never tell anyone about him."

Sadie sank down in the bedside chair and moaned.

Serena lay drenched in sweat, her hair plastered to her face. No one told her childbirth was like this. She'd expected sharp pains that cut like glass, not this. Not this unending, dull and relentless cramping starting like the very worst menstrual period from hell and accelerating into these unending, gut-wrenching gigantic waves of pain ripping her apart and drowning her.

"I promise," she whispered.

"I'll be back," he said, and raced out of the room.

* * *

Serena didn't know how long he was gone. She just held on with the last shards of determination left from five months of hard running. She saw the face bending over her in a semi-stupor, lamplight glinting off the blond hair.

"You got any forceps?" The voice sounded familiar somehow.

"No. Joshua doan keep 'em since both of us'd be scared to use 'em."

Where was Joshua, why hadn't he come back with the doctor?

"Chloroform? Morphine?"

"Nuttin' dat strong."

"I'll be right back."

"Son, we ain't got time to fool around here."

"Won't take me two minutes, don't worry."

"Where you goan get—"

"Gonna raid Dave Cabot's office. Hell, he don't need to be usin' 'em anyway, should've retired years ago."

Nothing made any sense to Serena but she was far beyond caring. It seemed only seconds until the strange, oddly familiar voice returned. Something covered her face.

"Breathe deep!" it commanded.

She breathed. And sank gratefully into the waiting dark.

She woke fighting new waves of nausea, nausea of a different type, sweeping up from her stomach.

"Here."

Joshua's voice. Thank God. He pulled her head over and held the basin while she gave in to the nausea.

Finally, she lay back. He wiped her forehead and mouth.

"It's the chloroform," he said, "makes you real sick."

"The baby?"

"Miss Serena, I'm sorry. You just both been through too much."

She sighed, too exhausted to feel much sorrow. "A boy?"

"No, a little girl."

She smiled. Even David Wentworth didn't get what he wanted every time. A daughter. The first twinges of loss swept over her. She would have liked a daughter.

"I'm so glad!" she said, and fell back into exhausted sleep.

Sadie leaned over when she woke again.

"So, you back in de land of de living?"

"Seems that way. I'm still not real sure right now."

Sadie stood. To Serena, Sadie seemed to soar in height until she approached the ceiling.

"Well, I jest wanta say one thing to you, girl. Joshua, he take yo' word last night 'bout dat doctor. De one saved yo' life and doan you make no mistake. He saved yo' life."

"I know. I remember. And I'm not supposed to say anything."

"Dat's right. You doan say nuttin' to nobody 'bout dat man. You make a solemn vow to my boy. But jest in case, lest something come up make dat promise slip yo' mind, you 'member dis. Do you even think 'bout slippin' up, I goan know. An' I'll tear yo' tongue out by de roots. You unnerstan' me?"

Serena sank back against her pillows, as frightened by the fierceness of Sadie's expression as by her words. She nodded.

"Dat's good."

* * *

Serena slowly recovered but made no move to leave. She felt curiously at peace at Gorley House and moved into the school rooms. She discovered a natural and unsuspected talent for children and teaching that surprised and pleased her.

Sadie didn't like her continued presence and she knew it. Just like she knew Joshua did. Everyone in the household carried their own weight, even the children. Chores spread out weren't a burden on anyone. Serena tried to pull her own weight, even if her presence wasn't welcomed by everyone.

One early April day she picked up a stack of Joshua's freshly laundered shirts from the kitchen table and toted them to his room. The door was open but the room was empty. She picked up the picture sitting on the bureau. Joshua in his teens. With a white man and a white woman. Joshua'd had a brother, a white half-brother, she'd heard that from somebody in the shelter, but that brother'd been dead for almost twenty years. She stared at the man in the picture. Light hair, obviously blond. Something about him seemed familiar. And he'd been a doctor.

Joshua'd found her a doctor. She remembered the man's voice more than anything. Something about it, not the voice so much as the tone, the inflection, the cadence of speech. He'd sounded very much like someone else she knew. Joshua. He'd sounded very much like Joshua.

You have to promise me, you have to swear, that you will never, never tell anybody—

Do you even think 'bout slippin' up, I goan know it. An' I tear yo' tongue out by de roots.

Impossible. Paul Devlin was dead. Wasn't he?

"What are doing with that?"

She hadn't heard Joshua coming up behind her. She started. It hadn't been her intention to snoop.

"I was just putting up your shirts. I didn't mean—"

"Paul Devlin and his wife," Joshua said shortly, "I'm sure you've heard the story from somebody. Paul's father Everett Devlin and Sadie raised me as a child. Paul finished the job. He and his wife are dead."

"Yes, I know the story," she said.

Joshua heard the slight hesitation.

"You listen to me, Serena," he said. His tone and his omission of 'Miss' got her attention. "Paul Devlin's dead. You understand?"

"Yes. I understand," she said. She did indeed. At least, she thought she did. He was no more dead than Joshua but for some reason the world didn't need to know that.

"Good. Please keep understanding it." He turned to leave.

"Joshua?"

"Yes?"

"Don't be angry with me."

"I'm not."

"Then can I ask you something?"

"You can ask. Doesn't mean I'll answer."

"You're half-white. Aren't you?"

Joshua smiled. He'd often noticed strangers found that quite obvious but the people he'd grown up with didn't. "I am."

"Sadie really is your mother, you don't just call her mama 'cause she raised you."

"Yes."

"Everett Devlin was your father. You use it because that's your name, not because they took you in."

"True. Anything else?"

"That man, the one in the picture?"

"My brother."

"You must have loved him very much."

"You have no idea."

She stared thoughtfully at his back as he walked away. So. Sadie'd raised his brother, too. In her mind, he was her son. And that explained Sadie's fierceness. Serena wasn't just an inconvenient problem for Sadie's living son. She could become a threat to her 'dead' son, too. Sadie needn't worry, but Serena knew there was no way to convince her of that.

Chapter Sixteen

Even without Sadie's constant reminders, Joshua knew Serena couldn't live in limbo forever. He sought her out the next night.

"Like some evening air? The swing out by Mama's roses?"

"Very much." They moved over and sat down.

"Miss Serena—"

"Don't do that."

"Don't do what?"

"Keep calling me 'Miss'. Considering the circumstances, I find it a trifle, well, affected."

He laughed. "I guess in private it wouldn't hurt nothin'. Serena, what are you going to do now?"

"I hadn't really thought about it."

"Gonna have to eventually. Might be time for you go back to Greenville."

"You don't know what you're saying."

"I said go back to Greenville, it's your home, your roots, your family. I didn't say go back to David Wentworth."

"It's the same thing."

"No. No, it isn't. Divorce is an ugly word and it's not all that common, I know, but—"

"Never. I couldn't fight him and win."

"Serena, your family has to have money, too. It's written all over you, the way you move, the way you talk."

"How conversant you are with genteel womanhood."

"Well, matter of fact, I am. My brother's wife. Chloe. I loved her almost as much as I loved him. You remind me of her. A lot. You were raised a society lady, it's all over you. Your family has to have some influence."

"Not anymore. It's why I married David in the first place. Papa liked to play poker."

"Oh, Lord," Joshua sighed, knowing what was coming.

"He gambled everything but our house and finally, he gambled that, too. Then he fell over dead. The doctor said it was his heart."

"And he was in a game with David Wentworth at the time."

"My mother had nothing left, Joshua. Nothing but me and my little brothers and sisters. What was I supposed to do? Where would they have gone? There's *nothing* worse than being a poor relation, you know that. And the Wentworths. Such a fine family. And David. He seemed such a gentleman! I had no idea." Her voice trailed off.

"But you're stuck in limbo. You deserve a life. A good one. Life's a great, good thing, Serena. Full of darkness sometimes, but full of love, too. And you could find it, marry a good man—"

"No, thank you!" She shook her head emphatically. "David loved me. He said."

"You can't judge all men by David Wentworth."

"And marriage, men, what they do! *Pahhh!*" She almost spat and shuddered.

He hurt me. In ways—I don't want to talk about it. She'd told him that. The first night. The words echoed in his head.

"Serena, it doesn't have to be like that, it's not supposed to be like that. It's not supposed to hurt. It's supposed to be a great pleasure."

"Maybe all men don't hurt on purpose," she conceded. "But I don't see how it could ever *not* hurt. Or how anything about that part of marriage could be remotely pleasant."

Joshua shook his head. Damn bastard. He'd scarred her for life, in a place where it couldn't be fixed. In her mind.

"You should at least think about it. You can't hide forever."

"Do you want me to leave? I'm sorry if I'm a lot of trouble, I love working with the children, I hoped it was a help—"

"*No!* No, I don't want you to leave because you're any trouble! I want you to have a *chance*! A chance at a good life! And you are a help, the children love you. I just don't want you to stay because you think you have nowhere else to go. And if money's a problem, I have money. Think about it."

"Oh, no, Joshua! I couldn't possibly accept—"

"Think about it."

* * *

She thought about it. As Joshua would say, know the truth and it will set you free. The truth was, she didn't want to stay just because she had nowhere else to go even though in fact, she didn't. She wanted to stay because she wanted to stay. Well, no, that wasn't exactly right either. She wanted to stay because she didn't want to leave Joshua. Which meant what? She didn't know. But she wasn't leaving until she did.

Joshua thought about it, too. And he realized he'd become the resident of some twilight zone between two cultures. He'd never be fully accepted by white society. That was a given and there was no point in wasting time crying over it. Black society accepted him, but it didn't understand him because his brother had done exactly what Everett and Sadie had worried so about all those years ago. He'd turned Joshua into a white man in a black man's body.

That man was lonely, especially since the usual physical releases available to most unmarried men were not available to him. He was, after all, a man of

God and it would not do *at all* to compromise that position by becoming involved with any young lady of any local church family, no matter the denomination. Nor, as a minister, could he frequent any establishments of ill repute for purely physical satisfaction because that would surely be out on the neighborhood grapevines before he ever walked back out the door of any such establishment. His usual solution to that problem was a week-long trip every six months or so to either Atlanta or New Orleans, which had always worked out well for him, at least, until now.

Now, there was Serena. He watched her in the classroom, saw her hanging clothes in the sideyard, heard her laughing with the children. She reminded him so much of Chloe. They didn't look alike at all, but they had a kinship founded in an inner core of steel.

Joshua finally broke down and admitted the truth to himself. *Know the truth and it shall set you free.* He found it humorous that he'd actually preached that line in his first sermon at St. Barnabas. He was dangerously, disastrously, magnetically attracted to— no, that was a bald-faced lie in the midst of what was supposed to be truth—he *loved* Serena Wentworth. He loved everything about her, her petite grace and lilting laugh, the way she moved, the way she talked. Most of all, he loved her spirit and the determination that had carried her alone and pregnant down the hard roads from Greenville, South Carolina to Macon, Georgia and Gorley House. To him.

He was in love but he wasn't *crazy*. Nothing would ever come of his feelings for Serena Wentworth and neither she nor anybody else would ever know he even had them. In his world, in the world where he'd worked so hard to build what he'd built—those feelings could get him killed. And too many people depended on him for him to let that happen. It had been over seven months since his last trip to New Orleans, and he resolved to schedule one immediately. As things turned out, he never got the chance.

Joshua woke abruptly. His eyes focused on the last person he expected to see. Something must be wrong.

"Serena! Are you sick? Is one of the children—"

She sat on the bed and placed her hand over his mouth.

"No. No one's sick."

The last traces of sleep cleared out of Joshua's brain. He allowed himself to look at her for only the space of a moment.

"Then I think it'd be a real good idea if you went back to your own bed. Right now."

"Joshua—"

"Now, Serena." His voice sounded harsh, even to himself. She had no experience with men other than her husband, he knew that, but didn't she have any idea what she was doing to him?

Serena didn't really understand why she'd been compelled to come to his room. And Joshua's tone crushed her like a fly unable to avoid the flyswatter. He'd never spoken to her like that. Like she was revolting, disgusting. David always sounded like that, especially when he had her in bed and started performing those disgusting acts men performed. Joshua'd said it didn't have to be that way between men and women, that it wasn't *supposed* to be that way. It was supposed to be a great pleasure.

She didn't really believe that, but she believed one thing. If there was one man who could make it even bearable for her, that man was Joshua Devlin.

For the past week, she'd been so engrossed in her own turmoil, her own conflicts, she hadn't stopped to consider the social consequences of this night's actions. She knew her husband detested her. She'd never pleased him and he'd sure as hell had never pleased her. She'd never thought she'd ever consider the act with another man. Now she had, and that man didn't want her. It never occurred to her Joshua was scared of her. Well, not of *her*. Of the possible consequences arising from the contrasting color of their complexions. She didn't even *see* the contrasting color of their skin anymore.

Her face crumbled. She backed away, embarrassed, humiliated, shamed.

"You lied." Her whisper stabbed his heart.

"Serena!" He almost stood up but remembered in time. It was May. He was naked beneath the sheets. He was in enough trouble now, he couldn't let his body touch hers, even through her nightdress. His hand shot out, attempting to catch her wrist.

He missed. His hand closed on the thin material of her nightgown as she fled. It ripped down the side seam. Her skin gleamed white through the tear, her body exposed to the gaze of a man who didn't even want it. She sank down to the floor and cried, hands clasped to her face.

"Serena." He leaned forward, but she was too far away for him to reach.

"Oh, *hell!*" He gathered the folds of the sheet around his waist and sat on the floor beside her.

"You lied to me," she whispered again, the words muffled by her hands.

"No!" Joshua pried her hands from her face. "I've never lied to you, Serena."

"You did! You told me, you said I couldn't judge all men by David—"

"You can't."

"You don't want me! You sounded just like him! So disgusted, so revolted! He said I wasn't a real woman and no other man would ever put up with me! He was right!"

"That's not it! For God's sake, Serena! *Look at us!* Will you just *look!*" Joshua reached out and held their entwined hands up into the streaming moonlight. In the moon shadows, their hands were caught in the striking contrast of ebony and ivory.

"I'm a nigger!" The whisper, if anything, intensified the significance of the words. "*Remember?*"

"You're Joshua Devlin and you're the finest man I've ever known, and if you can do this to me, if you can hurt me like this, I will *never, never* trust another man again!"

Joshua closed his eyes and moaned. He knew what he ought to do, what was necessary for his own continued good health and well-being. He knew what he had to do if he didn't want Serena scarred more deeply than she'd ever been scarred by David Wentworth, if she was to survive this night with any semblance of self-worth as a woman. And he knew what he wanted to do. Well, two out of three wasn't bad.

He stood up abruptly, releasing his hold on the sheet, and held his hand down to her. She stared, eye widened, terrified as she viewed the evidence of his obvious response. If David Wentworth had hurt her, Joshua was going to kill her.

Having no basis for comparison, she didn't know David Wentworth wasn't particularly well-endowed. In fact, he wasn't well-endowed at all, and therein lay the roots of his brutality. He carried an inferiority complex in reverse proportions to the size of his manhood.

Having no confidence in his sexual prowess, especially with a woman he hadn't bought and paid for, he only achieved erection through overwhelming physical force. He liked to slap, he liked to pinch. And he liked to bite, in especially sensitive places. She'd never told anyone any of it, especially Joshua.

Joshua pulled gently on her hand, bringing her to her feet.

"You can leave now, if you think you have to. Or you can stay. But I promise you, Serena. I promise. I will never hurt you."

She doubted that. But she stayed anyway. Frightened and determined, trembling with each new exploration, she stayed. And she trusted. Until his lips moved down and sought her breasts.

"No!" she pushed against him in panic. "Don't! Please don't. I can't stand that, not again!"

Joshua, determined to lay all her old ghosts to rest for all time, swung to the side of the bed and lit the lamp, adjusting the flame down low. What could be seen was often not as frightening. He turned back to her and tugged on the sheet she clutched in a death grip the moment she heard the flare of the match. His face hardened. If David Wentworth had walked into the room at that moment, he'd have killed him with his bare hands. Joshua had tended her in childbirth but he'd never seen her naked.

The ivory skin of her upper body was marred with scars. Scars rippled all over her breasts, especially around the sensitive skin of her nipples. Teeth marks. David Wentworth's.

Serena shrank back, frightened by Joshua's expression.

"It's ugly, I know," she whispered.

"The son-of-a-bitch! The bastard!"

She rolled over. "I'm sorry. I'll leave. You can't want me like this."

"Serena!" He pulled her back as she made to rise. "No, don't go. Please don't. *Trust me*, Serena, just try and trust me. I won't hurt you like he did. I won't."

He didn't. And afterwards, he lay on his back with her head on his shoulder, staring into the darkness and wondering just how in the hell he always managed to get in so damn much trouble.

* * *

He roused her before the first streaks of dawn streamed into the room.

"Serena."

"*Hmmm*," she purred, contented and secure, for the first time in her life, in her own womanhood.

"You have to get back to your room."

"Not yet."

"Yes. Now. House is goin' start waking up real soon."

The lingering sleep fog cleared from her brain. It really had happened. It was real. And she was terrified it would never happen again.

"You're not mad at me? You're not sorry? You don't want me to leave now, do you?"

He took the time to pull her close and offer reassurance. One night wasn't going to put a dint on the emotional scars running even deeper than the physical ones.

"No," he said. "And no and no. To all three questions. But Serena, we've got to talk about what we're goin' to do, we've got to think. Not now, we don't have time. You've got to get back."

She bent and kissed him quickly. She threw on her nightgown and pulled the torn seam together as she left. Joshua stared after her. Thinking and talking weren't going to be of much use in this situation. Nothing short of a miracle was going to be of much use.

Serena didn't see anyone on the way back to her room. But someone saw her.

Sadie didn't sleep well anymore, hadn't for some time. She didn't see any reason for anybody else to suffer because of her insomnia and moved with the silence of a jungle cat during the night hours. She frequently sat at the kitchen table as early as four-thirty in the morning, drinking her first cup of coffee in quiet solitude.

Sadie was aging. She didn't see well at a distance and her digestive system wasn't what it used to be. Her hearing, though—that was superb. Her ears caught the almost silent sound of a closing door. She moved to the kitchen door and saw the figure moving down the hall. Her eyes weren't so bad she didn't catch the gleaming ivory skin or the long, thick fall of black hair. Serena

Foxton. Coming from where? Sadie's eyes shot around, gauging the possibilities.

Joshua's room. The white woman, the one Sadie had judged to be trouble, bad trouble, at first sight was coming out of her younger son's bedroom.

Sadie closed her eyes and leaned against the door frame. Her stomach plunged to her knees. She hadn't felt this sensation since that long ago morning when she'd discovered Cain's poison tidbits in Joshua's pants pockets. Her sibilant whisper split the dark.

"Oh, God, son! Whut you done got yourself into this time?"

* * *

Joshua wondered the same thing. What to do, what to do? If he had half a brain, he'd put Serena on the Nancy Hanks for Atlanta. Though if he'd used half a brain, none of this would have ever happened in the first place. But it was way too late to consider that an option. He loved Serena. Serena loved him. And in Macon, Georgia that just wasn't going to work. It wouldn't work anywhere south of the Mason-Dixon Line. They wouldn't be the most popular couple in any neighborhood north of the Mason-Dixon Line, either, but at least folks would leave them alone. Maybe.

But while he was working out details for relocation to more hospitable climes, he needed to take care of another problem. Immediately. Because he definitely didn't want to bring a child into the world facing the problems that child would have to face. Possibly later, when they were settled wherever they settled and he could assess their situation more accurately. But sure as hell not now. Of course, abstinence was the best means of insuring that—provided it wasn't already too late—but he wasn't stupid enough to think abstinence was in his future anymore.

He went to the stables and saddled Twister, grandson of Paul's big stallion Cyclone. Joshua detested the noisy, blatting horseless carriages now appearing on the city streets and didn't think it'd be too smart to advertise his secret financial reserves with such an extravagant purchase even if he'd wanted one.

He rode downtown, heading for Sol Hogue's drug store and hoping like hell Fred Wenton was at the counter. He liked Fred, who'd been a stock boy back when Joshua ran in and out picking up things for Paul.

There wasn't much in the way of birth control in the early 1900s, but there were early forms of condoms, popularly known as 'French Letters'. Not infallible of course, but better than nothing. Again always providing he wasn't already too late.

Fred manned the counter, thank the Lord. He grinned.

"Damn! What's it worth to you for me not to tell your congregation?"

"Well, I tell you the truth, Fred," he said, throwing just a trace of black slur onto his speech. Not as much as Sadie would have liked but so far, enough to keep him out of overt trouble with the white folks. "This is just 'tween you and me, ain't it?"

"Sure."

"Well, see, there's this family I know, already got five young'uns and hardly able to feed 'em. So I sort of had a man to man with the daddy 'bout how it might be in the best interests of all concerned were there not six young'uns anytime soon and this gentleman, he wasn't real conversant with the topic. Didn't know there was any way to try to avoid that without deprivin' himself of his lovin' and he just wasn't real pleased with that idea."

Fred laughed.

"I swear, Joshua, I'll tell anybody I know. You my idea of a real preacher, you don't just preach, you really try to help. I mean that, Josh, I ain't just making sport."

"I 'preciate that, Fred, I really do. But see, after I explained the option, he allowed as how he might be willing to consider it but he sho' 'nuff didn't want anybody to see him buying 'em and besides, money wasn't exactly plentiful, so I told him I'd make a private donation."

Fred threw up his hands and still laughing, made his way to the back room. He returned with a goodly supply.

"You something, Josh. You really are."

"Well, thank you, Fred. I try hard."

Joshua's brain kept churning on the ride home. He didn't want to just live with Serena. He wanted to marry her, but now he knew she'd never be able to go back to Greenville and even attempt to divorce David Wentworth. Realistically speaking, Wentworth had the advantage. Joshua didn't have a trace of illusion about David Wentworth anymore. He'd probably kill her. Besides, legalities be damned. Wentworth renounced all right to claim Serena as his wife the first time he scarred her. She belonged to Joshua now, just as he belonged to her.

Boston was the logical choice. He'd made a lot of friends in Boston when he'd gone to school there. So he'd have to start over. He had the money and there were needy people everywhere. But who to leave in charge here?

And God, Sadie! He didn't even want to think about her reaction. She might even refuse to leave. Hell, she'd *probably* refuse to leave. But Tamara's little stone cottage was big enough for two and Sadie and Tamara would need each other. Paul would stop in to check on them every night. Paul. Oh, Lord. He couldn't imagine life without his brother. But the first thing to do was discuss this with Serena. Whatever they decided, it'd take some time to put into play because he wouldn't just abandon these people. But surely, somewhere, sometime, he was entitled to some semblance of normal happiness for himself? Just once?

He talked it over with Twister while he stabled him.

"You know, I could always get Paul to talk to Mama first. He's her favorite, after all." Joshua laughed. Sadie

didn't have favorites and Joshua knew it, but there'd
never been a set of siblings who didn't claim the same.
"But that'd be kinda cowardly, wouldn't it?" Joshua ran
the brush down Twister's side. "But you know what?
Damn right I'm a coward when it comes to my Mama.
Or maybe I'm just smart."

"Or might be you jest too stupid for words!" came
the voice behind him. It was Sadie. She'd kept watch
for his return, and she was furious. "You lost yo' mind,
boy?"

"Mama, I don't know what—"

"Then you let me tell you whut! I seen her! Last
night. Come out of yo' room. Now, do you know *whut*?"

Already. Lord, my God. He set his mouth firmly. "I
love her," he said.

"Dat *love* goan do both of you a lot of good when
you swingin' from a rope, boy! Dat *love* the stuff
lynchings made of, fool!"

"Hold it!" Joshua snapped. Last night's
sleeplessness, this morning's cyclical pattern of endless
consideration, and now his mother's attack. It was too
much. "I'm not a fool and I'm not a boy!"

"Den you quit actin' like one!"

"Don't you sit in judgment on me when you spent
twenty years in a white man's bed!"

"A white *man's* bed! You ain't noticed things kind
of *reversed* here?"

"Hell, yes, I noticed!"

"But not enough so's you got enough sense to stop
this foolishness, dat whut you tellin' me?"

"Mama, I didn't want to talk to you like this. And I
haven't talked to Serena this morning at all but there
are other places to go than here."

"You willin' to give yo' whole life up, boy? All dat
hard work, leave me and yo' aunt and yo' brother and
all de folks you done made depend on you? For dat
woman? Dat *married* white woman?"

"You don't know what he did to her! No merciful
God would ever hold that sham to be a marriage!"

"I know. I knows some and I can guess some more. I'm de one got her out of her wet clothes dat first night."

"And you can't understand—"

"I understan' you de only man whut's ever treated her decent and I—"

"Did my father's color matter so much to you? That you wouldn't have loved him if he'd been black? You don't think it's just a remote possibility that Serena looks at me and sees *me* and not my skin color? Or is it you just don't think anything's in me *worth* seeing past the black?"

Sadie closed her eyes. Dear Lord. She sounded like a black racist. She who'd loved Everett Devlin with every fiber of her being, not because of his color but in spite of it. She who counted as her oldest son a blond, blue-eyed prototype of the Anglo-Saxon race. She'd hurt this son needlessly, casting aside his good looks, his high intelligence, his compassion, his character, and all the traits making him the fine, good man he was.

She'd done Serena a great wrong, assuming a white woman couldn't possibly love a black man. Maybe Serena was Sadie in white skin. And maybe she loved Joshua not because he was white or black or even calico. Just because he was the man he was.

"I'm sorry. You and yo' brother and yo' Daddy, you all men any woman with any sense would love."

She turned to leave. They needed some time apart.

"Mama? It'll take a while, I'm not just going to pack up and leave, you know."

"But dat's 'xactly whut you *needs* to do, son. I wish you would. You right, ain't nowhere goan be easy, but other places, people more inclined to leave you 'lone. You goin' back to Boston?"

"Yes. I'll get everything set up here and I'll do the same thing in Boston I'm doing here, but probably not through a Church, Serena'd probably cause problems with that.. But I have friends in Boston, I can get set up."

"Son. Listen to me. Y'all go ahead and *leave*. Now. Travel separately, leave tomorrow. Leave tonight. I get things situated down here. Got folks to help, yo' brother can tell me whut I needs to do, do I not be sure."

"I can't do that. And I don't want to leave you. Come with us."

"To Boston? Now why for you think I want to traipse off to Boston at my age? New folks, new places, new start, snow? No, las' winter 'bout did me in down here, couldn't handle de cold. Me and Tamara, we do jest fine. 'Sides, yo' daddy and yo' brother. Dey here."

Joshua felt it. The relinquishment of the short rein Sadie had unconsciously placed around his neck, tethering him to her. Ever since Cain. He'd always known it was there and he'd never resented it or tried to escape it, even when it chaffed badly because he knew he'd created it himself. Now, in the first moments of its absence, he missed it.

"I love you, Mama."

"An' I love you. But you got de right to a woman's love, too. I bein' a foolish, selfish ol' woman, actin' like you a young'un can't tie his own shoes, like I think you ain't worth a woman's love. But son, you gots to be careful. 'Til you leave, you *gots* to be careful."

"We will be, Mama. I promise."

* * *

He watched Sadie move to the house, her head high and her back straight. He turned back to Twister. Serena's voice came from the door.

"Joshua, what's wrong? Sadie's been glaring at me all morning and just now she came through the kitchen and hugged me! And you've been gone all morning." She started towards him and he threw up his hand.

"Don't. Talk low, and don't *ever*, in daytime, in the open, act like you're about to touch me. I've been out and we have to talk."

Serena's fragile shell of happiness broke.

"I'll pack. I understand."

Joshua sighed. "Serena. Sit down, over there, on that bale of hay, and listen to me. And listen good, 'cause I don't intend to spend the rest of my life giving you three hours of reassurance anytime I'm gone for an hour. Know it'll take a while but you got to get over that."

"I don't understand—"

"Sit down and hush."

She sat.

"I've waited a long time to feel about somebody the way I feel about you. Pretty much gave up, in fact. You?"

"You have to ask me that?"

"Are you sure?"

"Yes."

"Sure enough to do whatever we have to do to stay together?"

Serena's eyes widened.

"Yes."

"It would mean leaving."

"Leaving Gorley House?"

"Gorley House, Macon, the South. Everything you've ever known. All of it."

"What would you do? Where would we go?"

"I went to school in Boston. I have friends there. And I have money. I already told you that. We're never goin' to be accepted, but I'm used to that, story of my life. You, though. Could you handle that?"

"I can handle anything with you."

"Easy to say now."

"Anything."

"It'll take me a couple of months to get things arranged here and set up in Boston."

"You'd do that? Leave everything and everybody, everything you've worked for? For me?"

Joshua laughed shortly. "I'm not that noble, so don't make me something I'm not. No, I wouldn't. I wouldn't leave everything and everybody for you. But I'll do it for us. If you're sure. If you want it."

"Oh, my God."

"Is that a yes or a no?"

She stood and he threw his hands out again.

"I told you, don't. Don't ever act like you're about to touch me. We've got to be careful."

Suddenly Sadie's actions of earlier that morning made sense. "Your mother?"

"She saw you coming out of my room last night."

"Oh. Oh, dear God! What she must think of me!"

"Darlin', she spent twenty years in my father's bed. The moralities of the situation ain't bothering her. She's scared. And she's right. And you have to be scared, too. We're not out of here yet."

"I understand. And I can do it. Whatever it takes. But Joshua! Your brother!"

Even knowing they were alone, he turned around and scanned the interior of the barn. He'd been certain she'd figured it out. At least, some of it. No way she'd figured out all of it, of course.

"Serena, when we're settled, I'll tell you about my brother. But for now, believe me. He can take care of himself and Mama, too. Go on back in, I got things to do."

He smiled and Serena's world lit up. And for the first time in her life she was happy.

* * *

Joshua's plans moved swiftly. They'd be leaving Macon sometime in the early part of September 1910. Sadie mourned silently. Everything was a trade-off. Nothing was free. It was Joshua's trade to make and he was certainly entitled to make it.

Paul shuddered at the consequences should this alliance ever come to public attention. More selfishly, he dreaded the nights of the coming years when he'd be miles away from his brother. Doubt haunted him, too.

305

For the first time he wondered if he'd done right by his brother, giving him the intense education that had consigned him to no-man's land between two cultures. Too damn late to worry about it now, though. Nothing left but to help Joshua as much as he could.

"I can buy you a mausoleum in Boston if we could just get you there," Joshua said, "so what kind do you want?"

"Italian Carrara."

"Damn! You ain't cheap, are you? Would you maybe consider it?"

Paul dropped his levity. "I can't. Not now. Mama and Tamara—"

"God, I hate to leave them."

"Both of us can't. Mama's in good shape physically but Tamara isn't."

"I know. Started sometime last year. How long you reckon?"

"Not long. And then Mama'll be by herself. I have to stay."

"God, Paul!"

"We'll still see each other. Sometime."

"How far do you think you can travel? And how fast? I mean when you—do that thing you do?"

"I'll start experimenting."

"We could always pay freight and ship a crate to Boston."

"Thank you, no. Don't much like the idea of being manhandled in a box. Joshua, does Serena know anything about me?"

"No. She ain't stupid though—"

"Don't know about that, fell in love with you, didn't she?" asked Paul. Brotherly love in action.

Joshua ignored the interruption. "And she sort of figured out who the doctor was when she was in labor. Your voice, more than anything, said she was hurting too bad to really see you. But the way you talked reminded her of me. Told her it should, I spent enough years imitating you."

Paul laughed.

"But she thinks you're in hiding for some reason or other, presumed dead. I told her you could take care of yourself and I'd tell her 'bout it when we got settled."

"That should be interestin'."

"Oh yeah, I'm really looking forward to it. Ain't took her to see Tamara yet, either. Can't you just hear that? 'Honey, this is my aunt, the Voodoo Queen. She specializes in exorcising Blood Drinkers. You know, Blood Drinkers. They got real bad manners and you just can't take 'em anywhere!'"

Joshua stood up and parodied an introduction worthy of the English court. "'And you've never actually met my brother, either. Dr. Devlin. He's the family vampire. Had a run-in with one of those Blood Drinkers and he just ain't been the same since.'"

"Let me know how that works out for you, little brother."

* * *

It was such a little thing, the thing that culminated in two nights more horrible in Paul Devlin's memory than the two summer nights in 1888 when life as he knew it ended.

Sadie didn't feel well when she woke one day in mid-July. Today was shopping day, though, and there was a house to feed. A big one. She got up and dressed and went to the kitchen to double-check her standard shopping list. She always started at Bone & Chapell, the grocers on Poplar and Fourth, then she'd go to Lieb's, on the corner of Cherry and Cotton, to pick up some special items Joshua loved, and then move to O'Gorman's Dry Goods to restock the staples. She'd finish at Jacques' Grocers on Fourth and Cherry. They had the best meats. It was her biggest day and she didn't have the time or patience for the growing swells of nausea rumbling in her stomach.

The nausea didn't take kindly to being ignored. She retreated to one of the bathrooms. One bathroom was a luxury at the time, multiple ones unheard of, but Joshua considered them a necessity when he built the shelter, given the numbers of people who'd be in the house at any given time.

Sadie came out and started firmly towards the door. Then she stopped in mid-stride, grabbed her stomach and retreated again.

Serena pounced when she came out from the second visit.

"Bed," she said firmly. "Now."

"Girl, get out of my way."

"Bed," she repeated, taking Sadie's arm and leading her down the hall. "Now."

"Got things to do, we almost out of dry goods and—"

"I'll do it."

"You doan know where I go an' what I buy."

"I know how to read a list. And I'll take Jerry with me to drive the wagon just like you do. He'll know exactly where to go," she declared. Fourteen year old Jerry Smith had been one of Joshua's first permanent orphans.

"You ain't got no business goin' out."

"I'll be careful and I'll wear a big sunhat. Besides, I'm going to the grocers', I'm not going to parade around in society."

"You needs to ask Joshua."

"Joshua's already left. Clara Cranton died this morning and he's out with the family making plans and all. "

"He ain't goan lik' dis," Sadie said, sinking gratefully down on the bed.

"He'll like it a lot less if the children don't have supper."

Mind over matter wasn't working, and the bathroom called again. Sadie gave in. "Girl, you watch yo'self."

"I will, don't worry."

* * *

Serena did watch herself. But someone else did, too. Serena wouldn't have recognized him if she'd seen him, but she never saw him. He'd been at her wedding. Kent Wentworth. A cousin from the Lexington, Kentucky branch.

Some months before, Kent's father entered into negotiations to purchase Findley Ironworks. He wanted one of his own to run it. He looked around the family and settled on his youngest son, Kent. Findley Ironworks sprawled over one block at the industrial end of Third Street in Macon, Bibb County, Georgia.

Kent didn't frequent grocers' establishments for fun and entertainment. However, his wife Miribelle wasn't terribly receptive to relocating. And she sure as hell wasn't relocating without some idea of the standard of living in Macon, Georgia, including the availability of certain imported food items. And she'd made it clear he needn't come home without answers to the list of questions she sent with him.

Kent liked Macon. Findley Ironworks would make the family tons more money, and there were some wonderful houses. Now he was checking the shopping scene. Miribelle was a damn Tartar when enraged. He wasn't about to go home without answers to every question on her list.

One shop's sign proclaimed *Leopold L. Lieb— Importer of Fine Groceries*. God was good. Life with Miribelle in Macon, Georgia might be tolerable after all.

He walked the aisles and thanked God again, and just as he was leaving, a laugh caught his ear. A good laugh, a pleasant combination of daintiness and heartiness. He glanced over at the counter. Fine figure of a woman, from the back, anyway, trim and small and reminiscent of Miribelle's figure before childbirth.

She'd never bounced back after the twins, turning Kent into a furtive but avid admirer of the female form.

Then she turned. Kent ducked back behind the nearest aisle. Lord God. Was that? Could it be? Yes. Definitely. His cousin David's wife, who'd run away in the dark of night, carrying David's unborn heir with her. Woman must have the luck of the devil, too, none of the Pinkerton agents ever caught the first scent of her. The child should have been born sometime in March and her figure definitely wasn't pregnant. When she left the store, he moved to the counter.

"Can I help you, sir?"

"Well, actually, my wife and I'll be moving to town real soon and I was just browsing through."

"Oh, that's wonderful, sir. I hope you've found everything you were looking for."

"Oh, I did. I surely did. My wife's goin' be real happy here, I'm sure of it. As a matter of fact, that lady that just left?"

"Yes, sir?"

"She looks real familiar to me. In fact, I'm almost sure she's a friend of my wife from finishing school days but her name escapes me right now. They were right close but they lost touch, you know how it is, and it sure would tickle me if I could go back and tell my wife I ran into her and she lives in Macon now. Life's strange, ain't it?"

"Yes sir, it sure is."

"You happen to know who she might be?"

"Well, to be honest, sir, I've never seen her before. Usually, Sadie shops for Gorley House."

"Gorley House?"

"It's a shelter, sort of. The preacher for the black Episcopal Church runs it, Joshua Devlin. A combination shelter, orphanage, school."

"But that lady's white."

"Well, Joshua Devlin's place, it's—different. See, he sort of works with folks nobody else wants, people don't have nowhere else to go. He don't bother anybody, I mean, it's not like he's one of them uppity niggers trying to be better than he is. He grew up here, raised by a real good white family who took him in, so I guess folks kind of overlook a lot of things they might not overlook otherwise. Besides, some of the white folks, the white churches, they give him a hand every now and then, one of their charities. Now that you mention it, she don't much seem like she's one of his street people."

"You sure she's from this Gorley House?"

"Oh, yes, sir. Charged it to the account and believe me, I wish some white folks paid their bills like Joshua Devlin does. And besides, she had Jerry with her. Jerry's one of their orphans, usually comes in with Sadie, that's Joshua's mama, to help out with the weekly shopping, so I'm sure."

"I see. Well, 'preciate your time. I'm sure my wife'll be adding to your business real soon now."

"We'll look forward to it, sir."

Kent walked out and stood on the streets, shaking his head. So that's how she'd avoided leaving any traces. Hiding out with the niggers. Probably did it in every town she ran through on her way here.

Kent grudgingly admitted to himself she had a lot of spunk. He further grudgingly admitted to himself that he didn't like his cousin, and he wouldn't want one of his daughters marrying any man who remotely reminded him of David Wentworth. But she'd birthed a Wentworth child with the niggers? And was *raising* him with them? He hadn't wanted to ask too many questions of the obliging clerk but if this Gorley House was a Church offshoot, he might ought to tour the local churches. He hadn't checked out Macon's religious circuit as yet. Actually, Miribelle hadn't mentioned it. Church for her was a social function more than anything else but she ought to be impressed with his thorough investigation.

A big Presbyterian Church stood on the corner of— now, what were those streets? Mulberry and First, that was it. God, new towns were hell. He collected his horse and rode on down the street.

He emerged from the minister's office knowing a lot more than he'd ever wanted to know about Macon's First Presbyterian Church. More important, he knew a lot about Gorley House and Joshua Devlin. Tolerant city, Macon. Basically, the white folks just let him take care of the business of needy folks so they didn't have to.

Visiting the police station probably wouldn't work, even if he flat out told them his cousin's runaway wife had kidnapped a child and demanded they make the recovery. He was pretty sure the residents of Gorley House would deny all knowledge of Serena and also pretty sure, unbelievable as it was, that the Macon police would take their word for it over his. After which, of course, Serena would be gone in about fifteen seconds. Besides, the Wentworths didn't go through channels. They made their own.

He consulted the street map, turned his horse and trotted down to Third Street, turning onto Congress Street.

He rode casually by Gorley House. The huge, clean clapboard structure wasn't at all what he'd expected. Well-fed, well-clothed children played in the side yard. But half the faces were white and half were black. And Serena was raising a Wentworth child here?

He rode back to Brown's Hotel. He needed back up. The Wentworths were simply going to go into Gorley House and take her and the child back where they belonged. The telegram to Greenville raced through the wires before noon. *Found her. Macon. Advise arrival time.*

* * *

Kent passed a profitable afternoon and evening waiting for his cousin's train to pull into the depot. Upper class Macon might be just fine and dandy letting

Joshua Devlin handle the problem of the needy. But he knew one class of Macon wouldn't be fine and dandy with it at all.

There were in-between folks, uneducated maybe, but not entirely illiterate and after all, Kent wasn't looking for Harvard graduates. These men weren't upper class, or even middle class, but they weren't trash. Fiercely independent, many were from farm stock whose families had been forced to the city streets and closely built houses by droughts or floods or failed crops or hoof-in-mouth disease. They didn't have a background of *noblesse oblige.* Most of them lumped all people with dark skin into one neat category: they were niggers.

Kent wasn't surprised to find the working class men who stopped in at the small bars on Third and Fourth Streets for a mug of beer on the way home didn't like Gorley House or Joshua Devlin. In fact, they were of the opinion Macon would be a hell of a lot better off if somebody rode that nigger out of town on the rails and burned the entire shootin' match to the ground. After all, nobody was giving *them* any hand-outs. Not that they'd take any hand-outs were they offered.

Kent smiled and disbursed liquid refreshment with a liberal hand. By darkfall, he had the bars incensed, ready to help in the righting of this terrible wrong. Things had come to a damn fine pass when a man's wife took off without a by-your-leave and stole his young'un. So what if the young'un wasn't born yet, didn't that damn woman have no idea what a man's first son meant to him? Didn't she have no respect, hiding out with the niggers? And that highfalutin' Joshua Devlin, who talked like a white man and acted like he thought his shit didn't stink, well, he'd just stuck his nose in one time too many where it didn't belong and if the rich white folks in this town didn't have the guts to put him in his place once and for all, they sure as hell did.

They'd like to see him try and stop them from helping their newfound friend and his cousin get that baby back. They purely would like to see it. They *hoped* they'd see it.

Kent left them at eleven p.m. to meet his cousin at the train depot. He'd meet them at Gorley House with David. Kent paced impatiently, checking his watch. Damnation. Almost midnight. Would the damn train never pull in? Finally, it did. David Wentworth stalked across the terminal platform.

"Where the hell is she?" he demanded.

For the briefest space, Kent, irritated as hell by David's attitude—no expression of thanks, no appreciation that his cousin had finally brought Serena to ground when battalions of Pinkertons hadn't been able to—almost told his cousin he'd been mistaken. That he'd thought he'd found Serena but it hadn't been her after all. But damn it all, a Wentworth baby was involved. Why the hell did there have to be a baby?

"At a church shelter," he said shortly. "It's called Gorley House. Now if you'll shut up, I'll tell you what we're goin' to do about it."

"Don't you talk to me like that!"

"I'll talk to you any damn way I please! I spent all damn day on this, I got the whole thing set up! Now you just shut up and listen to me!"

David did.

"What the hell you mean the police wouldn't be much help? We're Wentworths, by God, they'll do whatever the hell I tell 'em to!"

"I don't think so. And it don't matter anyway. I got better than the police. I got a whole group of liquored-up transplanted sharecroppers waiting down from the house ready to go in that door right behind us. Every last one of 'em despises niggers and hates this Devlin nigger's guts."

When they rendezvoused with the mob, David had to admit Kent had done himself proud. Nobody was going to stop this group. If Serena was in that house, they'd find her. And his son.

"All right," he said shortly. "Let's do it."

* * *

In this hour past midnight, Gorley House was dark. The children slept soundly in their dormitory rooms in the rear of the building, sprawled with the careless abandon of childhood between their clean cotton sheets underneath thin veils of mosquito netting.

The dormitory rooms reserved for those temporarily in need of shelter were empty. In high summer, seasonal farm work was plentiful and the nights were warm. No transient street people needed shelter that night.

Sadie was awake. She sat in the kitchen on the side of the house, sipping weak tea. The rumbling nausea had finally departed and she'd slept off and on through the day. Now, she couldn't sleep. She glanced out the window, looked away, and glanced back. Lantern light? Not out front, but she was sure she'd caught a lantern glimmer going around the side of the house toward the front door. Surely no one needed help at this hour in high summer. She groaned and got up to go check. Sometimes she wished Joshua had gone to medical school. She'd swear to the Lord fewer people had knocked for Everett and Paul in the middle of the night.

She stood by the door. Nobody knocked, but there was definite movement and low rumblings of mumbled conversation. Well, no sense letting them wake the house.

She opened the door enough to peer out. What on earth? Eight or ten men, all of them white.

Kent moved forward. He didn't trust David to handle this situation.

"Good evening, ma'am, we're sorry to trouble you this time of night."

"Yes suh?"

David pushed his cousin out of the way and shoved Sadie backwards. Caught off guard, she fell heavily and struck her head against the sharp corner of the low table standing against the foyer wall. She tried to fight off the dancing motes of lights behind her eyes and regain her balance but gravity pulled her on down. Her head bounced hard off the hardwood floor. She went limp, momentarily knocked unconscious by the successive blows.

"Goddamn, you idiot! This ain't no social event! I want that bitch! And I want my son!"

David started down the hall, his rag-tag vigilantes close behind.

"Goddamn it!" Kent exclaimed under his breath. The head-strong, stubborn, stupid son-of-a-bitch. And this idiot was the head of the sprawling Wentworth fortune? They'd best start stockpiling their money or it wouldn't last long. David was one insane little bastard.

Kent bent over Sadie, uncertain whether to pick her up. He heard the low mutters of the men and slamming doors as they moved throughout the house. He could check on the old woman later. Now he needed to follow David and see if he could keep the situation under control.

He froze at the bellow of rage.

"You whoring bitch! Ruttin' with a nigger!"

Kent shot down the hall. What the holy hell was going on? This wasn't the way he'd planned things, not at all.

He pushed his way through the crowd of men standing in the doorway, ignoring their mutters.

"Never seen the beat!"

"Did you ever?"

"My woman, I'd skin her alive!"

"Not 'fore I skint that nigger!"

"Starting at his balls!"

Kent pushed his way to his cousin's side. He stared in horror at the sight of the couple, their contrasting color staring in stark relief against the white of the sheets. The bedside lamp, lit hurriedly when the mob's search wakened them, burned low.

Its dim light served as the final macabre touch for this vision of a white man's greatest horror. He'd sympathized with Serena, he truly had. Only the thought of the Wentworth child had made him send the telegraph humming over the wires. But this? How in the hell had any white woman fallen to this?

He looked at his cousin's face and saw death. David's revolver was in his hand, pointed directly at Joshua. Joshua's eyes moved around the room, looking for something, anything. But there was nothing and he knew it. Nothing beat a bullet and even it did, he was staring a lynch mob in the face.

The hammer cocked. The trigger began to squeeze. Joshua turned to look at Serena's face.

"Love you," he said.

* * *

Paul roamed the woods, the blood fever upon him. The tensions of the past weeks, his worry over his brother—he hadn't even tried to fight it. He had to hunt, he had to stalk and capture, bite and tear. He knelt on the ground beside the big buck he'd strangled with his bare hands and tore open the jugular, feasting on the richness of hot blood.

Suddenly, he raised his head. Blood dripped from his mouth in black gouts and stained the front of his white shirt. He didn't hear the sounds with his ears. Some portion of his brain caught echoes, sending them out in a floodtide. He raised his arm and wiped his mouth with the sleeve of his shirt. The vibrations of a gunshot reverberated throughout every cell of his soul.

"No!"

The roar of the shout lingered long after he cast out into the dark.

David turned the gun on Serena. She sat immobile, carved from stone. She held the sheet, splattered now with Joshua's blood, tight over her breasts. She'd looked at Joshua once. She'd look no more. His face was gone. In a few seconds, she'd follow him and then she wouldn't feel the horrified grief and guilt she knew was coming as soon as the first numbed shock and disbelief wore off.

"David, don't!" Kent spoke urgently to his cousin, afraid to grab his arm for fear of the gun's explosion. "The nigger's one thing but—"

David Wentworth laughed.

"Like I'd make hers that quick," he told his cousin. He turned to Serena.

"Get your ass out of that bed and get dressed. Then you show me where my son is. But don't you dare touch him. You ain't never goin' to touch him again. You just about to find out what hell is, woman!"

"You don't have a son! The baby's *dead*, you bastard! *Born dead.*"

"*You bitch!* You killed my son!"

The hammer cocked again.

"And it was a *girl*!" she spat. At least she'd die carrying the look on David Wentworth's face with her.

Paul materialized directly beside Wentworth. The buck's blood still stained his mouth. His shirt dripped gore. The vigilantes' eyes bulged. As one, they started backing away, the mutters of the crowd blending into one voice of dismayed disbelief.

"Jesus!"

"Goddamn, did you ever see?"

"What the hell?"

"Let's get the fuck out of here!"

They turned as one to follow that last piece of good advice, their footsteps echoing down the hall. Paul grabbed the gun from Wentworth's hand, snapping his wrist bones. He flung the gun wildly. The force of its impact with the wall sent a bullet ricocheting around the room and Paul felt a sting in his right shoulder. He didn't stop to investigate.

Killing time. He was going to kill this man. He knew it. With his bare hands, he'd tear him limb from limb. A loud crack sounded in the room and Wentworth screamed, his left arm broken.

Serena flung herself off the bed as the gun flew through the air. She pounced on it the second the bullet exploded from the muzzle. She stood straight in the middle of the room, naked and caring not a whit that she was. No one who holds a gun is truly naked. Her long black hair swept across her face in a cloud and she shook her head impatiently, tossing it back.

Kent backed away, his eyes fixed on the furious, bloody thing closing in for the kill. He stopped at the sound of the cocking hammer.

"Don't you move!"

No general ever issued a firmer order. Kent didn't move.

Her voice broke Paul's concentrated attack. Wentworth fell in a crumbled heap at his feet. Paul bent down to grab his arm and haul him back up.

"No!" Serena commanded. "He's *mine!*"

"Serena, for the love of God!" Kent implored, his voice strangling in his throat.

"Look at me, David!"

Wentworth crouched in his huddle at Paul's feet.

"I said look at me!"

He raised his head.

"Meet me in Hell, you bastard!" She pulled the trigger.

Kent stood frozen against the wall, scalded by the heat of his cousin's brains spattering his pants legs. He closed his eyes, waiting to hear the hammer cock again.

"You. Now *you* look at me!"

Kent kept his eyes closed.

"I said, look at me!"

By God, if she was going to blow his brains out too, he'd be man enough to look at her. He opened his eyes.

Serena still held the gun pointed directly at him. But the hammer didn't cock. Keeping the gun trained on her target, she lowered her arms to give Kent a clear view of her body in the light of the kerosene lamp.

"You see me?" she asked. "You see David Wentworth's handiwork?"

He stared at her, at the scars marring her upper body and covering her breasts.

"Oh, my God!"

"You're a Wentworth, aren't you?"

He nodded.

"Yes. You have the look. Do I know you?

"I was at your wedding. I'm David's second cousin."

"No. You're my Judas."

His last nerve snapped.

"Why don't you go ahead and pull the damn trigger? Get it over with!"

Paul spoke.

"He's an extra body to get rid of."

Serena looked at Paul. So this was Joshua's brother, this vision who had appeared from nowhere looking as though like he'd bathed in blood, and knocked the gun from David's hand. How and why, she didn't know and she didn't care but she did know that no one needed to know he existed.

"All right, Cousin Wentworth." She moved to Kent and placed the gun's muzzle directly against his temple. "Tell me what happened here tonight."

"Ain't got no idea in Hell. Ain't seen David in two months."

"What about me?"

"Don't know where you are."

Paul spoke. "But if you ever remember, I'll know. And I'll find you."

"Do you understand?" Serena asked.

Kent was afraid to speak and with the gun to his temple, he was afraid to nod. His lips barely moved as he whispered.

"Yes."

Serena looked at Paul. He nodded.

"Go," she said, standing back and lowering the gun.

He went. And none of his father's raging threats of disinheritance ever brought him back to Macon again.

* * *

Paul looked at Serena. He couldn't look at his brother. Not yet. He walked to the dresser and lifted Serena's robe, tossing it to her. He dared not come near her. He wished he'd let her die in childbirth.

She caught it, realizing for the first time she was naked. She didn't care but she slipped it on. She stood and inspected him.

"You're hurt," she said. He shook his head. "Yes, you are," she insisted, moving nearer. "Your shoulder."

He moved away from her and looked down at the small, reddened hole in his shoulder. Must have caught a ricochet. He felt something move under his skin and as he watched the flattened lead popped out and fell to the floor.

He ignored Serena's gasp and maintained his careful distance. She caught the echoes of swirling ice in his voice.

"Where's Sadie?"

"I don't know."

The moan came from the doorway. He swirled around. Sadie stood, holding on to the door frame. She'd held on to the walls navigating her way to the room, refusing to give in to the dancing, dizzying motes floating behind her eyes. Paul rushed to her.

"Mama."

She sank down on the floor and sat stiffly, her eyes wide as they focused on Joshua's body. She folded her arms across her breasts and began to rock.

"Mama!" Paul knelt beside her and caught her swaying shoulders. "Mama, stop! Sadie! Look at me!"

But Sadie didn't stop. She didn't look. Her eyes stared, unseeing, at the still figure on the bed. She saw nothing. There was nothing in her world except darkness and the rocking sensation. She didn't know the swaying came from the motion of her own body. She knew nothing.

Paul slowly straightened. He turned and walked to the bed, picking up the bed spread from its bottom. He wrapped his brother in its folds.

"Get me a shawl or something. For Sadie."

"What are you going to do?"

"To bury my brother. And take Sadie somewhere."

"Where?"

"None of your damned business."

"I'll take care of Sadie."

"Like you took care of my brother?"

"Where will you bury him?"

"Are you deaf? None of your damned business."

"I deserve to know where he's buried!"

"So you can put flowers on his grave? Touching. You already killed him. That's not enough?"

She moved to Joshua's bureau and pulled out one of his shirts.

"Here." she said, holding it out. "Whatever you think of me, you can't go riding through town like that."

Paul looked down at his bloody shirt and shrugged. He ripped the buttons off and dropped it, pulling on its replacement. It was tight across the chest and the arms were a little too short. Both the Devlin brothers were lean and well-made but Joshua was smaller. No matter. It would do.

He picked Joshua up and they both disappeared, leaving Serena gape-mouthed. He materialized in the stables and placed Joshua carefully in the back of the small buckboard and returned to the bedroom.

He stared down at David Wentworth's body. Too bad he was dead. He'd died too quick. He bent and tossed the body over his shoulder and disappeared again. This time he materialized down by the Ocmulgee. Without ceremony, he tossed the dead man into the flowing current. Then he returned for Sadie.

"I asked you to get her a shawl," he said. He moved to Joshua's desk, opened the drawer and pulled out P. J. Devlin's checkbook.

Serena left the room. She refused to think about the mysterious appearances and disappearances of Joshua's brother. What did they matter after tonight? But the children. They must be terrified. She found them huddled together in one of the back rooms, and took a moment to reassure them.

"Miss Serena—"

"It'll be all right," she assured them. "I'll be back. Jerry, you watch them."

She went into Sadie's room for a shawl. When she returned to the bloody death scene, Paul held out a piece of paper. A check signed by P. J. Devlin representing most of the money held jointly by the brothers. The signature was neither his nor Joshua's, but a manufactured uniform script they'd practiced for just such purpose.

"Take it."

"I don't want it."

"I said take it. Joshua'd want you taken care of."

"What do you care? You'd love to kill me yourself, right this minute."

"Yes. I would. Now take this."

"How are we going to explain all this?" She waved her hand around the room at the pooling blood.

"We aren't. You are. And I don't give a damn how you do it."

She held out her hand and took the check. Paul moved over to Sadie and picked her up. Even in his arms, she swayed. Her eyes stared into the dark invading her brain. Paul had never tried to carry another living person with him when he cast out and sure as hell wasn't trying it with her. He walked swiftly down the hall, headed for the stables. The echoes of his boot heels floated back to Serena.

She walked over to the bureau and picked up the picture of Joshua and his brother and sister-in-law. She'd never seen another one. This was all she had. She laid it on Joshua's desk while she methodically tore P. J. Devlin's check into very small pieces. She threw them into the wastebasket where Joshua consigned the first drafts of his sermons. Paul wouldn't notice that it hadn't cleared the bank for several months. When he did, he'd merely shrug.

Then she picked the picture up again and walked down the hall to the children. Somehow she had to see them taken care of but she dared not do it herself. She didn't think David's cousin would ever breathe a word about her to anybody but she couldn't take the chance.

She knew, she'd known for several days, a small part of Joshua Devlin grew inside her. She wouldn't risk losing it. She'd make sure the children were placed elsewhere and then she'd disappear into the streets of Macon.

How she'd live, she didn't know. But she knew she'd live as Serena Devlin and that Joshua's child was going to carry his name.

Chapter Seventeen

Paul pulled the wagon up in front of Tamara's cottage at three o'clock in the morning. Light moved in the little barn at the rear of the yard.

He got down and decided he could leave Sadie for a few minutes. Her eyes still stared at nothing as she rocked herself back and forth. He found Tamara struggling to harness her team to her own wagon. She turned at his step. The malignant invader in her body had been working overtime. A death's head stared at him from gray-tinged skin.

"Son!"

"What the hell do you think you're doing?"

"I woke up and I knowed. I's got to get to Sadie."

"I brought her to you. She's in the wagon."

"Joshua—"

"C'mon." He felt the radial bone through its covering of skin and sinew when he took her arm. There was nothing else left. He didn't know how she still had strength to stand. He picked her up. She didn't weigh as much as a child.

"I ken walk!"

"Barely. Now hush." He took her to the wagon where Sadie still rocked on the seat, and set her on her feet.

"Sadie?"

"She doesn't hear you."

"Joshua?" Tamara asked again.

Paul stepped up into the wagon. He gathered Sadie into his arms and leaped down.

"Let me get you both inside. Then I'll bury him."

Paul stood back in the woods by the carved bench where Tamara, so long ago, had read his destiny in his palm. He looked at the neatly covered mound. His brother rested under the dark and healing earth. He wanted to pray but no words came. Tomorrow night maybe. For now, it was done. Just as he'd never remembered a word of Chloe's funeral service, he'd never remember actually digging Joshua's grave, never recall the sound of the shovel sliding through the moist earth.

He needed to check on the only two living people on earth who mattered to him. He cast back out into the dark.

"Sit down, son. Have some hot tea for you in jest a minute."

"Don't want it," he said. He walked over to Sadie, seated in the rocking chair in front of the fireplace. It rocked with the same rhythm Sadie'd mastered since viewing Joshua's body. He squatted in front of her and caught the arms of the chair in his hands, stopping the motion.

"Mama?" he asked again, expecting no reply.

Her eyes broke the fixed stare and turned to him. Her face split in a sudden smile.

"Now whut's dis? An' who you be, suh? You puts me in mind of my oldest boy! He a doctor, you know, and he an' dat pretty Chloe of his, dey fixin' to have a baby! I jest loves babies! Been a long time since my youngest boy been a baby. He workin' hard, my youngest boy, studyin' all dem books wid his brother and he goan go to school up north pretty soon. Goan come back and I be done raised two doctors. Ain't dat somethin'?"

Sadie smiled again. As suddenly as the blackness lifted, it descended. Her face went blank. Her eyes resumed their fixed stare at nothing. Her body tried to resume its sway and Paul turned loose of the rocking chair's arms and let the rhythm take over.

He lowered his head. Tears dropped onto his pants leg, leaving small, wet circles. Tamara watched as the circle was joined by another, and another. She moved behind him and put her hand on his shoulder.

"Son. Doan grieve for yo' mama. She happy again. She got both her boys back."

Paul choked on the muffled sobs caught in his throat. He turned and threw his arms around Tamara's legs, holding onto her through the folds of her long skirt.

She dropped to the floor beside him and held him in her skeletal arms. She let him cry out the first ripping tears of grief, and when Paul felt his strength begin to drain with the first hint of the sun's rays, she settled him in her root-cellar and soothed him as his own private darkness fell, just as she'd soothed him in the first dawns of his second life. She knew he felt neither heat nor cold but she covered him carefully nonetheless and went back to her sister.

* * *

Paul woke that sunset with the feeling something was wrong. Then he laughed harshly. His wife and infant son lay in a burial plot in Rose Arbor Cemetery and he'd never lie next to them. His father was dead of a heart condition precipitated by the sight of Isaiah Gorley's bloody head coming through the window. His brother lay in an unmarked grave with his face blown off because he'd dared love a woman he'd have never met if Paul hadn't insisted on turning him into a white man in a black man's body. The woman he called Mama sat in a rocking chair alternating between spells of complete blankness and total retreats into the past. She didn't even recognize him. And Tamara, the healer who dispensed comfort with her very touch, was dying quickly, inch by inch, before his helpless eyes.

Wrong? Now what could be wrong?

He materialized in front of the fireplace.

"Tamara, how's Mama doing?"

He broke off abruptly, staring at the two figures lying side by side on the bed. He'd never remember moving, but he found himself holding first Tamara's wrist and then Sadie's, searching for the pulse. Nothing. Either of them. He dropped Sadie's hand and backed away, his mind screaming denial.

When he had some semblance of control again, he looked around the room. A white piece of paper lay on the table, held down at the corner by Tamara's prized porcelain teapot, the one that sat on the mantle and was never used.

He picked it up. Tamara's handwriting had never been an example of copperplate penmanship but it had been firm. Clear and strong, it was an extension of her extraordinary personality. He'd seen it many times on the cards holding her scrawled notes and recipes for herbal remedies.

This handwriting was spidery, tentative, weak. Dying. He didn't read the words, he heard them. He'd never be sure but it seemed she spoke to him.

Son, I knows dis goan lie heavy on yo' heart and I wish dere was some way you didn't have to be de one to finds us. But dere ain't no other way. I doan got long, Paul, and I knows it. I ken feel it. My life's windin' down, de way all life winds down, and dere ain't but a few hours left. An' I can't leave my sister, son. Ain't nobody to take care of her and you jest can't tend to her. She wouldn't want dat burden on you. So's I's fixed her a pot of tea. Special tea. Right now, she think she visitin' me and she goan go home to you and Chloe and Joshua and yo' Daddy. She happy, son, and it be time. Time for both of us to go home. Know dat both of us loves you. An' know dis, too. I never tole you dis, 'cause I can't 'splain exactly how it goan happen, but somewhere, sometime, you goan find dat a part of us is still alive. All of us. Me and yo' Mama an' yo' brother an' yo' Daddy. Wait for us, son. We find you.

Paul folded the paper carefully and stuck it in his shirt pocket. He opened Tamara's cupboard doors and pulled out two quilts. He wrapped his last two links to human love carefully. Then his own merciful shroud of fog came over him again while he consigned the two bodies to the waiting earth beside Joshua's grave.

When memory returned, he stood in the middle of the big room of the cottage. Modern medicine would diagnose him as very close to a complete psychotic break. He wanted to cast himself out into the dark and materialize in the city streets of Macon. He wanted to hunt, to stalk and capture, bite and tear. And drink. And drink. And drink. But not among the shrouded trees of the thick woods. And not animals.

He wanted new territory, city territory, human prey. He wanted somebody else, anybody else, everybody else, to hurt as badly as he hurt.

He unleashed his fury in the confines of the cottage. He picked up every piece of furniture and smashed it against the walls. He grabbed every dish, every knickknack, every picture on the wall, and smashed them too, laughing as they shattered.

And when nothing remained but wreckage, he stood and surveyed his handiwork. He grabbed the kerosene lamps, which he'd saved for last, and jerked off the glass globes. He upended them and sent the kerosene streaming across the debris.

He went outside and struck a match, tossing it back in through the door. The cottage exploded like a tinderbox. The bonfire blazed high into the night sky.

It wasn't enough. He had to hunt.

He cast himself out, turning toward town. He materialized in an alley off Cotton Avenue and peered out into the streets. Good prey here. He could smell it. He started out and stopped as the hand touched his shoulder.

He swirled around. The night was empty but the voice was clear.

"You is God's own dark angel, son! You a child of de light dat walks now in de darkness an' doan you never forget it!"

He stood frozen.

"Tamara?"

"God's dark angel, boy!"

The voiced floated back to him.

He never hunted again. Not in the streets, not in the woods. In the coming years blood never touched his lips. Thus began his third cycle of life, which would last until the night he'd wake to a young woman asking, "Dr. Devlin, I presume?"

Chapter Eighteen

"And they found you," Ria said softly. "*I* found you. I'm the last living link. To all of them."

"Goddamn," said Dr. Knight reverently. He stood up abruptly.

"C'mon, Paul, let's go."

"Go? Go where?"

"My office. Can't do much tonight but I want some blood. Or whatever it is oils your motor. And some tissue samples."

"Daddy, it's past three o'clock in the morning!" Ria protested.

"Well, baby, let's just make him an appointment for ten-thirty Monday morning."

"I hate a smartass," Ria mumbled. "Let me get my pocketbook."

"No," said her father shortly. "You stay here. We got some heavy duty medical consulting to do. We need a lawyer, we'll call you."

"Daddy!"

"I don't stick my nose in when you're seeing a client, do I?"

"Stay here," Paul said. He leaned over and kissed her cheek swiftly. "Get some sleep."

"Will you come back here? When you get through?"

"If there's time."

She watched them walk out, two men from different ends of the time spectrum of the Devlin medical tradition.

Paul turned back and spoke in a sotto whisper over his shoulder.

"Everett Devlin lives," he said, gesturing toward her father's back. "God, he's Papa made over!"

An uncomfortable silence filled the car as Dr. Knight drove through the sleepy night streets toward the medical complex housing his offices. Paul didn't know how to break the silence. He was far younger than Charlie Knight in appearance, far older in years. He'd practiced medicine when Charlie wasn't a glint in anybody's eye, but this doctor could perform medical miracles Paul Devlin would never have believed possible. And he'd spent the last month and a half making love to the man's daughter. That by itself paralyzed Paul's vocal chords. He was from a different time.

Dr. Knight glanced over at Paul as he drove down the streets. He felt the turmoil pouring from his mind. He'd always been able to sense other people's thoughts and emotions but he'd never thought much about it. It was just part of him, like his dark brown eyes and his black hair, now threaded with silver. And a damn handy thing to have in the medical profession, too.

He'd been tickled pink, as Ria grew, to find she could do the same thing. Now he knew where it came from.

"What sort of time frame are we looking at here?" Dr. Knight asked suddenly.

"Sir?"

Dr. Knight laughed. "Sir. I don't think that quite works here. I'm Charlie and you're Paul. The man my daughter's in love with."

"*Shit*," Paul muttered under his breath, and Dr. Knight laughed again.

"You know, Paul, I think I've picked up on a few things Ria hasn't. Not 'cause she couldn't. 'Cause she don't want to. Joshua ain't the only Devlin's made a career out of being his brother's keeper. Thinking about consequences to other people—that's shaped your life more than maybe you shoulda let it. Like, for example, if you'd turned that police chief loose on Cain's circle—"

"I couldn't do that, I told you—"

"They'd have massacred everybody there. And as Sadie so accurately pointed out, neither one of *her* boys woulda been there. And then there's my grandmother. Serena. You wanted to kill her the night her husband blew Joshua's face off so what did you do? You wrote her a check for damn near the whole Devlin bank account. You didn't know she wouldn't cash it, and what the hell would you have done over the years if she had?"

"Joshua would have wanted her taken care of."

"Oh, fuck what Joshua would have wanted. Just one time, what does Paul want? Which brings us to my daughter."

"I don't intend for Ria to ever suffer because she met me, I promise."

"*Un-huh.* Thought so. So I ask you again, son, what self-imposed time frame did you give yourself to actually enjoy livin' and lovin' before you just pick up and boogey on out of her life?"

"How did you—"

"*Shit!* Anybody knows anything about you could figure that out. You just couldn't resist, but since you don't think you offer much in the way of normal lifestyle, there's no way you're going to make this a long-term thing. And what do you think that'll do to her? When you don't come back?"

"She won't remember me. Neither will you. Nobody will."

Dr. Knight sat thoughtfully under the parking lights.

"Yeah, I kind of thought there might be some mental domination thing. Goes along with the teleportation and all that."

"Alright, it's dishonest and it's selfish. But I thought maybe, just this once, just for a little while—"

"Shit, son. It sucks. I mean, it really sucks. You know?"

"And you'd like for me to just go ahead and disappear now? Is that it?"

"What I'd have *liked*, son, is for you and your Chloe to have lived out a long, happy life together with lots of kids and be side by side in Rose Arbor now. But since that just ain't the way it happened, let me tell you a few things about my daughter. First off, you might can make her forget. Make all of us forget. Well, you say you can, so I'm sure you can. But we're talkin' about Ria here. Last living link to the Voodoo Queen of Stone Creek Swamp, remember? And she'll *never* forget what she feels. And way down deep, she'll always sense— she'll always *know*--that there's something else, somebody else—somewhere. She won't know what and she won't know why but she'll measure every man she meets for the rest of her life by a man she doesn't even remember. And that I don't like. Not worth a damn."

"And your point is?"

"She's right. This was meant, Paul. She was *meant* to find you. Even Tamara said so, one of the last things she ever told you, over a hundred years ago. In other words, son, you're in for the long haul whether you like it or not and you better know it. Because no matter how bad you think you're fuckin' her life up by being in it, you'll *destroy* her if you leave. And that will *really, really* piss me off."

Paul laughed. He couldn't help it. He felt curiously lighter somehow, absolved of at least a little bit of blame for being irresponsible enough to start an actual human relationship.

"And if you're that pissed, then I better *hope* you don't remember where to find me, huh?"

"Damn straight. So what do you say, son? We have no idea what this thing is, but we won't ever know if I don't start tryin' to check it out. I'm not a research specialist but I have friends I trust who are. And if it can't be reversed—and we both know reversing something like this ranks somewhere between impossible and not a snowball's chance in hell, maybe we can mitigate it a little bit so you're at least a little more normal. We won't know how much more normal 'til we start lookin'. Can you trust me and the people I trust enough to try?"

Paul thought of the sun catching the reddish highlights of Ria's hair.

"You know how long it's been since I've seen sunrise, Charlie?"

"Right around a century and some change," Dr. Knight responded with barely a pause. "I was always good at quick figures. So can you try, you think?"

"Yes. I can try."

"But no matter what happens, you do understand what I'm telling you about Ria? Long haul. You got that?"

"You really believe that, don't you?"

"Son, I *know* that."

"All right. Long haul. Got it."

"Then let's get to it," Dr. Knight said. He threw open his car door. "And when I get through with you, you're gonna think I'm the vampire."

* * *

Paul materialized in Ria's bedroom. He had maybe an hour until dawn. As though she felt him even in her sleep, she stretched and turned. She smiled as her eyes opened and she held out her arms. He wiped all thoughts of the future from his mind and gathered her close. The house sighed in contentment, always happy to know its master was home.

Later, in the last minutes of darkness left, Ria purred contentedly into his shoulder.

"Well, you survived Daddy very nicely."

"Barely. He was right, he's the vampire," Paul said, flexing his right arm as it lay under her hair.

Ria turned her head, pulling his arm over her face and running her lips lightly along the sensitive skin of his inner forearm.

"Don't start something I don't have time to finish," Paul warned. "It's almost dawn."

"Wouldn't it be wonderful? If you could watch the dawn?"

"Ria, don't hope too much, darlin'.'"

"I know. But when did Daddy say he'd know anything?"

"Several days at least. Go back to sleep," he said, and grabbed one last kiss before the first rays broke over the horizon. He left.

* * *

Three nights later, Dr. Knight's voice sounded over the buzzer's intercom. Ria raced downstairs and hauled him up the steps.

"C'mon, Daddy! Lord, turtles move faster!"

"Jesus, baby! Give the old man a chance to catch his breath!" He pretended to stagger over to the couch and fell heavily on the cushions.

"Knock it off! You put in at least half an hour on the tredmill every day!"

"Do not!"

"Do too!"

"Children, children!" Paul called for order. "Ria, give your father a chance. And Charlie, just quit it! Nobody believes the old man act, all right?"

"C'mon, Daddy! What've you got?"

"Well, I can't tell you a lot, but I can tell you two things."

"Well, *what*?"

"Good news first?"

"Daddy!"

"Okay, okay! Well, the good news is I think I've discovered the cure for cancer."

"And the bad news?" asked Paul, with lifted eyebrow.

"Cure'll kill you."

Ria groaned and Paul laughed. Something in Charlie's face hinted at possibilities.

"Okay, seriously. Stu Harmon's 'bout to go crazy. That's my—"

"We know, we know. Big chief at the Atlanta Center for Disease Control." Ria knew her father had driven directly to Dr. Harmon's home Sunday afternoon with the samples. "So *give!*"

"Well, we're not sure about the DNA changes, too soon. But we think the big thing's the blood. Or whatever it is, 'cause it sure as hell ain't blood. It's a sterilizing agent. Sterilizes everything."

"Sterilizes?"

"It eats any foreign body that invades it. That's why there's no waste product to throw off. I gotta say Paul, you'd sure be my first choice for a traveling companion on a car trip. Wouldn't have to make any pit stops at all on your account, 'course you already know that."

Paul frowned. "And this means what in terms of doing anything to correct it?"

"Stu's introduced all sorts of cultures in the samples. So far, the samples have eaten everything. It's the universal cure for what ails you. Stu hasn't tried yet but we think it'll even eat the HIV virus. In fact, it seems to be pretty much the opposite of AIDS. The AIDS virus attacks the immune system and lets anything invade. This thing, Stu calls it the V-Factor, it completely overhauls the immunities and nothing seems to bother it, not even the aging process. 'Course, the side-effects, they'll—"

"Kill you," Paul supplied.

"Well, actually, maybe not. Think about it a minute, Paul. What actually killed you was exsanguination. That's blood loss to you, Ria. Maybe if you hadn't been literally drained dry—"

"No, back up. The V-Factor changes the immune system and that'll kill you anyway. Because then the system doesn't sustain normal life. It alters it completely. It isn't life by any of our definitions."

"But maybe if normal blood is reintroduced, it'll dilute the V-Factor to the extent that some amount of normal function is possible."

"But if it eats any foreign substance introduced," Ria broke in, "normal blood is a foreign substance and it'll absorb it immediately before any dilution can take place. And what the hell does any of this have to do with the night-time thing? Or the teleportation?"

"Well, shit, baby! It's been three days. We're not going to figure everything out in three days, or weeks, or months or years! We've got a lot more testing to do. But it's more than we did know. And we do have an idea."

"Which is?" Paul asked.

"Transfusions of normal blood."

"Daddy, you just said—"

"With some of the anti-rejection drugs developed for transplants. We got to start somewhere. What do you think, Paul?"

Paul looked at Ria.

"I think it won't hurt to try."

* * *

A week after her father's visit, Ria walked out to her car. Friday afternoon and she had three new appointed criminal cases, all three clients currently enjoying the hospitality of the local Law Enforcement Center, more commonly known as the jail. Ordinarily, she detested walking down its halls. Today, though, her spirits were high and not even the impending and annoying wolf-whistles and cat calls she knew she'd hear could dent her mood.

It was the first week of December. Christmas was coming, and after the holidays, they'd try the first of the transfusions. Of course, Paul and her father warned her every other breath not to expect much of anything this early in the research project. She still walked through the days in euphoric anticipation, though. It was a start. It was *something*.

A glazed ham baked slowly in her oven upstairs. Tonight was an early holiday dinner party. Sort of. Dennis Billings and his girlfriend were coming over. She liked keeping an eye on Dennis, that boy'd come around just fine. She was proud of him. And her law partner Johnny was footloose and fancy-free that evening, too, so he'd be there. Ria didn't enjoy cooking much but the holidays were something else altogether. Especially this year. Good friends, good company. And Paul.

Her mind was running over the night's menu to make sure she hadn't forgotten anything as she walked into the old carriage house, now the garage. She put her hand on the door handle just as the lights exploded behind her eyes. Her ears never registered the solid 'thump' of the gun butt as it caught her directly behind the ear. Her hand slid off the handle. She slumped, unconscious, to the concrete floor.

Justin Dinardo bent over. He laughed softly as he plucked the car keys from her hand. He'd driven into Macon for the past few afternoons, parking his stolen, ratty car up on College Street and walking down to crouch in the corner of the garage. Just in case. But good things came to those who waited. Sooner or later.

He opened the trunk and walked back to Ria. He picked her up and dumped her unceremoniously into the small space. He carelessly bent her arms and legs, folding her into a small enough package so he could close the trunk. He slammed the lid down and frowned. '65 Mustangs didn't have a lot of trunk room. He didn't care if she suffocated but his master wouldn't be happy if the cunt was dead.

He shrugged. It was a forty-five mile drive. If the air got stale, she'd stay unconscious. He settled behind the wheel and ran his hand over the leather interior. He caressed the gear shift.

Hell of a car. The speedometer was calibrated to 120 mph, just like all the old cars with V-8 engines. Shame to waste a car like this on the Knight bitch. Bet she'd never gotten it past eighty. And he couldn't either. Not this afternoon. Wouldn't do to get pulled over. Not at all.

He laughed suddenly and turned the ignition. The motor purred and he shifted into reverse, backed out of the garage, and headed towards Gray Highway.

Paul buzzed the intercom at six o'clock. He'd materialized on College Street tonight and walked down, as much for the pleasure of the crisp December air as for appearances sake. Everyone thought he rented one of the College Street apartments.

No answer. He glanced in the window. The foyer lamp was burning but the law firm's secretary Katie was gone because the main windows of her office reception room were dark. Ria must have had something out of the office running longer than she expected. If not, she'd be here. She was looking forward to the little party. Ria looked forward to everything these days. And he had to admit he did, too.

He buzzed Johnny's intercom as a courtesy, even though he had a key to the door—that appearance thing again. Johnny didn't answer either and it wouldn't do to dematerialize in full view on the front porch.

He had the key in the lock and was just about to turn the tumbler when Johnny drove his little sports car, hell-bent for leather, down the driveway and tooted his horn in greeting. Paul stood in front of the door and waited for him.

"Hey, man! What's the matter, key don't work?"

"Just got here myself when you pulled in. Happen to know where Ria is?"

"Yeah, but I'm surprised she didn't beat me back. She was going over to the LEC around three on some new appointed cases. She ought to be here." Johnny grinned. "Ria doesn't much like to linger around the LEC."

"I know."

"Well, come on in. We'll see if she called or something. If she didn't, she's probably on her way now."

Johnny unlocked the door to the reception room and strode to Katie's desk, grabbing the pink slips from the message slots.

"Call your mom," he muttered to himself. "Call Karen in the DA's Office. Pre-trial on Harris set for two next Friday. Shit! I wanted to leave early next Friday, my folks are going to the beach house. Well, that's all mine, let's see what's in Ria's. *Hmmm.* Call your mom. Our mothers, I swear. Sometimes I feel like I still live at home. Another appointed case. Shit! You'd think we were the only two lawyers in Macon on the damn list! And Dennis says they're running late, be here at six-forty-five. That's it. Did you check your cell phone?"

"Didn't have a chance. Let's see." Paul pulled his phone out and checked. "Nope, nothing."

"Well, she didn't try me, either, I just checked my phone. No voicemail, no missed calls. Let's see where she is." Johnny hit her cell number and the call went straight to voice mail.

"She'd have her phone off in the LEC. Might have forgotten to turn it back on, I do that all the time. She's probably on the way, though."

"I'm sure she is. Let's go on up, I'll check the kitchen out."

Johnny sniffed the air all the way up the stairs.

"Damn, that ham smells good. Just like Christmas."

"C'mon over when you're ready," Paul said. "I'll go organize."

Paul flipped on the light switches and crossed to the kitchen. He was a better cook than Ria was anyway. No reason for dinner to be delayed.

Dennis and Lori arrived earlier than expected in spite of the message to the contrary they'd be late.

"We hurried so much not be any later than we thought we'd be, we're early," Dennis explained. They settled on two of the bar stools at Ria's kitchen counter and watched Paul move around the kitchen.

"Where'd you say Ria was?" Dennis asked.

"LEC. I call it the jail," Paul laughed. "And if she isn't here in just a few more minutes, I think Johnny needs to call down there and see if we can track her down."

"You know, if it weren't for Ria, I'd probably be there myself tonight. In some jail somewhere, anyway." Dennis shook his head. "Man, I just can't believe I was ever that stupid!"

"You learned a hard lesson this year, Dennis. Ria's real proud of you."

"Yeah, and that bothers me a little."

"It does? Why?"

"'Cause I don't think I really deserve it. I mean, I didn't do anything about Justin until I absolutely had to and I never would've had the guts to break away from him at all if it hadn't been for—" Dennis broke off abruptly.

"Oh, c'mon, Dennis!" Lori exclaimed. "You always say you'll tell me what happened that night but you never do! You always stop short like you don't want to think about it!"

"I don't," he said shortly.

"I didn't know anything in particular happened, Dennis," Paul said, glancing at the clock. He'd give her five more minutes and then some calls were starting.

"Neither does Ria. But it did. And if I'd told her about it, she'd have thought I was on something myself."

"Maybe you ought to go ahead and get it off your chest, Dennis." The boy looked as though he needed to tell, no matter how much he'd rather not.

"You'd think I was crazy. But you might be able to put it to use. What are you writing, Paul? Is it a horror novel?"

That cover story of his might present future problems. Eventually, someone was going to expect to see some actual product. Ria'd damn near written a book, though, when she'd transcribed his story for her father. Maybe he'd borrow that. And it was sure as hell a horror novel.

"Sort of. Why?"

"'Cause you could probably work it in there somewhere. Damn sure the most horrifying thing ever happened to me."

"And with that kind of build-up, you're still fartin' around about it!" Lori exclaimed. "Not fair. Now give!"

"Well, it happened out there where we stashed the stuff. Out by Stone Creek Swamp."

Tingles like icy water dripped down the back of Paul's neck and ran down his spine.

"There was this cave, sort of, you see," Dennis said. "All covered over with rocks." His words tumbled out, faster and faster. He described everything. The stake, the dancing particles of dust settling over the moldering bones.

"And while we were tearing down the path, I swear I don't know how in the hell I didn't roll that damn dirt bike, or crash into a tree, I swear I don't, I heard it. This voice, this goddamn roar. It came from everywhere and the woods stood still. I mean, everything stood still. Nothing else moved. Nothing else made a sound! And it shouted, *'I'm aliiiiiive!'* Except it didn't sound like that, it just kept echoing! Over and over, on and on and on."

Dennis finally stopped and looked at his audience. "Paul?"

Paul attempted to speak and couldn't. He cleared his throat and tried again.

"And Justin? You noticed he started getting worse? Right after this?"

"Yeah. I ain't defending what we were doing, Paul, honest to God, I'm not, but before then Justin didn't go around terrorizing girls and leaving dead rats in their lockers and all that sort of shit. I always knew something was off with Justin and deep down, I got to admit I was always scared of him somehow, but after that night, man, shit! He said the next day that it was all our imagination but it's like, it made me wake up. And it turned him into a nightmare that didn't stop. Paul? Where are you going?"

Paul headed to the door.

"I think Johnny needs to call the LEC. He knows who to talk to."

Johnny was standing in the doorway when Paul opened it, just about to knock.

"Man, that smell's killing me!" he exclaimed, as Paul opened the door. "Ria, I didn't know you could cook like this!"

He glanced around the room.

"She still not home?"

"No. You know who to call, Johnny, do you mind?"

"Hell, no," Johnny said, whipping out his phone. "Desk, please." He put his hand over the mouthpiece. "This really is taking her too long. Deputy Graves? Oh, good, guys!" He stated to the room at large. "I got one of the big boys on the phone." Johnny was a people person, he knew how to get service. "Mike, this is Johnny Bishop. My law partner seems to have misplaced herself this evening, do you think you could run her down over there for me? She hasn't? At all?"

Johnny's tone changed abruptly.

"And you're sure? I see. Thanks, Mike."

He hung up the phone and bit his lip.

"She hasn't been there. At all. He ran down the whole day's sign-in sheet to be sure."

Paul started for the door.

"Paul, wait! Maybe something else came up and she had to change plans. Let me ask Katie."

Johnny hit another number and pushed the speaker button so everyone could hear.

"Katie? Sorry to bother you but where'd Ria go this afternoon?"

"The LEC. You know that."

Johnny grimaced. "What time did she leave?"

"Three or so. Like she told you was goin' to do."

"Oh. Well, thanks, Katie."

"Johnny! Wait! Don't you hang up this phone! What's the matter and something is or you wouldn't be calling!" Katie's voice came in over the noise of her toddler's rendition of 'Jingle Bells'.

"Well, the thing is, she's not back and she hasn't called. And Katie, she ain't been to the LEC this afternoon. At all. I just checked."

"But she left at three-fifteen and I heard the car when she pulled out of the driveway. Can't miss that Mustang when it's shifting gears. And it was funny. Because when she shifted, it—what do y'all call it? The gears were grinding. Like when it doesn't catch right, or somebody's not familiar with the car. Ria's never done that. Ever."

"Well, maybe she was distracted."

"Maybe. Call me when she gets home, okay?"

"Okay."

He hung up.

"Folks, we got trouble. Because there's one thing Ria Knight doesn't do in that Mustang. She doesn't grind the gears. And she'd chew anybody else's ass off that did, *if*—and that's a big if—she even let anybody else drive it at all. I mean, driving an old-style stickshift is pretty much a lost art, not that many people even can anymore."

* * *

Ria swam slowly back to consciousness. It was cold and she felt dampness through the thin sleeves of her blouse. Her coat was gone. Her head ached like an abscessed tooth. And it smelled. Wherever she was, the air smelled stale and musty, closed and unused. She knew this smell but she just couldn't place it, so she stopped trying. Of course. It smelled like the Knights' cabin on Lake Sinclair smelled when they opened it every spring to dispel the winter chill.

Something, no, somebody, had knocked her out in her own garage as she approached her own car. A spurt of anger flickered. Its heat helped fight off the stiffness of her joints.

Her own garage, damn it, she'd been attacked in her own garage. But that smell. Wherever she was now, it wasn't the garage.

Fear sprouted and leapt up in bright flames, mingling with insulted outrage. The mixture was peculiarly nauseating.

She stretched. No rope or cord. Fine kidnappers her assailants were. Didn't even bother to tie her up. She pulled herself up on her knees as her eyes raced around the room. A bedroom, but not one that saw frequent use. And the mattress sucked.

It was dark, but that didn't help much in figuring out any timeframe. December brought full dark by six o'clock. It could be six-thirty or three o'clock in the morning. Or six o'clock in the morning. One window. Nailed or locked, for sure, but it was her only shot. She had to try it.

The door opened and she froze. A gigantic shadow loomed in the doorway, casting a pool of deeper black across the floor. Behind the shadow, the reddish-gold glimmer of leaping flames danced in a fireplace. She heard the *hiss* of cracking wood, smelled burning hickory. The shadow spoke.

"My name be Cain," it said. "An' my color be sebben."

* * *

346

"There wasn't anything out of place in the garage when I parked," Johnny said. "But then, there's not much in it."

"On TV, when something happens to a lawyer, it's because of a case. A crazy client or something," said Dennis.

"Dennis, this is not TV!" Johnny snapped. "And we're small time!"

"But Ria had a case with somebody crazy!" Dennis snapped back.

"What the hell are you talking about?"

"Justin," Paul said quietly. "He's talking about Justin Dinardo."

"Nobody's seen Justin since he skipped bail."

"Which doesn't mean he's not around."

Paul headed for the door. He had to get out of this room, away from these witnesses, and cast himself out into the night. He had to hunt. Not for blood, for Ria. He needed to catch every smell, every sound. He didn't have Justin Dinardo's scent, damn it. But it would be lingering in the garage. And he knew, as surely as he had ever known anything in his life, that wherever he found Justin Dinardo, he'd find Cain. Cain's scent still burned in his brain. He'd never forget it.

"Paul, wait!" Johnny grabbed his arm. "First, let's try her cell again," he said, punching his phone as he spoke. Nothing. Just voicemail. He flipped it closed and looked at Paul. "You don't know where in the hell you're going. We've got to call the police. That's the first thing."

"I thought people weren't considered missing until they'd been gone 24 hours," Dennis observed.

"Dennis, take Lori home," Johnny ordered. "There's nothing you can do here. Except, would somebody please cut off the damned oven so we don't burn the house down on top of everything else?"

"No. I'm not going."

"Goddamn it, I don't have time to argue with you, Dennis!"

"Lori can take my car. I'm staying with Paul!"

"I'm just about to beat your ass, boy, so help me!"

"You and who else?" Dennis snapped back. "I know Justin. You don't."

"Wait! Both of you!"

Paul needed to get away from Johnny and he didn't think he could, short of just casting out in front of him. Johnny was in for the count, he would stick like a leech. Dennis would be easier to handle. And if push came to shove, he'd much rather cast out in front of Dennis than Johnny. Dennis had already seen the unbelievable. He'd watched Cain rise.

"Well, what?"

"You take Lori home, Johnny. I need Dennis."

"What the hell you think he can do?"

"He does know Justin. A lot better than we do. And he knows where he'd most likely be. He just has to think about it."

"You got any idea how many crack houses and sleaze joints there are in this town?"

"That's not where he is. Not if he's got Ria. And besides, you know people, you know who to talk to. I don't. Probably lose my temper and piss somebody off."

Dennis kept quiet. Paul was trying to get rid of Johnny. Dennis didn't know why, but there had to be a reason. And there was something else, too. The look on Paul's face when he'd listened to the story of the skeleton clothing itself in new flesh. Paul knew something he didn't want to tell Johnny or the police.

"We're wasting time," Paul said impatiently.

Johnny reached in his pocket for his keys and patted his cell phone to make certain he had it.

"Okay, I'll take Lori home and I'll make some calls. Dennis, give me your number so I can get y'all."

Dennis crossed to Ria's desk and scribbled hastily on a note pad, tearing it off and handing it to Johnny while Paul paced impatiently.

"C'mon, Dennis. Let's cruise."

"You're dead!" Ria whispered hoarsely. "You're dead!"

"I be hard to kill, pretty white lady," the shadow said as it approached. "Mighty hard."

The blackness loomed over her. A steel vise clasped over her arm when he hauled her to her feet. He dragged her across the floor toward the door and threw her into the center of the big room. The walls and furniture wavered in and out of focus, lit only by the flicker of the fire dancing in the big stone fireplace. Another figure rose from the shadows of the couch.

"You said she was mine," the voice whined. "You said I could have her."

"Justin!"

Ria stared up at the boy as he came closer. His face was pallid in the firelight, his eyes wide and staring. His lips had thinned into nothing and his cheekbones jutted strongly forward under his skin.

She'd seen that look before, many times, as she walked hurriedly down the halls of the LEC. It had looked back at her across a table as she interviewed appointed cases charged with possession. The look worn by an addict in the advanced stages of addiction.

"Yeah, it's me. You fucked up, bitch. Bad."

She turned and stared up at the dead man who proclaimed himself Cain. A giant of a man, six foot six, at least. It hadn't been a trick of the shadows. His massive shoulders really had filled the doorframe. His shaved head gleamed in the firelight.

He stretched his arm out and pointed a finger at Justin. The sleeves of his shirt were rolled back to his forearms and she saw white scars marring the black velvet of his skin. Scars such as left by burns. Burns sustained when Paul threw him furiously around the cleared circle on the banks of the Ocmulgee River on a hot August night in 1888, without regard for the seven fires burning in their circles of stone.

"You have her when I say you have her, boy!" He dropped his arm and laughed. "Knows my name does you, white lady?"

Ria nodded. A shaking hand pushed the hair back out of her eyes.

"Fancy white doctor you keepin' time wid, I reckon he done tol' you *all* 'bout me, ain't he?"

Ria didn't answer. His ham-like hand shot out and caught her on the side of the jaw. Her teeth clicked together sharply and she felt the grit of a broken back tooth disintegrating under the impact.

"I say, ain't he?"

"Yes," she spat, gritty residue grating sickeningly between her teeth. "He told me."

"He tell you whut he done to me?"

Pure and righteous fury boiled up in welcome replacement of the numbing terror.

"What he did to *you*? You're *insane!*"

Her head snapped back as he struck. For the moment, she felt nothing. Her jaw was broken.

Cain crossed to the wooden crate standing by the hearth holding tinder for the fireplace. He selected a long, slender piece of kindling and thrust it into the flames. He turned back to her.

"Had my druthers," he said, grinning as he approached her, "I'd heap rather him be here to see dis. But since I 'spect were he to show up in de next few minutes, I ain't goan be able to finish dis right, I believe I's jest better let him see you when I through."

He bent forward and grabbed the material of her blouse below the shoulder seam. He ripped downward. The material sagged down her arm as the seam parted. He brandished his flaming torch and smiled.

The screams poured out of the cabin, down to the shoreline of the huge lake stretching in front of the house. They bounced across the surface of the water like a stone skimming across the waves. Other vacation lake houses stood nearby, but in this winter season, they were empty. There was no one within a five mile radius to hear.

* * *

Paul tore out the front door and around to the back.

"Where you goin', man, my car's in front!"

"I have to check something first," he called back from the garage, and sniffed the air. The familiar rushing sensation overwhelmed him, as it always did whenever he opened his perceptions to this degree. He struggled to eliminate the known scents from the unknown.

He paced the concrete floor. Ria's scent. Light, delicate, unmistakable. Johnny's scent. Heavier than Ria's, as all masculine scents seemed heavier than feminine scents.

And here. He stopped and stood in the corner where Justin had crouched waiting. An ugly, secretive scent, carrying hints of madness and desperation. He sniffed lightly, imprinting the smell in his brain, and staggered suddenly. Echoes of a high-pitched, pain-filled scream exploded in his brain.

"What the hell are you doing?" Dennis frowned as he looked in the door.

"I'm through. Let's go."

Paul pushed past him and strained to catch the lingering vibrations of that psychic scream. He couldn't do it. It was too far away.

"You want to drive?" Dennis asked, unlocking the passenger door.

"Hell, no."

"Okay," Dennis said, coming around and jerking his own door open. "Then you better buckle up. I think I know where to go."

"You do?" Paul asked, and gripped the armrest as another scream ricocheted around his brain, and another, and another. God, what were they doing to

351

her? The screams were over to the right, but so far away.

"Yeah. And I had an idea you didn't want Johnny to know. So I didn't say anything."

"Dennis, you have the makings of a good man. Though I guess your phone's going to ring every five minutes."

"No, it won't. I told you, I knew you wanted to get rid of him. I reversed the last two numbers I gave him. I mean, if I just turned my phone off, he'd know it was on purpose. This just looks like I screwed up."

"A real good man. Where are we goin'?"

Dennis headed down the short stretch of Orange onto Walnut. He paused briefly at the red light on College before the right turn onto Riverside.

"My folks and Justin's folks have a cabin they own together up at Lake Sinclair. You did want to get rid of Johnny, didn't you?"

"Yes. Nothing personal." Paul's knuckles turned white as he gripped the armrest. The psychic voice kept screaming. "Now where are we going?"

"Lake Sinclair. It's a big, manmade lake up by the power plant near Milledgeville. Miles of shoreline and lots and lots and lots of summer cabins. Some of it's real developed and lots of folks live there all year. But our folks got together and bought a big lot up at one of the real remote parts to build on. The only house even sort of close is Dr. Knight's, he bought a big lot beside it. Nobody'll be there. I've been up in the winter before and it's dead up there in December, man. Really, really dead."

"How far?"

"Forty-five point seven miles. I checked once. But the last couple are over dirt roads that'll shake your kidneys out."

Paul sat and considered. Thank God Dennis knew where to go. He knew they were headed in the right direction. But if he asked Dennis for specific directions, they'd be in terms of road. Useless for his purposes.

Paul didn't understand the mechanics of the casting out process but he knew he had to visualize a specific spot if he wanted to arrive at a specific destination. Miles of shoreline. He could cast out and hit in the general area, he had the scents. And the woods would be full of other smells, wood scents of game animals big and small, their scents overwhelmingly stronger than the scent of man. He could search all night, casting out over and over, and never get a direct hit. Dennis was his best bet.

"You can't go any faster?"

"I will when I get out on Gray Highway. Don't have time to get pulled over for speeding."

Dennis risked a glance at his companion. He liked Paul, he'd liked him instantly. Not just because Ria was obviously head-over-heels in love with him. Paul was a laidback dude. Most of the time. Dennis almost didn't recognize him now. His mouth was set in a thin, hard line, his chin jutted forward in determination.

"Why me?" Dennis asked.

"Pardon?"

"You didn't want Johnny. Why didn't you mind taking me?"

"I do mind taking you. But you're the lesser of two evils and when we get there, you're goin' to park back. Far back. And you won't get out of this car. Understood?"

"You going in by yourself? And what are you, an action hero's stuntman or something? A ninja in drag?"

Paul didn't answer. Dear God, the screams had stopped. Was she unconscious? Worse? Was she dead?

"You know something. I know you do."

Dennis left the lights of the parking lot of the Super WalMart, last stronghold of Macon proper, behind in his tail lights and stepped on the gas. He zoomed down the highway toward the neighboring small town of Gray, toward Highway 129 to Eatonton and the cutoff to the first of the backwoods dirt roads.

They ran through a cavern of shadows.

"Paul, tell me! *What is it?!*"

"Dennis, I hope to hell you never know," Paul said. He stared fixedly forward into the darkness.

* * *

Cain paced the big central room of the lake cabin impatiently, glancing now and then at the battered, bleeding lump of flesh he'd tossed casually into the corner by the fireplace. The arms lay in an unnatural angle, the broken bones giving the figure the appearance of a rag doll whose floppy extremities had been braced by sticks. The skin of the arms was raw and blistered and bleeding, the face swollen and distorted. She lay mercifully unconscious.

Cain held himself back by a supreme effort of will. Every action he'd taken since slaking his first thirst of rebirth had been calculated toward finding the white man and having found him, to exacting revenge. He knew his prey well. Devlin would rush in foolishly, with no thought of protection, intent on retrieving his new woman.

And the new acolyte who'd served Cain, in the main, fairly well, would attack from the rear, driving the thick, carefully sharpened stake through the doctor's back, puncturing the heart. But not piercing it, no, just impaling him like a bug on a pin. He'd be helpless. But he'd see her agony, see the havoc Cain wrecked by Cain. And he'd live long enough to watch Cain feast on her blood.

He'd almost ruined it. The scent of the girl's blood, pumping furiously through her veins, the rate of its flow accelerated by the adrenaline of agony—he'd actually placed his mouth over her jugular vein. He had to drink. Just a little. And then just a little more. He felt the first rush of an orgasm he'd never known with any woman. And he knew. He knew if he began to drink, he'd guzzle. No way to stop. And the doctor wasn't here to watch yet.

But shit. The night was young. First things first. The white man had to get here, in Cain's own stronghold. And when he got here, when the white man'd learned his lesson, he'd drain the girl dry. And she'd rise. His. His ready-made consort. The first of his new congregation. Time to speed things up a little.

* * *

The voice thundered in the close confines of the Camaro. Dennis heard it rushing through his brain, not through his ears.

White doctor! I know you out dere! We gots us some unfinished biz'ness, white man!

Shockwaves ran down Dennis' arms into his hands. That voice. He'd heard it before. The skeleton celebrating rebirth. The same voice. Jesus Christ. It was the same voice.

The car swerved across the center line of the highway. Dennis jerked the wheel to the left just in time. An outraged horn screamed a long protest as an oncoming car ran off the road onto the median, narrowly avoiding the Camaro's left front fender. Dennis heard the driver's roar through closed windows as the cars passed.

"You goddamn drunk! Get off the fuckin' road!"

Paul reached over and grabbed the wheel to straighten up, issuing furious orders.

"Take your foot off the gas! Brake, damn it! Now, pull over. Right now. *Right now! Pull over!*"

Dennis concentrated. *Foot off the gas. Don't slam the brakes. Easy. Brake easy. Pull over.* The car shuddered to a stop on the right hand median.

Paul leaned over and cut the ignition. Dennis gave a half-sob and leaned his head forward on the top of the steering wheel.

"That voice," he managed to say. "I know that voice."

I got her! The shout was loud and victorious in the small interior. Yo' new woman! I got her! Whut you goan do about it, white man!

"But it's me you want, Cain! Where are you? Me and you! Right now! Wherever you say! You don't want her!"

I gots her, I do got you, white doctor! Damn do-gooder Devlin, always stickin' yo' nose in my business! I knows you! Ain't no way to make you hurt lik' you suffer knowin' she sufferin'! An' she sufferin', sho' 'nuff! Jest lik' I did. Dat night. 'Member whut you did to me, white doctor? I does! An' I ain't leaving nuttin' out! Follow me, white man! Iff'n you dare!

Raucous, mocking laughter filled the car. Dennis clapped his hands over his ears. He'd go insane if he had to listen to that laughter another second. And then the laughter, too, died away into the dark, leaving no sound except the slow tick of the car's cooling engine.

Paul reached up and grabbed Dennis' wrist, jerking the protective hands away from the boy's ear.

"Stay here! *You hear me?* Don't you move this car an *inch!*"

Dennis tried to protest and bit his tongue hard as his mouth snapped shut. Paul was gone. Just gone. The door hadn't opened. He was certain of it.

He leaned his head against the steering wheel. He moaned and struck his forehead, over and over, against the padded leather.

* * *

Johnny Bishop, frustrated and furious, damned all law enforcement protocol to hell and back. He'd butted heads with three police officers while taking Lori home. True to Dennis's observation, they'd refused to consider taking a report.

"We're sorry, sir, but we can't take a missing person's report on the basis of two or three hours.

Maybe she had car trouble. Did you call all her friends?"

Now, heading back to the house, he dialed the Assistant DA assigned to Justin Dinardo's case home number. Ted Dorry's cavalier attitude didn't help Johnny's temper a damn bit.

"Johnny, calm down! Ria's a big girl, she probably went shopping or something and lost track of time in the Christmas crowds."

"Ted, goddamn it, she was having a dinner party tonight!"

"Maybe you got the date mixed up and it wasn't tonight."

"There was a goddamn *ham* baking in the fuckin' *oven*, Ted! She did *not* lose track of time and I *don't* have the wrong date! And she *damn* sure didn't grind the gears in that Mustang when she pulled out of the drive! Somebody else was driving that car!"

"Johnny, now listen—"

"No, you listen! Justin Dinardo—"

"*Skipped bail.* Nobody's seen or heard from him since. He's long gone, Johnny. Long gone."

"*Bullshit!* Now you get somebody off their asses and get them out lookin'!"

"And where the hell you suggest we look?"

"Did you even *try* to find him when he skipped town? Did anybody even check the places he might have gone?"

"Johnny, that's damned insulting!"

"He was small time! You got a big backlog of cases! I wanta know if y'all just put out an APB and forgot about him or whether there might be any notes somewhere about where he could be!"

Several seconds of silence ensued. Finally, Ted spoke again.

"Okay," he said with a sigh. "You're right. On ninety-nine percent of cases like this, we do just put out an APB. We just don't have the manpower to do much else."

"Ted, goddamn it, nobody's pointing any fingers! I know your caseload. I just thought maybe—"

"But this time, since Ria was so insistent that Justin might be, well, abnormal, and since Dennis was the informant and his family's sort of, well, you know—"

"His daddy's a bigshot surgeon with a big bank account and friends in high places. So you checked a little harder."

"Johnny, that's not fair!"

"No, just accurate. I'm not yellin' at you, Ted, I know you can't help it, but it sucks anyway. So you got any ideas?"

"Not off the top of my head. But since it's Ria and since you're so worried, I tell you what. I'll go back down to the office and pull the file—no, wait a minute. I brought a stack home to go through before we throw them completely into pending. Let me check there first. I'll call you back." The call went dead.

Damn. Johnny hated being one-upped. He pulled back in the yard to check the apartment in case anybody'd come back. His phone rang.

"Ted?"

"Johnny, I had the file at home. The Dinardos and the Billings have a cabin at Sinclair they own jointly. Do you know it?"

"Shit! Sure they do! Right down from Dr. Knight's! Only been to the Billings' place once or twice but I been to Dr. Knight's a lot."

"We had it checked out every couple of weeks right after Justin disappeared but when he didn't turn up anywhere we gave up."

"Okay, so how fast can you get somebody up there?"

"Johnny, are you totally crazy? Okay, scratch that, forget I even said it, of course you are. She's not even officially missing!"

"I hope to hell that soothes your conscience when a couple of deer hunters stumble over her body in the woods! But I guess it won't be an *official* body, so that's all right!"

"I don't have anything to connect Justin with this and even if I did, there's no reason to think he'd do anything like that!"

"Sweet Jesus, Ted! Nobody hides out for weeks and then abducts somebody for nothing! You think he's just going to let her *go* after he gets his jollies?"

"Wellll—"

"Do this unofficially. Surely to God, there's some way you can get somebody up there!"

"In the morning, maybe."

"In the morning!"

"Johnny, I can't mount a manhunt on what we've got! Now, I tell you what—"

"No, I'll tell you what! Get somebody up there as soon as you can if you don't hear back from me by morning. And if I call you before then and say I need help, you better by God get me some!"

"You can't just go chargin' up there yourself!"

"Watch me!"

Johnny regretted that you couldn't slam down a cell phone like a landline. He wanted to hurt Ted Dorry's ears. He headed for the house to grab his pistol from his nightstand drawer and dialed the number Dennis left him.

Damn it! "Hi, this is Cindy! You know how this thing works!" Shit! Dumb-ass kid gave him the wrong number! He charged up the steps to the apartment doors, both left standing wide open, and heard the insistent ringing of Ria's house phone. He almost didn't stop to answer, but just maybe it was Ria. Or somebody that knew something.

He raced inside and grabbed the phone.

"Hello?"

"Johnny?"

"Yeah."

"Charlie Knight. You got secretarial duty?"

Johnny danced impatiently, shifting from one foot to the other. "Well, I was closest to the phone."

"Let me speak to Ria or Paul, please. Whoever's handy, neither of 'em are picking up their phone."

"Well," Johnny hemmed and hawed. This was Ria's father. Should he tell him? Did he have the right not to tell him?

"Johnny, do you mind?"

"Well, they can't come to the phone right now."

"Neither one of 'em? They havin' an orgy while company's over?"

"They're not here right now."

"Then pardon my French, son, but what the hell you doin' in her apartment if nobody's home?"

"Dr. Knight, the thing is, we're not sure where Ria is."

"Say again?"

Johnny decided to come clean.

"The lake house? And you're charging off by yourself?"

"No choice. Ted won't call the Sheriff's Office up there and Paul left with Dennis to see if he could come up with anything! And they gave me the wrong damn cell number! I don't know where the hell they are!" Johnny exclaimed in exasperation.

"Bet I do. Smart kid, Dennis. He'll hit on the lake house. They're probably almost there already. You stay put by the phone. I'm goin' up."

"I am *not* going to stay put by the *fuckin'* phone!" Johnny shouted.

On the other end of the line, Charlie Knight grimaced. He'd watched Johnny grow up. Hell, he and Ria'd practically lived interchangeably in each other's houses. And no, Johnny wasn't about to stay put by the fucking phone. He'd charge up to the lake house and interfere with—what?

Dr. Knight thanked God for police procedure. He could just see a bunch of deputies surrounding the lake house where Justin Dinardo might have a gun pointed at his daughter's temple, just as he could see Paul, materializing silently behind him. But Johnny was going no matter what, and he'd best not charge in alone. Especially if Paul was either there or on the way.

"Then meet me. Park at the barbecue place outside of Gray and I'll meet you there. Ought to hit about the same time. You probably couldn't find the road, anyway."

"I've spent lots of time at your place."

"Different road to get to that cabin, further down. Meet me. I'm leavin' now. And Johnny, you goddamned well better wait on me! You got that?"

"Yeah, yeah. Just hurry!"

* * *

Paul soared over the nightscape, straining every sense to catch a lingering scent, an echoing sound.

Nothing. Goddamn it, there was nothing.

He'd spread too wide, too quick. He'd never done this before, never rushed forward in such furious haste without knowing exactly where he was going. His disincorporated molecules streamed too far apart. He concentrated, trying to bring the invisible particles of his being back together.

Too far. He'd spread too far.

He fought to correct his mistake, a pilot guiding a private airplane with frozen controls.

* * *

Cain strode furiously back and forth across the braided rug, much like he'd paced furiously across a cleared circle, waiting for a group of followers who'd never come. Where the fuck was he? Ought to be here by now.

"Damn!" He muttered under his breath. "Wouldn't turn tail and run. Know he wouldn't. So where the fuck do he be?"

Justin's whining voice broke his concentration.

"You said she was mine," he protested. "And you said I'd be the first. The first you took and made like you."

Cain crossed to the boy and grabbed him by the throat with his enormous hand. The pressure caused the boy's eyes to bulge forward. Cain saw traces of red as tiny capillaries burst.

"*Shut up!*" he roared, shaking the boy. "*Shut up, fool!* You do whut I say! You gets whut I *say* you gets!"

The smell hit his nostrils. The rich, heavy scent of pumping blood.

He was too close to the boy. Too close. During his assault on Ria, he'd almost given in completely to the overpowering blood lust commanding him to feast fully, to drain her completely. He'd had the barest taste of the ultimate orgasm, so powerful it had shaken his entire giant frame, waves of sensation he knew would culminate in a brilliant burst unlike anything else he'd ever experienced. And he wanted to experience it again. Fully. Completely. From its beginnings through the end.

He stared at Justin's neck. His mouth gaped open and the points of his gleaming incisors glinted in the firelight. Cain had never been fussy about his sex partner, seven years in that Louisiana prison camp had taken care of that. A hole was a hole. Anyway, this type of orgasm was an asexual act. The gender of his partner didn't matter.

His furious tone modulated to a soft caress.

"But den, I did promise, didn't I?"

* * *

"Dennis."

Paul grabbed the back of the boy's neck, stopping his forehead from making further contact with the padding of the steering wheel.

Dennis shuddered at the sudden touch, his body jerking. He snapped his neck to the right and stared at Paul. In his wild, wide eyes, Paul caught the memory of Sadie's eyes, immediately before her retreat into the dark of catatonia.

"Dennis, it's me. It's all right."

Paul spoke softly, wondering why in the name of God humans always assured each other everything was all right when it was clear things were going to hell in a hand basket.

"Listen, Dennis, we don't have much time. You've got to get a grip on yourself."

"You—you disappeared! That voice, it came out of nowhere and then you just—and now you're back and—"

"Dennis! Listen, we have to move. I can't find him by myself. You'd better let me drive."

Paul reached for the door handle. Wouldn't do to dematerialize again, Dennis would go berserk. Besides, he was pretty shook himself after surging forward out of control and almost spreading himself into eternity forever. He hadn't known that could happen but then he'd never cast out in such a state of desperation with no certain destination in mind.

He thanked God for the nights he and Ria had ridden the back roads while she laughed and scolded and called him names for grinding the gears of her prized Mustang classic.

He came around to the driver's side and opened the door. Dennis collected himself enough to scramble over the console into the passenger seat.

Paul sat down and inspected the controls.

"Why bother to drive? You sure don't need a car to travel."

"I can't hit an exact spot if I don't know exactly where I'm going. And I don't have time for trial and error."

He cranked up and but sat and looked down at the floorboard as though something was missing.

"Dennis, where's the clutch?"

"This is an automatic, it doesn't have one."

"So how, exactly, does it work?"

"You've never driven an automatic?"

 "No, I learned how to drive on the Mustang."

Dennis didn't register the significance of that statement at first. Then he did.

"Ria's Mustang? You mean, that's the car you learned to drive on, not just learned to drive a stick?"

"Yeah."

"Jesus," Dennis muttered. But then someone who could appear and disappear at will wouldn't have a lot of need for cars. "Just mash this button on the gearshift and put it in D, that's drive. That's all there is to it till you stop. Then mash the button and put it in P, park. R is reverse."

"And that's it?"

"That's it."

Paul pulled back onto the highway and increased his speed. He risked a glance at Dennis. The boy's face was white and pinched. He still stared fixedly forward but he'd managed to have a conversation about the car's controls. Paul supposed that showed a continued grip on reality.

"That voice we heard—it's the same one I heard this summer. That night."

"I know."

"It—he—you called him something."

"Cain."

"He called you *white man*." Dennis supplied the emphasis. "Like it was a dirty word, worse than motherfucker. And he called you something else, too. *White doctor. Do-gooder Devlin.*"

"Yes."

"Your name's Paul Everett. You're a writer."

"No."

"Then what the hell are you? Who are you, really?"

Paul searched for words and in the end, found nothing better than the ones used to introduce him to this world of endless dark.

"Dennis, this world as we know it, it's ringed with worlds on worlds. And some of them are bright and beautiful and some of them are nightmares beyond imagination. And sometimes, people of great power can cross the boundaries between the worlds. And that power, by itself, it's neither good nor evil. The people who possess it are. And if that person is evil, they can break the barriers and things cross over into this world that weren't meant to be here."

"And Cain, he's from one of the dark worlds?"

"No. He's part of this world but he possessed great power, the power to break the barriers. One night, he broke through them and something crossed over. Something that—changed me."

"Into what?"

"Dennis, there really isn't a word that exactly describes me. There's a word that comes close but it'll scare you if I use it."

"There was a stake," Dennis said. "I told you. A stake stuck in his rib cage, just resting there between his ribs. It was a skeleton, man, just a skeleton, had to have been there for years and years and years."

"Since 1888."

"How the hell do you know that?"

Paul hesitated. "My brother put it there," he said.

"1888!?"

"Dennis—"

Dennis was beyond listening. His words tumbled out in partial sentences, struggling to make logic out of the most illogical things he'd ever heard.

"And when Justin pulled it out, it was just like in the old Bela Lugosi films, the old silent movies, the ones they show sometimes at the Pizza Parlor on Friday nights when the vampire—Cain's a vampire?"

"Not originally. Just extraordinarily powerful. Powerful enough to break the barrier between the worlds."

"Then what happened? You said he let something loose. Whatever it was changed him into a vampire?"

"No," Paul said shortly. "It changed me."

Dennis inhaled deeply and bunched his muscles tightly. The smell of sudden terror filled the car.

"*Oh, shit*," he moaned.

"Dennis, this isn't an old Bela Lugosi movie. Some of the old legends are right about some things, but they're mostly wrong. What I am, in and of itself, isn't good or evil, just like the power that can crash through worlds isn't by itself good or evil. It can be either. It depends on what you do with it."

The car flew silently down the dark highway, nearing the little town of Gray. Paul was a vampire but he was one of the good guys?

"Slow down," Dennis warned. "You're almost on top of the city limits."

Paul lifted his foot off the accelerator and lightly tapped the brakes.

"Are you all right?" he asked. How lame, those words. Misused and overused and totally inadequate for most situations.

"I think I'm maybe gettin' there," Dennis said. He sat straight and peered ahead. The old two story stores lining Gray's oldest main street threw alternating shadows through the car windows. "After this light, there's another one, right past the railroad crossing. Cross the tracks and turn left. Puts us on Highway 129 to Eatonton."

Paul complied.

"Okay." Dennis sat back. "We're clear. You can speed up."

The powerful engine of the sports car sent it surging forward as Paul accelerated.

Dennis bit his lip before he asked his next question.

"So if the thing changed you and not Cain, what made him a vampire?"

"I did. The next night. No human would've stood a chance against him."

"And then your brother hid him in the cave where we found him and drove the stake through his heart."

"Yes."

"Paul, he said he was doing to Ria just what you did to him. That night. That he wasn't leaving anything out. What did you do to him? Before?"

Paul's lips tightened and he pressed the accelerator harder. The car surged forward.

Dennis sank back in his seat.

"I was afraid you were going to say that."

* * *

Johnny'd gotten a late start but he didn't have any sudden voice roaring into his car and scaring him shitless. As fast as he was driving, he'd be dead if he encountered a deer taking a stroll across the highway. He wasn't much worried about that right now. When he passed Gray and headed on toward Eatonton, he'd have to worry about it but he was by God making as much time as he could until then. He pulled into the parking lot of the barbecue place outside of Gray, parked, and fumed.

Damn it, where was Dr. Knight? He cranked back up and threw the car into reverse, narrowly avoiding ramming the Ford Explorer pulling up behind him. Charlie Knight got out, slammed the door viciously, and stalked up to Johnny's window.

"Boy, I *told* you to wait on me!" Dr. Knight was furious. "Don't you listen?"

"You were taking so long."

"Get your ass in my car!"

Dr. Knight stalked back to the Explorer. Johnny, chastised but unrepentant, got in the passenger side.

Dr. Knight didn't speak as he pulled back onto Gray Highway and sped toward the city limits. He still didn't speak when he turned left slightly past the railroad tracks and increased speed.

"Dr. Knight—"

"Shut up," he ordered shortly. "I have to concentrate. Easy to miss in the dark."

"What?"

"This," Dr. Knight said, slowing abruptly and swinging right with a bone-shattering bounce onto a dirt road forking off from the highway. He reached down and engaged the Explorer's four-wheel drive.

"What the fuck?"

"Loggin' roads. Going as the crow flies. Cuts off miles. Drives Don Billings crazy. He never has figured out how I get to the lake so damn fast."

The Explorer bounced and rattled. Johnny double-checked his seat belt.

"Jesus!" He exclaimed. That bounce damn near sent his head into the roof. He grabbed onto the armrest for further insurance.

"That's right, son, you better hang on. Ain't never taken it this fast and never plan to again. So hold on."

* * *

Cain caught himself again. Barely. The scent of the fool's blood almost got him, but he needed the boy right now. The white doctor wouldn't be watching his back, he'd be focused on his woman. This fool was necessary back up for the rear.

Cain threw the boy down and Justin crouched into a ball on the sofa. He wanted the power, the eternal life promised by Cain but his close inspection of Cain's incisors brought home to him one important aspect of the transformation he hadn't previously fully considered. He'd die in the process. Maybe he should re-evaluate the pros and cons.

Cain resumed his pacing and then stopped, standing stock still in the middle of the rug.

Of course. He'd spoken to the white man by psychic transmission, purely by the power of thought. He hadn't left a trail for him to follow, no scent, no actual voice echoes.

Shit. But of course, there was a good side to everything. His years-old nemesis was probably casting out, over and over, looking for a trail that wasn't there. Cain spread his arms and cast out himself. Then almost instantaneously he reappeared. The walls shook under his roar. He'd been practicing his new powers for only six months, still learning their expanse and limitations.

And he'd just realized something Paul had known and worked around for many, many years. He had to know exactly where he was going to get there.

"Goddamn it! I doan got his trail, neither! I cain't find him! Motherfucker!!"

He raged through the room. He stopped in front of Ria's body and kicked. The crack of snapping bone was loud as her rib cage splintered. Even in her unconscious state, she moaned. Behind him, Justin moved slowly, attempting to slip off the couch and slink out of the room. Slink out of the house, actually, and as soon as possible. Tonight he'd seen Cain in a different light. Time to reconsider the benefits of his continued association with the man. Definitely.

Cain turned at the whisper of Justin's jeans sliding over the nubby material of the couch. His shiny blueprints of vengeance were shredding around him. The white man might not even find him tonight. The girl wasn't going to live much longer and if he wanted her for his consort, he'd have to take her soon. Even if the white man wasn't there to watch. And now this fool looked to be sneaking off.

Damn! Couldn't trust nobody. Well. He'd serve as a nice appetizer before the main course.

* * *

Dennis brought the car to a halt some ways back from the cabin. He'd insisted on reclaiming the wheel when they hit the dirt roads.

"No offense, man, but you ain't the world's most experienced driver and these roads can be bad-ass mothers in the winter when nobody's usin' 'em."

Paul hadn't protested. And Dennis had sure been right. If his kidneys had still been subject to shaking, they'd have shaken out.

"I can get closer," Dennis said.

"I know where the cabin is now, I don't need you any closer. Now you listen. I want you to stay here."

"*Here?* No way, man!"

"Here, goddamn it, here! You'd just be in my way!"

"But there's two of them!"

"You can't do shit against Cain, Dennis! And as for Justin, do you have a gun? A knife? Could you use 'em if you did?"

"I could if I had to."

"Maybe, if you had 'em. But you don't, do you?"

Dennis shook his head.

"And *you're* not a ninja in drag, are you?"

Dennis shook his head again.

"Then stay here!"

Paul disappeared and left Dennis staring into the silent darkness.

Suddenly the darkness wasn't silent anymore. The screams rolled out from the cabin, oddly neuter in gender. Definitely not Paul or Cain, which left Justin and Ria, but he couldn't tell if the screams were masculine or feminine.

And why would Justin scream anyway? Suddenly Dennis remembered something. He got out of the car and ran down the crunching gravel of the road as fast his running shoes could carry him.

370

*　*　*

Paul materialized behind Cain's back. Justin's screams would've disguised an approaching elephant herd. Cain bent the boy backwards, his mouth approaching the vulnerable neck. Justin's arms flailed wildly and something grayish white and speckled with blood waved in the firelight. A broken bone. Without thought, Paul made the medical translation. Compound fracture of the ulna, the point protruding some two inches out of the broken skin.

Paul didn't know or care what Justin did to provoke Cain's fury. It provided him his edge and he wasn't wasting a minute of it. He cast out like a speed swimmer kicking away from the wall of a pool and materialized by the fireplace.

He reached into the fire for one of the smaller burning logs. He wasn't depending on wood alone. He wanted fire, too. Then he saw her from the corner of his eye. Ria's body, thrown in the corner. Broken and bleeding and burned.

Too late. Oh, God, too late. He almost started toward her but a cold, detached voice speaking from the base of his brain stopped him.

If she was dead, there was nothing he could do. And if she wasn't, then she would be, very soon, unless he sent Cain back to the dark. He reached into the fireplace again, just as Cain, momentarily sated, dropped Justin's body.

*　*　*

Dennis crept around the rear windows of the cabin toward the largest bedroom on the right hand side. His father kept a .38 pistol in the nightstand and always ignored Dennis's pointed observation that the first thing any winter thief looked for was firearms. The cabin had never been vandalized until tonight though, and Dennis was the vandal.

371

He reached up, tore the screen off and smashed the glass of the pane. He thrust his arm inside to the window lock. God, it was stiff. The broken glass caught on the quilted sleeve of his jacket. Dennis jerked and scored a long gash across the back of his hand.

He didn't have time to worry about it. He grunted and tried again and finally felt the catch give. The first thing he'd do this spring was spray all the goddamn window latches with WD-40. There. Finally.

He jerked the window open and climbed in just as the screams faded into nothing. He heard the hard *klump* of a falling body.

The drawer of the nightstand clattered to the floor when he jerked it open. Where the hell? There. His fingers identified the cold, oily feel of gun metal while his eyes adjusted to the shadows. Not loaded, of course. His father kept the ammunition on a shelf in the closet, like he thought any intruder would politely wait for him to retrieve the ammunition and load the gun.

Damn, his fingers wouldn't stop shaking. Finally he grasped the fully loaded gun in his hand. He crept to the bedroom door.

Justin's body lay in an inert heap on the floor. Cain's gigantic figure moved silently toward the fireplace. There was something in his hands, but Dennis couldn't make out exactly what. He moved toward Paul, who stared at something in the corner.

Oh, God. Ria's body. Paul seemed to collect himself and reached into the fireplace, but he'd never make it. He'd never turn in time to avoid Cain's great hands, raising over Paul's back. In horror, Dennis identified the sharpened stake, aimed directly at Paul's heart.

"Look out!"

Dennis fired. A flower of red bloomed on Cain's back but Dennis knew better than to think the bullet had any more effect than a bee sting. But it did get Cain's attention.

"*What de fuck?*" Cain swung his head around to check his rear and Dennis fired again.

Paul lunged for the fireplace and retrieved a burning piece of hickory. The flames scoring into his hands didn't faze him.

Dennis fired again and again, until the chambers were empty. Cain's body sprouted flowers of slowly spreading red from the ineffective bullets. He grinned at the boy.

"Worl' jest full of do-gooders, now ain't it? Well, you jest got to wait yo' turn, boy."

Dennis smiled. Paul stood behind Cain. He raised the flaming wood high, aimed between Cain's shoulder blades. Cain's words cut off and turned into a gurgling scream as the burning wood plunged into his back. The material of his shirt caught fire and blazed.

Cain tried to turn and pull away from the blazing, unsharpened stake but Paul moved with him, pushing harder, harder.

The scream increased in volume as the spurting red liquid spouted out of Cain's back in geysers, sizzling as it came into contact with the flames. Finally, it peaked in an astounding crescendo. The end of the firebrand poked through the front of Cain's shirt and still Paul pushed.

Why didn't he fall? Damn it, why didn't he fall?

"Paul!" Dennis shouted. "Let go! You're holding him up yourself!"

Paul abruptly turned loose of the hickory and Cain's body crashed to the floor.

"Oh, man!" Dennis breathed. "Oh, man!" He crossed the floor at a run to grab Paul's wrists. "Your hands, Paul, your hands!"

The skin of his fingers was gone. Nothing remained but bare, blackened bones.

"Oh, God!" Dennis choked back a retch. "Com'ere, sit down."

"It's nothing," Paul said. "Just give me a minute. Check Ria. I couldn't feel a pulse point right now."

"But what—"

"Just do it!"

Dennis dropped Paul's hands with a half-sob and flung himself toward Ria's body. The door crashed open. Charlie Knight and Johnny Bishop gaped, surveying the bloody, fiery battleground.

"*Oh, shit!*" Johnny pointed at Cain's giant body. It lost substance before their eyes. The flesh flew off the bones in a flurry of small dancing motes that floated on the air and then disappeared until there was nothing left but a skeleton.

The still burning brand fell against a bare rib and sent streamers of fire into the rug. Johnny ran over and looked for something to give him a hand-hold on the wood that wouldn't fry his hands. Paul knocked him back.

"For God's sake, *don't!*" he shouted. Dr. Knight came from the kitchen with a slopping dishpan of water and tossed it directly onto the flames.

The four rescuers stared down at the mottled bones of the skeleton, the blackened stake protruding from the ribs.

Paul flung himself towards the corner. His hands hovered over Ria, hesitant to touch.

"Paul, your hands!" Dennis exclaimed. "Your hands—" Dennis stopped and stared. "My God," he said softly.

Paul's hands were normal, clothed in new and unmarked flesh.

Dr. Knight joined Paul in the corner. "Oh, baby! Oh, God, Ria!"

"My fault." Paul barely managed to push the words out. "My fault."

Dr. Knight stared at him a moment, his expression unreadable, his eyes veiled.

"That skeleton. Cain?"

Paul nodded. "My fault," he said again.

"Wastin' time," Dr. Knight said, and bent over his daughter, feeling carefully up and down her body. He sat back again. "Oh, Jesus!"

"Is she—is she dead?" Dennis asked softly. Johnny stood behind them, not speaking.

"Not yet," Dr. Knight said, and stood up. "But she will be, very soon. Some of the rib bones are puncturing her lungs. I think one's right at her heart. We'll kill her for sure if we move her and she'll die in the next few minutes if we don't."

Johnny finally spoke.

"There's nothing you can do?"

"There's nothing I can do. But Paul can."

Paul raised his head, his eyes filled with horror.

"You don't know what you're saying!"

"Yeah, I do. I'm saying I want my daughter and you're the only way I can have her."

"No! I killed her already, I won't do this!"

Dr. Knight reached down to grab his shoulders and shook furiously.

"You shut up! You get out of that goddamned hair shirt and stop feeling sorry for yourself! I don't know how Cain got here but you didn't resurrect him! And without you, *nobody* could have stopped him! Not the first time, not this time! So there's no blame here. There's only the next few minutes to decide if Ria lives or *dies!*"

"You don't know what living like this is like! You don't know how it hurts!"

"I know you survived."

"Don't you understand? That she'd *never* see another sunrise?!"

"But she'd see moonrise," Dennis said. "Forever."

Paul looked down. Then he picked up her hand and turned her palm upward. He stared down into the duplicate tracings of the lines of his own palm.

The lifeline didn't disappear, it submerged and ran faintly under the skin, all the way down her palm, and then around her thumb and back, circling continuously.

He stared at her face, battered and swollen beyond recognition.

He heard a voice he'd never thought to hear again speak over his shoulder.

"God's dark angels, son! Both of you!"

"Get out," he said shortly. "All of you."

* * *

Paul walked out of the lake house half an hour or so after issuing his terse command. Ria's body, drained of all blood, lay carefully arranged and covered on the couch.

"...don't understand one goddamn thing that's happened and I want somebody to tell me what the fuck just happened here right now!" Johnny exclaimed as he approached the group standing by the Ford Explorer.

"Johnny," Dr. Knight's voice was weary, drained of all emotions. "You got to take this on faith right now. I'll explain it all. Later. I just can't right now. I just can't."

"Here's Paul," Dennis spoke, alerting the group to his arrival.

"Well?" Dr. Knight raised his head.

"It's done. She'll need blood. Tomorrow night. For God's sake, not human. It'll be twice as hard to control if she ever tastes human."

"I'll get it."

"What the *fuck?*" Johnny's sibilant whisper hissed in the darkness. "Has everybody gone stark, staring crazy?"

"Leave it in the mausoleum. Before sunset."

"No, I want to see her."

"No. You don't. You really, *really* don't."

Dr. Knight bowed his head. He'd never heard ice spew when Paul spoke, but he heard it now. He recognized it for what it was. Inhuman. And no human could argue with it.

"I'll have it there."

376

"What about all this? What can we do? I mean, he rose once." Dennis waved his hands toward the cabin.

Johnny's running commentary continued under his breath. "Everybody I know is a lunatic. They've all gone stark, starin' *crazy!*"

"Johnny, shut the fuck up!" ordered Dr. Knight. The running commentary stopped.

Paul answered Dennis. "I've thought about that," he said, leaning heavily against the Explorer's hood. "The thing is, to make sure the vampire doesn't rise, you not only have to stake it, you have to—"

"Cut off his head," Dennis interrupted. "And throw it in running water."

Johnny stared at the boy in horror.

"I read a lot," Dennis defended himself.

"Yes," Paul confirmed. "And my brother didn't manage the last part."

"Why not? Didn't he know? I don't understand that."

"Dennis, he was only seventeen. He did his best."

"Well, that's not a handicap I've got to contend with." Dr. Knight's voice was cold. "And I'm not only going to cut off the skull, I'm going to tear his bones apart and beat them into dust with a sledge hammer. We can throw the bone shards in the lake. We need to find some tools, some bags."

"There's some croaker sacks in the boathouse," Dennis offered. "Lots of 'em, With the tools. Dad wants to redo the sandbags at the pier this spring. We can weight 'em down with rocks."

"Good. That'll do fine. And we can throw 'em in the middle of the lake. Have to row out in the damn rowboat, I guess. I sure never thought about needin' a boat and motor tonight and we damn sure ain't waitin' for tomorrow."

"But Justin?" Dennis asked.

"Cain drained him," Paul said. "He'll rise tomorrow if we don't do it tonight."

"I'll handle that, too," Dr. Knight said. "Don't worry about it."

"Wait a minute!" Johnny broke in. "You're going to shove a stake through a dead body and cut off its head? The skeleton's one thing, but a body, that's—that's—"

"Johnny, take the Explorer and go. I'll ride back in with Dennis. You haven't seen us do anything yet. Much. I know your legal code of ethics or whatever y'all call 'em wouldn't stand up to watching us mutilate a dead body. Felony or something. Go on."

Johnny looked at Dr. Knight. He still didn't understand but he knew he had to take this on faith. A long night of rowing over the surface of the cold, black lake lay ahead. Dennis was a teenager. Dr. Knight was sixty-five. And whatever was going on with Ria, that was obviously Paul's department. They needed him.

"No, I'll stay."

"You sure? You can't argue and you can't ask questions. Not tonight."

"I'm sure. But I'm asking questions later."

"'Course you are. And I'll answer 'em. Thank you, son."

Johnny nodded and added his own observations of details to clean up.

"The inside of the cabin, that rug. Got burn marks and blood all over it. We'll have to toss it, too, with the bodies. Get a replacement up here, maybe nobody'll notice."

"Mom'll notice," Dennis assured them. "Soon as she walks in. But don't worry about it. I'll tell her I brought Lori up here and the fire sparked. Hell, I'll tell her we were so hot, we set the rug on fire. She won't say anything else."

"Dennis," Dr. Knight put his hand on the boy's shoulder. "Your Dad's a good surgeon but I swear, boy. You're already twice the man he ever thought about being."

"Oh, shit!" The exclamation came from Johnny. "I got the idea about the lake house from Ted Dorry, made him go through Justin's file. He's goin' to have somebody up here in the morning if I don't call him back. I think. He wasn't real happy about it."

"Well, you'd best be calling him, then. We got to get this place lookin' just like it looked and we sure as hell don't need anybody up here in the next day or two."

"Okay. I'll tell him he was right and Ria was out shopping and had car trouble. Damn, I hate lookin' like an idiot!"

He paused. God, he'd give anything right now to hear Ria ask, *What? You're not used to it by now?* No way she'd pass up an opening like that.

"Humility's good for the soul, son. Let's get moving. Paul?"

"I'm takin' Ria now. Don't try and see us. We'll come to you. When she's ready."

"Right. And Paul, there might be something. We never even got started on any of Stu Harmon's ideas—"

"No. That's over. Nobody's experimenting on Ria and if something changed me for the worse or killed me, she'd be alone. And Ria will not go through eternity alone."

Paul spoke firmly. Again, Dr. Knight deferred.

"And Johnny," Paul continued. "In the next few nights—if you hear anything in Ria's apartment—don't come over. We'll come to you. When she's ready."

"But guys—what are we goin' to say about it?" Johnny asked. "After this weekend. I mean, Ria has a law practice, clients, friends."

"I got a job offer I couldn't turn down," Paul improvised quickly. "On a newspaper somewhere. Wyoming, Oregon, hell, Idaho, I don't care what you say. Ria and I got married, spur of the moment, and headed on out. We'll be back on visits. Ria's impulsive enough for that to be believable. And all of you know— we have to leave. Won't take long for somebody to notice they never see Ria in the daytime anymore.

"Hate to miss the wedding," said Johnny.

"Wedding was half an hour ago, Johnny. And believe me, you didn't want to see the ceremony."

Paul turned and walked back towards his new bride, whose consciousness was floating somewhere in the black void between the worlds while her body furiously healed.

He turned back.

"Charlie?"

"Yeah?"

"Would you get me something? Won't mean much to Ria for a few weeks but it'll mean a lot to me."

"Anything."

"I want a set of wedding rings," he said, and reached for his wallet.

"Paul, I'll get whatever you want, don't—"

"No, I have to pay for these."

Dr. Knight closed his eyes. No white wedding gown, no white roses, no white cake. Yes, they needed this.

"What kind do you want?"

"Something unusual, as unique as you can find. Wide gold bands, I think, set with stones, but not diamonds."

"Then what?"

"Rubies. Blood red rubies."

"Okay. I'll leave them when I get them."

Chapter Nineteen

In the confines of the closed coffin in Paul's mausoleum in Rose Arbor Cemetery, two bodies stirred instead of one. Paul shook off his day sleep quickly, rising from the coffin and looking for the supplies he knew Dr. Knight would have waiting.

Ah! There it was. Sitting next to an elegant tumbler. Paul poured the contents of the thermos jug into the glass. The stirrings from the remaining occupant of the coffin increased. He moved to stand beside it.

Ria sat up abruptly, a sleeper emerging from a nightmare.

"What—" Her voice cracked, harsh, unused, as though passing through sandpaper. "What's happened to me? I—it *hurts*!"

He thrust the tumbler into her hands.

"Drink!"

* * *

During the first nights, the blood fury raged through Ria with the force of Hurricane Katrina. The butcher's blood left by Dr. Knight was a poor substitute for the hot, pumping blood she craved in her state of existence, a mere stop-gap and nothing more.

After she slaked her first thirst with the nightly offerings her father left like clockwork, they cast out and Paul flew beside her through the woods on the banks of the Ocmulgee as she stalked and captured, bit and tore. And drank. And drank. And drank.

When he sensed the approach of sunrise, he pulled her back to the mausoleum, folding her in his arms in the cramped confines of the satin lining of the coffin, and closed the lid after them. He didn't want her father to see her yet and hoped Dr. Knight didn't raise the top to gaze at her when he left the blood.

A week after her first waking, Paul saw the jeweler's case lying on top of the small chest of drawers. Ria, behind him, flitted impatiently from one side of their small residence to the other, appearing and disappearing in a feverish ballet.

"Let's go, Paul, let's go!"

He held the open case in his hand and turned around.

"Ria, you've had blood already. You've got to start getting this under control. You have to start tapering off."

"I can't!"

"You can! You can do this, Ria. Look," he held the case out to her. "I asked your father to get them for us."

She gave the rings the barest glance.

"I have to hunt, Paul! I have to!"

"Try to get by tonight, Ria. You've got to start sometime."

She snarled and drew back her arm. "*I won't!* Just because you're Mr. Perfect and don't need it doesn't mean I don't!" With all the strength of the vampire in its early bloodlust, she slapped him across the face with such force his head snapped back.

Paul dropped the jeweler's case. He'd been in agony these past nights, the mental agony of guilt as he watched her rip and tear. Dear God, why hadn't he just let her go? The mental agony melted and merged with the raw, burning physical agony assaulting his nerve endings while he fought to regain control of his own thirst.

He'd kept it dormant for so long. It was dormant no more. The taste of Ria's blood, the coursing heat of it as it pumped into his waiting mouth! Ah, that unleashed wild, furious waves of need he'd struggled to crest and ride when he'd stood outside the cabin talking to the three humans. The smell of their blood almost overpowered him, the urge stronger than it had ever been, even immediately after his own transformation. Then the nights of following Ria as she stalked and gorged, wanting more than anything to stalk and gorge with her. And now she dared taunt his control?

He lifted his arm and struck back with all the strength of his enraged and tortured abstinence. She flew backwards and her body struck the marble wall with such force a mere mortal's spine would have cracked on impact.

She lunged forward, spitting and hissing in her own fury. Her hands caught his shoulders and threw him back with equal force against the opposite wall. She fell on him again. They growled and snarled. Incisors gleamed as they locked into combat, a battle of immortal Titans.

Suddenly Ria dropped her hands and her expression changed. Paul saw the first surface glimmer of his Ria, the Ria who'd cried silently in empathy as he painted pictures of Cain in the night air.

"You want it, too. Don't you? I didn't realize—it was me, changing me, it brought it back. Didn't it? How bad?"

"Bad. Horrible. I don't think it's ever been this bad."

She looked down at the floor, her eyes searching and then finding. She bent and retrieved the rings. Taking the larger of the two, she reached for his hand.

"With this ring," she said softly, placing it on his finger, "I think we're more than wed, Paul." She lifted his finger to her lips. "And will you wear my ring as long as you wore Chloe's?"

He took the smaller ring and placed it on her finger.

"Longer," he said. "For eternity."

"Come," she said, and tugged at his hand. "Let's go."

"Ria—"

"Not to the woods. I need to find a store."

"A store?"

"Yeah. I just thought about it. You know what we got here, darlin'? The psychologists call it an oral fixation. Know what smokin' is? An oral fixation. We need a carton of cigarettes. Two or three of 'em. I mean, it's not like we're goin' to die of lung cancer."

The first smile Paul had smiled in the last week flitted across his lips.

"Somehow, I don't think it's goin' to be a real satisfying substitute."

"Well, maybe we can find something to go along with it."

"Let's go."

They materialized within the walls of Ria's apartment, plastic bag of cigarettes in Ria's hand. They moved to the bedroom and physically consummated this new marriage sanctified in blood.

Always before, Paul had made love gently, sometimes almost tentatively, well aware that his great strength, unleashed, could injure her badly. Now there was no need for restraint and they reveled in the new physical freedom like an old married couple who, after years of intimacy, suddenly discover new passion in bawdiness.

"Good Lord," Ria said softly, lying against his side with her head on his shoulder and her leg thrown over his thigh, and he knew. They were all right again. Both of them.

* * *

Paul handled the wheel easily and naturally as the silver Camry skimmed over the blacktop surface of Highway 41, headed for the Alabama border and points west. The Mustang rested in Dr. Knight's garage. It was simply too conspicuous an automobile to take on the road.

He glanced over at Ria. She was turned slightly toward the right, gazing thoughtfully out the window over the nightscape with one elbow propped against the arm rest. Her head rested on the palm of her hand. Feeling his eyes, she turned and smiled and he was struck again by the miracle of her renewed beauty, emerging triumphant from the wreckage left by Cain.

Her flowing sleeve rippled slightly as her arm moved. She'd never appear in public again without long sleeves. The burns left by the flaming kindling had left mottled, puckered scars which, having been inflicted prior to her transformation, would never disappear. She'd carry them forever, just as he carried the white ropy scars of Cain's knife cuts on his chest. Battle trophies.

He smiled as they sped out towards unknown destinations. They'd go wherever the wind blew them, to whatever town took their fancy.

As the old protective circle of Sadie and Everett, of Tamara and Joshua, had closed around Paul in the first days of his new existence, so had the new protective circle, the circle of Charlie and Liz Knight, Johnny Bishop and Dennis Billings, closed ranks behind their departure.

Ria lifted her arm and shook back the cuff of her long sleeve.

"Bastard," she observed mildly.

"What did I do now?"

"Not you. Cain. My arms. I'll never go sleeveless again."

"I don't mind."

"I know you don't."

"You are so much stronger than I was," Paul said suddenly.

"How so?"

"Three weeks and look at you. Took me months to get that far."

Ria smiled. "But it has nothing to do with strength. I have you. Oh, look darlin'!"

She pointed to the golden orb that was pulling out onto the night sky over the tall stands of trees crowning the low hills.

"Moonrise!"

* * *

In the depths of the silent, shrouded world of departed spirits, Tamara stirred restlessly. She didn't know what was disturbing her. She'd cast her vision out through the veil on the night of Ria's change and spoken to her boy, offering assurance that destiny waited for the birth of another dark angel.

He had his wife now, the one she'd foreseen in his palm years before, whose line paralleled the line representing Chloe but stretched, unbroken, all the way across his palm and circled back around. She'd never told him of his coming bride but it had been a source of great comfort to her, this knowledge that her beloved dark angel wouldn't always walk alone. But now something was disturbing the cosmic peace and she couldn't return to her placid rest. Something. But what?

Suddenly lightning shot out from the spirit world, cracking wildly in the night sky nestling the earth. The men had done their jobs well. Cain's bones, what remained of them, rested in a weighted croaker sack, lying on the murky bottom of Lake Sinclair, sunk in the deepest part of the lake. His skull rested in another croaker sack, a half-mile further down.

But Justin. They hadn't waited for the transformation before staking his body.

Transformation must be complete. Otherwise the body, furiously engaged in healing itself to a state of physical perfection, would slowly push the intruding stake right out of the heart muscle, knitting new tissue as it did so. The presence of the stake would slow the

386

process down. The vampire wouldn't rise in one night, not even in two or three.

But he would rise.

And in the depths of the black lake bottom, in the deepest center of water between the stretching shores of Lake Sinclair, the tip of a stake finally squeezed itself from a headless body shrouded in a croaker sack. The wood trembled in the water and then floated momentarily before dropping to the bottom of the rough material.

Two hands ripped the burlap apart and impatiently pulled the gaping split open as the body emerged. The hands began their slow, blind groping over the floor of the lake, looking for their head.

The End.

Published by BWL Publishing

The Witch - War-N-Wit, Inc. Novella 1
Resurrection - War-N-Wit, Inc. Novella 2
The Coven - War-N-Wit, Inc. Novella 3
MeanStreet, LLC - War-N-Wit, Inc. Novella 4
The Witch Wars – Compilation of the Novellas
Vanished

With Jude Pittman
Mother Shipton and the Sister Witches

Gail Roughton is a native of small town Georgia whose Deep South heritage features prominently in much of her work. She's a retired paralegal who lived in a law office for over forty years, during which time she raised three children and quite a few attorneys. She kept herself more or less sane by writing novels and tossing the completed manuscripts into her closet, most of which have now emerged in published form. A cross-genre writer, her books range from humor to romance to thriller to horror and she's never quite sure what to expect when she sits down at the keyboard. She usually has a project or two on the backburner but doesn't discuss any for fear of jinxing them. Given her affinity for the supernatural, this should come as no surprise to any reader.